Praise for Claire Delacroix's
Medieval Romances

"Claire Delacroix is a shining star of the romance genre. Cleverly original, emotional and fast-paced, full of twists and turns, her books will sweep you off your feet!"
— Julianne Maclean, USA Today bestselling author

"A beguiling medieval romance...readers will devour this rich and compulsively readable tale."
— Publishers' Weekly on **The Rogue**

"When you open a book by Claire Delacroix, you open a treasure chest of words, rare and exquisite!"
— Rendezvous

"An engaging tale of lost love found."
— Booklist on **The Rogue**

"Enthralling and compelling!"
— TheBestReviews on **The Scoundrel**

"A delightful romp through medieval times in a game of cat and mouse...The Scoundrel is an enjoyable read, mixed with passion, humor and an unexpected plot that kept me turning the pages."
— Romance Junkies

"[Claire] Delacroix's satisfying tale leaves the reader hungry for the next offering."
— Booklist on **The Warrior**

*"**The Beauty Bride** is a book that captures you from the first page...a magical and inspiring story. Four hearts!"*
— Pink Heart Reviews

"A lyrical medieval-era romance!"
— Publishers Weekly on **The Beauty Bride**

THE
CRUSADER'S
KISS

THE
CHAMPIONS
OF
ST. EUPHEMIA

CLAIRE
DELACROIX

NEW YORK TIMES BESTSELLING AUTHOR

The Crusader's Kiss
Claire Delacroix

Printing History:
Deborah A. Cooke trade paperback edition
January 2016

This work has been published in a simultaneous digital edition.

છ

Dear Reader;

One of the most interesting things about writing stories all the time—and one thing that frequently surprises people who aren't writers—is that I don't always know how the story is going to work out. Some stories seem to have an energy of their own, and with those books, I feel like the last one to know what's going to happen. Bartholomew and Anna's book is just such a story. I knew Bartholomew had a secret. I guessed that Anna had a grudge. I believed that they would have to work together to see everything resolved, but couldn't see how it would happen. They seemed too different to me, yet their dialogue showed the energy of attraction right from the outset.

I knew the book would be set in England, so I began to compile images for my storyboard on Pinterest that were evocative of medieval England. Quickly, I saw a theme in the pictures that I was choosing: they reminded me of the Robin Hood story. As I delved deeper, I saw that there were similarities between that story and Bartholomew's history, but even more interesting, I discovered (or rediscovered) that the true story behind that of Robin Hood is believed by some scholars to be almost concurrent with the story of the Champions of Saint Euphemia. (As is often the case, there are several possibilities for the origin of the legend, and there are other scholars who insist that the legend has no basis in truth whatsoever.) I enjoyed using elements of the legend in this story.

It was easy to see that Anna would be the leader of the thieves in the woods, just because of her rebellious nature. Does she have a justification for seeing herself as a leader? I love how her disregard for the laws of the nobility contrasts with Bartholomew's respect for justice and order. What a wonderful time I've had with this pair: the woman who accepts no authority and the man who must learn to assert his own. I hope you enjoy their story as well.

*One of the other projects I'm enjoying is the writing of Duncan and Radegunde's story, **The Crusader's Handfast**, which is being published in monthly installments between December 2015 and May 2016. I had thought that the arrival of Gaston and Ysmaine at Châmont-sur-Maine would be part of Bartholomew's story, but it really wasn't. Whose story was it? When I saw that Radegunde had an eye for Duncan, I knew. Like so many servants, this pair knows a great deal more about their knights and ladies than those nobles realize, and they also work to ensure that their lords and ladies win their happy endings. The reader letter for The Crusader's Handfast is on my blog, so you can read a bit more about how* *this story evolved.*

There's an excerpt from The Crusader's Vow at the end of this book, which is Fergus and Leila's story and the final book in the series. It's the fourth book but being published fifth, since Radegunde and Duncan jumped queue.

As of this writing, **The Crusader's Bride** *and The Crusader's Heart are both available in audio. Check my website for links and updates on that process.*

As always, please follow my blog or subscribe to my monthly newsletter to keep up to date on all the news. The newsletter contains advance notice of most sales on my books, as well as chances to win audiobooks, cover reveals, and updated news of releases. You can also choose which news you'd like to receive, in case you don't read in all of the same sub-genres in which I write.

Until next time, I hope you are well and have plenty of good books to read.

All my best,

THE CRUSADER'S HANDFAST

Short Stories
BEGUILED

Apocalyptic Romances:
The Prometheus Project:
FALLEN
GUARDIAN
REBEL
ABYSS

❧

Deborah Cooke Books

Contemporary Romance:
The Coxwells:
THIRD TIME LUCKY
DOUBLE TROUBLE
ONE MORE TIME
ALL OR NOTHING

Flatiron Five
SIMPLY IRRESISTIBLE

Paranormal Romance:
Dragonfire:
KISS OF FIRE
KISS OF FURY
KISS OF FATE
WINTER KISS
WHISPER KISS
DARKFIRE KISS
FLASHFIRE
EMBER'S KISS
THE DRAGON LEGION NOVELLAS
SERPENT'S KISS
FIRESTORM FOREVER

The Dragons of Incendium:
WYVERN'S MATE
NERO'S DREAM
WYVERN'S PRINCE
ARISTA'S LEGACY
WYVERN'S WARRIOR

Paranormal Young Adult:
The Dragon Diaries:
FLYING BLIND
WINGING IT
BLAZING THE TRAIL

❧

THE
CRUSADER'S
KISS

THE
CHAMPIONS
OF
ST. EUPHEMIA

CLAIRE
DELACROIX

NEW YORK TIMES BESTSELLING AUTHOR

Sunday, December 6, 1187

Feast Day of Saint Nicholas.

❧

Prologue

Châmont-sur-Maine

Bartholomew was torn between his loyalties. He knelt in the chapel all night before his investiture as a knight and wrestled with his decision.

When Gaston offered to dub him a knight, Bartholomew had immediately thought that he might return to England. As a knight, he could challenge the villain who had stolen the holding that had been his birthright. As a knight, he could defend justice and ensure that his parents were avenged. As a knight, he could claim his family holding of Haynesdale if it had been abandoned and appeal to the king for its return to his hand. His first thoughts had been all of opportunity and triumph.

Still, there had been a seed of doubt. Gaston had been more than good to him. That knight had found Bartholomew, orphaned in the streets of Paris, when he had been only a young boy. Gaston had not only ensured his welfare but trained him as a squire when he was too young and small to be one. Though there was only a little more than ten years between them, Gaston could have been Bartholomew's father, given the role the older knight had played in his life. Now, Gaston not only would knight Bartholomew—at considerable expense—but had offered him an opportunity as Captain of the Guard, defending the borders of Châmont-sur-Maine.

Did he not owe it to Gaston to take this role?

Bartholomew's doubts had increased when the party arrived at Gaston's newly won holding to discover that the husband of Gaston's niece was displeased to find Gaston arriving home and hale. It was clear to all that Millard had aspirations to claim Châmont-sur-Maine for his own, and might well have done so already if Gaston had been further delayed. Though the matter had been resolved in Gaston's favor, Bartholomew was aware that his good friend could face additional challenges. Gaston might well need every blade he could summon to his side.

Which duty should Bartholomew fulfill? Was it better to right an old wrong or to ensure that another matter did not go awry in future?

Just days before, Wulfe had arrived for Bartholomew's investiture as a knight, a radiant Christina by his side. That former Templar's tale of returning to his family abode and being accepted by his father had been an inspiration. Wulfe, to Bartholomew's surprise, had been not only a bastard but one spurned by his sire. He had won a title and the hand of Christina in his own.

Because Wulfe had dared to hope for it.

Nay, because he had dared to seek it out and claim it.

Indeed, the fact that this fine holding of Châmont-sur-Maine came to the hand of Gaston argued in favor of Bartholomew going to England. A younger son without a legacy, Gaston had believed he would serve as a Templar for all his life. That such a rich reward had come to the knight Bartholomew admired most in all of Christendom was a welcome indication that he might prevail himself over the villain who had stolen Haynesdale.

It would have been easier to be certain of his path had he known what awaited him at Haynesdale. What had truly happened all those years ago? Bartholomew had been too young for his memory to be reliable. He knew he had been sent away. He dreamed of fire and he bore a scar, burned into his own flesh. Who had attacked their abode? Did his mother still live? Did the villain still hold the estate?

Would the king heed Bartholomew's appeal? He knew that the Angevin kings demanded that all holdings in England revert to their control upon the death of a baron, so that the king could see the responsibility bestowed anew. This practice was to ensure that the king's faithful men were always in power and always rewarded. Henry and his kin did not recognize inheritance in those lands beneath their control—save by the gift of coin. The escheat could be bought but Bartholomew had no coin to secure his claim.

If he departed from France, would he betray Gaston's trust and fail in his own quest, as well? He could argue the merit of both courses and see the risks of both.

Bartholomew eyed the reliquary on the altar and wondered whether Saint Euphemia had interceded for Wulfe and Gaston. Their party had defended the saint's remains all the way from Jerusalem, at some peril. Would she do as much for him?

How could he chose between two paths, both honorable yet both filled with peril?

He supposed this was the task of a knight.

Perhaps this decision was his true test.

That evening, Bartholomew had been washed and shaved, and his beard had been shaved. He had donned a new chemise and chausses and entered the chapel in reverent silence. The reliquary had been revealed and the priest had kissed it, then placed it upon the altar. Gaston had placed the sword with which Bartholomew would be girded before it, and he had been left in silence to prepare himself for his vows.

The portal had been locked and the chapel had become both dark and cold.

It had been hours. Bartholomew's knees hurt. His belly was empty. His mouth was dry and his fingers were cold. Still, he prayed, hoping for one choice to offer itself as more important than the other.

The night passed slowly. He might have dozed, yet on his knees, save his thoughts were churning. The chill of the stone rose through his body and seemed to close around his heart.

Gaston or Haynesdale?

It seemed Bartholomew had knelt for an eternity when he saw the sky lighten beyond the windows of the chapel and heard birds stirring. He raised his gaze yet again to the altar, to the sword that would soon be his own. Its pommel gleamed in the darkness. It was a fine blade of Toledo steel, its hilt simple and strong. Gaston had chosen a weapon that would serve Bartholomew well all his life. The pommel had a round crystal in it, much like Gaston's own, but this orb had a fragment of the True Cross trapped within it. The sword and the spurs Gaston would fit to Bartholomew's boots on the morrow symbolized his new role and responsibility.

Behind the sword was the golden reliquary they had carried from Jerusalem to Paris for the Templars. The tale was that it remained in Paris, but to ensure its safety, Fergus would take it secretly to Scotland. The Grand Master in Paris had agreed that it might grace the chapel here, at Gaston's request, so long as the portal was barred and none outside their party saw it—save the priest.

Bartholomew had not seen the marvel himself until they had reached the Paris Temple and still he could not believe its richness. The reliquary was large and wrought of gold and gems embellished its surface. It was adorned with the name of the saint whose sacred relic was sheltered within.

Saint Euphemia.

Just the day before, Christina had recounted the tale of Euphemia's life, including the miracle attributed to her at the Council of Chalcedon. There had been a dispute about the correct doctrine, so two scrolls, each describing one perspective, had been placed in the sarcophagus containing the saint's relics and sealed there. In the morning, one scroll had been in Euphemia's hand, the other beneath her feet.

She had chosen which doctrine would be orthodox.

She might help him to choose. Aye, it was her blessing to bestow.

Bartholomew recognized this impulse as the right one. Should the first beam of sunlight to touch the altar land upon the sword— the sword given to him by Gaston—he would remain to defend Gaston's legacy. Should the sunlight touch the reliquary first, he would choose greater risk and uncertain reward, the path of justice for his lost father. A martyr like Euphemia, after all, had become a saint by following her faith and holding to her convictions, no matter how uncertain the outcome.

Aye, Bartholomew resolved, it would be so.

His heart beat a little faster as the sky lightened yet more beyond the windows. Finally, a shaft of sunlight pierced the shadows, painting the west wall of the chapel a rosy gold. The sun rose higher and the beam of light eased closer to the altar. Bartholomew prayed as he watched its progress. He could not guess where it would land.

The sunlight was slanting over the altar when he heard a footstep outside the portal. The priest spoke softly to another, probably Gaston, and the key was turned in the lock. The sunlight touched the corner of the altar cloth in that moment, and still he could not anticipate whether reliquary or sword would be illuminated first.

The priest murmured a prayer from the back of the chapel. His soft footsteps came closer, the tread of a knight's boots following behind. Bartholomew watched the sunlight move slowly, nigh holding his breath.

The flare of light when the sun touched the gold was so bright as to blind him. The reliquary shone so vividly that it might have been ablaze, and truly, Bartholomew felt as if the saint's will set his own blood afire.

He would ride for Haynesdale, determine the truth of its situation, and strive to see his father avenged.

Justice it would be.

No matter what obstacle stood in his path.

It would be his first quest as a knight.

Saturday, January 16, 1188

Feast Day of the Five Friars Minor (Saints Berardus, Peter, Accursius, Adjutus, and Otto).

❧

Chapter One

Haynesdale in Northumberland, England

Anna was on her belly in the snow, watching the party that camped in the forest she knew as well as the lines in her own hand. She was perfectly still, her crossbow loaded and hidden beneath the sheepskin pelt that disguised her figure from view. She might have been chilled, if her heart had not been pounding so hard in anticipation. Little Percy was nestled beside and partly beneath her, his eyes bright as he awaited her instruction.

They were both dressed in simple dark garb that would blend with the shadows. Anna had bound her long hair beneath a cap and wore a man's chausses and boots. She liked that she could run more quickly in such garb, and that she oft gained liberties when perceived to be a boy that might be denied her as a woman.

It had been months since a party had ventured along this road, and longer yet since one had been fool enough to take their rest within the forest. It had been a hard winter and would likely be a harder spring. There were rumors of new taxes and tithes, though the harvest had not been a good one, and Anna would not be the sole one hungry.

In truth, they had expected a party to ride in the other direction, away from Haynesdale keep, for the baron always paid his taxes to the king after the Yule. Well aware of the thieves in his forests, Sir Royce always sent out scouts the day before the wagon laden with coin left for the king's hall. Anna and Percy were watching for that sign.

Instead, they had discovered a party of knights riding towards Haynesdale. It was most unusual. Sir Royce was not a frequent host. Anna debated the merit of summoning some of the others, but decided she and Percy could manage alone.

This party's wealth was clearly considerable. Their horses were remarkable beasts, so fine that Anna knew they would be readily recognized in any town's market she might try to sell them—or even en route to those towns. She would have to forgo the temptation of the horses. Fortunately, the palfreys were heavily burdened with saddle bags and parcels.

What did these men carry?

The men were armed more heavily and more richly than was typical in this corner of Christendom. They wore mail, each and every one of them, not merely boiled leather jerkins. Their boots were tall and polished, and they had helmets of fine design.

Who were they?

There were two Templar knights in the party, their white tabards adorned with red crosses that identified their order. Both of them had a squire, and both squires slept atop their knight's belongings. Anna had little interest in them. They would have good swords and sturdy hauberks, but would have to be killed to be parted from those prizes. Beyond that, the wealth of a Templar was in his destrier, and she had already decided against taking the horses.

There were two other knights, who appeared to be of an age with each other. Both were handsome enough, if she had possessed an affection for their kind. One had russet hair and had a pair of squires himself. Anna had heard snippets of conversation and enough of his words to conclude that he was from the north and returning home to Scotland from a voyage afar. The majority of the bundles belonged to him, by all appearances, and he had spoken of his betrothed.

Gifts for a lady, then. Anna would guess he brought cloth for rich garments, as the packages were too numerous to all contain jewels. If there were jewels, they would likely be hidden on his person. He looked young and virile, and she was not certain she could best him in a fight.

It would be harder to sell jewels than horses, to be sure. What she wanted was coin, and food.

The other knight had darker hair and was more quiet than his fellows. He alone had a short beard, which gave him a rakish air. Indeed, Anna had feared more than once that he had discerned her in the shadows, though she knew it could not be so. There was something more intense and alert about him, to be sure, and Anna trusted her instinct to leave him and his squire be.

Finally, there was one more warrior, an older man with a little silver at his temples. A Scotsman, for he wore the plaid wool so favored by his kind. He carried two saddlebags and Anna had noticed that he kept a hand upon one of them.

There was something of merit in that bag, she knew it well.

She thought she could outrun him, if not outwit him.

Anna had chosen a spot close to the Scotsman but downwind of him. She pointed to the bag in question and Percy nodded, biting his lip.

The moon was setting, the forest as still as it would be in the night. Since the sky was clear, Anna waited for the moon to dip below the uppermost branches of the trees, for then, the small camp would be cast into shadow. The wild growth of the forest beyond the road would be her friend, then, for she knew a path through it that no stranger would be able to discern in the night. She and Percy would part ways and her brother would run quickly and quietly to the cavern, while she led the hunt astray.

If there was one.

It would work perfectly.

The Scotsman had been keeping the watch, but he dozed. The horses dozed. The squires slept. One Templar snored. The Scottish knight murmured in his slumber. The moon slipped ever lower and the men's camp fell into shadow.

It was time.

Anna touched Percy's shoulder and the boy eased forward. She gripped her crossbow and aimed at the Scotsman, in case he awakened and tried to stop the boy. Percy showed uncommon stealth for a boy of his age and could move with a silence that impressed Anna every time she watched him.

Her brother might have been born to be a thief. Percy inched toward the sleeping man, silent and sure. Finally, he reached out and touched the saddlebag, resting his hand there for a moment to ensure the Scotsman did not react. Anna sighted her bow, her heart thundering as she watched and waited.

Percy eased the bag away from the Scotsman's side, slowly at first. The man murmured in his sleep and shook his head, but did not seem to be aware of the boy. Percy tugged the bag more quickly, sliding backward across the surface of the snow in silence.

He was almost at Anna's side, and cast her a triumphant glance, his eyes dancing with his usual mischief. It was but a game to him, and one at which he often won. She might have given a nod, but the Scotsman snorted in that moment. He rolled over, reached for the saddlebag and his eyes flew open at the realization that it was gone. "Hoy!" he cried and his party stirred.

Percy ran.

Anna fired her crossbow and the bolt would have gone through the Scotsman's hand if he had not bounded to his feet in that same moment.

"Thief!" He roared in outrage, pointing after Percy, and the entire company was alerted. The quiet knight leaped from his bed and lunged into the forest. Anna thought to lie low and let him try to chase Percy, but he headed straight for her.

She had been seen! Anna clutched her crossbow and ran, taking a different direction from Percy and abandoning the sheepskin. The knight was closing fast behind her, so noisy that she had no doubt of his location. She guessed that he was a good foot taller than her, and that height gave him an advantage. She was taking three strides for his two, after all.

Percy's escape was of greatest importance, she told herself. This man was a knight, pledged to defend women and orphans, of which she was both.

On the other hand, Anna had witnessed how readily a knight could disregard those vows. Her heart was racing and not just from her flight.

Not again!

"Stop!" he cried. "Thief!"

Anna ducked beneath a branch, hoping it was too low for him. She could not hear Percy and hoped he was safely away. Anna ran in the opposite direction of the cavern, ducking branches, taking a labyrinthine course, dodging around shrubs, and diving through the bracken. The knight was not deterred. He was cursed quick, too, even though he wore his hauberk. The sound of his boots on the dead undergrowth was louder and closer. The darkness did not seem to be aiding her.

If she could shake him from her trail and reach the haven of the cave, he would never find her.

Anna doubled back and crossed a small stream. Her boots slipped on the wet rocks because she moved too quickly. Though the stream was not wide, it was cold and deep. She flailed her arms for a moment to regain her balance and was certain the knight would emerge from the forest and spot her. To her great good fortune, he did not. In fact, she heard a thump and a muttered oath. Ha! She found her footing and leaped into the undergrowth on the opposing bank, then paused.

There was no sound of pursuit.

Had he abandoned the chase?

Had he fallen and injured himself?

She stood motionless, halfway certain the sound of her heart would reveal her, then slowly smiled. There were fading footsteps, then the forest was silent again. Anna waited a long while, listening, but there was no sound of the knight.

They had succeeded again! The knight had been deceived by her turning back and had continued in the same direction. He might make the keep by daybreak, or spend the rest of the night wandering through the forest, lost.

Anna spun, intending to find Percy, only to discover the dark-haired knight standing behind her, his arms folded across his chest. He had moved as silently as Percy could. He was patient as no man tended to be.

"Where is the boy?" he demanded.

Anna caught her breath and made to run, but the knight seized her around the waist, lifting her feet from her ground. She aimed a kick at him, but he anticipated the move. Her fear rose that she was at his mercy.

To her surprise, he wrestled the crossbow from her grip, then flung her aside. He took a bolt from his own belt and cocked the bow, moving with such surety that his gaze never wavered from hers. Too late she saw that there was a hook on his belt and realized that he was an archer himself. He aimed it at her—her own bow—then smiled with wretched confidence in his own skills.

"Where?" he murmured, the single word hanging in the air between them on a breath of vapor.

"I will never tell," she growled and took a step back even as her thoughts flew. She could dive into the river and swim to the cave. If he shot at her, he might miss, and it would take time for him to load another bolt.

She met his gaze and saw the resolve in his eyes. His thumb was on the release. "I do not want to kill you, boy," he said softly. "But I want Duncan's property returned."

Boy. He thought she was a boy. Of course. If he knew her sex, would he spare her?

Or would he abuse her? Fear quivered in Anna's belly.

The surprise might slow his reaction. She had to gamble upon that.

"Boy?" Anna echoed in challenge and saw his confusion. She smiled at him as she reached up and tugged off her hood, shaking out her hair so that it fell over her shoulders. She saw his eyes light with surprise, but did not give him time to recover.

It was a fleeting advantage, after all.

Instead, she dove into the pool of the river beyond the rocks and let herself sink below the surface. She could hold her breath a long time, and though the water was fiercely cold, she did just that. Anna swam into the hollow by the opposite bank, where she had hidden to surprise Percy the previous summer and waited. When her chest felt fit to burst for lack of air, she slowly rose to the surface, knowing she would be concealed behind the ice at the banks.

There was no sign of the knight on the opposite side of the stream.

Anna had learned to be wary of him, though. He was stealthy and possessed of a rare cunning. She remained still and watchful, certain he had not abandoned the chase. He would reveal himself, she was certain, and if it was a question of patience as to who was revealed first, she could wait him out.

He was noble and a knight, after all, and Anna knew such men had naught of merit in their veins.

¿&

She was gone, as surely as if she had vanished into the air.

Bartholomew knew better. He stood silently and waited. No person could vanish. No person could hold their breath forever. Sooner or later, the surface of the stream would ripple and he would spy his prey.

While he waited, he marveled.

He had been convinced that he pursued a boy.

His prey had been quick, that was for certain, and agile as well. Bartholomew was fast on his feet, but he had been hard-pressed to close the distance between them. The boy clearly knew the forest well, and all its hidden pathways. If not for the snow and the contrast of the boy's dark clothing against it, Bartholomew might have lost him completely. Where the snow had been blown aside or melted into mud, it was a challenge to keep sight of him. He ran quietly, too, making little sound even on the dried leaves underfoot.

There was no doubt about it: this boy and his companion had stolen before and were well practiced in their trade. Bartholomew might have felt sorry for them, if they had stolen out of hunger, or even granted them coin out of compassion, but they could not abscond with the precious reliquary entrusted to the party.

He had to retrieve Duncan's saddlebag.

When the boy had started to cross the river, Bartholomew had anticipated his destination, doubled back and reached that point before his prey. He had not expected an easy triumph, but neither had he expected to be so surprised by the boy's removal of his cap.

And the spilling of long chestnut hair. The sight of that gleaming curtain of hair had changed his perception immediately. In that moment, Bartholomew saw how slender the "boy" was, how finely boned the hands and face. He could explain the curve he had felt upon seizing his prey, for it was not some bundle as he had anticipated.

It had been her breast.

She had clearly delighted in his astonishment, then taken advantage of either that or his chivalry to escape anew. Diving into the stream was folly in this season, to be sure, and Bartholomew knew he would have to ensure that she was warm and dry when she finally emerged. His reaction to her became protective, courtesy of that glimpse, and he realized that he was prepared to give greater heed to her side of the story.

It was shocking to realize how a pretty face, even a dirty one, could so affect his thinking.

Still, there was no sign of her. He crouched and scanned the surface again, cursing that the moon was too low to grant much illumination.

She might have planned as much. Why else wait until this hour to strike? Certainly, she and her accomplice had not just happened upon his party.

Had they been followed for long? Bartholomew could not credit it, though he knew that Duncan had been convinced all the way from Paris that some soul pursued them. She had looked too poor and too much a resident of the forest to have followed them from much distance. Also she had no steed.

At least not one he could see. Who was to say where she had hidden her various treasures away? And who was the other one? Was he truly a boy? Where had he gone with the saddlebag? Bartholomew frowned, convinced as he was that this one knew the other's destination. He would wait.

Was that a ripple on the surface on the far side of the stream? The bank overshadowed the water there, but it seemed to Bartholomew that that the ice was disturbed. It was too dark to be certain. He eased closer, watching.

She emerged suddenly and took a gasping breath, her horror clear in her expression when she spied him. She made to climb the opposite bank, her movements slow given the weight of her wet garb. Her agitation was so obvious that Bartholomew felt some compassion for her.

But not enough to let her evade him. He leaped the stream and seized her, hauling her out of the water. He shed his cloak and wrapped it around her tightly, seeing that her complexion was already pale. "Where has he gone?" he demanded.

She glanced over her shoulder, clearly considering the merit of making a confession. He was glad she did not dwell on the matter overlong. "Where is my bow?"

"There. And it is mine now."

"Yours?" Her eyes snapped in outrage. "You have no right..."

"Just as you had no right to take Duncan's saddlebag."

Her eyes narrowed as she assessed him, and Bartholomew held tightly to her upper arms. "I will trade you," she offered with a boldness he thought undeserved.

"Trade me?" Bartholomew echoed. "You have stolen from me, yet I have just ensured that you will survive this night. You owe me and twice over. I see no reason to return your bow, for you have little to offer in exchange."

"I did not steal from you..."

"But the boy did and you are allied together."

Her lips thinned and her gaze turned mutinous. "You did not save me..." she began with scorn.

"You had trouble making the bank, and you are chilled to your marrow. Without this cloak, you would catch a chill and that might be fatal." He arched a brow and did not loosen his grip upon her upper arms. "Indeed you might still fall ill."

"My disposition is most strong," she said hotly. "I owe naught to you and your kind..."

"Then I will take my cloak back and leave you to yourself."

She clutched it tightly and glared at him. "It *is* warm."

"And?"

"And what?"

"And you should thank me for so graciously sharing it with you."

"Graciously?" She laughed, as if she would have preferred not to do so. "A knight is never gracious to a person of the woods."

At that, Bartholomew spun her out of his cloak, tripped her, and let her fall back into the stream. He knew the water was not deep, and he guessed that naught would be injured but her pride. If she wanted to be without him, the matter could be arranged. He leaped over the stream again and picked up the crossbow, acting as if he meant to leave her. She came up sputtering, looking fit to shred him from his bones.

"It is mine!" she cried.

"It is forfeit," Bartholomew replied. He waved to her. "Since you have such a strong disposition, I will leave you now."

"Where are you going?"

"To retrieve what was stolen, of course." He made to stride away, hearing her labor to climb to the banks again.

"Cursed wretch," she muttered and he glanced back to see her shake like a dog. With her garb wet, Bartholomew could see that she was a woman in truth, though slight of stature. She wrung out the hem of her tabard and glared at him anew. Then she sneezed and shivered convulsively. That did not stop her from marching after him, fire in her eyes. "I will trade you the bow for Percy's location," she offered again, a challenge in her tone.

Bartholomew laughed. "Because he is already rid of the prize. I would be a fool indeed to give you the ability to dispatch me when you clearly hold me in such affection."

She snorted, in a most unfeminine way. "It is not yours." The way her gaze lingered on the crossbow told Bartholomew how important it was to her.

Why? It was not common for women to have proficiency with the weapon.

"You shot at Duncan," he recalled, deliberately taunting her because she seemed inclined to reveal more when she was irked. "Or maybe I should say that you missed Duncan? Perhaps your skill is not very great. Perhaps you stole this weapon and have no skill with it."

Her eyes flashed anew and she spat at the ground, before shuddering again. "Luck favored him. The miss was no mark of my incompetence." She was proud of her skill, to be sure, and he wondered whether her pride was warranted.

He provoked her anew. "Perhaps I would take no risk in returning it to you. Perhaps you could never fell me."

She blinked, battled with her reaction to the insult, then smiled and extended a hand. "Perhaps not."

Her sudden smile made Bartholomew blink, for she was even more pretty than he had realized. He had seen the war of her thoughts in her eyes and had the instinct to trust her. She was not witless, but she was a thief without guile.

What an intriguing woman.

"But what need has a woman of such a weapon?" He let his voice fill with derision. "Should you not leave your defense to a man? Your husband or father?"

"I have neither," she declared and snatched for the bow.

Bartholomew easily held it out of her reach.

She sneezed again, then considered him with displeasure. "I might die of this chill, as you say," she declared. "And then your path to Percy would be lost forever." She put out her hand, ever optimistic.

"If there is a wager, it must be on my terms," Bartholomew said, finding remarkable enjoyment in this discussion.

She scoffed. "Doubtless, they will be enticing."

"What do you expect?"

She took a deep breath of forbearance. "You will want to bed me, as well as have the saddlebag returned, and then you will cheat me of the crossbow, for you will declare it unfitting for a mere woman to hold such a weapon. You will leave me soiled and bereft of all I value." Her lip curled in disdain. "I know how your kind wagers."

Bartholomew was astonished that she could think so poorly of a stranger and a knight. He looked past the mire and the grubby clothing to the shape of her face and lips, the narrow indent of her waist, and the beguiling flash in her eyes. She had an appeal, to be sure.

But he would prove her assumptions about his nature to be wrong first.

"Here is the trade I will make with you," he said, keeping his tone reasonable. "I will return the crossbow to you when I have Duncan's saddlebag returned to me, its contents intact."

Her lips set. "So, we would have taken the risk for naught at all. Would you not sweeten the offer with a coin or six?"

He eyed the crossbow. "Even in the darkness, I know this is a fine weapon, and it would fetch a good price. Perhaps I should take it to York and sell it."

"You would not get your bag back then."

"It sounds as if I will not get it back at any rate. You have drawn out this conversation to ensure that Percy has had plenty of time to reach some refuge."

Her smile flashed. "I did not think you had the wits to notice."

"I think you have sufficient wits to know that not all men are the same as the one who taught you such distrust."

For the first time, she looked both surprised and a little bit uncertain. She eyed Bartholomew with new interest, and her lips parted. He took a step closer, snared by her gaze yet wary of her intent. She stretched out a hand. "Might I borrow your cloak, sir? You were so gracious to lend it to me earlier, and it was warm."

Bartholomew smiled. "Are you only charming when you desire something?"

She smiled back at him. "Perhaps I have learned one thing from your kind." She sneezed again, most violently. Bartholomew could not risk her welfare. He swung the cloak from his shoulders and dropped it over hers. She clutched it and shivered beneath its weight. She spared a glance at its fur lining, then eyed him anew.

"Are you rich?"

Bartholomew shook his head. "I have a generous friend."

She cast him a coy glance and might have spoken again. Indeed Bartholomew found himself leaning closer to better hear whatever she might utter.

Then a child screamed in the distance.

They both straightened and stared into the shadows of the forest. Bartholomew noted that his companion was stricken. "Percy!" she whispered, and then she ran in pursuit of the cry.

With his cloak yet upon her back.

Once again she fled, and once again, Bartholomew chased her through the shadows and bracken of the forest. Was this a feint to see him robbed anew? Or was Percy truly in peril?

And what had happened to Duncan's saddlebag? If any soul looked within it, Bartholomew doubted he would retrieve the relic readily.

If at all.

He could not so betray the trust of Gaston and of the order of the Temple. He had to recapture that bag, no matter what the price.

Even if this defiant wretch of a maiden held the key.

&

Percy was panting with terror.

He did not know what had happened to Anna. She was not behind him and he could not hear her at all. He hoped she had taken another path to lead their pursuers astray, just as she usually did.

He ran on, making for the cavern as was their usual plan.

He leaped over a log and flung himself through the forest, then paused. Had he heard sounds of pursuit? Percy leaned back against a large rock for a long moment, letting his heartbeat slow as he listened.

Naught. He was safe.

Anna would follow him soon, but he could take his time reaching the cavern.

After all, he had the prize.

What was it?

Percy licked his lips and hunkered down to unfasten the saddlebag. It was heavy, and he had imagined its contents as he ran.

22

A mound of silver coins. Jewels fit for a king. Even a stack of pennies would be welcome. His fingers trembled with cold and excitement as he unfastened the ties. He made a wish, as always he did, and cast back the flap.

Percy's mouth fell open in astonishment at the sight of the golden item within. What was it? It was as large as his head, maybe larger, studded with gems and covered with writing. He had never seen the like of it.

He might have removed it from the saddlebag, but he heard a sharp intake of breath that revealed he was not alone.

"I will take that," declared a man, his voice familiar. Gaultier, the baron's Captain of the Guard, stepped out of the undergrowth, and his smile made Percy feel cold. "I knew you would return when you had made another theft, but this is an exceptional prize."

"Nay!" Percy cried and clutched the bag as he bolted.

The silhouettes of three more knights blocked his view, and he knew himself to be trapped. Still, he tried to fling himself through their ranks, then kicked and screamed when he was seized. The saddlebag was claimed by Gaultier, while the others trussed him and carried him away.

"Help me!" he roared.

"Please do summon your associates," Gaultier said smoothly. "I should very much like to see your sister again, if she lives."

Percy clapped his mouth shut. He did not know what had happened when Anna had been imprisoned, but Gaultier had done her some injury before her escape. He could not cast her into that knight's power again.

Gaultier chuckled. "So, she does live. I had wondered. We shall search for her on the morrow. Let her have time to realize you are gone."

The horses had been hidden behind the hill, and Percy was carried easily toward them.

"Hoy there!" Gaultier shouted. "Whoever is allied with this brat can find him in Haynesdale's dungeon, if you would care to make a bargain for his survival."

With those words and the knight's chuckle of satisfaction, Percy had the wits to say no more.

‿❧

Not Percy!

Anna knew that her brother would not have cried out without good reason. He was notoriously silent. That ensured he was a good partner, but made his shout doubly troubling.

The cry had come from the direction of the cavern, which was no good portent. He should have met her there and should have been safe.

Had their refuge been discovered?

Or had Percy not reached their sanctuary?

There was only silence after that cry and Anna feared the worst.

As she ran, she had no doubt that the knight would follow her. He was naught but persistent, to be sure. She dared to hope he might actually be useful, but that seemed overly optimistic. At least he managed to move with relative silence, though she could discern him behind her.

She paused to steady her breath when she drew nearer to the cavern. The knight halted behind her, their breath mingling white in the night air. She cast him a quelling glance and touched her fingertip to her lips.

It was an unnecessary warning, for he was already silent. His lips tightened and he reached out, seizing her wrist to keep her from fleeing anew.

Too late she wondered whether she had stepped into a trap.

Then Gaultier shouted, in close proximity, and offered a challenge. "Hoy there! Whoever is allied with this brat can find him in Haynesdale's dungeon, if you would care to make a bargain for his survival."

Anna froze and feared for Percy's fate.

The dark-haired knight watched her with interest. She heard the horses riding through the forest, heading back to Haynesdale. There were four of them by the sound.

Perhaps she could save Percy before he was trapped in the keep. Gaultier and his knights were riding back to the keep by the easiest route and would have a long gallop on the curving road. Even better, the road was exposed near the village. There was naught she would have liked better than to have taken Gaultier down with an arrow.

Anna eyed her crossbow pointedly.

The knight smiled and held it out of her reach, his eyes glinting with such satisfaction that she yearned to do him injury.

His grip was firm on her wrist, but he did not hurt her. She twisted a little and realized she could not free herself.

He was larger and stronger than she, which was frightening.

She took a breath and leaned closer to him, even though the sound of the horses had faded. "We can cut through the forest to the village, and maybe stop them from entering the keep."

He nodded once in agreement, awaiting her choice of direction. When she tugged at his grip, he touched the rope hanging from his belt with his other hand, as if inviting her to be trussed like a wild creature. Anna let him see her dislike of that notion and was rewarded by a fleeting smile, one that set her heart leaping despite its brevity.

He was fiercely handsome.

She pointed and he nodded, keeping a grip upon her as they hastened through the woods. There was no visible path, but Anna knew the way, orienting herself by the shape of the land and the location of old trees. The knight did not release her, but neither did he hinder their progress.

Anna halted where the forest thinned near the village, then crept forward to the edge of the shadows.

All was quiet.

All she needed was that crossbow.

How badly did her companion want to retrieve that saddlebag?

Could she make a wager with him?

She watched the knight through her lashes as he peered ahead of them into the shadows. He must have noted the thin trails of rising smoke because his gaze trailed upward. At least some of the villagers were sufficiently awake to have kindled a morning blaze. Anna noted the huts and knew it was Finan the apothecary. Doubtless, he and his wife felt the cold more in their later years. Smoke rose from Denley the baker's abode, as well as that of Cedric the tailor. Both widowers with infant children, they did much to ensure the welfare of their young children. She would have to see if Esme could spare some eggs. Perhaps Regan would trade some cheese for the eggs.

Anna watched the knight beside her inhale, sampling the air, and respected that he gathered information much as she did. His eyes narrowed. Aye, he would smell the pigs and the latrines, as sure a sign of human habitation as there could be.

He met her gaze and lifted a brow in silent query.

Anna edged closer to the road, which was on the far side of the bracken, the knight's grip fast on her wrist. They hunkered down in the overgrowth, and she knew she was not the only one straining her ears.

Where was Gaultier? The forest was too quiet for all to be right.

She leaned forward to peer down the road. Suddenly there was a flurry of racing hoof beats. Anna recoiled, colliding with the knight. If not for him, she might have fallen backward, but he caught her against his chest with one arm and did not move at all. The hoof beats became louder as Gaultier shouted for the gates to be opened. Anna ducked low with instinctive speed. The knight remained utterly still, his grip tight upon her.

The horses raced past them, not four strides away. Even in the darkness, Anna knew it was Gaultier. She heard the jingle of the knight's trap and heard his armor, saw the gleam of fine horseflesh and heard the gallop of a destrier.

She saw the golden-haired boy cast across the knight's lap and struggling.

Percy!

The knight clapped his hand over Anna's mouth before she could make a sound and ducked lower, fairly tucking her beneath his strength. "Percy?" he whispered in her ear.

Anna nodded vigorously and tried to reach for the crossbow. He kept it out of her reach, even though she did kick him.

"Be silent! There is not a clear shot."

Anna peered through the growth to realize that he was right. Gaultier rode to the gates of the keep, his men clustered behind him. She could have struck the last one, but his armor might have repelled the arrow at such a distance. It was better to remain unobserved.

Even if she disliked that her captor was right.

"What is this place?" the knight whispered.

"Haynesdale keep."

He frowned and eyed the keep again, as if he would argue the matter with her. What did a French knight know of her home? "It cannot be," he murmured. "There is no mill."

Anna frowned, astonished by his comment.

Why was he here?

What did he care about a mill?

What did his company want in these parts? They must be passing through, but why?

Anna thought furiously, recalling the detail of what she had seen even as the sound of hoof beats faded. Something had bounced behind that last knight in the party, a saddlebag of familiar size and shape, and she knew that Percy's prize had been claimed, too. What had it been that Gaultier had decided to take Percy as well as the bag? Why would he take the boy to the baron?

Because there was something of import in that bag.

She twisted in the knight's grip, wanting to see his eyes when he answered her. "What was in the bag?" she demanded, her words as silent as a breath.

"A prize beyond compare," the knight murmured, his eyes narrowed so that she could not guess his thoughts. "Since you are responsible for its loss, you are going to help me to retrieve it."

Before she could argue that, he hauled her back into the forest. He still held her wrist and she still wore his cloak. He marched through the undergrowth until they were well away from the village. "Let me go."

He laughed. "And never see you again. I think not."

She wrenched her hand free, pulling him off balance, then bent to bite him. His lips thinned and his eyes flashed, but Anna was free. She managed four steps before he caught her from behind. He had unfurled the length of rope and bound her with astonishing speed, securing her within his cloak with her arms trussed against her sides. She might have panicked at his intent, but he knotted the rope around her knees as well, hobbling her so that she could not run.

It also meant that he could not abuse her.

"Fiend," she snarled as she struggled and wondered at this. "You dropped the crossbow."

He only grinned. "Into a nice bed of leaves and snow. It is undamaged." He picked up the crossbow and held it before her to prove his words. He slung it over his back. Then he spun her around, his hand on the back of her neck as they moved deeper into the forest.

"Guide me back to the camp of my fellows, and no trickery," he commanded. "Speed is of the essence if Percy is to be retrieved before much befalls him."

As much as Anna would have liked to have defied his command, he spoke good sense. Would he and his fellows truly help to retrieve Percy? She supposed they wanted that prize back.

But she wanted both crossbow and brother.

Anna guessed that this knight's price might be higher than she would have liked.

Still, she did not have a choice, and he would be the kind to both recognize as much and use it against her.

How she hated knights!

Chapter Two

"Explain your terms to me, clearly," Anna demanded when they were out of earshot of the village. She thought it better to act as if she were in a position of power than to acknowledge outright that the knight had much advantage.

"Why?"

"Because you and your kind are deceptive," she said, her tone cross. "I would know your intent before I am of assistance to you, the better to ensure that I am not tricked."

"You think little of knights."

"I do."

"Yet you would make an agreement with me."

"Aye. I perceive that I have little choice, for I will need aid to retrieve Percy."

"Have you no other allies?"

She shook her head, choosing not to betray the others in the forest, then spared him a backward glance. "If you would treat with a woman."

He smiled. "Only one who keeps her word."

"I do!"

"I have no way to know as much. You have promised me naught thus far so owe me naught." He marched in silence for a moment, as if mustering his argument. "As I see it, we each have something of interest to the other, or have contributed to the loss of something possessed by the other. Together have a better chance of retrieving both."

"Agreed," Anna said, though it nigh killed her to agree with one of his ilk.

"To state it clearly, so that no one believes themselves deceived, you stole the saddlebag that is now in the keep of Haynesdale. I and my fellows would like it and its contents back."

"My brother was taken by the baron's men. I should like him back." She granted him another glance. "Hale and free."

"You are skeptical of my intent," he said mildly. "I cannot vouchsafe for his state until he is in our company, but I will not do him injury. Does that suffice?"

"What of your fellows?"

"They will not do as much either. It is against our nature and our vows to injure a child."

"Even a thief?"

"Even a thief." The knight's agreement was so easy that Anna eyed him, knowing her doubt was clear. He smiled at her, which was most discomfiting. "Who would have taught him how to behave with honor?" he asked with humor. "You? Having poor instruction and not knowing the difference cannot be his fault, not at such an age."

"I do not grant poor instruction!"

"Then you think a life as a thief has merit. An interesting moral code."

"I think life has merit, when the alternative is to starve."

"Is this not a prosperous holding? The land seems most bountiful."

Anna snorted again. "It depends who you are, that much is certain. I hear the baron's table groans with plenty and that his coffers overflow with the taxes he is determined to collect."

"Have you no love for your overlord and baron? Surely his powers are rightfully gained?"

"Surely not! These lands were stolen from the rightful baron, stolen by a Norman knight who coveted both the holding and the wife of the Baron of Haynesdale. The villain was triumphant in claiming Haynesdale and now rules with disgust and disdain for all those beneath his hand." She lifted her chin. "One day, the seed of Nicholas will return, so it is said. One day, the son of the true lineage will return to Haynesdale and reclaim his legacy and bring justice to all those who have remained loyal to his family name."

The knight was particularly quiet after this utterance, and Anna assumed he was skeptical of such optimistic omens.

She continued in a scathing tone. "But then, you come from France yourself. I see it in your garb and hear it in your voice. Doubtless, you would ally with him and sit contentedly at his board, oblivious to the suffering of those upon his lands."

"Perhaps I will," the knight mused.

Anna gasped outrage, then saw the Templars step out of the shadows ahead. The knight spoke to them quickly and in French, which Anna did not understand. They nodded and scanned the forest behind her, then followed the knight and herself into the camp. All of the party were awake, and their expressions were not welcoming.

"One of our thieves," the knight said, giving her a push toward the middle of the clearing. Did he speak English for her benefit? "She works with her younger brother, who fled with Duncan's saddlebag and was captured by knights in the service of the baron who holds title to these lands. Percy and the bag have been taken to the baron's keep."

The Scotsman winced and sat down heavily. The other knight laid a hand upon his shoulder as if to reassure him. "And so? We visit the baron together to retrieve our respective prizes?" he asked, that Highland lilt in his voice.

"Take the lass like that and she will be dispatched to join the boy, whatever his fate might be," the Scotsman said, his tone dour.

"Precisely," the knight who had captured her agreed. He smiled at her, which Anna did not trust a whit. "Which is why I would propose that we visit this baron, as a party on our way north to attend the wedding of Fergus, once a Templar and now a noble friend."

The other knight, who must be Fergus, smiled. "We arrive as friends, then, not foes."

"And the lass?" the older man asked. "No one could take a look at her and think her a boy in truth."

"Nay, they could not." The knight's eyes gleamed. "Which is why she will travel as my wife. Might we trouble you for the loan of some of that fine garb you bought for your betrothed, Fergus? Your generosity is such that Isobel cannot miss the sacrifice of one kirtle."

Fergus laughed, his manner so merry that Anna found herself liking him even though his amusement was at her expense. "Particularly if Duncan regains his property."

"I will not pretend to be your wife!" Anna protested hotly.

The knight smiled with infuriating confidence. "Then I am in possession of a fine crossbow," he countered with a shrug. "And Percy cannot rely upon our ensuring his rescue. Ah well."

"I will see to my brother myself."

He leaned close, his eyes shining with intent. "Not if I leave you trussed in a tree."

"You would not!"

But his expression did not change and Anna knew he would. "Fiend! Knave and blackguard! You compel me to do your will, with no regard for my own choice..."

"She sounds like a wife," commented one Templar, then made to tend his steed.

"I hope she is worth the trouble," replied the other and they laughed together.

"I will not welcome you to my bed!" Anna cried, struck with new fear.

The knight slid a finger down her cheek. "We will be compelled to share a bed," he murmured. "In order to ensure that our ruse is not discovered." There was a twinkle in his eyes that Anna did not trust. Did he intend to take his pleasure? "But I vow the bed will be chaste, unless you insist otherwise."

The words could only be a lie.

"Wretch!" she muttered and tried to kick him. She only lost her balance from her efforts but the knight did not allow her to fall. He caught her up and his gaze bored into her own, his manner solemn. His grip was uncommonly strong.

"And so we make our wager. Alliance in the baron's hall, the goal being the retrieval of both bag and boy, and on our successful escape from that place, our paths will part. We will have safe passage through the forest, and you will have the return of your crossbow on the northern borders. Have we a wager?"

"Have you a name?" she demanded, unable to fully hide her resentment that she was compelled to accept his terms.

Even though they were not unfair.

"Bartholomew de Châmont-sur-Maine," he said. "And you?"

"Anna of Haynesdale village. The smith's daughter."

"And have we a wager, Anna?"

"Aye, sir."

"Bartholomew," he corrected, that smile quirking his lips in a most alluring way. "We are to be wed after all, Anna."

"Bartholomew," she echoed, liking the sound of his name. She wriggled pointedly. "I regret that I cannot seal our wager with a shaking of hands."

"It is of no matter," he said easily. "I have learned well how to improvise."

Then without waiting for her to agree, the cur bent and kissed her soundly. The other men hooted and clapped approval, and Anna was flooded with new terror. She froze, convinced that his intent was to claim her fully and feared a repeat of her past.

To her amazement, Bartholomew seemed to be aware of her reaction.

To her greater astonishment, it changed his deed. He lifted his head and broke their kiss almost immediately, but did not release her. His eyes gleamed as he surveyed her, seeking an explanation. Anna tried to kick him as a reward for his cursed confidence and his audacity.

This time, he let her fall.

And his fellows laughed.

Curse him to Hell and back again!

è▲

Bartholomew was not an impulsive man, but Anna's audacity tempted him to be so. Her attitude and her assumptions irked him as little else had done in a long while, and there was a perverse pleasure to be savored in surprising her.

He also had been startled to hear her speak of the seed of Nicholas, and the ultimate return of that baron's son. He was surprised that the tale of his father had survived, no less that his own arrival might be anticipated. Even more oddly, it survived in this place that did not look in the least bit familiar to him. Had he forgotten all he had known? What of the mill? He could see it clearly in his memory, but there was none here. How could that be?

And what of this baron who held Haynesdale now? She said he was the villain and treated those beneath his hand unfairly. Did that mean he was out of favor with the king? Bartholomew suspected not, which meant the current baron would have to die before there could be a question of making a claim. Did he have a son?

Of greater import, could this maiden help him to claim his

rightful due? Would she believe any claim he made to be the son of Nicholas?

Would anyone else?

And why had a kiss so terrified her?

Anna tumbled to the ground and rolled a little, struggling furiously. Her eyes were filled with loathing when she glared at him, but Bartholomew crouched down beside her.

"Reconsidered?" he asked lightly.

"You take pleasure in vexing me."

"In truth, I do." He admitted the truth easily, marveling in it even as he did so.

"Knave," she repeated. "Cur, blackguard, and scoundrel."

He smiled, untroubled by her words. "Insults will not improve your situation."

"There is no reason for us to pretend to be wedded," she argued, the heat of her reaction making him wonder if there was more merit in the impulsive suggestion than he had anticipated.

"There is every reason for such a feint," he countered mildly. "What I desire is within the keep. What you desire is within the keep. The only way to release both is to enter the keep."

"I am not a simpleton."

"So, how would you propose we enter the keep, without arousing suspicion of our intent?"

"You go as you are, a French knight visiting one of his own kind, and I will go as a boy, perhaps as a squire."

Bartholomew shook his head. "No one with any wits about them would fail to note that you are a woman. Your disguise, if that is what it is, works only in darkness."

There was no question of having another woman disguised as a squire in the company. Anna would be quickly revealed, and that might prompt their host and his men to look more closely at their guests. Bartholomew would not so imperil Leila, who was garbed as one of Fergus' squires and had answered to the name Laurent all the way from Jerusalem.

He pushed to his feet. "I think that our pretending to be a wedded couple might serve our needs well."

"Which needs?" Anna demanded with obvious suspicion.

What had happened to her? Bartholomew might have guessed that she had been used by a knight for his pleasure, given her hostility toward his kind.

He spoke reasonably. "You do not trust me. I do not trust you. I can see no other way for us to be sure of each other's actions at all times than to pose as a wedded couple."

"Your arguments would give the tale credence," commented the Templar Enguerrand and his companion laughed.

"And visiting as guests will give us the opportunity to learn more of the keep and how well it is armed," Fergus noted, to general agreement.

"There is another option, lass," Duncan said. "You could remain bound and be taken as our prisoner. Doubtless, the baron has a dungeon for villains."

Bartholomew nodded approval, even as Anna looked daggers at Duncan. "A fine notion. I should know the precise location of our thief then." He smiled at Anna, savoring her vexation a little more than he knew she appreciated. Aye, it was amusing to tease her, when her eyes made her thoughts so clear. "Perhaps you would find your brother there."

Duncan grimaced. "Although it is likely the pair would be compelled to face the baron's justice."

"It might be a fitting solution," Bartholomew mused. "Plus I could keep this crossbow," he added, purely to annoy Anna.

It worked perfectly. Her eyes flashed and she struggled with new vigor.

"You are an irksome man, even for a French knight," Anna growled, wriggling in her bonds. Aye, there was no hiding the ripe curves of her breasts and hips. Was she older than Leila?

She had kissed like a frightened maiden, though. Bartholomew found his interest growing.

"I shall take that as a compliment," he said, as if disinterested in her fate. In truth, he was quite certain she would cede to his suggestion. "To the baron's keep and his dungeons then at first light." Bartholomew strode to the fire, intending to stir it up, even as his fellows began to prepare themselves to depart. "Even better, Fergus has no need to be generous with the gifts intended for his lady."

"I cede!" Anna cried, and Bartholomew ignored her for a moment. "I said I cede, sir!"

"Did you hear something?" Bartholomew asked Duncan, who

chuckled.

"I addressed you and you know it well," Anna said with that same fury.

He looked upward. "The wind in the trees, perhaps." The other knights chuckled then, and Anna fumed.

"You heard me well, you cursedly confident man!"

Bartholomew turned to face her, placing his hands on his hips. "Fear not, Anna. I will make as much haste as possible to see you reunited with Percy in the baron's stronghold."

He thought he heard her swear under her breath and fought the urge to laugh.

"We have a wager, sir." Anna caught her breath and corrected herself. "*Bartholomew*," she said through gritted teeth. "And I will not be the one to break it first."

"So, we do have a wager."

"We do." She glared at him. "Sealed even with a kiss."

He rubbed his brow. "But you are of these parts. What if you are recognized? We could all be cast in peril, then."

"I daresay a wash will remove any chance of that," Duncan said grimly. The men in the party laughed, and Anna fumed visibly.

"Surely your friend has a veil for his lady?" she suggested with hope.

"Surely he does," he agreed. He reached for the knot of the rope. "We have a wager and now you must be made presentable."

"I can garb myself."

"But Duncan's argument is a fair one. You are filthy and likely infested with vermin." He made an elaborate grimace, just to see her eyes flash.

"I am not!"

"You do not look like any woman I would take to wife." Bartholomew shook his head sagely. He was enjoying this encounter far too much. "Nay, if this ruse is to be plausible, I will see you scrubbed clean myself."

"Oh! You will do no such thing!"

He lifted his hands away. "I thought you were *not* the one who would break our wager?"

"But you did not mention this earlier. I would not be displayed nude before you all."

"Not before all." He smiled. "Simply your lord husband."

Anna looked willing to flay him alive.

"A wife should be biddable, Anna," he reminded her gently. He knew he heard her teeth grind.

Then she smiled at him, the smile of a woman who preferred to see him thrashed. "A knight should be gallant, Bartholomew."

Bartholomew laughed for he could not help himself. "And where is it writ that I will not be? Be easy, Anna. I do not partake of any feast unless it is willingly offered."

She lifted her chin, her manner yet indignant. "I bathed at Samhain," she informed him. "That is sufficient until Beltane."

"A bath twice a year?" Bartholomew made a face. "That explains much of your scent, Anna." Duncan chuckled at that and she glared at the men in turn.

"How oft do *you* bathe?" she demanded.

"As oft as possible," Bartholomew replied and took note of Anna's surprise. He stood her up then and felt the vibration of rebellion in her body as he untied her bonds. He met her gaze steadily, his manner serious in his intent to ensure she took his warning to heart. "Know that if you flee, I will catch you, and our discussions will not be as friendly as they are now."

"I do not find our discussions so friendly as that."

"I will destroy the crossbow and abandon your brother." He fixed her with a look and her lips tightened. "Are we understood?"

"Swear it to me," she demanded. "Swear that you will treat me with honor, and swear it on something of import to you. I have not known much good when at the mercy of knights."

Bartholomew wondered what she had endured, for he saw a flash of vulnerability in her eyes. That fleeting expression changed all for him. He drew his sword and she flinched visibly, but he supported the weight of the blade on one palm. He showed her the pommel, which was formed of a rock crystal orb. The sphere had been halved once and a shard of wood trapped between the two halves. It was snared in a setting shaped like a dragon's claw, which held the orb securely together.

"This is a splinter from the True Cross," he informed Anna, whose eyes widened. "And this blade a gift from my patron and friend, who blessed me with such a weapon that I might always strike true." He kissed the orb, then held the sword up so that the first rays of sunlight illuminated it. He heard Anna catch her breath.

A shadow was cast upon the snow by the upraised blade, a cross with fire at its summit. She looked from the shadow to the sword to Bartholomew with obvious awe.

"Upon this talisman, I pledge to defend you as if you were my wife in truth, and to treat you with honor. I vow to do all within my power to see Percy set free, Duncan's belongings returned, and you left safely wheresoever you desire."

Anna swallowed visibly. "I swear to show you the same honor," she whispered. Bartholomew offered the orb to her and she eyed it for a long moment, then touched her lips to the crystal. Her eyes closed and her lashes fluttered against her cheeks, the expression making her look angelic and sweet.

Her manner changed in that moment, for her defiance seemed to melt after her lips touched the token. She took a steadying breath before her gaze locked with his and her animosity was gone. "Thank you, Bartholomew," she said quietly and he smiled at her.

Indeed, his heart gave a strange lurch, and he wondered if there would be more gained in this adventure than the return of Duncan's saddlebag.

He sheathed his blade and untied her bonds, feeling that the fight had gone out of her. He did not trust her, that was certain, but he was glad to have reassured her.

And truth be told, he was looking forward to seeing her clean and suitably garbed. Was Anna a fair maiden? Bartholomew was curious indeed.

ð

A shard of the True Cross.

Anna had never thought to see such a marvel. Given that assurance from any other, she would have doubted the relic to be genuine, but the reverence in Bartholomew's gaze could not have been feigned. He could not have seen that the Templars both dropped to one knee when he held up the sword. Both Duncan and Fergus bowed their heads and crossed themselves, while the squires stared in awe. It was clear they all believed this prize to be what Bartholomew claimed.

It had seemed that a divine finger had touched the orb of crystal, sending a beam of light through it as if to approve of the marvel, or to endorse it. Either way, Anna had found herself convinced of the relic's merit.

And much closer to acknowledging that the knight might have some merit as well. What manner of friends did he have, if one granted him such a prize as this for a gift?

He took her back to the river, the weight of his hand heavy on the back of her neck, leaving his armor behind. He also left his fellows behind and she was glad that she would not be exposed to all of them.

Could she trust him?

Bartholomew shed his tabard and boots while the last of the rope was still knotted around her knees and wrists. Anna could not resist the urge to steal glances at him but dared not look fully upon him. He tugged his chemise over his head and she saw that he was yet tanned from the summer's sun. A fleeting glimpse revealed that he was also finely wrought and muscled. He returned to her in his chausses and she averted her gaze, blushing as he made quick work of the last knots.

Anna's heart was thundering and her mouth was dry. There was no seduction in his manner, though, merely purpose, as if seeing her clean was merely a task to be done. His cloak was cast aside and he frowned at her wet and dirty garb. "You *are* filthy," he muttered.

"It is easier to hide in the forest when one smells like the forest," she countered.

He arched a brow. "I suppose that is one excuse for it. All of it, off. It will have to be burned."

Anna hesitated to undress before him. Though she was not shy about nudity, she felt so in such a man's presence. She did not wish him to see the token she kept hidden between her breasts. "Will you not turn your back?"

Bartholomew grinned. "Would you in my place?"

"You wish to look upon me."

"I wish to ensure you do not take advantage of me." He fixed her with an intent glance. "Would you turn your back upon me, were our roles reversed?"

She could not help but smile, for she would not have done so. "Still, I would keep some modesty," she said, trying to sound haughty. The weight of the ring on the lace around her neck was sufficient reminder of the truth. Anna turned her back upon

Bartholomew and kicked off her shoes, then untied her belt and tugged her tabard over her head. She hesitated before unknotting her chausses and he cleared his throat behind her.

"Do you have need of assistance?" he demanded with impatience. "Because I should be glad to be of aid, if you have trouble with the knot."

"Not I," she said and shed the chausses with speed. The chemise was long enough to cover her hips, and she glanced over her shoulder at him.

"All of it," he commanded and grimaced. "I cannot even see what color your chemise once was. God's wounds but this water is cold!"

Anna untied the lace at the neck as she stepped into the water. It was icy cold. She tugged the garment quickly over her head, flinging it toward him, then ducked into the stream so that her nudity was hidden from view.

She did not flee, although she wished to do as much. Instead, she turned in the water to regard him. "I will stay here," she insisted. "And you will stay there."

"You will be quick," he countered. She shivered, having no doubt of that. "Timothy!" he called over his shoulder and Anna sank lower into the water. A boy, clearly his squire and the one he had summoned, scrambled down the slope. He presented several thick cloths to Bartholomew and a small piece of something pale. The boy glanced at Anna but she crossed her arms over her breasts, remaining low. Bartholomew cleared his throat and the boy raced back up the slope.

"Soap," Bartholomew said, crouching on the bank to offer the lump to her. "And a thick cloth to scrub away that mire. Be quick or I will do it myself."

Anna eased closer, not truly trusting him, but he granted her both. Their fingers brushed and he scowled at her. "You are already chilled. Show some haste, Anna, and a care for your own welfare." Then he straightened and stared down at her, his arms folded across his chest, as imposing as she might imagine any man could be.

Under his watchful gaze, Anna worked the filth from her flesh. The soap smelled wonderful, finer than any she had ever be so fortunate as to use, and the cloth was both thick and woven as if for this very purpose. She had never felt the like. It was most luxurious.

She scrubbed so hard that her skin warmed. Had she not been so cold, it might have turned rosy. As it was, she found it most welcome to feel clean again.

"Your face," Bartholomew instructed and she washed it as bidden. Her face was buried in the cloth when he spoke again.

"Do you need assistance with your hair?"

Anna jumped at the sound of splashing water in close proximity. Evidently, he had not awaited her reply, for she felt his hands in her hair. She stiffened, thinking he meant to dunk her, but he did not. He rubbed some potion into her scalp and through her hair, then dipped her into the river for a moment to rinse. She came up sputtering and heard his chuckle as she wiped the water from her eyes. She kept low in the water to hide her treasure, knowing he would assume she meant to hide her breasts.

"Are you a lady's maid or a knight?" she demanded, and Bartholomew dunked her again.

"You are not the first ruffian I have seen cleaned," he said with humor in his tone when she came up for air. Anna shook her head and wiped the water from her face to find him close beside her, a twinkle in his eyes as he studied her. "Well, well," he murmured. "There was a pearl in the mire after all."

Anna felt her cheeks heat and might have retreated from the warmth in his eyes but Bartholomew reached for the lace around her neck. "What is this?" he asked, his curiosity clear.

Anna closed a hand around the ring. "A token from a loved one," she said. "And no matter for you to see."

His eyes narrowed. "The lace is dirty, as well."

"The lace will remain."

Their gazes held for a long moment and she feared he would challenge her anew, Instead, his expression turned stern and he stepped back. "Recall your vow," he said, then scrubbed his own face and hair. He was not two paces away from her and she knew she would not get far if she chose to run. In truth, she did not wish to break her pledge.

She took the opportunity to survey him and was even more impressed by his vigor. Indeed, Bartholomew was more well made than any man she had ever seen. She dared to take a better look while he could not observe her boldness. There was a scar on his chest, one obscured by the dark tangle of hair that grew there, but she could see that the flesh was puckered and reddened there.

Of course, it would have been strange for a knight to have not been scarred. To have had a wound so close to his heart, even a small one, could not have been a minor injury. She thought to ask him after it, but wagered he would want to see what hung on the lace around her neck in exchange.

He was one for bargains, to be sure.

And not a displeasing man. Anna found herself recalling that kiss and feeling an unfamiliar warmth flow through her body. If he did it again, she might allow herself to enjoy his touch a little. She wrung out her hair, wondering how she would see it braided as a lady's hair should be. She had no idea how the feat was accomplished.

"Don the cloak," Bartholomew advised, as she made for the bank. "Timothy will bring me clean linen and you should be covered when he returns."

Anna did as instructed, well aware that he watched her with care. Once she was wrapped in the fullness of his cloak, she sat on a stone and tucked her feet beneath its folds to stay warm.

Bartholomew smiled that she did not flee and she felt a curious pleasure in his satisfaction. He strode out of the stream, shaking his head like a great dog, and she had ample opportunity to see his nudity. The water beaded on his tanned flesh and she took note of his obvious strength. He would be a formidable foe in battle, and she was glad to be entering the baron's keep under his protection. His confidence was deserved, for he moved with an ease she found most alluring.

Timothy returned, once again moving with haste, and offered a heavy cloth to his knight. He gathered up the soap and cloths while Bartholomew dried himself, then presented clean linens. Bartholomew donned the chemise, which was whiter and finer than any Anna had seen before, then clean linen braies. His dark chausses went over the braies, then he donned his boots. He indicated that Timothy should gather her discarded clothing, then strode toward her and scooped her up into his arms before striding back to the camp.

"I can walk!"

"In bare feet, in winter?" He shook his head. "Hardly fitting for my lady wife." He winked at her then, and Anna considered that this wager might have unexpected benefits. It had been long indeed since any soul had fended for her. Usually, she cared for others.

Her dirty clothing was burned, despite her protests, upon the fire that was now blazing. A thick smoke rose into the morning sky and the Scotsman shook his head. "Our presence is not a secret any longer," he murmured, and it was true.

Fergus and Bartholomew conferred over that Scottish knight's collection of gifts for his betrothed, then Bartholomew brought Anna a linen chemise as fine and white as his own. A pair of stockings with red garters, fine leather shoes, and a splendid crimson kirtle with gold embroidery on the hem was also offered to her.

"I could not wear such a gown!" Anna could not hide her astonishment, which made Fergus laugh aloud.

"Consider it a wedding gift," he teased.

"A necessary concession to see justice served," Duncan agreed. "The hue would not favor Isobel, in my opinion."

Fergus laughed again. "I fear you speak aright, although I like it well."

Bartholomew considered Anna. "It will favor Anna, I believe."

For her part, Anna was flustered by the generosity of the loan. "I shall ensure all is returned to you as pristine as in this moment," she vowed.

"Do not pledge what you might not be able to see done," Bartholomew said, and she wondered what they expected to find. They were all so suddenly grim that a chill struck her heart.

"What *was* within that saddlebag?" she asked and all but Bartholomew turned away.

"It is not for you to know," he said tersely. "But any who looks upon it will not surrender it readily."

What burden did these knights carry?

Would Percy pay for it with his life?

The notion was terrifying. She had to aid Bartholomew in making this ruse work.

కా

Anna was beautiful.

Astonishingly so.

There could be no doubt that she was a woman, and once again, Bartholomew wondered at her age. Younger than him, he would guess, but not quite as young as Leila. Perhaps of an age with Lady Ysmaine's maid Radegunde. Once garbed in the finery intended for Isobel, she would indeed look to be a noblewoman. Bartholomew dressed, donning his aketon and hauberk, glancing at Anna at intervals. She donned the stockings and shoes, then the chemise and he saw her marvel at its weave.

"It is so fine," she murmured, then impaled him with a glance. He had just tugged on his hauberk and Timothy was fastening his belt. He noted again the shadow between her breasts, the one caused by that token that hung upon the lace, and wondered what she treasured.

Anna sat down, drawing his cloak over her shoulders again. "But there is one matter I cannot see done," she said. He thought she meant to defy him, but she lifted the weight of her wet hair. "I do not know how to braid it as noblewomen do."

Bartholomew was flummoxed. "Nor do I," he admitted, seeing the flaw in their scheme.

"She should have a maid," Fergus added, though his tone was more indicative of a man with a solution than one finding a problem.

Of course. Bartholomew turned to Leila, who was watching him keenly. The Saracen girl had been his friend in Jerusalem and had journeyed this far in their company disguised as a squire.

She cleared her throat and spoke gruffly. "My cousin oft asked me to braid her hair," she said, maintaining the guise of being a boy. "I could be of aid."

Bartholomew knew that Leila had fled a marriage arranged by her uncle and, though she had never confessed the details, he was certain she must have good cause to have left all she knew. Fergus had offered Leila the position as his squire. He said no more, for the surrender of her disguise had to be Leila's choice. He assumed the tale of the cousin was a lie, meant to disguise the fact that she had braided her own hair once.

What did she intend to do in Scotland? Had she considered her future, now that Outremer was far behind them?

Leila rummaged in her small bag of possessions and removed a comb. It was carved of a fine golden wood. Duncan started at the sight of it and Leila smiled at him.

"Radegunde gave it to me," she admitted and he nodded. Apparently, the man-at-arms had seen it before. Fortunately, none of those unaware of Leila's truth found it odd that a maid would give a comb to a squire.

Yet.

Leila went to Anna's side and reached for the ends of her hair. Anna wrinkled her nose and gave Bartholomew a disparaging glance. "What is the point of a bath, if the squire who aids me smells of dung?" Before he could reply, she turned sharply to face Leila. Her eyes narrowed, her gaze dancing from Leila's hands to her face.

Bartholomew knew the moment that Anna realized the truth, for her lips parted in surprise. She tried to hide her reaction, but he had already noted that she had little talent for subterfuge. Indeed, she turned to him, a question in her eyes.

Leila, meanwhile, put the comb in Anna's hands. She straightened and turned to Fergus, then bowed. "My lord," she said in her usual voice, speaking French. "I believe it is time."

"The choice was always yours to make," he replied, inclining his head and smiling approval.

The Templars looked between them with evident confusion, a reaction shared by their squires. Anna clearly did not understand the exchange, though she had guessed the truth of Leila's sex.

Leila retrieved the small bag that she had carried since their departure from Châmont-sur-Maine, and Bartholomew realized that Radegunde must have given her more than a comb. The two women had seemed to become friends after the party's departure from Paris. Had that been Duncan's doing? He looked indulgent in this moment, as if all came to pass as he had anticipated.

Leila put out a hand before Timothy, requesting the soap. The boy surrendered it after confirming with Bartholomew that he was permitted to do so. He looked no less confused than the Templars, but Hamish and Duncan were unsurprised.

Leila made for the stream with purpose, even as the rest of the party stared after her. Moments later, she could be heard splashing, out of sight. At a nod from Fergus, the boys served the last of their bread and cheese that they might break their fast. There was a wineskin with a last measure of red wine from Gaston's abode, and a few apples yet, but it was time for them to find more provisions. Bartholomew doubted that he was the sole one who would have welcomed a hot meal.

Anna ate with haste, showing an astonishing appetite and one that made him wonder when last she had eaten at all. By the time Leila strode up the slope from the stream, they were preparing to depart. Every man and boy in the company turned at the sound of her footsteps and each one of them stared.

Anna was not the sole one transformed. Leila wore a simple kirtle of a green hue and a leather belt. She wore yet the same boots and her dark hair curled around her face. Though she had cut her hair in Jerusalem, there could be no doubting that she was a maiden, and an alluring one.

Bartholomew smiled, even as many of his fellows stared in astonishment.

Chapter Three

"But, but, Laurent," Timothy whispered, his shock clear.

"Leila," Leila corrected as she returned the soap to the astonished squire. She cast her filthy garb on to the fire with evident satisfaction. She plucked the comb from Anna's fingers and set to work on her hair, as the Templars began to consult with each other in agitated murmurs. They were both frowning when they raised their voices to confront the other knights.

"So, we have unwittingly journeyed with a woman in our company?" demanded one.

"It is against the Rule!"

"It is not against the Rule to protect those in need of our defense," Fergus replied.

"But it was a lie!"

"It was a scheme to protect this maiden, and one endorsed by the Grand Master in Jerusalem," Bartholomew supplied. The Templars appeared to be slightly more at ease with this additional information, but still eyed the remainder of the company warily. He wondered whether they expected more women to be revealed in their ranks.

"Not all was a lie," Leila said softly, smiling at Fergus. "I do have a cousin whose hair I braided." She combed Anna's hair deftly, braiding it and coiling it with all speed. "You will need to open your bags again," she said to Fergus. "A lady has need of a wimple, a veil and a circlet."

"Glad I am that I brought so many trinkets for my betrothed," Fergus jested, even as he unfastened his saddlebags anew.

"'Tis no coincidence, lad, and you know it well," Duncan murmured. Fergus smiled in acknowledgment.

"What do you mean?" Bartholomew had to ask for he did not understand.

"This lad was born to the caul. He has the Sight, though he seldom tells what he has seen."

"Witchery," whispered one Templar, and they crossed themselves as did their squires. The other scanned the forest, seeking yet more unwelcome surprises.

But the sole one for Bartholomew was the sight of the thief transformed. He could not tear his gaze from Anna as Leila finished the braiding and coiling of her hair, for the elegant length of her neck was revealed. She looked fragile and feminine, as he had not guessed her to be. The wimple and veil gave her an alluring mystery, and it seemed to him that her eyes sparkled in new awareness of her charms. She cast a shy glance at him, then smiled and blushed a little, evidently noting his reaction and finding it discomfiting.

She had been abused by a man then. He would have to treat her gently.

Truth be told, Bartholomew found the blend of traits in her nature most beguiling. Perhaps he had never been smitten with a woman because they seemed to be concerned with their garb and their embroidery, or their likelihood of bearing sons. He admired that Anna possessed a crossbow and acknowledged that she had given him a fair contest in the woods. He doubted that any who had known her as a ruffian would recognize her like this.

Bartholomew was intrigued by this maiden and sensed that state would not abandon him soon.

Anna rose to her feet as Leila laced the sides of the crimson kirtle, then turned in place with obvious delight at her garb. "Sir, I thank you for your generosity," she said to Fergus and bowed low in her gratitude. Even her way of speaking had changed, as if the garb wrought a transformation in her very nature.

"You will earn it, if we retrieve the saddlebag with your aid," that knight replied. He smiled at Leila, who was hastily breaking her fast.

"Which means we must know all you can tell us of this baron, his household, and his defenses," Bartholomew said. "His keep cannot be far by the road." He was looking forward to seeing the keep in daylight, for there had been naught familiar about it in the night. Perhaps he would recognize it better this morning, and from the vantage point of the road.

Surely there could not be two holdings called Haynesdale? Nay, it could not be so, for Anna had shared the tale of his own father. Bartholomew was the seed of Nicholas, and his arrival was evidently anticipated by Anna.

Still, it was disconcerting to have no memory of this place at all.

He watched as Anna considered the height of the sun. "This road leads directly to his gates. With such steeds and a stately pace, we will reach it by midday."

"An excellent time for guests to arrive," Fergus said with satisfaction.

"A hot meal would be welcome," Duncan said, echoing Bartholomew's own thoughts.

"Not a cup of ale?" Fergus teased and they laughed together.

Bartholomew nodded. "Then we should set out, that we are at his gates before we are discovered and believed to be trespassers." He smiled at Anna. "As you have no steed, my lady, it seems you must ride with me."

"I could ride with my maid," she countered with familiar defiance.

"You could, if I trusted you." Bartholomew strode to Zephyr, who stamped in anticipation of a run. "Or if I did not wish to confer with you about our host."

Anna folded her arms across her chest, showing no inclination to do as he suggested. "But what of this company? Who are you all and from whence did you ride? How did such a company come to be assembled? And what is your destination?"

"We ride from Jerusalem," Fergus said to Bartholomew's relief. "For I return to Scotland for my nuptials, after the completion of my service with the order."

"We brought tidings of events in Outremer to the Temple in Paris," Bartholomew added.

"And once there, the gratitude of the Grand Master was such that he granted Fergus an escort to his home," Duncan said, gesturing to the two Templars. They bowed their heads to Anna.

"Enguerrand," confided one.

"Yvan," added the other.

"Jerusalem?" Anna echoed in awe. "You rode from the Holy City itself?"

Bartholomew nodded. "We did."

"And why do you go to Scotland?" she demanded of him.

"To witness the nuptials of my friend, of course."

"But you are not of the order?"

He shook his head.

"Do you have a holding?"

"I praise God that you are not overly curious," Fergus drawled, and Duncan chuckled.

Anna turned on him, fire in her eyes. "If I am to be his bride, then I should know some detail of his life."

Fergus shrugged. "We should all like to know more of Bartholomew's secrets," he drawled and she turned to Bartholomew anew.

"I have no secrets," he said softly.

"Nay?" Fergus asked. "Then why the insistence upon this road?"

"And why the departure from Gaston's abode?" Duncan added.

Bartholomew held his ground. "I wished to see your home and more of the world, no more than that," he said, though he imagined Fergus remained skeptical. He bowed to the other knight. "But perhaps you, when you come into your inheritance, will see your way to offering me a post in your keep."

Fergus lifted a brow. "After you declined a similar offer from Gaston? It might well be a waste of breath."

"And it might not." Bartholomew had not told them of his hope for Haynesdale, but he had insisted they travel by this route. He knew that both men were curious beyond all, and was relieved when the subject was dropped. He felt a strange conviction that to express his dream aloud would reveal the folly of it.

Anna bit her lip. "So it is the promise of goodwill that keeps you by his side."

Bartholomew chose to tease her. "I am only practical. We must eat something, wife, particularly if we are to have sons." Duncan smiled and turned to his steed.

Anna held his gaze for a long moment, her intensity making his heart leap. It was almost as if she guessed the truth that he did not wish to utter aloud, as if she discerned the secret he hid from all.

But that was impossible.

"You are a wretchedly confident man," she said with a shake of her head. "To take a bride with no means of supporting her is most audacious."

Bartholomew grinned despite himself, for he would never have committed such an impetus deed.

"Perhaps he trusts that the course of love will run true," Fergus teased.

Anna flushed. "Perhaps he is fortunate that our match is but a tale," she countered. "Were I truly a bride and learned as much of my husband's scheme, I might well abandon the match."

"You could not if it had been consummated," Bartholomew observed.

"Then I am the fortunate one," she retorted. "For I have yet a choice."

Bartholomew grinned at her. "Was that a challenge, my lady? Shall I see you seduced this night to ensure that your choice is made?"

Though his tone was teasing, again her reaction was vehement. "You could not. You would not!" She even retreated from him.

"I might convince you."

Anna flushed furiously and strode toward the horses. It proved that her elegant manners were readily abandoned, for she moved with her former purpose. "Vexing man," she muttered.

"'Tis why you love me," Bartholomew countered. "I see the truth of it in your eyes."

"Wretch," she whispered, but her blush deepened.

"Their match was destined to be," Fergus teased but Anna ignored him.

Bartholomew swung into the saddle, then urged Zephyr toward a fallen log. Anna climbed atop it, more agile than any lady he had ever known. He held her hand and she used the stirrup to climb and ride pillion behind him. She had donned his cloak again and flicked it out of the way as she positioned herself, then draped it over Zephyr's back with Leila's assistance. Then the younger woman climbed into the saddle of her palfrey.

"You will have to touch me, my lady," he advised quietly when Anna did not lean against him.

She gave a sigh of forbearance. "I suppose it is inevitable, my lord," she ceded with such feigned deference that he could not bite back his smile.

"Is my wish not your command?" he teased.

"Do not vex me overmuch, sir," Anna countered. "Not if you mean to sleep in my company."

"Surely Leila will defend me," he retorted.

"Surely she will," that maiden replied with vigor. "For there are no more noble knights in Christendom than those of this company, particularly my lady's lord husband. No woman could ever find a better man."

Bartholomew felt Anna's surprise at this endorsement of his character and realized there might be additional benefit to having Leila act as Anna's maid. Anna's arms wound around his waist and she leaned cautiously against his back.

Bartholomew felt a strange satisfaction to have her weight against him. He clicked his tongue, and Zephyr tossed his head, prancing toward the road. The party arranged itself in pairs, Bartholomew and Fergus at the fore, and the Templars at the rear. Duncan rode in the midst with Leila, Timothy and Hamish ahead of them and the Templars' squires behind. They reached the road, which was of pounded dirt but even and straight, and the steeds began to canter.

Bartholomew swallowed, both anxious for a better glimpse of the keep that might be his birthright and fearful of what their arrival would bring.

❧

What a remarkable company. The more she learned of Bartholomew and his fellows, the more Anna was inclined to believe that they might succeed in retrieving both their saddlebag and Percy from the baron's keep. They did have unexpected advantages and seemed most intrepid.

Indeed, her terror was rapidly being replaced with anticipation.

Her curiosity about the contents of that saddlebag also grew with every passing moment.

"Now tell us of this baron," Fergus invited her.

"Nay, first my lady wife has need of a name," Bartholomew said. "You cannot simply be Anna, the smith's daughter."

Anna bristled that her name was insufficient for him. "Because a knight of your stature, with no holding to his name, would not

52

deign to wed so low?" she asked sweetly.

Bartholomew laughed and surprised her with his response. "Nay, because you will be betrayed by the familiarity of your name and recognized despite the change in your appearance. Then Percy shall not escape the dungeon and that is not our goal."

"I do not advise the use of another name," Leila contributed. "Lest you err and fail to respond to a summons. It is the easiest error to make and a most revealing one."

Anna guessed that Leila had made such an error in their journey. "But Anna is a common enough name," she said.

"Can we create a title?" Fergus asked. "Do we dare to be so bold?"

"The baron is most well connected," Anna said. "It must be a name he knows but not a person he has met."

"She could have ridden with us from Outremer, or even France," Duncan suggested.

Anna shook her head. "But I have never seen either of those places. I believe Sir Royce has gone to the king's court in Normandy. And I do not speak French."

"A small question could reveal the ruse," Leila said.

"So, we have need of a noblewoman unknown to the baron, perhaps because she does not exist, with a title known to the baron." Fergus ran a hand through his hair.

"There will be a riddle to solve," Bartholomew agreed. He glanced over his shoulder at Anna, his eyes gleaming. "Unless you know the solution already, my lady."

Anna smiled at him, glad she did and equally glad that he had anticipated as much. "There was a widow, Elizabeth of Whitby, whose wealth was much coveted after her husband's demise. She had a daughter, name of Anna, and feared they both would be forcibly wed once they had no defender. She fled their holding with her daughter to seek refuge at the abbey of Saint Mary."

"When was this?" Fergus asked.

"More than ten years ago. My mother used to recount the tale as a mark of foul times."

"How so?" Fergus asked.

"The lady Elizabeth died, for they were betrayed and assaulted upon the road. But her maid took the child and reached the abbey. Once there, the abbess saw them both defended. It was said that the girl took her vows young and meant to live her days serving God. She would be of an age with me, and none have seen her since she was a child."

"And none will see her soon, if she remains in the abbey," Bartholomew mused. "So, you would suggest that she had changed her thinking?"

"She might have been stolen by a wicked knight," Anna replied and felt Bartholomew's chuckle beneath her hands.

"Aye, she might have," he agreed, then twisted the tale. "But she was rescued from such dire peril by our company, it is clear."

"Nay, she was snatched from the villain's clutches by the knight, Bartholomew de Châmont-sur-Maine, a valiant crusader if ever there had been one, and a warrior much concerned with justice," Fergus suggested, even as Anna sputtered in protest.

Bartholomew lifted a fist to his chest. "Do not tell me that she lost her heart to him?"

Fergus nodded sagely. "Smitten with but a glance. She cast aside her vows and begged him to wed her. I witnessed it all."

"Nay!" Anna protested, but heard laughter in her own tone. "You two steal the tale."

"Only to create a finer one," Bartholomew said. "I would not be cast as a rapacious villain."

"No knight of merit could endure such an assault upon his nature," Fergus agreed so solemnly that Anna wanted to believe him.

"Must I have begged him to wed me, though? It is not like me to make such an entreaty."

"Aye, I can believe as much." Fergus shook a finger at her. "But such is the power of love. It turns us all into fools, desperate for the favor of our beloved."

"So speaks a man who has lost his heart," Anna guessed, and Fergus winked at her, unashamed of his state. He had brought many gifts for his betrothed and she admired that he was unafraid for others to know his affection.

"Although I should like to see Anna beg for my mercy," Bartholomew said, once again teasing her. "Would you oblige me, my lady wife?"

"I will not!"

"But then," Fergus dropped his voice low. "Perhaps the maiden only so entreated the knight because she saw that in his eyes that he had lost his heart to her."

Bartholomew gave a snort.

"A knight must have a heart to lose it," Anna replied. "And I am skeptical that it is thus. It seems a dubbing does destroy all compassion in a man."

She felt the shock ripple through the company and realized belatedly that in speaking her thoughts aloud, she had insulted them all.

"We must show Anna that she has not seen the true merit of our kind," Fergus said quietly.

"Indeed, we must," Bartholomew said, and Anna could discern no playfulness in his tone. His hand closed over hers for a moment and gave her fingers a squeeze.

She did not know how to account for the influence of this fleeting touch upon her pulse.

"I must protest this scheme," huffed one of the Templars. "We cannot perpetuate such a falsehood."

"Not even to ensure that the lady's welfare is defended?" asked Fergus.

"Or the property regained that we hold in trust?" Duncan asked.

What had been in his saddlebag?

"Or the lady's brother saved from what cannot be a good fate?" Bartholomew added.

The pair of knights looked uncomfortable with the situation, but reluctantly ceded that there was merit in the plan. Anna assumed that they would neither aid in the ruse nor reveal it, and supposed it was the best to be hoped for.

After a few moments, Duncan cleared his throat. "And so, you shall be Anna of Whitby?" he asked.

"Anna de Beaumonte," Anna replied. "That was her name."

"You would feign to be French?" Bartholomew asked. "But you do not understand the language."

"I would scarce be the first in such a situation."

"Particularly if she had come of age in an abbey," Fergus replied. "Perhaps the nuns spoke only English."

"And Latin at their prayers," Bartholomew added.

"I do know my prayers," Anna said.

"Praise be," Bartholomew teased.

"You would not wish to be seen as a heathen," Leila said, and Anna wondered at the heat in her words.

Fergus nodded approval. "No solution is perfect, but I think this one that will work sufficiently well."

"I fear she will be tested and revealed," Bartholomew said, and his concern had merit.

"We will not linger overlong in the baron's hall," Fergus replied.

"Just long enough to collect our due," Bartholomew agreed.

"And you have said that we must always be together, husband mine," Anna reminded him sweetly. "Surely you can ensure that any error on my part is turned aright?"

"I shall have to try," Bartholomew said grimly and she could feel that his body was more taut.

Was he afraid for her?

Did he truly mean to defend her?

The possibility sent a strange warmth through Anna, though she knew she could protect herself. She spared a glance to her own crossbow hanging from Bartholomew's saddle and wished for its weight in her hand once again.

But she would keep her word to this confounding knight.

If only because she suspected that Bartholomew anticipated otherwise.

"Now tell us of this baron," Fergus invited again. "We must know all we can of the lion before stepping into his den."

❧

Haynesdale forest was utterly unfamiliar.

Bartholomew had hoped that the lands of his home estate from the road would conjure some memories of his past. He had hoped that a glimpse or a view or a hillside would inspire a recollection that proved his connection with this holding. He had the name memorized, and he knew its seal, but he yearned for a sense of homecoming.

Like the one Gaston had experienced at Châmont-sur-Maine, or the one that Fergus anticipated at Killairic. Bartholomew wished above all else to know where he belonged.

To be home and know it well.

Yet these forests were no different from any other.

It was true enough that he had been taken away from Haynesdale when he was but a young boy, but still he reasoned that he should recall *some* detail. There was none. The forests were clearly lush with game, the land gently rolling, and he had occasional glimpses of water through the barren trees.

But as much as Bartholomew admired the view, he could have been anywhere between Scotland and Constantinople. He could have ridden a road he had never visited before. He could have erred, but he knew the name of the holding as well as his own name. His mother had impressed that upon him, at least.

In more ways than one.

It was strange to have his return anticipated, even in a tale, and he recognized that revealing his truth too early could be a fatal error.

How did *any* know that he had survived?

Was it just a hope of the people who disliked the new baron?

Or could some person betray him? He fought an unwelcome sense that it might be Anna herself who could do as much and resolved to confide as little as possible in his unexpected partner.

They would see Percy free, retrieve Duncan's bag, then his path and Anna's would part forever. Indeed, visiting the hall might provide him with an inside view of how best to recover his lost legacy. Without learning the situation, he could not devise a plan.

There was always a chance that the baron would step aside in the name of justice.

A small chance, to be sure.

"Sir Royce Montclair is known for his greed hereabouts," Anna said, unable to hide her scorn. "He shows great enthusiasm in gathering taxes, purportedly for the crown, though there have been those who doubted that all the coin went to the king's court."

"But there is doubt no longer?" Fergus asked.

Anna gave a short laugh. "There are no longer any who express their doubt. He is...*thorough* in eliminating dissent in his holding."

Bartholomew saw her lift a finger and point into the forest. He frowned as he followed her gaze, seeing there was an area to one side of the road that was blackened and burned. It was strange to see the blackened stumps of the trees amidst freshly fallen snow, the sky clear overhead, in the midst of such a vigorous forest.

"There was where he routed those who last rose against him in rebellion. They fled into the woods and he had a great circle set ablaze. His men stood around the perimeter, waiting for the fire to consume them all." She shuddered so that Bartholomew gripped her hand beneath his once more. "I still hear their final cries in my dreams," she concluded, her voice husky.

"When was this?"

"Two years ago." He felt her straighten, and she pulled her hand from his grasp.

Who had she lost in that blaze?

"Where were you?" he asked quietly, but she did not reply.

"Has Sir Royce a wife? Or family?" Duncan asked.

"He has a wife, for his marriage was arranged by the crown. He returned from Winchester with her eight years past."

"Her name?"

"Lady Marie de Naumiers. She has yet to bear him a child, though, and is seldom seen outside the keep's walls. There is no gossip, for she brought her own maids, and they seldom leave the keep either." She paused. "He is said to have been wed before, but that his first wife died after the death of their only child. He remained unwed for so long that the king arranged the match with Lady Marie."

The village appeared ahead of them, its location evident because the trees were cleared and huts were visible. As they rode closer, Bartholomew saw that there were few people for a village of such size. They were dirty, as Anna had been, more dirty than been the case in other villages where their party had stopped. Those villagers who watched their progress were wary. He saw an older couple step out of one house, then two men of roughly his own age, one with a single infant and the other with a pair of very young children. What had happened to the mothers? He heard goats bleating but could not see them.

A sturdy man looked up from his garden, which could only have had cabbage at this time of year and that beneath the snow, and glowered at them. His wife watched sullenly from the portal to their hut. The company rode closer together without exchanging any words, for there was hostility in the manner of those who observed their progress.

"Where are the children?" he asked Anna softly.

"Who would willingly bring a child into this realm?"

It was but half an answer, though Bartholomew guessed she would not confide more. Were these the survivors of the fire? Or the only ones who had not fled?

Had Anna and Percy been alone in the forest? He would have to ask her later.

"Pull up your hood to be sure you are not recognized," he murmured.

"Aye, husband," she said, her tone as close to biddable as he might have expected. In other circumstance, he might have smiled at her manner.

But they passed through the last of the forest and he saw the keep of Haynesdale in its full majesty. The sight drew him to an astonished halt. In contrast to the hard scrabble and dirt of the village, the wooden curtain wall around the keep was high and straight. The keep sat on the top of a mound, commanding the entire area, a vivid pennant snapping from its square tower. The keep was large, far larger than he might have imagined, and it bore no resemblance to any place he recalled. It seemed that Anna's notions of coin for taxes remaining in the barony were not unfounded, for such a fortress would have been costly to build.

"What a fine keep," Bartholomew said, unable to hide the wonder from his voice. "Is this holding so likely to be assaulted as it appears?"

"A man with few allies and fewer friends might fear as much," Anna whispered. "Construction began before the wedding and took years."

Worse than being newly constructed and large, the keep would be heavily armed. Bartholomew knew a moment's dread, for he would make his future within these walls or ensure that he had none. How would they find and free Percy? How would they reclaim the prize in Duncan's saddlebag? How would they escape?

How would he avenge his father and assert his birthright? The odds were considerable against Bartholomew's success, greater than any man of sense might have hoped. He had expected a manor house, perhaps a small motte and bailey, but not a fortress. An appeal to the king's court would be doomed to failure, if this baron was so allied with the crown that his marriage had been made by the king.

Nay, he must prove himself worthy, by proving the baron unworthy.

Somehow.

He was the seed of Nicholas.

He had to ensure that Anna and Percy were safe, even if all went awry.

Bartholomew touched his spurs to Zephyr's side, sending the destrier forward more quickly. He led the party to the gates and raised his voice. "Hoy there! We seek shelter in the name of Christian charity!"

At his cry, the porter came forward. Their names were taken and in but moments, the portcullis of Haynesdale was raised in reluctant welcome.

"Into the very gates of Hell," Anna murmured, and Bartholomew could only close his hand over hers and give a minute squeeze of encouragement.

&

Marie, Lady of Haynesdale, had believed for years that there could be no worse fate than to be an heiress. Paraded before men deemed to be suitable husbands day after day, compelled to be charming at meal after meal, forced to visit holding after holding had been a particular kind of torment. To always smile at the arrangements made for her approval, regardless of her thoughts on the matter, had left her cheeks aching and her attitude poor. She had been convinced that naught could be worse than to be well known as a bride with a hefty dowry—or to have had such an exacting guardian.

Now she knew better. To *have been* an heiress was far worse.

She was but a wife. A barren one. And this life was horrific.

Marie stood at the window and looked over the bleak forests of her husband's holding and despised what her life had become. There were no dinners, no visitors, no excursions, not even any parties led to hunt since her husband had vexed every living soul beneath his hand. Or executed them. There were no fawning suitors, no adoring troubadours, no men staring after her with such yearning that her heart raced. Even if a man with blood in his veins had dared to come to their hall, her husband's foul repute would ensure that the guest never raised his gaze to hers.

There were only barbarians and brutes as far as she could see.

No doubt the greatest barbarian and brute was the one who came to her each night, took his due, then left her alone in that broad, cold bed.

The mercy was that she had only once been compelled to look upon him without the patch over his eye. To think that she had once imagined his appearance dashing and mysterious. Dangerous and alluring. Seeing what was beneath the eye patch had curdled her heart.

He was marred.

He was unworthy of her.

He gave her no sons. She began to think he did as much apurpose, the better to keep her captive in this abode.

Marie supposed Royce had guessed the resentment in her heart, for he had ensured that there was never a weapon in her proximity.

How she loathed him.

How she hated his desolate holding.

No number of furs could keep her warm as she slept. No brazier could pierce the chill of her chambers. The floors might have been wrought of ice. The chill emanating from the stone floor was so vehement that she swore it would never be driven from her bones. Even the so-called summers in this foul abode offered only rain and tepid warmth.

She was tired of meals that filled the belly but did not delight the senses. She yearned to hear music again. She longed for the warm caress of the sun upon her face, the sound of laughter, the flavor of good wine.

She yearned even more heartily for the company of handsome young men. Knights. Troubadors. Princes and dukes. A king on occasion.

But there was only Royce, and as finely wrought as he once had been, knowing the truth of his nature vastly diminished his appeal. He had looked more appealing at the king's court, where he had stirred himself to converse and to charm.

Marie *had* been charmed, more fool she.

And now, she had no power, no control over her days, no ability to make demands or be heard. She was her husband's property and so was all the lovely wealth her father had accumulated. Royce spent it with gusto and used the tale of it to borrow more.

She sat in a keep built with her father's coin, as much a prisoner as that poor brat who had been dragged to the dungeon earlier in the day. Marie felt sympathy for the boy only because his plight was so similar to her own.

Granted, he had no food, no light, no bed, and likely shared his chamber with vermin, but Marie was inclined to overlook such petty details.

She had been wronged, in her view, and there was no way to change her circumstance save to deliver to Royce a son and heir. She had tried to conceive, she truly had. She allowed him to do what he desired to her, as disgusting as it might be. She was certain that a little more masculine company would be vastly encouraging, but after that regrettable incident in Winchester on their wedding night, Royce was disinclined to trust her.

He had vowed that she would not leave Haynesdale until she bore him a son, for then the boy would undoubtedly be of his blood.

She doubted that he had imagined it would take so long.

Perhaps she should fight him again on this night. It did arouse them both when they argued before mating. Marie pursed her lips, considering.

And then she straightened. There was a party on the road headed toward the gates of the keep.

Strangers.

Guests.

Knights!

God in Heaven, there were even two Templars in the party. What a feast!

She had to intervene before Royce dispatched them from the gates.

"Agnes! Emma!" Marie spun from the window and called again for her maids. She tipped open her trunk and began strewing garments across the floor. Royce could not keep her captive if there were guests. Nay, she must greet them as Lady of Haynesdale and he would not dare to rebuke her before strangers.

And perhaps one of them would plant the seed that Royce apparently could not sow. At this point in time, Marie was prepared to do any deed to return to the pleasures of the king's court and abandon this festering backwater. Let Royce remain here, in the place he valued more than aught else, let him rot here with their son, and she would dance in palaces again.

The gold kirtle. She cast it across the bed, eyeing the shimmer of the silk with approval. Aye, she would look like the prize she had once been in this garb.

Marie smiled. If Royce were so overcome with desire at the sight of her in all her finery that he felt compelled to visit her bed this night, that deed might well disguise the contribution of a guest to her lord husband's quest for an heir.

&

Anna would never have expected to enter Haynesdale willingly. But here she was, riding beneath its portcullis as she endeavored to look accustomed to such affluence and perhaps a little bored. It was a better choice than revealing that she was terrified. She was glad to have Bartholomew's solid strength ahead of her and welcomed the feel of his mail under her fingers.

She hoped by every saint that the baron did not guess the truth.

She had to find Percy quickly. But where? The keep was enormous. There could be more than one dungeon in this place.

Despite her impatience to achieve their goal and depart, noblemen, it seemed, did naught with speed. Bartholomew dismounted, then lifted her down to the ground, his fellows dismounting as well. She chafed to hasten ahead but Bartholomew's movements were leisurely. He smiled down at her, as if they were a loving couple, and pressed a kiss to her hand. "Patience, my lady," he murmured and Anna exhaled in an attempt to calm herself.

She doubted her success, for Bartholomew's eyes danced with humor.

She touched her fingertips to her crossbow, slung from his saddle, in an apparently absent gesture. She saw from his slight smile that he understood.

"Timothy, if we are to be entertained here, I would have you ensure that Zephyr is brushed down. Please bring our bags and the bow to us when you are done."

"Aye, my lord."

Bartholomew ran his fingertips over the crossbow. "You know that I cannot bear to let any prize from my sight, be it weapon or wife."

"Aye, my lord."

Anna glared at him. Bartholomew smiled.

The squires kept custody of the reins, after the knights dismounted, and Anna noted that no one stepped forward to escort the steeds to the stables. They stood together in the middle of the bailey, horses behind them, the baron's men keeping to the perimeter. Leila remained behind Anna with her head bowed.

"Such a breach of hospitality," muttered one of the Templars. "Are we to be treated like vagabonds instead of guests?"

Anna tugged her hood over her brow, just in case any soul looked too closely. In the forest, it had been easy to trust in the protection offered by a change of garb, but now that she stood within the bailey of Haynesdale, she was terrified that she would be recognized.

There was a sudden fanfare, then Sir Royce himself appeared in the portal to the hall. He was much older than Bartholomew and not as tall. His hair was white, though he looked virile and hale. There was the patch over his one eye, but despite that—or perhaps because of it—he was a striking man. He was garbed richly and stood with confidence, a trim man who had earned his way with his blade.

And his savagery.

Anna had to restrain her urge to spit upon him. Bartholomew tightened his grip upon her fingers, evidently having guessed her reaction and granted her a quick sidelong glance of warning. She smiled at him, though she knew her anger showed in her eyes when he arched a brow. She stared at her toes then, apparently demure, and fumed. If they had hurt Percy...

Bartholomew put her hand in his elbow and closed his fingers over her own.

"Welcome to Haynesdale," Sir Royce said, his manner not particularly welcoming. The men bowed to each other, then exchanged introductions. Anna kept her gaze downcast, even as her heart thundered in fear.

"To what do I owe this unanticipated honor and pleasure?" Sir Royce demanded. Though his tone was fulsome, a sharp edge of suspicion touched his manner. Anna spared a glimpse at him, only to see that his eye had narrowed and he surveyed the company assessingly. Aye, it was easy to recall his brutality when his expression was as forbidding as it was in this moment. He considered the two Templars, and Anna wondered whether it had been their presence that had seen the gates opened at all.

"Circumstance alone," Bartholomew replied with apparent cheer. "We ride north but my lady wife tires. We had hoped for a night of rest and would beg your hospitality."

Anna grimaced, disliking that the stop should be blamed upon her supposed feminine frailty. At least with her head bowed, none could see her expression. Bartholomew's grip tightened upon her fingers as if he had guessed it.

He was cursedly observant.

"But why are you on this road?" Royce asked. "Few appreciate its charms."

"And so we were fortunate to do as much," Fergus said, his Scottish accent more pronounced than it had been. "For I thought I recalled the way to Carlisle, but discovered I had erred. This is the mark of my years in Outremer. I nigh forgot my way home!"

The men laughed together at this, though Royce only smiled.

"Your holding has fine forests," Duncan said with approval. "Are they held in trust for the King of England?"

"Of course they are," Royce snapped. "Still, you do not tell me why you are here."

"I return to my own wedding in Scotland," Fergus explained with ease. It was as if the knights had not noted the rudeness of their potential host, but Anna knew they could not have missed it. He gestured to Bartholomew. "And my good friend from France accompanies me to wish my lady and I well."

Bartholomew bowed. "And I have been so fortunate as to find a bride myself."

Anna curtseyed low, keeping her head bowed. She could feel Royce looking at her and prayed silently that he would avert his gaze without realizing who she was.

Fergus indicated Duncan. "My man, of course, escorts me as ever he does, and we have been blessed by the companionship and defense of these two noble knights."

"Templars," Royce huffed. "I do not mean to be rude, but why do you have such companions as these?"

"These two knights have served with the order," replied one Templar, his manner so resolute that none would dare challenge him. "So great is the respect of our Grand Master that he insisted we escort Laird Fergus to his home."

Royce was unconvinced. "I have never heard the like," he protested, and Anna feared he would send them from the gates. "I regret that I have no space for guests on this night..." he began, but there was a flutter of activity at the portal to the hall. Sir Royce fell silent and Anna dared to hope they had won a reprieve.

Chapter Four

All eyes were drawn to the portal as a woman of considerable beauty emerged from the shadows. Truly, she could not have timed her appearance better.

It was Royce's lady wife.

Anna had not seen her since her triumphant arrival at Haynesdale, but Marie was just as slender and her hair just as dark as it had been eight years before. She appeared to be just as elegant and poised, as well.

Truly, there could not have been a woman more different than Anna. She slanted a glance toward Bartholomew, for he must be accustomed to women like Marie. She felt aware of her own shortcomings.

At least in posing as a noblewoman.

Marie paused on the threshold, as if ensuring that all appreciated her beauty before she proceeded. She was lovely. She was garbed in silk of a golden hue, the fabric shimmering even in the wan sunlight. She might have been an angel setting foot upon the earth. She might have been a vision from afar; Anna was aware that every man and boy in their small company caught his breath in awe.

Marie, Lady of Haynesdale, deigned to greet them. There had been speculation that Marie no longer drew breath, that she had been imprisoned by her husband or even that she had fled. All of those situations would have explained the lack of a son.

The way Marie floated to Royce's side, an adoring smile upon her lips, did not.

Anna glanced up to find Bartholomew apparently transfixed by the lady and did not like it a whit.

"Guests, my lord husband," Marie cooed. Anna could not describe her voice otherwise. "What a marvel, and so thoughtful on your part. I yearn for an evening of good company." The lady fluttered and spoke with a slight accent, her dark lashes dropping demurely even as her rosy lips curved in a smile. "What a delight it shall be to have guests at the board on this dreary winter night."

Before Royce could protest, the lady swept forward to greet the new arrivals. That she targeted Bartholomew did little to improve Anna's mood. "Sir! I am Lady Marie of Haynesdale, and I am delighted to welcome you and your party to our humble abode."

Humble? Anna recalled how the carpenters and laborers had been driven to build this keep with all speed, and the estimates of how much coin had been expended. There had been word in the village that the king himself did not possess a keep so fine.

Marie meanwhile offered her hand to Bartholomew and addressed him in fluid French. Anna fumed in silence, doubting it was a coincidence that the lady's wimple was so sheer that her pale throat was fully visible through it, as well as the pale swell of her breasts.

And Bartholomew, curse him, not only replied with charm and grace, but *looked*.

Though he did reply in English and turn almost immediately to her. "And this is my lady wife, who has recently put her hand in mine, to my own good fortune," he said, gesturing to Anna. "Anna de Beaumonte."

Marie barely spared Anna a glance. "Charmed, I am sure," she said, then encouraged Bartholomew to introduce her to the others. Somehow the lady contrived that he was the one to escort her into the hall. Anna disliked how she laughed and flirted with him in French. She did not have to understand the words to recognize the lady's intent.

Nor it seemed did Royce. His brow was dark when he offered Anna his elbow. The sole benefit of his sour mood was that he did not deign to converse with her or even grant her more than a cursory glance. She might have kept her head down had she not been astounded by the splendid interior of the great hall. Lavish tapestries hung on each wall, larger than she might have believed possible to weave. There were two fireplaces and servants were stoking the fires in them both.

Royce said something to her. It had to be French, for Anna did not understand.

Anna smiled. "What a welcoming hall you have, sir."

He frowned a little at her and she ducked her head, letting her hood hide her features from him. "You do not converse in French?"

"I was raised in an abbey, sir, that of St. Mary in Whitby. The nuns chose not to speak French, so I never learned it."

"I see. And your kin?"

"My mother died when I was young, sir. Perhaps you knew of her? Elizabeth de Beaumonte was known to many, so the sisters have told me."

"Indeed. A beauty much admired, and one who died too young."

"I thank you, sir." Anna crossed herself, in memory of her own mother as well as Elizabeth, whom she had never known.

"Raised in the convent," Royce mused. "Of course, one heard that was your fate, but it seems you have left that life behind."

He turned a piercing gaze upon her and Anna's heart fluttered. That eye patch did make him look menacing, and what she knew of him did not temper the impression. "Aye, sir, and not by choice. I was abducted by a villain of foul intent, but was so fortunate as to be aided by a noble knight." To her relief, she blushed easily. "He fair stole my heart with his gallantry, and I chose to wed him rather than return to the abbey."

"And is this a defiance of your mother's plan for your future?"

"Nay, she merely wanted me to be raised in safety and to learn my prayers well, that I might one day be a good wife to a better man." Anna smiled. "And so that day is come, and I have proof that God has held me in the palm of his hand, all these years."

"Not so many years as that," Royce mused. "You are young."

"The better that I might give my husband more sons, sir," she dared to say.

"And there is a fine sentiment," the baron said with approval. He cleared his throat and she felt the weight of his gaze land upon her again. "Elizabeth de Beaumonte," he repeated, considering the name anew. "What happened to your father's wealth?"

Anna did not know, so she contrived a plausible tale. "The crown claimed it, sir, and the king holds the seal."

"Your husband should appeal for it to be granted to him."

"I could not say, sir. It is not a woman's place to be so concerned with the worldly matters of her lord husband."

He arched a brow. "Indeed? And what is her place?"

"To obey, sir. Of course."

Royce sniffed. "I should have found a convent bride," he muttered, then raised his voice. He called for wine and for ale, then seated her at his right hand at the board. Anna could not believe that she would be compelled to make conversation with this man, above all others. She glanced toward Bartholomew, but he was leaving the hall with Royce's wife. That woman laughed lightly at some jest he made and Anna found herself seething that he was so quickly gone.

What of his pledge to remain by her side?

What of his defense of her? The baron lifted her cloak away from her shoulders and she lost the protection of the hood. Leila accepted its weight from him, then bent closer to adjust Anna's veil. She felt exposed before the baron's keen gaze and bowed her head, averting her face slightly.

Royce laughed. "Surely your lord husband has banished your shy nature by now."

"I am not accustomed to the company of men, sir," she said, pretending to be very modest. "I do apologize if my modesty gives offense."

"On the contrary, I find it most refreshing."

Anna gritted her teeth and stared at her hands, as Royce lifted his chalice and drank to her health.

She would murder Bartholomew with her bare hands when he returned.

If he returned.

If she survived.

To her relief, Fergus leaned forward and asked about the keep and its construction. He professed a need to improve the defenses of the keep he would inherit and admired Haynesdale with such fulsomeness that Anna felt Royce thaw. In a matter of moments, their host was explaining choices made in construction, likely to show his own cleverness and the weight of his purse. Fergus and Duncan encouraged him with their curiosity and expressions of envy, so that Anna could look down at her hands in silence.

And seethe that Bartholomew was evidently so taken with the charms of Marie. Was it not just like a man—or a knight—to forget all but his own pleasure? What of Percy? What of the entire reason they had entered this cursed place? Anna bit down on her disappointment, telling herself that she was the fool, for she had begun to hope that Bartholomew might be different.

She had been right about him from the first and it was not a realization that gave her pleasure.

≥◆

Bartholomew did not know why Lady Marie was so determined to be alone with him, but he was not one to cast aside an opportunity. If they were to save Percy and recover the reliquary, he needed to know the location of both. When Marie hovered at his side like a butterfly, he dared to ask to see the marvels of the keep.

He did not have to feign that he was impressed by its size and construction.

He did ignore the press of her breast against his side, and the dance of her fingertips over his arm. He professed a fascination with the keep's defenses, and she granted him a tour in excess of what her lord husband might have found fitting. He was shown the chapel, the kitchens, the staircase to the tower. He was shown the curtain wall, the defenses and the stores of weaponry for the guards.

He counted the Captain of the Guard, four knights, and either seven or eight men-at-arms, all employed in the guarding of the keep. It seemed that Sir Royce believed in stout defense. There had to be a dozen squires, but they hastened this way and that, and were of so similar a size and age that he was not confident of their exact number.

It seemed long odds to escape this keep without detection or pursuit.

It would be longer odds to claim it by force.

The castellan was a tall, thin man with a grim countenance, and it was more grim as he warned the lady that there was only sufficient flour for bread for another month. It was evident to Bartholomew that the castellan would have preferred not to have had to share that bread with guests.

"We shall eat venison," the lady declared, dismissing the concern, and Bartholomew watched the seneschal frown.

Aye, he had never known a castellan who liked to see his counsel disregarded.

In the kitchens, there was a cook and a saucemaker, neither of whom were plump, and a number of serving maids. A stocky woman appeared to be in charge of the cleaning and bullied the younger maids to do her will. He did not have an impression of a happy household.

Two elegant maids trailed behind Marie in silence, until she dismissed them to await her at the board.

Bartholomew was told the location of Marie's chamber, as well as that of her lord husband, and she made a jest as to how readily he might find her chamber from his own.

Indeed, she had commanded that he and his lady wife should have the chamber directly beside her own in the tower, while her lord husband's solar was at the summit. Bartholomew saw Timothy taking the bags and Anna's crossbow to that room and nodded approval at the boy. The others were to be quartered in the chambers over the stables. The kitchens were in the space between the stable and tower, the chapel on the far side of the bailey, the well in the middle and the high wall around all.

The dungeons were below the tower, and Bartholomew took note of the location of the stairs. The keys, he had to assume, were either near the dungeon entrance or in Royce's possession.

They did not enter the chapel, and he was not shown the treasury. Was the treasury at the summit of the tower? The reliquary had to be secured in one or the other. He could not think of how to ask without arousing suspicion.

It was Saturday. Perhaps they would stay to mass the next morning.

Bartholomew was so consumed with creating a plan that he did not pay much attention to the lady's chatter. She ushered him through a doorway, and he realized only once he had crossed the threshold that it was a storage chamber. He turned to depart, thinking she had erred, but the lady closed the door behind them. They were plunged into darkness, and the click of the key in the lock seemed overloud.

Had she guessed his intent?

Marie collided with him suddenly, backing him into the shelves. Did she stumble? Bartholomew took a step back and found a wall behind him, then the lady's lips at his ear. "Sir, I must cast myself at your mercy," she whispered. "I entreat you to aid me in my distress."

Was this a trick?

"Of course, I should be glad to be of service to my noble hostess," he said with care.

Her hands were on his tabard and he could smell her perfume. He decided to believe that she wished to confide in him quietly, but her hands began to rove across his chest.

In a caress.

"You are most finely wrought, sir," she whispered. "And I have need of the services of such a man."

Should he cast her aside?

Was there more to be gained by remaining in place until she had her say? What would be lost if he spurned her and she was insulted?

"My husband's seed does not take root, despite these many years of his efforts," she continued in a heated whisper. "I have need of a child. I no longer even care of its gender, but a son would be best."

Bartholomew blinked. She wished for him to lie with her?

Her voice dropped lower, her frustration clear. "There are never men in our hall, never noblemen at our board. No knights, no guests, no barons, no hale men within three days' ride!" She seized fistfuls of his tabard and shook him. "Sir! I must have a child!"

Bartholomew tried to recall the example of Gaston's diplomacy and chose his words with care. "My lady, I have much sympathy for your plight, but I am a wedded man. I would be faithful to my wife and my vows."

"She was raised in a convent!" Marie hissed. "What pleasure can she give you?" Her hand was beneath his tabard before he realized what she did. Her fingers closed over him, granting him an intimate caress.

Bartholomew seized her shoulders and pushed her away. "She is my wife. You must know that what you suggest is wrong."

"Wrong? It is wrong for me to rot in this filthy burg! It is wrong for me to be denied the one thing that would deliver me from this place!" Marie made a growl under her breath, then seemed to steady herself. She continued with low heat. "Sir, do not imagine that my relief will be lightly won. There are those who do not survive the peril of bearing a child, and certainly all women endure the curse of Eve in so doing. Your part would be trifling."

"But..."

"But I ask for naught you cannot spare." Her tone turned pleading. "But one visit. Perhaps two. While your lady wife sleeps." Her voice dropped lower than it had been thus far. "She need never know."

"It would be wrong."

"No one need ever know. Indeed, I will welcome my husband to my bed on the morrow. No one will ever guess that it is not his child."

"There are others..."

Marie interrupted him crisply. "I have no taste for Scots, and the red hair that appears suddenly in their children might reveal my deed. Your coloring is like mine and that of my husband. I choose you."

"The Templars surely share my coloring..."

Marie laughed. "I have but one night to see this done. Even I do not imagine my charms to be sufficient to tempt such a knight to abandon his vows so readily. It must be you."

Bartholomew did not know what to say. He would not do it, but telling Marie as much might put the entire party in peril.

She slid her arm into his elbow, as sinuous as a snake and as sly as a fox. "You must think about it, I see," she said smoothly. "I like a man of principle. Your seed will have integrity."

She led him forward, and he heard the key turn again in the lock. Marie opened the door a crack and listened, then urged him into the corridor. Her manner changed immediately, though the invitation lurked in her eyes.

"But you must be famished!" Marie declared, speaking so loudly that any might hear her. "A knight so robust as yourself has need of every fine morsel we can summon."

"Indeed, it has been a long ride this day," Bartholomew acknowledged. "And even longer since we have dined on fine fare."

"Then come, come to the hall," she insisted, tugging him by the hand with such a playful manner that they might have been courting. She leaned close to him before they entered the hall once more and dropped her voice low, her gaze filled with invitation. "I find my husband's hall is quite dull after the revels I knew in France," she whispered. Her hand trailed across his chest. "Perhaps you, sir, since you are said to be so gallant, might amuse me later this eve with some tales from the court."

"I should be glad to regale the hall with any tidings from afar."

Marie's laughter was throaty and her gaze was knowing. "That was not my meaning, sir, and you know it well," she murmured. "I will summon you once your lady wife sleeps."

How would she know?

Was there a means for Marie to spy on their chamber from her own? There must be. Bartholomew no longer wondered at their being granted the chamber beside the lady's own. How would he evade her scheme? He had no desire to aid in her quest, though he could well understand that her situation was troubling. He also had no wish to set her against their small party.

Nor did he want to anger his host. He would need every memory of Gaston's talents to see them free of this place and unscathed!

In lieu of a comment, Bartholomew only smiled. He stepped into the portal to the great hall, that he might be in view of her husband, and bent low over her hand. "I thank you, Lady Marie, for your kindness in showing me the stables. I have relied long upon the goodwill of my steed and would ensure his comfort wherever he rests."

"Knights and their steeds," she laughed, complying with his excuse. "I know your habits well."

Bartholomew bent lower and brushed his lips across her fingertips. "You are most indulgent, my lady. I thank you for it."

"How could I resist?" she murmured for his ears alone. "And now I await your indulgence."

Bartholomew pretended not to have heard. He straightened and turned, escorting her to her husband's side, well aware that Anna eyed him with disgust.

She could not hide her thoughts to save her life, to be sure, but in this case, her manner could only aid in their deceit.

Indeed, Marie chortled under her breath. "I see that the old rumor is true, sir."

"Which rumor is that?"

"That the plain ones are the most easily driven to jealousy, for they are not confident of their hold upon a man's affections." She shrugged. "I suppose it is only reasonable."

Bartholomew did not reply. He seated Marie beside her

husband, aware of the intensity of that man's interest, then took his place beside Anna. She gave him a look that could have cracked a stone.

Was she truly irked with him?

Or did she feign as much, because she thought it appropriate?

Bartholomew was surprised by how much he wanted to know. He drank his host's health, then let the weight of his hand fall on the back of Anna's waist. He could fairly hear her thinking and guessed that she wished to fling the weight of his hand aside. Her gaze flicked to his and sure enough, there was fire in her eyes.

"Did you miss me, my lady?" he murmured, as if trying to improve her mood. He smiled at her in warning.

"Of course, my lord," Anna replied, her tone sweet. "You know I am fearful when we are parted." She put her hand on his thigh just as he lifted the chalice to his lips. To his astonishment, Anna slid her hand over his chausses slowly.

Seductively.

Upward.

Bartholomew nigh spilled his wine when she eased her hand beneath his tabard and tightened her grip on his thigh. He met the challenge in her gaze and smiled back at her, more than willing to best her in this game.

"You have wine on your lip, my lady," he murmured, then dragged his fingertip across her bottom lip slowly. Anna's eyes widened in a most satisfactory way and Bartholomew liked how her cheeks flushed.

This ruse might result in a most interesting night, indeed.

"You looked to have seen a ghost, lad, back in the forest," Duncan said to Fergus in Gaelic when they two finally had a moment alone. They were in the hall of the baron, but to one side and with no listening ears in their vicinity. They gave every appearance of warming themselves before the fire and admiring the hall's design. Duncan ensured that the many squires and men-at-arms were not sufficiently close to eavesdrop.

By all that was holy, the keep was well-defended!

The younger man seemed to deliberately avoid his gaze as he

stared into the flames. "That is as good an explanation as any," he murmured, responding in Gaelic.

That Fergus did not pretend to be uncertain of the moment in question told Duncan he was right.

"Or was she a vision come to life?" he asked, pressing the lad a little more.

Fergus glanced up then. He appeared to be agitated, as seldom he was. "You know I never speak of it."

"I do. And it is curious, to my thinking," Duncan acknowledged. "Most with such an ability would share much of what they perceived to lie ahead, if not all. Some would do it for coin."

Fergus shook his head with rare vehemence. "It is curse, not gift, Duncan. I seldom see what is good, only what peril lies ahead. And sometimes, it does not come to be. It is irksome how mysterious it all can be, although in hindsight, it makes perfect sense."

Duncan considered his charge, the son of the man to whom he owed the greatest debt of all. "Did you see peril for this Anna? For Bartholomew?"

Fergus grimaced. "I have seen her, several times, but did not recognize her as the maiden in my visions until she had changed her garb. Indeed, I bought the crimson kirtle knowing full well that Isobel would never don it." He sighed. "Her fate is bound to that of Bartholomew, this much I would swear upon my own life."

"That is why you ceded to his request that we take this road," Duncan guessed.

Fergus nodded. "I knew we should find her upon it. Bartholomew's destiny." Duncan saw the concern in the younger man's eyes. "Whether she means him good or ill, though, is unclear."

"And is her fate bound to yours?"

Fergus shook his head. "My heart is claimed, Duncan. You know that well. I had but a contribution to make to this tale, though whether it is good or ill has yet to be seen."

Duncan made a jest, endeavoring to lighten the other man's mood. "Then I shall be certain not to mention the crimson kirtle to Lady Isobel, lest she believe your affection was tested."

Fergus forced a smile. "So speaks a man wise in the ways of

women."

"Do you see your own fate?" Duncan had to ask, for he felt a bad portent for the future of Fergus and his betrothed Isobel.

"Nay, that is the puzzle of it," Fergus said. "My own life could end in a moment, and I would never have had a glimpse of it." He shrugged and surveyed the hall. "I suppose I should be glad of that mercy."

Duncan smiled and gripped the knight's shoulder. "It means you must use your own eyes to see what is close at hand, just like the rest of us," he said with false cheer. "It is not such a handicap as that, lad."

ૐ

The man tormented her at the baron's board.

Anna was convinced that it was no accident. Bartholomew, it appeared, knew far more of amorous games than she—although his touch made her long to learn more. In the hall, amidst the company, she knew he could not take more than she offered. Such dark deeds happened in privacy, not in the bright light of a busy hall. She was safe, so long as they remained with the others, and that meant she could savor the sensations he kindled within her.

She had been bold in her first gesture, wanting only to claim his attention and knowing no other way to do as much. It was clear she had ventured out of her own depth and that Bartholomew could play such games far better than she.

She felt as if she had no defenses against his assault.

If he thought she would be an easy conquest, though, he could reconsider the matter. If he thought to seduce her in truth, after abandoning her in the company of Royce, she would delight in showing him the truth. If he thought to take what she had vowed not to share, she would ensure he regretted it.

Bartholomew was beyond attentive. He kept his thigh pressed against Anna's own, his hand resting often on the small of her back. She was nigh in his embrace, right at the board! He leaned against her to speak to their host on her other side, ensuring she could not evade the heat of his body or the scent of his skin. His removal of that drop of wine was but the first caress. He fed her venison stew from his own fingertips like a besotted husband, granting her the most choice morsels. He ensured her cup was full and her every need satisfied.

Except the fire he had lit within her belly.

It was curious to be so aware of a man, and so desirous of more. Anna found herself thinking of the kiss he had tried to bestow upon her earlier, and her own inability to enjoy it. What if she trusted him? What if she had another chance? She resolved that she would welcome a kiss, if that was to be the sum of it, and if it was offered in such circumstance as this.

Aye, Anna wanted a kiss from Bartholomew.

Just to know what it could be like. Though her experience with intimacy had been one of violence and pain, she knew her parents had made merry together when they met abed. This man and his attention made her wonder if it were possible for her to enjoy the same pleasure with a man.

The truth was that she wanted more than a kiss.

It was unsettling, to feel her body at war with her reservations, even undermining them. Was this a kind of sorcery? Anna might have pulled away from Bartholomew, but guessed this was his means of disarming their host and hostess. Also, pulling away from Bartholomew would put her closer to Royce, which was not an enticing prospect.

Did Bartholomew know how much he distracted her? It might not be kind, but Anna could not regret that the lady of the hall was so displeased by Bartholomew showing fascination with his wife.

Had he only gone with Marie to learn the location of the stables and to check on his steed? They had been absent for a goodly amount of time, in her view, too long for such a venture. Or would any interval of time have felt like an eternity in Royce's company?

Perhaps Bartholomew had learned the location of both Percy and Duncan's possessions.

Perhaps he had paid the lady for that knowledge with a kiss.

Or more.

Why did she wish to know so badly?

Anna burned to ask him for the truth, but she could not do as much so long as they were at the board. Some event had made his manner more attentive and more amorous. She feared to think how the Lady Marie might have inspired such an inclination.

Not that it should matter to Anna what amorous adventures

Bartholomew might pursue, on this night or any other.

Her thoughts and fears were as troubling as his persistent touch. She found her agitation growing and her voice growing higher. She was out of familiar circumstance and felt that her own reactions spiraled from her control.

By the time they left the board, Anna was humming with a newfound need. She had consumed an unfamiliar quantity of wine, which made her feel both daring and warm. Bartholomew's touch had left her desirous of more, and she was glad to take his hand and be escorted from the hall.

They walked in silence to the chamber, and she noted how watchful he appeared to be. That drove the heat of the wine from her veins.

It was only when the door to their chamber was closed behind them that Anna dared to take a full breath in her relief. "Praise be," she whispered, but Bartholomew gave her a sharp glance. He rapidly touched his ear, then his eye, and glanced toward the wall that was common between their chamber and that of the Lady of Haynesdale.

Anna felt her eyes widen even as she understood.

There were knots aplenty in that wooden wall, and she could readily imagine that some of them were holes. The hair prickled on the back of her neck.

Were they being observed?

She amended her comment quickly by yawning with vigor. "As kind as you have been on our journey, husband, I am fair glad to see a plump mattress awaiting me this night."

"Are you then?" Bartholomew mused, a twinkle lighting his eyes.

Emboldened by the knowledge that she was not truly alone with him, Anna laughed. "You, sir, will never be sated."

"Not soon, wife of mine, not soon." He caught her up and spun her around, and Anna enjoyed the charade of being a happy couple. "Perhaps you will be warm enough this night that you will have no need of me in your bed," he teased and she laughed again.

"Oh, husband, how can you suggest such a possibility?" she murmured, pulling back to watch Bartholomew's eyes darken. She caught her breath when his gaze fell to her lips and felt his fingers spread across her back as he gripped her more tightly. He held her above the floor but she dared not struggle, as willing a wife as any man might want.

Her heart thundered with the possibility of another kiss.

Even as a quiver began in her belly. She licked her lips and he watched her with a hunger that made her shiver.

He bent and touched his lips to her ear, causing a most delicious sensation. "We must create no suspicion," he murmured. "But I have given you my vow."

Not to touch her.

Anna nodded as she looped her arms around his neck. She looked up at him, giving every sign of doting upon him. In truth, it was not that hard to pretend. "Is it true, husband, that some couples do not share a bed each night?"

"I have heard it said," Bartholomew acknowledged. He pulled her against his chest so that she caught her breath. "It seems wrong to me, I must admit." His hand slid down her back, pressing her against him, even as he kissed the side of her neck. Anna felt shivers run over her skin and a warm thrum between her thighs.

"I cannot imagine being without your warmth all the night long," she agreed, trying to look flirtatious. Her heart was racing with the prospect of him lying beside her.

Would she sleep?

Would he?

Did she dare to trust his sworn word? Anna thought she could.

"I think it is more than my warmth you desire at night, wife," Bartholomew murmured. He considered her, smiled a little, then lifted her to her toes. He held her gaze, his own gaze dropping to her lips for a moment.

Anna understood. He was asking permission. She took a breath and nodded quickly, knowing that their ruse had to be maintained.

Bartholomew did not give her the chance to change her thinking His mouth sealed over hers with such purpose that Anna was momentarily startled. She dared not pull away, though, so compelled herself to lean against him as if she truly were a submissive bride, and open her mouth to him. Bartholomew made a little growl in his throat, one that sent a thrill through Anna, and deepened his kiss.

The mood changed between them in that moment, their kiss becoming heated as it had not been before. It did not matter then whether any soul watched them, for this was no feint. Bartholomew kissed Anna as if he truly desired her, and she could not resist the urge to respond in kind. Her fingers were locked in the thick waves of his hair, and he feasted upon her lips with ardor. She had never been kissed with such passion and found her body responded of its own accord. She closed her eyes and capitulated, surrendering to sensation.

He scooped her up into his arms and made for the bed, and Anna clutched at him in uncertainty. It would look like passion to an observer, but her heart was racing. She was on her back on the bed, his weight pressing her into the mattress in a most terrifying way, when suddenly there was a rap at the portal.

Bartholomew broke their kiss with obvious regret. He took a deep breath, as if he, too, had been affected by their embrace. He left the bed, pacing to the window as he composed himself. Anna sat up in haste, feeling guilty and disheveled.

But they were believed to be wedded.

Leila entered the chamber, carrying a bucket of steaming water. Anna thought that Bartholomew and Leila exchanged a quick glance. About what?

Were they lovers?

Another serving woman followed Leila with a brazier filled with coals. Leila gestured that it should not be lit as yet, so the woman put it down near the bed, then left. The dog from the hall was at the portal and the woman made to shoo it back down the stairs, but Bartholomew stepped forward.

"What is the dog's name?" he asked.

The woman sneered. "Cenric, for he is a Saxon dog. Of course, all Saxons are dogs." She laughed at her own jest, then made to kick the beast, even as Anna yearned to strike her. The creature was nimble and evaded her easily, much to Anna's relief. "Come along, varmint," the woman said to the dog. "Out to the stables with you."

"Leave him," Bartholomew ordered and the servant eyed him with surprise. "I like a dog in the chamber. If this one has no place to sleep, he can remain here."

"If you so wish it, my lord," the woman said with a curl of her lip. "I would not welcome the fleas, but the choice is yours." She then bowed and left.

Not a moment too soon, in Anna's view.

Saxon dog. Anna felt her lips tighten in disapproval. Bartholomew gave her a look, and she knew her thoughts were clear. She turned away from the common wall and fluffed the pillows so that no others noted her reaction.

Cenric watched the woman depart, then eyed them warily. Bartholomew crouched down and put out his hand. The dog had clearly been kicked by others, for he sniffed at the air, before padding cautiously toward Bartholomew. He was a large dog, the kind of wolfhound that lords used for hunting, and his shaggy coat was a hundred shades of silver and gray. He seemed to have great eyebrows, like an old man, which gave him a friendly appearance. When he sniffed Bartholomew's hand, his long tail began to wag like a ragged banner. When Bartholomew scratched his ears, he sat down beside the knight and leaned on his leg. That tail thumped against the floor.

"I once knew a dog like you," Bartholomew told him. "The most faithful creature in all of Christendom. I miss him heartily."

Leila turned to look at him. "When did you have a dog?" she asked, apparently surprised. At Bartholomew's gesture, she recalled herself. "My lord," she added. "I do not recall ever seeing you with one."

"Nor I," added Anna, wanting to buttress the other woman's words for any who eavesdropped. "Though we have only known you a few weeks, in truth."

Leila nodded. "That is true, my lady. The days have been so merry that I lost track of the time."

"It was when I was a boy," Bartholomew admitted. "Indeed, I scarce recall it myself, but when I saw this Cenric, I remembered that hound so vividly." His tone was thoughtful, even dreamy, and Anna wondered at his manner. "He was as friendly as this, though I think he might have been larger."

"Was this in France, my lord?" Anna asked.

"Normandy or Anjou?" Leila added. "You said you had been to both."

"Before that," Bartholomew said softly. "Long before that." He straightened and surveyed the chamber, a new glint in his eyes that Anna could not explain. "I ask for your indulgence in this, my lady. I would not see a dog that looks so much like my former one dispatched to the cold."

"I have no argument with a dog in the chamber. We always had several—"

"At the foundation," Leila interjected.

Anna nodded. "Though they were smaller than this one."

Bartholomew looked so pleased that she was surprised. He might have been a child on Christmas morn granted an unexpected gift. "He is too thin," he mused, running his hands over the dog. "Particularly for one so young."

"Perhaps the baron has no use for him," Anna suggested. "And could be persuaded to part with the creature on the morrow."

"He might sell the animal, if there are too many hounds in his stables," Leila added.

"It would be suitable for you to have a hunting dog, my lord," Anna agreed.

"Or even one to slumber in the hall," Bartholomew agreed. He straightened from patting the dog, and Anna could not explain why he seemed to be more resolved than previously. He looked taller, even.

Because of a dog?

It made no sense.

The hound made for the brazier, clearly aware of its purpose even though it was unlit as yet. It circled half a dozen times before lying down beside it to sleep. Leila struck a tinder and lit the coals, patted the dog cautiously herself when it lifted its shaggy head to watch her. Anna wished she had saved some meat from the board for the hound did look thin and the meat had been plentiful.

"Oh!" Leila pivoted to face Anna, her hands rising to her lips in dismay. Genuine or feigned? Anna could not say. Truly, the other woman was far better at disguising her true intent. Perhaps Anna could learn from her. "My lady, you have not made your prayers this night."

Anna was uncertain why the other woman had made this suggestion and was momentarily uncertain of what to say. She was supposed to be a woman raised in a convent, after all. Perhaps Leila meant to reinforce the tale.

"I would not trouble our host and hostess," Anna said with a smile. "I can pray here."

"Nay," Bartholomew said with unexpected heat. "There is a chapel in this keep. I will escort you to it that you might pray as is your custom."

Before she could agree or disagree, the knight claimed her elbow and led her from the room. He set a sharp pace and seemed to know his destination. Anna could only scurry along beside him, wondering at his intent. "I do not need to pray," she whispered.

"Of course, you do," he whispered back. "I believe I have found Percy, but we still have to find the contents of Duncan's saddlebag."

Anna's heart thrilled that he had discovered her brother's location. He *had* been using Lady Marie to orient himself!

She considered his words but was confused. "And you think to find those contents in the chapel?" What had been in the bag? Anything of value would have been taken the treasury. Any foodstuff would have gone to the kitchens or pantry. Anna frowned.

"Without doubt," Bartholomew murmured with conviction. "The difficulty will lie in retrieving it from there." He spared her a quick sidelong glance as they stepped out into the bailey. "You may need saintly intercession this night, my lady."

Anna felt her lips part in surprise. Saintly intercession? That could only come from a saint's bones.

Which meant Bartholomew's party had been carrying a holy relic.

Who *were* these knights?

Chapter Five

Cenric. The dog had his father's middle name.

It could not be an accident.

And the dog itself was the image of the hound Bartholomew had known as a toddler. Hours before, he could not have described the beast for he recalled only its loyalty, but one glimpse of this dog, and he knew it to be his Whitefoot's twin.

Perhaps his descendant.

He had to take the dog with him on the morrow.

Along with Percy and the reliquary. There would be cause for celebration if their party managed all three, that was for certain. He knew more of the keep's defenses, which was good, though he still had need of a plan.

Leila's suggestion had been a most sensible one. He hoped that taking Anna to her prayers on this night would give him the opportunity to discover the location of the reliquary, which might provide a better idea of how to retrieve it. He spoke to a servant of their scheme, and that man ran for the priest. He took Anna to the chapel, and they found the heavy wooden portal locked securely.

"Too many keys," he said under his breath.

"She will have them," Anna replied, flicking him a hot glance. "You might put her interest to good use."

"I already have learned the layout of the keep from her, sweet wife," he murmured, then bent to kiss her forehead. "She wishes for more, but I fear you will exhaust me with your passion this night."

Anna stiffened as if dismayed by this prospect, but Bartholomew had no opportunity to reassure her. Again, he sensed that she had known abuse by a man and would have reaffirmed his own intent, but he heard the sound of approaching footsteps. He had to content himself with squeezing her hand, then turning to greet the priest.

ào

Anna was disconcerted by Bartholomew's words, and might have argued his assertion, but they were no longer alone. When Bartholomew released her from his embrace, he turned a smile upon the approaching priest.

Anna caught her breath. It was Father Ignatius.

From the village.

Of course, it was. There was no other priest closer than York.

Anna's heart leaped for her throat, then plummeted. Father Ignatius had been priest in the village all of her life. He had baptized Percy and buried her parents. He likely had wedded them and baptized her. There was no soul more likely to recognize her than Father Ignatius.

And no soul with less capacity for deception.

Anna bowed her head, her heart hammering. Surely he would not reveal her? Anna averted her face, that her veil might conceal her features, even as her panic rose. Was it too much to hope that the change in her garb would keep the priest from looking too closely?

Anna feared that it was.

"I do apologize for so troubling you, Father," Bartholomew said smoothly as the priest sorted through his keys. Father Ignatius carried a ring with five keys of various sizes. What would they open? Anna could account for two. The chapel here in the keep and the village chapel. What of the others? There was no gate on the cemetery and Father Ignatius did not lock the portal to his own home, as a matter of principle. He might have a key to some entrance to the keep.

Did she dare to hope that one key might be for the dungeon?

As her thoughts flew, Bartholomew continued to charm the priest with the false tale of Anna's background, and her enthusiasm for prayer. "Morning, noon and night," he confided in the priest. "She prays most frequently."

"I am not one to find fault with that," Father Ignatius said with his usual amiability.

"Again, I am sorry to trouble you so late," Bartholomew said.

"It is no trouble to administer to the faithful, my son. It is my calling." The priest unlocked the portal, revealing a chapel of simple elegance. It had high windows, though at this hour, no light came through them. The priest strode forward to light beeswax candles. There was clean linen on the altar, but naught else.

Not a relic to be seen.

There must have once been one, to see the chapel blessed. Had it been lost? Stolen? Sold? Or was it hidden here? Perhaps beneath the floor.

There was no other door and the windows were too high to be reached easily from outside. They were also small, undoubtedly due to the cost of the glass.

"Come, come, my child," Father Ignatius encouraged. "God's house is always open."

Anna dropped to her knees before the altar and folded her hands. She did say her prayers, asking first for their safe escape from the hall and the retrieval of Percy, for the future welfare of all of them, and the restoration of the knights' prize. She was distracted by the possibility of their carrying an item of such value. How would it be retrieved from a locked chapel, even if they could find it?

Was it not wrong to steal from a chapel? She had to think it would be.

She had to think it would be worse yet to deceive Father Ignatius, a man who had only been kind to her.

Bartholomew was on his knees at her right, making every sign of praying himself. Perhaps he was. Father Ignatius knelt on Bartholomew's right, saying his own prayers. After this had continued long enough for Anna to repeat her prayers three times, Bartholomew nudged her with his foot.

She thought it an accident, but he did it again. Harder.

She was supposed to do something.

Ask for saintly intercession, she supposed.

Bartholomew stood, genuflected and thanked Father Ignatius again. "I leave you to your prayers, my lady," he said with a bow, then retreated, leaving her alone with Father Ignatius. Anna heard the doors close behind her, and knew that she was supposed to ask after a reliquary, if not find it.

Without knowing what it was.

Without revealing that she fully expected it to be in this chapel.

And she was to trick a man who had only been good to her. A

priest!

Curse Bartholomew again!

৵

Anna took a deep breath. "Father," she said, speaking in a high voice that Father Ignatius might be less likely to recognize. "I would ask for your aid."

"Indeed, my child."

"I fear to disappoint my husband."

"Why would you fear such a situation, my child? He seems most amiable."

"But I grew up in the company of nuns, Father, and know little of a man's needs and desires."

"I am certain that your noble husband will make his expectations clear. You have only to cede to his requests."

Anna had the urge to grind her teeth. Father Ignatius was also one of the most tolerant and understanding people she knew. Now that she considered the matter, he always counseled patience. She let her voice rise a little higher. "But I know little of administering a secular household, Father. What if I err?"

"But I am certain the nuns taught you of such duties. Did you have no tasks while in their foundation? I know that the sisters of Saint Mary cleave to the rule expecting each to contribute to the welfare of all."

"I helped in the tending of the gardens, Father," Anna lied, halfway expecting that some higher authority might smite her for lying to a priest in a chapel.

There was no bolt of lightning.

"And doubtless your husband's holding will have gardens, too," Father Ignatius continued in a soothing tone. "You will find solace and familiarity there."

"But, Father, I am so fearful. I have no one, neither kith nor kin, other than my lord husband. If he turns me aside, what shall I do? Where shall I go?" She tried to sound even more agitated. "What if I anger him, without knowing what I have done? What if I fail to conceive his child? What if I bear him only daughters? Father! I am so afraid!"

The priest laid his warm hand over hers and Anna ensured that her fingers shook. "You have led a sheltered life thus far, my child. It is only reasonable that you should feel trepidation on this change in your circumstances." He paused for a moment before continuing. "Is your husband cruel to you?"

"Nay, Father. He has been only kind." Anna could not lie about that. She let her voice tremble. "But still, that could change if I err."

Father Ignatius gave her fingers a little squeeze. "Let us pray together, my child," he said with his usual calm confidence.

"I wish I could ask for the aid of a saint," Anna whispered, hoping she sounded desperate. "The sisters would have let me kiss the finger bone of Saint Mary. Even the prospect of her intercession always soothed my fears." She shook her head and bent more deeply over her hands, pretending to weep. She could feel the priest watching her.

Anna had time to think that her efforts had been for naught when he abruptly stood up.

One key on his ring proved to open a door set into the wall to the right of the altar. Anna had not even discerned it, for it was so well crafted that it was nigh invisible. She could not see its contents when Father Ignatius opened the door, for his figure blocked her view, but when he turned, she saw something gold in his hands.

It was not small.

It was studded with gems and gleamed in the candlelight.

She ducked her head to hide her astonishment. Was this what Bartholomew's party had carried? Where had they gotten it?

Was this what Percy had stolen? No wonder it was missed!

"Do you know the legend of Saint Euphemia?" Father Ignatius asked.

Anna shook her head for she did not have to lie. "Nay, Father."

She peeked to see that he regarded the reliquary with some wonder of his own. "She was a virgin sworn to purity in her love of Christ. At her father's command, she was tested and tortured, but she refused to worship false gods as he so desired. She died a martyr, but her relics have done wonders. She defends the righteousness of good choices."

Anna stole a look through her veil as Father Ignatius paused before her.

"This treasure is lately come to us, by some divine design, but perhaps you are the reason why."

She feared then that he had guessed the truth. "I do not understand, Father," she said in that high voice.

"That you might ask for her aid, of course. That the saint might give you confidence in your choice of husband. But a day ago, I could not have offered you this solace, my child." He held the reliquary before Anna. "Perhaps Saint Euphemia will give you strength."

"I thank you, Father," Anna whispered. She leaned closer, her eyes downcast, her gaze flying over the marvel before her. She had never seen an item so richly adorned or so precious. It must contain the saint's head, for it was of the right size.

It was also the right size to account for the bulk of the stolen saddlebag.

How had Bartholomew's party come to carry this prize? Surely they had not stolen it?

Anna watched her breath fog the surface of the gold, knowing she had never seen any thing so fine as this. She bent and touched her lips to one large amethyst. She could smell the scent of roses, which was said to emanate from holy relics, and felt awe to be in the presence of Saint Euphemia herself. Anna prayed in truth then, that Bartholomew and his companions were not thieves, that they might succeed in freeing Percy, that they might all escape unscathed.

Father Ignatius leaned closer.

"Lady Anna, are you certain you have confided all of your concerns?" he asked softly. "You seem most troubled and I would be of assistance."

"I am much recovered, Father. Thank you."

And Anna made the mistake of looking up.

She met Father Ignatius' gaze and saw that he had recognized her. He frowned and her mouth went dry.

"Anna?" he asked, clearly astonished.

"Father Ignatius," she managed to say, an entreaty in her tone. She felt her cheeks heat as she flushed in guilt.

Before she could defend herself or request his support, the door creaked at the other end of the chapel. Father Ignatius straightened, and the door was flung wide just before Royce's voice filled the chapel.

"What is this?" the baron demanded. "I told you to keep that secured!"

Anna heard his footsteps as he strode toward her and she closed her eyes, praying for salvation in truth.

è▲

It *was* here.

Bartholomew followed Royce into the chapel, relief flooding through him at the sight of the reliquary. His first reaction was profound relief that the reliquary had been located.

His second was the realization that something had gone awry. The priest was staring at Anna, as if he had seen a ghost. Anna was utterly motionless, apparently frozen in place.

There was only one possible explanation: the priest had recognized her.

The priest took a cautious step backward, his gaze still fixed upon Anna, and opened his mouth.

Bartholomew had to do something to keep him from uttering the truth.

"Zounds!" he cried heartily. "What a prize you have hidden in this place!" Royce turned to look at him. Bartholomew cast up his hands and kept talking. "What a marvel! Sir Royce, you are indeed blessed to have the custody of such a treasure. No wonder your estate prospers as it does!" He laughed heartily. "We should all have the blessings of the saints upon our worldly deeds." He marched forward and dropped to his knees before the priest, narrowing his eyes as if he read the inscription. "Saint Eu...."

"Euphemia," the priest said. "It contains a relic of Saint Euphemia." He cleared his throat, his gaze sliding to Anna again. Her eyes were wide and she shook her head minutely. The priest frowned.

The sooner that man was left alone, the better.

Bartholomew kissed the reliquary, stood, then genuflected, his hand locking around Anna's elbow. "Come, my dear wife, you have had a long day and are in dire need of your sleep. Your morning prayers will come soon enough."

He gave the priest a hard look and to his relief, that man seemed to have composed himself.

"Sir Royce, surely your lady wife awaits you?" Bartholomew

continued in the same jovial manner. To keep Royce from speaking to the priest, he seized the baron's elbow and urged him from the chapel. He set a brisk pace, compelling both Anna and their host to make haste across the bailey.

And away from both priest and chapel.

"What a day this has been!" he enthused. "We shall sleep well this night, my lady, thanks to our gracious host. Sir Royce, I must thank you for your hospitality. Never have I seen such a marvel as this keep, or that sacred treasure you hold in trust. You should send word to the king that he might come and worship in your chapel, for surely he would be glad to cast his eyes upon such a prize."

"Perhaps..." Royce began but Bartholomew interrupted him.

"Of course, you might be concerned that such a marvel would tempt him, and so it might tempt many a man. I would be so bold as to suggest that you invite the archbishop as well as the king, along with all their retinues, that they might each ensure the other's good conduct. You might host quite the festivity at Haynesdale." He gave a laugh as if anticipating that event with joy. "Indeed, my dear wife, we might have to return to Haynesdale for it. You have not yet seen me joust and I do not doubt that the king would appreciate such entertainment."

"I do not think," Royce managed to utter at the base of the stairs.

"Oh, the revenue," Bartholomew mused, interrupting the baron. "One thinks often of the cost of hosting such a venture, but one must expend coin to earn it."

"Truly?" Anna prompted.

He beamed at her. "I have never told you, my lady, of the coin that flows into the coffers of those barons who host tournaments. It is true that the events come with expenses, for there must be feasting and there must be wine, and there must be ransoms paid, but the bounty that is earned in taxes and wagers. I knew a lord who hosted a tournament, invited all the best knights, then put a high toll on all roads leading to his gates from his borders." Bartholomew laughed. "He told me he had earned tenfold the cost of the event before it even began! Can you imagine? Tenfold!" He paused before the portal to their chamber and wagged a finger at the very interested baron. "And his repute!" Bartholomew gave a low whistle. "The bards sang of him. The ladies yearned for him. The knights honored him. The king favored him. Truly, there was naught he could do wrong. 'Twas clever beyond all." He leaned closer to Royce, his manner confidential. "When I have a holding, you may be certain that I will host such a tournament, for I know it would be a sound venture."

Royce frowned in consideration of this. "My wife might enjoy it," he allowed.

"Indeed, she might." Bartholomew smiled down at Anna. "And now, my lady wife, your duties are done by God but not by husband." He winked lewdly at her. "To bed! Good night to you, Sir Royce." He swept Anna into the chamber, only to be greeted by Cenric. He leaned back against the door for a moment and dared to meet Anna's gaze.

She smiled at him, a twinkle in her eyes. "I have never known you to be so fulsome, my lord," she whispered, then reached up to touch her lips to his cheek. The press of their softness against his skin sent a surge of heat through him and made his heart pound.

"Well done," she whispered, her eyes glowing. "Thank you."

Before Bartholomew could savor her rare approval, Anna pivoted and walked toward Leila. "Dare I hope the water is yet warm? It was always cold when I lived with the sisters, but truly, husband, I grow spoiled in your company." She sat on a stool and unfastened her stockings, as if he were not watching her with such interest.

But then Anna lifted the hem of her kirtle and granted him a fine if fleeting glimpse of her legs. It must have been unwitting, for her gaze flew to his in sudden dismay. Their gazes met and held, and a bewitching flush rose over her cheeks. She untied the garter and removed the stocking with haste, then smoothed down her kirtle to hide her legs again. She turned her back upon him so abruptly that he wondered whether her fears of men—of knights— were restored.

The bed *was* curtained. They could draw the drapes and make a great deal of noise, as if vigorously making love. It was the sole way to keep from offending Lady Marie, Bartholomew reasoned, for then he could argue that his wife had exhausted him.

The trick would lie in convincing Anna to cooperate. It would have been untrue to say that he had no desire to lie with her, because he did, but he knew what was right and what was not. He could not touch Anna in that way. He had given his word.

But that did not mean that Marie had to know the truth.

Were they being watched even now?

Had Royce gone to his wife or retired alone?

There was a rap at the door, and he found Timothy on the threshold. The squire bowed and entered the chamber, for he had come to help Bartholomew disrobe. All set to the business of making ready for bed, although Bartholomew's thoughts were spinning.

There would be little slumber this night and a hard race on the morrow to escape.

And what then? If they succeeded, would he ever see Anna again? Or would their paths part forever? If naught else, he wanted to leave her with one good memory of a knight.

And he had this night together to grant it to her.

❧

Father Ignatius had learned long ago to keep his counsel when he was uncertain of his situation. Prudence was a necessary trait for any who would survive in this holding when it was under Sir Royce's command.

Indeed, Father Ignatius' nature was such that he could weigh the merit of two competing possibilities for months on end, if not years. He preferred to make as few decisions as possible, and ignored the conviction that doing naught *was* a choice in itself.

Truly, the only thing Father Ignatius had ever known without doubt was that he should take holy orders.

He had, for example, been troubled for years by the departure of so many from the village of Haynesdale. That they were compelled to take to the forest and live like outlaws, when few of them had committed any crimes worthy of such a punishment, would have been of sufficient concern. That he, by remaining in the village, was losing the flock he had been charged to tend was even more troubling. There were days when he thought he should follow the survivors into the woods, seek them out, and ensure that they were provided with the services of his office. He knew there had to be some of them out there, even after the great fire.

Father Ignatius knew however that if he did as much, he would be in violation of the baron's express orders to forget their existence. There would be no return to his home and hearth, even if he went once. This might have been one thing, but he in his role as village priest was responsible for the tithes being submitted on time from Haynesdale. He feared that Sir Royce would simply add the tithes to his own treasury, for that man had offered several times to do as much.

Caught between the tending of his flock and the defense of tithes owing to the church, Father Ignatius was not certain what to do. He believed that the ultimate administrator would value souls over tithes, but he was far less certain of the bishop's preference. So, he lingered, and he debated, and he did not choose.

And now, here was Anna, the smith's daughter, in Sir Royce's private chapel, dressed as a noblewoman and apparently wed to a French knight. He would have given the young woman the benefit of the doubt, for she was pretty and he had not had tidings of her for two years—indeed, he had feared her dead, as had many others—but Sir Royce's comments revealed that he believed her to be Anna de Beaumonte.

She was no more Anna de Beaumonte than he was the Archbishop of Canterbury.

Father Ignatius said nothing, because he did not know what to do. He had wondered whether the arrival of these knights had any connection to the sudden appearance of this remarkable relic in Sir Royce's collection. Both the knights and the reliquary seemed exotic, too exotic for Haynesdale. He had shown it to the lady because he had thought she might know something of it.

She had seemed to be hinting.

But he had been so surprised to recognize Anna that he had failed to notice much else. In mere moments, he had been left alone with the reliquary to lock it away, while the knight and Sir Royce left with Anna.

How had Anna conspired to arrive as the knight's wife?

And why?

"While you are here, you might as well give last rites to the prisoner in the dungeon," the Captain of the Guard said to him when he would have returned to his modest home.

"I did not know there was a prisoner in the dungeon," Father Ignatius said with a mildness he did not feel.

"Well, there is, and he dies tomorrow," Gaultier snapped.

Father Ignatius fought against the horror that rose within him, even as he inclined his head.

That another prisoner should be executed was deeply wrong, for there had been no court, but it was also a warning of the price of dissent.

Father Ignatius believed he could make more difference in Haynesville alive. "Then I shall be glad to visit him," he said, bowed and made for the dungeon.

So it was the Father Ignatius finally found himself making a decision. For him, it was remarkably impulsive. But when he unlocked the dungeon and found young Percy alone in tears in the darkness of that dank cell, his resolution was made.

This was the fearsome villain who was condemned to die?

Percy was but a boy, and a frightened boy at that. Father Ignatius then understood Anna's appearance in the keep, if not her disguise. He knew her to be fiercely protective of her younger brother. Was the knight she accompanied in league with her? Why would he aid her?

"Father Ignatius!" Percy cried in amazement, his face streaked with tears. "Can you help me?" He must have been terrified to be confined here in darkness, with only rats for company.

Rare anger rose inside the priest, an outrage that was only awakened when the strong abused those weaker than themselves.

The priest crouched down beside the boy, who seized his robe. Father Ignatius dropped his voice to a whisper. "Of course, I can help, Percy," he said with newfound resolve. "But first, tell me how you came to be in this place."

❧

Exhaust him with her passion.

Anna could not push Bartholomew's suggestion from her thoughts. He had pledged to keep their bed chaste this night. Had he changed his intent? That kiss might have been a hint of what was to come. Leila had said he was honorable. Was it true? He had caressed her in the hall. Had that been a feint or a hint of what she could expect this night? It was her nature to simply ask for the answers she desired, but her awareness that they might be watched—and overheard—precluded that.

Anna wished she knew him better.

She wished she had some experience of expecting good from knights, instead of the pursuit of their own interests.

Her hands were shaking when she folded away the fine stockings, and she knew she took too much time with disrobing and washing. She thought it likely a lady might linger over the task and did not wish to reveal her truth. She also wanted to delay the inevitable as long as possible.

She did not dare to look at Bartholomew as his squire aided him in removing his mail and garb, though there was little reason for shyness. She had seen him nude in the river that very morning, but the chamber was more intimate. She felt herself in greater peril where there were fewer witnesses, and fewer to respond to a cry.

Not that she had gained much aid when she had cried out on that fateful night. Anna shuddered in recollection and realized Leila was watching her closely. The other woman pressed her hand briefly, as if to encourage her. Anna took a deep breath and smiled for her. She wished she was not so easily read, but it was her burden.

Bartholomew meanwhile had been divested of his hauberk. She was keenly aware that he was shedding his boots and chausses. It was hard to believe she had met him less than a day before, but Anna reminded herself of it repeatedly.

She knew so little of his nature.

He was kindly to the boy and thanked him, then drew the curtains on the bed on the side of the common wall. Did he mean for them to have privacy? Or that none could see his deeds? Anna wished she knew! He placed a lantern on the far side of the bed. The dog returned to sleep by the brazier, which now burned low, and Leila dragged a pallet alongside it. Anna's hair had been combed out and she wore only her chemise. The chamber was cold but she stood there, hesitating to join Bartholomew in that great bed. Though she yearned to seize her cloak and curl up on a pallet alongside Leila, she knew that any observer would find the choice curious.

She lifted her own crossbow from the neat array of Bartholomew's belongings and rounded the bed on silent feet. Both Leila and Cenric watched her.

Was Bartholomew nude in the bed? Was he asleep already? Her mouth went dry.

"Husband," she said softly. "Do you not always sleep with your weapons nearby?"

"I have both sword and knife, my lady," he said. When Anna took another step, she could discern him in the shadows of the bed. He was sitting, his back braced against the wall behind the head of it, his eyes glowing as he watched her. The sword was on the floor, in its scabbard. The knife, she could not discern. "But if you would prefer I have the crossbow as well, then I will keep it to hand. Did you bring the bolts?"

She had and offered them to him, keeping one herself. He was watching her and she could not guess why he smiled when he saw what she did. The weight of the bolt was reassuring in her hand, cold and solid. She could stab with it, if necessary.

Bartholomew had to know as much, but he appeared to be untroubled. His chemise was open and he had shed his boots. His chemise covered him to his thighs, which she found encouraging, and she could see the tanned flesh of his chest. His sleeves were rolled up, and he smiled at her, as if knowing her trepidation. The light from the lantern painted him in shades of gold. She had never seen a more alluring man, noble or common.

"You must be cold, wife," he said. "Come and let me warm you."

A part of Anna longed to do just that.

The greater part of her was more sensible. She would not begin what she could not halt. She would not give encouragement to any urges. She eased into the bed, ensuring that she was at the foot of it. She placed the crossbow on the mattress between them. It was not loaded, but still she thought its presence would make her feelings clear.

Indeed, Bartholomew smiled. He lifted the bedclothes and patted the mattress beside himself. "Come and be warm," he invited again. When he leaned forward, Anna saw his shadow on the closed curtains on the far side of the bed.

Would the silhouette be visible to anyone watching from the other room?

He beckoned to her, the motion of his finger clearly displayed on the drapery. Anna crawled toward the empty spot beside him and saw how it appeared that she moved into his embrace. He rolled over, as if pinning her beneath him, though in truth they were alongside each other and not touching at all. "Oh, my lady," he murmured, then kissed the pillow and moaned in pleasure. He embraced the pillow in apparent rapture.

Anna had to bite back a giggle. He did mean to trick Lady Marie!

And he did not touch her, just as he had pledged. Relief flooded through her.

He winked at her and moaned again. "My lady, how I have longed for you this day!"

"My lord!" she replied in kind, his game restoring her confidence. "Cease your chatter and kiss me!"

Bartholomew dropped his face to the pillow to smother his chuckles. Again, he embraced it with ardor. Anna clapped a hand over her mouth and had to avert her gaze from his dancing eyes when he braced himself on his hands. The shadow made it appear that he was looking down at her.

"Have you lost your passion for me, my lady?" he asked as if perplexed. "Methinks you are uncommonly shy this night. Do you yearn for another?"

"Nay, my lord. Never!"

"Then what is amiss, wife of mine?" he growled. "Tell me what I can do to feed your pleasure."

Anna shivered at the intent in his tone. "I prefer such deeds be done in darkness, sir," she dared to say.

"The sisters cannot see you now."

"But I, sir, fear to look upon nudity."

"Your every wish is my command," Bartholomew replied, then leaned out of the bed. He licked his fingers and pinched the wick on the lantern. The flame hissed as it was extinguished, then they were plunged into darkness.

Anna had a moment to fear that she had erred, then Bartholomew groaned anew. She could not feel him or even his heat, and knew there was distance between them.

"Oh!" he cried. "Oh!" He began to move so that the mattress rocked, and Anna blushed in the darkness at the familiarity of the rhythm he set.

She had heard that sound many a time, to be sure.

But it was an illusion, and she should do her part to help.

"Oh!" Anna gasped, ensuring her cries were in time. She had heard her mother cry out thus and tried to mimic the memory. "Oh, oh, *oh*!" The ploy felt ridiculous to her and she feared she did it badly.

But Bartholomew seemed to understand. He seized her hand, the warmth of his fingers closing over hers. "Slower then faster again," he whispered, his voice close to her ear. "'Twould not be mortal to endure long at this rate." Then he raised his voice to a roar. "My lady, you will ensure my demise this night! Oh, oh, OH!"

Anna giggled. She could not help it. The notion that she might kill him with passion was as preposterous as his performance.

Then she had to account for the sound she had made. "Sir! That is a treacherous tickle!"

Bartholomew laughed. "Atop me, my lady," he commanded. "I will show you a treacherous tickle."

He began to rock again, his motions making the bed thump against the floor. He grunted and groaned with his apparent pleasure, then gave her fingers a quick squeeze.

She had to say something or make a similar sound.

"Sir, you are as vigorous as a boar!" she cried, and she felt Bartholomew shake with laughter. His rhythm faltered and she feared she had ruined all.

"My lady, you are insatiable," he retorted. "I fear I will not survive the month in your bed."

"That is why we will not spend the whole of the month abed, sir."

"Who would have imagined an innocent to be so lusty?"

"Who would have imagined a bold knight would so complain?"

"I do not complain, lady mine. I simply savor the marvel that you are."

Anna was surprised by his words, for his tone had dropped low. She wished she might have believed them, and even so a warmth suffused her heart. He held fast to her hand and kept his pledge, which gave her great pleasure. She was close enough to smell his skin and to feel his warmth.

Rather than considering the intimacy of their situation, she thought about their plans. What would happen in the morning? How would they save Percy? How would they escape? She wanted to ask him but Bartholomew's finger suddenly landed over her lips.

"Moan," he advised quietly.

"I do not know how," she confessed quietly.

"Everyone knows how," he countered and moaned with gusto to prove his point.

Anna listened, then tried to do the same. She was certain she sounded more like a lowing cow than a woman in raptures.

Or a sheep with bloat.

That Bartholomew was trying to disguise his chuckle did little to help. She could feel him shaking and swatted him. "Oh my lady, you are demanding!" he cried, and she swatted him again.

"I feel foolish," she whispered. "I like it better when we bicker."

"We cannot bicker all the while we pretend to make love."

"I am certain there are those who do."

"Should I silence you with kisses?"

He was teasing her and Anna knew it. Her face burned. "I think not!"

"Shall I compel you to moan, then?"

Anna caught her breath. "You would not."

"Not unless you asked me to."

She could imagine how he would look in this moment, his hair tousled and his eyes sparkling with mischief. His confidence was clear, and she wanted to challenge him in return. "You cannot do it," she insisted. "And you will not do it."

"I will. I pledge it to you." His lips brushed across her knuckles. "You have only to ask, and your wish will be my command."

But Anna did not dare. "You wish only for me to agree so that you can see to your own pleasure."

"Nay, I will ensure yours alone."

"It cannot be done."

Bartholomew chuckled. "Then dare me to do so, Anna," he whispered, his suggestion making her shiver with desire. "Or moan on your own. The choice is yours."

Did she dare to trust him?

She was surprised by how much she wished to do so.

But that would be folly. She fell under his spell, no more than that.

"Nay," she said, and heard the tremor in her own voice. "Not that, sir. I cannot."

There was a moment of silence then and she feared she had revealed too much.

"You must tell me who so injured you, Anna," Bartholomew murmured finally and with heat. "And I shall see you avenged."

It was a promise to thrill her heart, but not one to make her lose her good sense. Anna closed her eyes and recalled all the lovemaking she had ever overheard, then tried once again to moan with supposed pleasure.

They had an agreement, after all, and she would do her part to see both Percy saved and the reliquary relieved.

In the darkness, at least, Bartholomew could not see her blush.

Sunday, January 17, 1188

Feast Day of
Saint Antony of Egypt.

Claire Delacroix

Chapter Six

It was clear to Bartholomew that Anna had been compelled to welcome a man and that against her will. The notion infuriated him, but there could be no doubting the meaning of her reaction to his own touch. She was not shy. Indeed, she was a bold maiden, more willing than most men to accept a challenge or a dare.

But when she was caressed, she recoiled in terror. He would have expected her to meet him touch for touch, to be as fearless abed as elsewhere, but she shrank from him in terror.

Even when they jested.

She had been raped. There could be no other explanation. He would have wagered his own life upon it. The notion sent fire through him, along with a need to see her revenged. He felt a cur for having teased her with a kiss, and a fool for not having guessed this secret sooner. Worse, he imagined that her dislike of French knights was rooted in this experience.

Aye, many a nobleman believed that pretty maidens in villages were there for his pleasure. The fact that it was commonly done did not diminish Bartholomew's outrage that it had been done to Anna. It was wrong for any woman to endure as much, and he was appalled that Anna should have been so misused.

If naught else, his awareness of her past ensured that he gave her what she desired. He kept his distance in the great bed and held only her hand as they feigned the achievement of their satisfaction.

He was fiercely glad that he had made her laugh, even a little, in such circumstance.

When they had appeared to couple beyond all human endurance, he roared with his apparent release, thumping the mattress with his fist. The dog came to look upon them then, its curiosity aroused and Anna giggled again.

Bartholomew began to snore loudly, like a drunken lout who

had had his pleasure and cared for naught else. He felt Anna pat the mattress and Cenric was quick to accept the invitation. The dog was large and warm, and Anna curled up with the beast between them.

That was no accident, he would wager.

Indeed, she would only sleep if they were not alone.

"Call Leila, too," Bartholomew advised quietly, between his raucous snores. The bed was big enough for all of them, and he could see no reason for Leila to be cold. None could doubt that the bed would be chaste this night, with four of them sharing it.

Leila slipped into the bed at the invitation, and Bartholomew felt her settle on Anna's other side. They four were nestled against each other and quite warm. To his relief, he heard Anna's breathing slow. Within moments, he knew he was the sole one awake.

And that gave him the opportunity to consider the puzzle of Anna.

Bartholomew had always thought that village women knew more of intimate matters than noblewomen, for their chastity was not defended with the same vigor. They were often given young to a partner, whether wedded or not, and could have half a dozen children by Anna's age. He supposed that also meant that they might be abused more readily, as Anna had evidently been.

Who had been a French knight who had taken advantage of her? Had the man been a guest in Royce's abode? Had it been Royce himself?

Only in the darkness of that night did Bartholomew wonder whether Percy was truly Anna's brother or her son.

There was no doubt that she returned his kisses as if she expected only pain to come from such an embrace, and he knew that she had little talent for subterfuge. Anna might be a good thief, but she would make a poor spy.

That was part of what he liked about her. She was honest and blunt. Her wits were quick and she showed no hesitation in sharing her views. He liked that he knew where he stood with her, at any moment. He liked that she was intrepid and that she was loyal to her brother. Aye, she would be the kind of person who stood by her word, regardless of what transpired.

He liked that well.

What if he could teach her that not all knights were fiends and knaves? It was a legacy Bartholomew wished very much to leave her, but their paths would likely part on the morrow.

Could he see her avenged? Would she name the villain? Or was that man long gone from Haynesdale?

Bartholomew should have been planning his own triumphant claim of his father's holding, but instead, he found himself thinking of Anna. What token hung from the lace upon her neck? It had a weight, to be sure, and he thought he had seen it glimmer through her chemise.

What jewel could she possess that she would not sell to see her brother fed and warm? It would be sentimental, to be sure, a token of her parents, perhaps.

But her father had been a smith, not a jeweler.

It was yet another riddle in all the many riddles of his unexpected companion. Bartholomew wished to unravel them all, though he knew he would not have the opportunity.

He dozed hours later, when the keep was quiet all around him.

He should have anticipated that the nightmare would return.

೨♣

They were running in the darkness, his hand held fast within his mother's own. It was dark and cold, the ground wet beneath his feet. There was only darkness ahead. He looked back to see fire blazing behind them, consuming all within view. He had been awakened in haste, seized by his mother and hastened from their home.

Was that what burned?

Where was Papa?

Where were the men who guarded the hall? He heard the clash of steel upon steel but could not see anything beyond the fire. His mother fairly dragged him onward, her feet bare and her hair unbound. Her breath was frantic and she murmured his father's name like a prayer. He could taste her fear and ran as fast as he could, not wanting to disappoint her. Her hand was soft and warm, her breast softer when she finally swept him into her arms.

Still, she ran, her arms wrapped tightly around him. She was weeping, he could tell by the sound of her breath, and he reached up to feel the wetness on her cheeks. He could see the fire over her shoulder, the way it spread, the hunger and the brilliance of it.

"Papa," he said and she shook her head.

"Not now," she whispered to him in French. "Not now."

She stumbled into a cabin, the darkness closing around them so suddenly that he blinked. "Help me," she appealed and he was passed to the embrace of another. It was a man, his arms thick and heavily muscled, his skin smelling of iron and fire.

The smith! He smiled for he liked this man well and often came to watch him work. The smith handed him to his wife, who always smelled of fresh bread, and fired up his forge. A smaller fire lit there, burning brighter and whiter with the smith's every mighty push of the bellows.

He was transfixed by this fire, controlled and contained, yet just as fiery and powerful as the one that had raged behind them. His mother offered a token to the smith, who accepted it with a nod.

It was a ring.

It was his father's ring.

"He must be able to prove his birthright," she said softly. "Mark him, over his heart."

The smith hesitated for a moment, but the sound of swordplay came closer. He exchanged a look with his wife, then worked the bellows with greater vigor. The fire was hot. It was white. It made them all narrow their eyes against its power.

The smith took the ring with his great tongs, and plunged it into the fire on his forge. The ring seemed to glow. It heated like a spark of the sun snared within the greater fire. He wanted to watch it but his mother opened his chemise as the smith's wife held him fast on a table.

"You will be quiet," his mother urged. "As silent as a hare hiding from a fox."

He nodded agreement, not really comprehending. The smith removed the ring from the fire and it was glowing. He was fascinated by the way it had changed, how it looked like a star, but in the shape of his father's ring.

The smith took it in his smaller tongs, then pressed it into the skin over his heart.

There was pain, radiating consuming pain, and the smell of burning flesh. He opened his mouth, then recalled his mother's request, choking back the scream that he wanted to make.

The pain.

The burning.
The searing of his very soul.
The fire that could not be evaded, at any price.

ॐ

Bartholomew awakened with a jolt, his fingers locked in a fist over the scar on his chest. He was breathing quickly, as if he had run miles, and there was perspiration on the back of his neck. He could smell again the burning flesh and feel the heat on his skin. He touched the scar, recognizing that it had been a long time since he had dreamed of its making. He could feel the indent of it, the shape of his father's signet ring, the mark that had been burned into his body that night.

His throat was tight with the memory. It had been the last time he had seen his mother. He had been dispatched from Haynesdale before the wound had cooled, entrusted to a loyal group of knights.

He had lost everything that night.

It took him a while to calm his breathing.

Why did he recognize only the dog?

The dream was a reminder that he had a quest to fulfill, that he had arrived at Haynesdale, that he had to finish what had been begun.

Then he realized the dream had given him a gift. Anna said she was the daughter of the smith. Was it the same smith? Could she take him to her parents that he might be recognized as the son of Haynesdale?

Was this the aid he needed to reclaim his legacy?

ॐ

Leila awakened to the sound of the dog snoring. She was nestled in the great curtained bed along with Anna, Bartholomew, and the dog, and there was a faint light coming through the shutters. When she sat up, the dog's tail thumped against the mattress. Its expression was so entreating that she imagined it expected her to abuse it.

Instead, she rubbed its ears. She didn't know much about dogs, but Bartholomew evidently did. This one had his favor and was both large enough and mellow enough to put her at ease. She was accustomed to horses, after all. She wondered what the dog had endured in this place—for she thought little good of Sir Royce and Lady Marie—and was glad that its past had not made it vicious. It seemed well content to nestle amidst them, though she could see that its ribs were too prominent.

She felt as strongly as Bartholomew that they should take the dog with them. She rose and stirred the coals to life then opened the shutters. The sky was a pale hue and it looked as if it would be a fine day. The dog followed her, putting its paws on the sill to share the view. It wagged its tail at her again and tried to lick her cheek, which made Leila smile.

She supposed it was hungry.

So was she.

There was only the sound of slumber from the curtained bed, but then, after their race through the woods and their performance the night before, Leila could believe that Bartholomew and Anna were tired. She knew she should act like a maid and picked up the bucket she had used to bring water for Anna to bathe the night before. The lidded bucket with the slops had been left outside the chamber door, and she hoped someone had taken it to the sewer.

She straightened to find the dog watching her with a hopeful expression. She supposed it had matters to tend in the morning, as well. Would it return to her when she called it? She did not want Bartholomew to be disappointed by the dog's disappearance. It had seemed to matter greatly to him to let the dog remain with them.

Leila rummaged in his belongings and found a bit of rope. She made a loop at one end, ensuring the knot could not slide and slipped it over the dog's head. They left the chamber together and she was glad the dog walked calmly beside her, because she ended up with two buckets. She dumped the contents of one into the sewer at the back of the stables. The dog cocked a leg and relieved itself, then darted ahead and watched her expectantly as she stepped into the bailey again.

"He must be hungry," a man said softly, expressing her own thoughts aloud.

Leila spun to find the priest watching her from the shadows. He carried a sack and removed a loaf of bread from it. Leila was certain there could be no fresh bread already baked this morning, for the keep was quiet. The priest tore off a piece of bread and offered it to the dog. It was sniffed and then quickly devoured. The dog sat before the priest, waiting for more.

"I think it *is* hungry," Leila said. "What should it eat?"

"Meat, but not so much fat. Some like other fare, but they are wolves in truth and meat is what they all like best. He does not look to have had much, but then the hounds of Haynesdale tend to be kept hungry."

"My lord said he was too thin."

"Some of this will not do him more injury than a hollow belly." The priest gave the dog more bread.

"Will they mind?" Leila asked.

The priest smiled. "The bread is old, given by the baker Denley as alms to the poor. But there are few remaining in Haynesdale village. They are poor enough, but Denley has already shared with them. I thought the squires might have been given less last evening, since the baron had guests, and they are mere children." The priest looked up suddenly. "You are Lady Anna's maid."

"I am." Leila bowed.

The priest considered his words as he fed the dog more bread. He took his time about it, ensuring the dog chewed and swallowed each portion before granting another. "I understood that she prayed in the morning, so I thought to linger and unlock the chapel for her."

"That is very kind, sir. I shall be sure to tell her."

"Please do." He gave her a sharp look that Leila could not interpret.

"Do you think it would be possible for my lord to buy the hound?" she asked. "He is much taken with it and if there are too many here..."

The priest smiled. "I think that if it follows you, it will not be missed."

Leila was pleased to hear as much.

The priest handed her the rest of the loaf of bread. "Take this for the hound. Mind you break it into pieces before you give it to him. He might eat too quickly otherwise." He picked up the sack of bread.

The hound followed the loaf to Leila, fixing its gaze upon her.

"I thank you, sir," she said, even as she looked down at the bread. It was hard, at least a day old or maybe two. But the strange matter was its weight. What did they put in their bread to make it so heavy? She glanced up to find the priest's eyes sparkling.

There was a gap on one side. Leila's fingers slid into the crevice made on one side of the loaf and touched something cold. The priest's expression tempted her to look, and she peeked to see the end of a large iron key hidden inside the bread.

The key to the dungeon.

"I shall return directly to my lady and tell her of your thoughtfulness." Leila bowed again. "And I thank you again, sir, for your kindness to the dog. I will be very sure to feed him slowly."

He nodded once and turned toward the portal to the hall. A woman's voice rose from the kitchens and a clatter of pans announced that the day's work had begun. Leila left the dirty bucket and took both dog and bread back to the chamber, along with a fresh bucket of water. The dog bounded up the stairs and waited every dozen steps for her, licking its chops in anticipation.

If any questioned her haste, she would say her lady was impatient.

&

Duncan was awake when he heard the door to the stables creak. He rolled over in the loft so he could see the crack of light at the portal. To his surprise, the priest slipped through the gap and closed the door behind himself. Duncan did not move but watched with interest. What would the priest seek in the stables? What did he carry? And why did he close the door again?

It seemed unlikely that a priest had a nefarious scheme, but Duncan made few assumptions about the choices of others without evidence.

He waited and watched instead.

Once his eyes had adjusted to the darkness, Duncan saw the priest moving down the line of stalls. He seemed to know the layout of the stables and was able to find his way with only the glimmer of daybreak that shone between the boards.

He also moved toward the horses of their small party, not the baron's own steeds.

Did he mean to do the beasts ill?

Duncan eased down the stairs of the loft. The priest did not glance up but seemed to be counting the horses. When he reached the destrier of Fergus, he looked around himself. Duncan felt his eyes narrow. The priest peered around the horse, his agitation clearly growing, and Duncan unsheathed his sword.

Duncan cleared his throat as he touched the tip of the blade to the priest's back. That man jumped and spun to face him, his eyes wide. "Might I be of service?"

The priest gaped at the sword, then lifted the sack he carried. "I have bread, alms for the poor. I had thought you might be glad of it on your journey."

"We have bread enough," Duncan said, his suspicion unallayed. "Although I thank you for the kindness."

The priest straightened. "I think you should take this bread."

"What of your poor?"

"There are few of them in these days, not because Haynesdale prospers but because there are so few in the village at all. They will not miss it."

"I think it a foul thing for a guest to cheat his host's villagers."

The priest's eyes flashed and his lips tightened. Duncan was intrigued by this glimpse of his frustration. The other man leaned closer, his gaze boring into Duncan's. "I advise you, my son, to take the bread." He bit off each word and Duncan could not account for his manner.

He took the sack cautiously. The bulk in it was about the size of two round loaves, put base to base. The weight of it, though, was all wrong. This could not be bread alone. Duncan frowned but the priest smiled with a strange confidence.

"I believe you will find it a most welcome souvenir," he said. "Though I would suggest you not mention it to anyone else. As you say, the baron might not approve of my generosity in this matter." The priest glanced down at the sword then turned his back upon Duncan. He walked slowly back to the portal, gave Duncan a parting glance, then peered into the bailey before he left the stables.

Duncan could not find it within himself to strike down an unarmed priest.

And he was glad of it. For when he opened the sack, he found not two loaves of bread, but the reliquary, shining gold in the base of the sack.

Duncan swore softly in his amazement.

Then he crossed himself and said a prayer of thanks before rousing Fergus. They had to depart before the loss was discovered!

૨૦

Anna found Father Ignatius in the chapel, just as Leila had said she would. They exchanged a nod and he turned his back to the door, kneeling to pray. Anna crossed herself and knelt by his side, wondering what he would say to her.

She felt as if she had been summoned.

After a few moments, presumably time granted for her to pray, he murmured softly to her. "You ride in uncommon company, Anna."

"Aye, Father."

"And your husband..."

"Is not my husband in truth." Anna spared a quick glance over her shoulder but the door to the chapel was still closed. "Percy and I robbed his company yesterday morn. We thought they would have coin or food, but—"

"They carried the reliquary."

"Apparently so. I did not see it. Percy and I divided our paths, as always we do, and the knight who pretends to be my spouse pursued and caught me. We were arguing when we heard Percy shout for aid, then followed to see him brought here. The scheme was that of the knight, to retrieve both Percy and reliquary."

"I see."

"Thank you for the key, Father."

"Percy told me much of the tale himself last night in the dungeon. I assume the knight will retrieve him?"

"He does so now." Anna clutched the priest's arm. "What of the treasure? We have a wager and I would see both prizes retrieved."

"You trust this knight," Father Ignatius observed. "Despite..."

"I believe he is different, Father. He has treated me well thus far." Anna took a quick breath. "But I do not see how the reliquary can be reclaimed."

"It is done, Anna."

"Father! If you aid in our quest, you will be caught." She

clutched his arm. "If it is missing, they will know you were the culprit. I would not see you punished..."

"Do not fear as much, my child." The priest patted her hand. "I will not linger to be caught."

"But your part will be discovered! They will hunt you."

"And so they might." His expression filled with new resolve. "It is time I tend to my flock in the forest. You will leave by one gate and I will leave by the other."

Anna stared at the priest but there was no doubting his conviction.

And she knew those who had taken refuge in the forest would welcome him gladly.

"There is a trail four paces to the right of the road," Anna advised in a whisper. "Await us at the large crooked elm. It grows in the midst of the trail. You cannot miss it."

He kissed her brow, just as the door was opened behind them. "Bless you, my child. May you bear many sons to your lord husband and walk in the way of the Lord for all your days and nights."

"Then you are ready to break your fast," Sir Royce said. "Good morrow to you, Father." He bowed and Anna went to his side with no small trepidation. "I am informed that your party will ride out early this day, in order to reach Carlisle with all speed. I am sorry that you cannot linger for mass, but at least, you have been blessed."

"Aye, sir, I have been indeed," Anna said, then put her hand in his elbow.

"Then come to the board with me, I beg of you. We have fresh bread and fresh honey this morn."

"How kind you are, sir. I thank you for your generosity."

Royce chattered to her as they walked, his fingers stroking the back of her hand as if she were a pet. Anna set her teeth, kept her head down, and struggled to be polite.

The sooner they were away from this hall, the better, in her view.

᠃᠍

Bartholomew had escorted Anna to the chapel and closed the

door behind her. There was no one afoot in the bailey, though he could hear sounds of activity in the stables. Fergus laughed and Duncan grumbled, Hamish protested, and Timothy must be brushing Zephyr.

Gaultier, the Captain of the Guards, was walking the curtain wall, the other knights of the household following closely behind him as he inspected the ramparts. They were occupied, but only for a short time.

He had but moments to use the key.

Bartholomew sauntered across the bailey as if he had naught but time to spare and slipped into the hall. He quickened his pace then. The kitchens were busy, for he could hear preparations being made for the morning meal, and there were maids sweeping the rushes in the hall. No fires had been lit there as yet, and he stepped back as a maid hastened up the stairs with a bucket of steaming water.

For Marie? Or for Royce? Either of them might appear at any time.

Bartholomew hastened to the portal to the dungeon, looked up and down the corridor, then unlocked the door. He looked down into the darkness. "Percy?" he whispered.

"I will not go quietly to die!" the boy wailed.

"You will be quiet if you mean to live," Bartholomew retorted. "Anna bids you heed me."

"Anna?" Hope mingled with skepticism in the boy's voice.

Bartholomew could discern the pale orb of the boy's face in the darkness below.

"Anna." Bartholomew tossed the rope ladder down the hole. "Climb quickly!"

The boy needed little encouragement to do as much and scrambled up to Bartholomew's side. Bartholomew wrapped him quickly in his cloak, folding him against his chest beneath the wool. The boy had a fearsome smell, but there was little to be done about that. He closed the trap door and locked it, then stood and held his cloak about himself.

"Be still and be quiet," he advised sternly and felt Percy nod.

Again he strolled into the bailey, moseying toward the stables. No one took any notice of him, until he stepped into the stables.

Fergus turned with a grimace. "Where have you been

sleeping?" he demanded, then Bartholomew opened his cloak to reveal his burden. "The thief!"

Percy's eyes rounded. "The party of knights!" He punched Bartholomew in the stomach and made to flee. "Anna never gave you a message for me!" Duncan shut the door and leaned against it, blocking the boy's passage. Percy spun in place, eyeing the three knights as if he would fight them all.

"Anna is with us," Bartholomew said. "We mean to see you returned to the forest, hale and whole."

"Why?" Percy demanded, his suspicion clear.

"We needed Anna's help to retrieve what we value, and her price was your rescue," Bartholomew explained.

Instead of being reassured, the boy caught his breath in alarm. "She did not come into the keep, did she?"

Bartholomew wondered at his concern. "She did, in disguise, and I will thank you not to reveal her."

"Not I!" declared Percy. His mouth took a grim line. "I would not put her in peril again." He strode to Bartholomew and shook a fist at him. "And if you have done her injury, I shall see her avenged."

"The lady has a champion," Fergus said with amusement. The boy glared at him.

"They have endured much, I believe," Bartholomew said. He crouched down before the boy. "We mean to garb you as a squire and hide you within our company. It is the best way to see you freed of this place, but the scheme will only succeed if you cooperate."

Percy looked between them again with hostility. "If I see Anna abused, I owe you naught."

"Fair enough," Bartholomew said and stood. "I think we should break our fast."

"Not all at once, lad," Duncan said. "You go first. We shall tend to the boy."

Bartholomew thought he might collect Anna from the chapel, but found that portal locked. He crossed the bailey to the keep and opened the portal there, blinking at the sudden darkness.

"How strange that you wrapped yourself tightly against the cold just moments ago," Marie said softly. "Yet now you have abandoned your cloak completely."

Bartholomew froze, realizing too late that he had left his cloak in the stable. He saw Marie sidle toward him from the bottom of the stairs, a knowing smile upon her lips. She paused before him and sniffed.

"And even more curious, you have a definite scent of dungeon, though I know for a fact that you slumbered in a fine bed with your lady wife." Her fingertip landed on his chest. "Surely, you do not deceive your host, sir?"

"Surely I do not. I was cold but am so no longer."

"You carried a filthy child but do so no longer," she corrected. Her hand flattened against his chest and eased to his shoulder. "Such a fine man." She took a deep breath, then met his gaze. "You may have been exhausted last night by your lady's passion, or you may have been avoiding my offer," she purred, her gaze unswerving. "But now I believe we can negotiate."

"I do not understand your meaning," Bartholomew lied. "You are right about the scent. I should change my chemise before my baggage is all packed." He made to move past her, but Marie stepped into his path again.

"You will not leave here with that *baggage* unless I contrive it to be so," she whispered. "And I will not contrive it to be so unless you pledge to meet me four days hence and give me what I desire."

The intent in her eyes could not be doubted. She would reveal them to Royce, without a moment's hesitation. If Percy was found, they doubtless would be searched completely, and the reliquary would be found. Anna might be identified and the priest might be cast into peril.

They could all end their days in Haynesdale's dungeon.

Bartholomew bowed his head as he surrendered. He believed her request was wrong, but maybe some other course would become clear to him. If they did not escape from Haynesdale with Percy and the reliquary, there would be no future for any of them.

"Where?" he asked quietly and the lady smiled in her triumph.

"The mill," she decreed, much to Bartholomew's confusion. There was no mill, not that he could see. But he had no chance to ask, for the others joined them in that moment.

He supposed he should be relieved that he could not keep such a promise to the lady, not if he could not find her assignation, but in truth, it troubled him to have given his vow when he could not fulfill it.

❧

"All will be well, lad, so long as you keep your head down," the older Scotsman advised Percy in an undertone. There were three knights, including two Templars, and four squires loading the horses and checking their trap. Percy did not know whether the Scotsman was knight, Templar, or man-at-arms. He was gruff, to be sure. It was early in the morning, and Percy's stomach was growling because he had not eaten much since the previous morning.

Father Ignatius had not been allowed to bring him food the night before.

Percy did not know who these men were and he could not understand why they would even make a wager with Anna to help him to escape the baron's dungeon. He and Anna had robbed them just the day before. After being brought to the stables, he had been commanded by the Scottish knight to quickly dress in the garb of one of the squires, while the other Scotsman watched. He was lifted into the saddle of a palfrey behind the red-haired boy before the Scotsman granted him such advice.

Percy nodded agreement.

He had few choices, and he had given the French knight his word.

The Scotsman pulled Percy's borrowed hood forward, the better to hide his face. "Best if you do not speak at all, lad. We shall be outside the walls soon enough."

"Did you get it back?" Percy had to ask. He should have held his tongue, but he could not do it. They were being kind to him, for whatever reason, and it felt wrong to deceive them.

The Scotsman peered at him. "And what business would that be of yours?"

"You might think I can lead you to it, but they took it. It is here. If you want it, you should not leave without it."

The Scotsman's smile broadened. "It will only be within these walls for a little longer, lad."

So, they had found it and reclaimed it. Percy liked the sound of that. He hated when Royce claimed anything of merit. He also would like to have a better look at what they had been carrying. He had seen that it was big and it was gold, that it was studded with gems, but not much more than that. What was it exactly? It might be a big bowl...

Percy wanted to ask the Scotsman about Anna, but he feared that doing so would put her in peril. What if she were hurt? Why was she with them? Where was she? He had been hoping that she was safely back at the cavern or with the others, but knowing she was in Haynesdale keep, even with these knights, made him uneasy.

The party of horses was led into the bailey, where the baron stood with his lady wife. The other knight was there, holding the reins of a horse with a woman in the saddle. Her face was veiled and a maid rode a palfrey behind her.

Percy frowned. There had been no women in the party when he and Anna had robbed them. Had they come to Haynesdale to retrieve the women? He had expected Anna to be with them, but there were only the noblewoman and the maid. The maid wasn't Anna. There were few souls living in Haynesdale keep who Percy did not know, but he did not recognize the maid at all. He peered at the lady, for he had never seen another noblewoman in Royce's holding. Who was she?

It was sufficiently curious that he wished to ask a question. The Scotsman seemed to guess as much, for he gave Percy a stern look.

Percy held his tongue.

Many compliments were exchanged between the knights and the baron, and Percy wished they would just move toward the gates. It all seemed to be taking so very long.

A knight came from the hall to join them, bowing low to all the knights in the party. Percy caught his breath and stared. It was Gaultier, the Captain of the Guard, the most evil of all the men in the baron's employ. Percy hated him more than any other soul alive.

Even more than the baron.

He wished he had a knife so that he might strike Gaultier down and repay him for all the ill he had done their family. He would kill the villain for Anna in a heartbeat.

The Scotsman gave him another look, this one even more quelling than the last.

Gaultier surveyed the party. "Do you not have an extra squire on this morning?" he asked with suspicion.

"Do they?" Royce asked, then visibly counted the number of the party.

The Scotsman's horse moved then, sidling through the group as if impatient to be gone. Percy guessed that he meant to confuse the baron's count.

The Scottish knight laughed. "An extra boy? I have ridden to Outremer and back with two squires, my dear sir, and scarce have need of another."

"But I was certain..." Gaultier began.

"Who counts boys?" the Scotsman scoffed. "Save when it is time to feed them?"

The knights laughed, but not the Templars. They looked so grim that the baron appeared to find support in their view. Royce stepped toward one Templar. "I beg of you, sir, tell me how many squires your comrade had yesterday."

The Templar looked so discomfited that Percy wanted to roll his eyes. All he had to do was declare that there were two squires. It was not that big of a falsehood.

Though Percy supposed they were sworn to tell the truth.

The Scotsman made a sound of disgust and glared at the Templar.

"Two, of course, sir," the Templar said, but his delay had fed Royce's doubts.

"Look at the height of the sun!" the knight with the lady exclaimed. "It will be midday before we are away, and night will have fallen long before we reach shelter. My lord, we must depart!" He swung into his saddle and reached to offer a hand to his lady that she might climb to the saddle behind him. She seized his hand and he made to pull her bodily up behind him.

"Let me be of aid," Gaultier offered. The Captain of the Guard linked his gloved hands together and created a step for the lady.

She hesitated, as if she knew him to be the lecher he was.

"I thank you, sir," she said, and put her foot onto his hands.

Anna? She sounded almost like his sister.

But Anna could not be so close to Gaultier! Percy made a sound of consternation, which drew the Scotsman's eye.

It also drew Royce's attention. "That boy," he said with resolve and pointed at Percy. "*That* boy was not with you yesterday. Step down, boy, and show me your face."

"We will be late, sir," the Scottish knight protested, but had no chance to say more.

"We must reach Carlisle with all speed," the Scotsman insisted.

Anna had just put her weight upon Gaultier's linked hands, when a chance gust lifted her veil. Gaultier had been looking up at her, undoubtedly hoping to peer up her kirtle. He gasped aloud.

Anna caught her breath and stared at him in obvious terror.

"It is the smith's daughter," Gaultier declared and seized her around the waist. "I knew you were not dead!"

"What is this?" Royce demanded.

Gaultier made to cast her to the ground, but Anna kicked him hard in the groin. The knight turned the horse and struck Gaultier in the back of the head with a mailed fist, then snatched for Anna. She leaped toward his saddle and managed to grasp his belt. The other horses stamped and the rest of the party turned to ride out, giving their spurs to their steeds.

"Ride!" Anna cried, even as Gaultier lunged for her. The maid kicked Gaultier as her palfrey cantered past him, but Gaultier still managed to catch hold of Anna's kirtle. He tugged at her and she slid backward on Bartholomew's horse, then he grabbed her ankle.

He would pull her to the ground! Percy gasped in horror.

"Filthy wretch!" Gaultier roared. "You are no lady, and you will not ride from this keep without my leave!" Anna hung on to the knight, even as Gaultier held fast to her ankle. The horse was sufficiently strong that the Captain of the Guard was dragged behind them. Gaultier would keep Anna behind! The knight tried to dislodge the captain's weight, but Percy saw that he was constrained by Anna's position.

Percy had to help. He gave the squire's palfrey his heels.

"What are you doing?" cried the squire before him, but Percy did not heed his protest. They rode straight for the Captain of the Guard and he seized the squire's short blade from his scabbard that he would be ready. As the horse drew alongside Gaultier, Percy stabbed at him.

"Knave!" he cried.

The blade was diverted by Gaultier's coif, though, and only scratched his face. "Vermin! My lord, it is the smith's other brat!"

the Captain of the Guard roared and swung a fist at Percy. He struck the squire's palfrey, which danced sideways, then bolted for the gate. Percy could only hold on and look back, helpless to do more.

Indeed, he had not done enough.

"Halt!" Royce bellowed. "Close the gates!"

Percy heard the creak of the portcullis being lowered. As the squire's palfrey galloped beneath it, he looked back in time to see Anna kick Gaultier again. Her kirtle tore before the knight's grip loosed and she pulled herself closer to the knight.

"Ride!" she cried again, and neither the knight who accompanied her nor his steed needed more encouragement. The Templars raced forward, the Scotsman falling to the rear. The portcullis was lowering quickly, but those riders bent low over their saddles and sailed beneath it.

"Ride!" the Scotsman roared and slapped the rump of the palfrey that the other squire rode, hastening the others ahead of him.

They had escaped!

"You will not depart so readily!" Gaultier bellowed and snatched at the Scotsman, who was the last rider in the bailey. That man clung to his saddlebag and Percy feared he knew what was within it. The pair fell to the ground, the saddlebag clutched to the Scotsman's chest, and his steed raced on with the reins trailing.

The portcullis clanged to the earth right after the Scotsman's horse. One of the squires snatched its reins and led it onward. The Scotsman and Gaultier were wrestling in the dirt, the saddlebag between them. Percy saw three more knights step forward and knew the Scotsman would have to surrender.

"Nay!" Percy cried, for the Scotsman had been kind to him. He wished he could have made his blow count and killed Gaultier, as that man deserved. He did not want Royce to have the treasure, either.

"God in Heaven," the Scottish knight muttered, his destrier slowing its pace as he looked back.

"Ride on!" the knight with Anna insisted. The maid's palfrey galloped behind them, and the squires followed in a tight pack. They knew how to ride quickly, that much was for certain, and their horses were accustomed to it. The palfreys were followed by the

Templars.

"We must save ourselves that we can later save him," one of the Templars said.

"Naught will be gained if we are all taken," the other agreed.

"We will return for him," the knight with Anna insisted, and the Scottish knight reluctantly turned his steed to follow.

"And the prize," he muttered, and Percy noted that all the men in the group were grim. For some reason, they carried that treasure, and he guessed that they would not readily abandon it.

Or their comrade.

But where would they hide?

Surely Anna would not reveal the refuge and compromise the safety of all of Haynesdale's outcasts? Percy watched the way his sister looked at the French knight and could not be certain.

How could she abandon her hatred of Gaultier's kind so readily?

Chapter Seven

Anna was torn.

She knew they could not outrun the baron's men. It was too far to another sanctuary.

Yet, as much as she wanted to ensure the safety of Bartholomew and his companions, she could not help them to hide.

Because that would mean revealing her fellows in the forest. Such a large company of horses could not be hidden in the forest for long, even if they were taken in by the outcasts from Haynesdale village. The baron's knights would not rest until they had found Bartholomew's party. Already she heard the baying of the hunting dogs and trembled that those who had been safely hidden in the forest until this day would pay the price for her deeds.

Again.

Who could have guessed that one theft could have led to so much going awry?

And now Duncan was still held captive in Haynesdale. She wanted to be of aid, but she could not betray those who trusted her. It seemed there was no good solution, only choices that endangered all.

She remained silent, hoping Bartholomew and his friends had a scheme.

Otherwise, she would have to save Percy first and leave them in peril.

Anna felt trapped, as if there were no good solutions. "The dog!" she recalled belatedly, thinking of another matter gone awry.

"There was no opportunity to ask for him," Bartholomew said, regret in his tone. "And no chance of gaining him now."

"Royce will hunt us to the ground when he realizes that we nearly reclaimed the treasure," Fergus said, drawing his steed alongside.

"Or do injury to the priest," Bartholomew agreed. He glanced back at Anna. "He will guess that we had that man's aid. Will he be safe?"

"Sir Royce will not find him," Anna could assure him with confidence. "Father Ignatius left the hall and village after helping us."

"Can we find him?" Fergus asked. "I would not leave him undefended."

His gallantry only added to her dismay. "He will fare well enough," she said, not wanting to admit more.

"You have a haven, then?" Bartholomew said with satisfaction. "Those are good tidings."

Anna did not make the obvious offer and to her relief, he did not pursue the question.

For the moment. Bartholomew or one of his fellows would return to the matter of refuge and she must decide what to do. The location of the hidden sanctuary was not her secret to tell, for doing so would compromise the safety of all. On the other hand, these knights had saved Percy, and at considerable risk to themselves. They had lost one of their own and the sacred relic. She owed them much and came to believe she could trust Bartholomew's word.

What should she do?

"They will pursue us within moments," Enguerrand declared, drawing alongside Fergus and Bartholomew. "All they must do is saddle their steeds and open the gates. And he must know these lands better than we do. We are lost!"

Even as the Templar spoke, a hunting horn was sounded from the keep behind them.

Without exchanging a word, they all urged their horses to greater speed. Anna's heart raced, and she was glad to see that they approached the bend in the road. She felt Percy watching her and knew she must decide.

"It is only a matter of time until they catch up to us," Fergus said. "There is but one direction to look for us until the road forks!"

"And that is in several miles," Bartholomew agreed.

"I cannot think there is a refuge to be found nearby," Yvan said, glancing at Bartholomew. "It was *you* who advised this road. Do you know where we might find sanctuary?" Anna noted how that knight considered Bartholomew.

Why would Bartholomew have brought his party through Haynesdale? She knew little of him, but in this moment, she realized she knew almost naught at all. Why would he have come to Haynesdale?

"What of Duncan?" Fergus asked. "We cannot abandon him."

"We must leave him there for the moment," Bartholomew said. "Anna? How far must we ride this day to safety?"

"The lands to the north are Royce's former holding," she said with care. "And it must be nigh two days ride to a town." She shrugged. "They must have thought you mad to have believed you could reach Carlisle in a day. It takes at least three to arrive there."

Fergus swore. "Never did I think I would curse the wilderness so! We have need of a town."

"A cave," Yvan suggested.

"We are doomed!" moaned Enguerrand.

"Nay, I think not," Bartholomew said, glancing back at Anna. "You have a suggestion, I would wager. Perhaps we might share the sanctuary used by the priest."

"He is not there yet. Just ahead, there is an old crooked elm off the right of the path. He awaits us there."

"We cannot all hide in an elm, no matter how old or crooked!" protested Yvan.

"Anna knows of a haven," Bartholomew reminded them quietly.

"Will you take them *there*?" Percy asked and all the men looked at him.

Anna sat straighter behind Bartholomew, knowing the men would protest her one condition. "There is a haven, but it is not my right to reveal it, for others take sanctuary there." She saw Bartholomew's disappointment. "I cannot take you there."

"What madness is this?" Enguerrand demanded. "We saved your thief of a brother!" He was as outraged as if he had made the plan and taken the risk, though Anna knew he had been a reluctant participant.

"We imperiled our companion in that quest," Fergus reminded her gently.

"And lost the relic," Leila said, her tone more scathing. It was clear she thought little of Anna's choice.

"I cannot do it," Anna said. "And the horses cannot be hidden.

They will bring dogs and all will be lost."

"But..." Fergus began.

Bartholomew held up a hand for silence. "Anna speaks with sense. If her refuge offers no hiding for the horses, we will be found, along with those she would defend. Remember the burned forest we saw yesterday and the tale of it."

"But still," Enguerrand protested.

Bartholomew rounded the curve and slowed his destrier. "Of course, we will let you return to the forest and ride on to draw Royce's men away." To her surprise, he leaped from the saddle then lifted her down.

"You have no time," she argued, fearful for his survival.

He granted her a sparkling glance and seized her crossbow from where it hung on the back of his saddle. "You will give me refuge, or never see this again."

"Curse you!" Anna said.

"Ride on," Bartholomew said to Fergus. "Meet me where the forest is burned at the next new moon." He seized Percy from behind Hamish and put him on the ground. "I will find a way for us to retrieve the reliquary by then, and Duncan, too."

"Can you trust her?" Enguerrand demanded.

"So long as I hold her prize, aye, I can," Bartholomew said, then spared Anna a glance. "And she knows more of these lands than we do. Alliance may offer our sole chance."

It was a compromise that Anna did not like—though truly, she was glad that this would not be the day she saw the last of this knight.

And she admired that he would finish what he had begun.

"Fair enough," Fergus agreed and reached for the reins of Bartholomew's destrier.

"But my lord!" Timothy protested.

"Ride with them," Bartholomew instructed. "You will be safer."

"But your hauberk!"

"I will find a way. Fear not and ride on!" Bartholomew cried and slapped the rump of his destrier. That beast sprang forward with a nicker, and the entire company gave their spurs to their steeds. The horses galloped down the road, both Timothy and Leila looking back in concern. Bartholomew gave them a jaunty wave, but Anna seized his arm.

"We must hide!" she hissed, and he followed her immediately. Percy had already ducked into the undergrowth and she turned her steps toward a large crooked elm.

Father Ignatius was there, his hand upon Percy's shoulder. He carried a large sack, and Anna assumed he had brought some provisions and perhaps a Bible. Bartholomew held up a hand as the sound of hoof beats became louder. They ducked down in the undergrowth and watched the shadows of the passing horses. Dogs ran with the steeds, baying and barking after the departing party.

She wished that they had not left Cenric behind. Of course, there had been no opportunity to ask for the dog or to offer to pay for it, and she already knew this knight well enough to understand that he would not have simply taken it.

"Four," Bartholomew whispered when they were gone.

"They will double back," Anna said. "We will be found." She fixed Bartholomew with a look. "You must be blindfolded to go farther."

His lips parted. He looked back to the road, then to her. "A fine time to mention such detail."

"I cannot betray them," Anna said with ferocity.

"Them?" Bartholomew echoed, looking between her and the priest with obvious curiosity. "How many hide in these woods?"

"At least half the village of Haynesdale," Father Ignatius said. "I did not think so many were killed in that fire as Sir Royce maintained." He nodded at Bartholomew. "They have learned a distrust of knights and noblemen. Decide, my son, for it must be this way if you are to continue."

"And make haste!" Percy said. "Or we shall abandon you here."

Bartholomew nodded once, then sat on a log. Anna tore a length of cloth from the hem on her chemise and wrapped it several times around his head before knotting it securely. "You will have to trust my guidance," she said quietly.

"If I trip, I will be sure to break the weapon you so value," he countered, and she had to admit that it was not an unreasonable reply.

"Once again, we make a wager to see the goals of each of us achieved," she said and was rewarded by his quick smile.

"Quickly, now," she urged then, and Percy gathered some

boughs. Fortunately, there was little snow on the ground here where the trees were dense overhead even in winter. They moved with haste, Anna leading Bartholomew by the hand and Father Ignatius steadying his other elbow. Percy trailed the group, sweeping over the marks of their passage and tucking bracken across the path to disguise the way. The deeper they went into the forest, the quieter the air seemed to be. There was no smell of wood smoke or any notable signs of men.

Anna saw the bent twigs that were left as signals and the quick movement of shadows on either side of the established route. Word of their party would reach the haven before they did, and she anticipated a full greeting.

Father Ignatius would be surprised by the size of his flock that survived in the forest.

> ❧

The sorry truth was that Duncan had seen worse prisons.

This dungeon was not so fine a place, but the vermin—thus far—were neither numerous nor bold, and the dampness was constrained to one corner. It did not smell fair, but it was not a dung heap either. It was damp but not as cold as he might have expected.

Aye, he had seen worse.

That was precious little consolation now that he found himself trapped in this one. Indeed, it said much about his life, and little good.

The realization disgruntled him.

The entry was from above, a trap door in the floor, which was the height of three men above him. There was a rope ladder that could be lowered into the dungeon but he had simply been cast through the hole. It was a blessing that he had not broken a bone on impact with the packed dirt floor.

Duncan had paced the space to confirm what he already suspected. It was roughly square and offered no other way out than the trap door: There was not a foothold or a handhold to be found in the walls, which were cursedly smooth—not that it mattered for scaling one even to the top would still leave him too far from the trap door to escape. He did not even imagine that a trio of men could work together to escape this place.

It was of simple but cunning design.

To think he might have still been with Radegunde.

Duncan paced the dry end of the dungeon, then he stood beneath the door for a while. He refused to sit while he had a choice, and he was determined to remain alert. Curse duty and obligation! Curse his own integrity! If he had not been so resolved to keep his word and escort Fergus home, as promised, he might have been with Radegunde.

Radegunde.

Of course, he would not have been the man he was, if he had been able to so readily discard a vow, and Radegunde might not have felt affection for him, as a result.

Still, it was more than sobering to realize that he might never see her again.

Would she learn of his fate? He did not believe that Fergus would abandon him readily, but was not certain how much the party would risk. Certainly, they would try to regain the prize of the reliquary for it was their mission to deliver it safely. But given the choice between relic and himself, Duncan knew there would be only one decision they could make.

They were sworn to the saint's defense, after all.

He wondered whether he would ever see daylight again, when he heard a key turn in a lock. The trap door was flung open, emitting sudden light into the dungeon so that he squinted at its brightness.

"Sir Royce would speak with you," said a man gruffly, then kicked the rope ladder down into the hole. "Hasten yourself, for if you cannot climb on your own, you will lose the chance to beg his mercy."

Duncan had no intention of begging for Royce's mercy. He suspected he would have little chance to speak. He feared he might be tortured or worse, executed. Still, there was no point in flinching from whatever would be. He seized the rope ladder and began to climb.

৯৯

It seemed to Bartholomew that they walked for hours, though in truth, he knew it could not have been so long. Deprived of his sight, his other senses were more keen. He felt that they moved deeper into the forest and that the land changed shape. For a long time, their progress was over level ground, then they crossed a stream and it began to rise. He felt that the air moved more, as if they climbed a hill that stood in the wind.

Anna periodically paused to spin him around in place, undoubtedly hoping to muddle his sense of direction, but Bartholomew was not so easily disoriented as that. He also guessed that she would not take a circuitous path, because the baron's men were hunting them. At intervals, he heard the thunder of passing hoof beats or the barking of dogs. When the baron's men could be discerned, Anna pulled him low and froze in place until the sounds faded again. He could hear the footfalls of Father Ignatius on his other side and the sounds of Percy disguising their path behind him as they progressed.

There could be no doubting the tension in Anna, for her grip upon his elbow was tight and her breathing was quick. Bartholomew knew she was afraid of being caught, and he guessed that her fear was based upon a past incident that had not ended well.

Was Gaultier the French knight who had abused her? That would explain Percy's decision to attack the Captain of the Guard, and perhaps even Gaultier's seizing Anna.

Perhaps Gaultier had simply ordered the assault.

As they walked in silence, Bartholomew could not ask Anna. He would not have asked her in the presence of the priest and her brother, at any rate, and he reasoned she would not have answered no matter how or when he asked.

Still, he wanted to know.

Finally, they entered a clearing, and Bartholomew knew it because he felt the sunlight on his shoulders and head. Unless he missed his guess, it was midday for the heat came from overhead, which meant the sun was at zenith. He felt Percy leave them and race ahead, then heard the boy circle back through the undergrowth.

"Now you must climb," Anna said, just as dogs began to bark at closer proximity. She caught her breath. "There!" she said to someone, probably Father Ignatius for that man left Bartholomew's side.

The older man grunted as he endeavored to do some feat, the dogs barked more loudly, and Bartholomew had sufficient of the game. He pushed off the blindfold and shoved the piece of cloth into his belt.

"Nay!" Anna protested, but he ignored her and seized the end of the rope ladder that Father Ignatius was trying to climb. It hung from a nearby tree and swung so with the older man's weight that he was having difficulties in ascending it. Bartholomew put his weight on the base of it, ensuring it was stable and vertical. The priest cast him a smile of gratitude and made better progress. Bartholomew could see that there was a platform built high in the tree's boughs.

"You expected me to climb this while blindfolded?" he asked Anna. "Or maybe you meant to abandon me to the dogs?"

"I did not!" she retorted. "But you cannot see our haven."

"I have no notion of where we are and could not find this place again. It is sufficient," he assured her, although he was not nearly as lost as she might believe. Father Ignatius made the platform overhead, and Bartholomew beckoned to Percy. "Go." The boy scampered up the ladder, then Anna came to his side with some wariness.

"You should go next," she said.

"Ladies first."

"You are not the lord of the forests," she countered. "All follow my dictate in these woods."

That was a marvel in itself, but Bartholomew did not budge. "Perhaps they follow the dictate of whoever carries the crossbow," he suggested, just to see her lips thin in displeasure and her eyes snap. The crossbow in question was slung on his back. "Shall we discuss it for the remainder of the day, or do you mean to climb?"

"Vexing man," she grumbled, then seized the ladder. She paused when they were eye to eye. "Do not look up my skirts," she warned him.

"Aye, for that would be a fearsome fate." He teased her, for he could do naught else. "Never mind Royce's men or the dogs or the prospect of incarceration or execution. For me to see the sweet curve of your legs would be a most dire situation. Make no mistake: you offer your share of vexation, Anna." He made a face and she swatted his shoulder. He held her gaze with intent, knowing why she insisted thus, and dropped his voice low. "Climb, Anna. I will not look."

And though he might have savored the view, Bartholomew kept

his word.

He was about to climb the ladder himself when he heard some beast running through the forest. He paused to look back, for it came from the same direction they had come, just as a large gray dog burst into the clearing. It had its nose to the ground, but looked up and headed directly for him.

Cenric!

Other dogs barked but he could not abandon this hound dog. It might well reveal their location, but more than that, he wanted its company. It jumped toward him with joy and he seized it, casting it halfway over his shoulder before he climbed the rope ladder anew. In this moment, he was glad that the dog was too thin, for it was a formidable weight and size even as it was. He was panting with exertion when he reached the summit of the ladder and the others helped to pull the dog onto the platform.

Cenric was none too pleased with the situation. His eyes were wide and he sat in the midst of the platform, as if terrified of falling from its edge. Percy and Father Ignatius patted the dog in an attempt to reassure it and it cautiously laid down. Bartholomew was certain the dog's nails were digging into the wood.

"You risk your life for a dog," Anna chided, though he knew she was pleased. "Whimsy!"

"I defend what I take to heart," Bartholomew said even as he caught his breath.

"And so it is with a man of merit," Father Ignatius said with approval. "Well done, my son."

Anna granted Bartholomew a level look, then advised them all to be quiet. Percy whisked the rope ladder up to the platform and they all ducked down, the dog in their midst, to peer through the tree's branches at the ground. Bartholomew imagined that in summer, when the tree was in full leaf, they would be completely hidden. As it was, he felt exposed.

Still, a hunter would have to think to look up. Who would expect a platform to be built in a tree in the midst of the forest? Who had built this one? He peered into the other trees around the clearing and thought he could discern another platform in a large oak tree opposite them. Were there people on it? He could not be certain. If there were, they were garbed in plain clothing and very still.

He removed the crossbow from his back as the sounds of pursuit grew louder and loaded a bolt under Anna's watchful eye.

A trio of dogs raced into the clearing, barking as they followed the scent. Though Percy had brushed a bough over the party's footprints, the snow looked different where they had walked. Two dogs passed by, following the false trail, but one slowed its steps to sniff beneath the tree. All on the platform held their breath as one.

The dog below took a step back and looked up the tree, its eyes glinting, and growled.

Cenric growled in return, though he could not have seen the other dog. He must have smelled it. Bartholomew felt the vibration of the dog against his side.

He could have killed the dog below, but its corpse would draw more attention than its growl. He aimed the bow and waited.

The dog's ears flicked at the sound of Cenric's growl.

It took another step back and its ears flicked, as if considering the puzzle of a dog in a tree.

A man whistled and the other two dogs raced back across the clearing. The one beneath the tree gave one last look upward, then heeded the summons as well. The dogs could be heard bounding through the scrub, and slowly the sounds of their passage diminished to naught.

The sun passed its zenith.

The snow melted in the clearing.

An owl hooted three times.

An owl? In broad daylight?

Anna stood up and hooted in reply. Her eyes were dancing as she watched Bartholomew's reaction. "How many are hidden here?" he asked, still keeping his voice low.

"More than you will believe," she replied. "Come, Father Ignatius, you will be most welcome."

ॐ

It was good to be back.

Anna always felt more at home in the forest than anywhere else. Here, she could trust her fellows. Here, she was safe. Here, she knew every man, woman, and child, what they believed and what they would do in any circumstance. It was a haven in every sense of the word.

Esme's chickens were the first to surround them, clucking and pecking. Cenric bent to sniff them and they fluttered away, scolding with a confidence that was the result of Esme's protection. The dog looked bewildered by their manner, but walked at Bartholomew's side and left them alone.

Willa, the wife of Esme's son, shooed the chickens out of the path of the new arrivals, her eyes bright with curiosity. Her husband, Edgar, was fast by her side, his eyes narrowed with suspicion. Anna understood that they two had stepped forward to discover the truth of her companion, while the others remained hidden. "Look at you!" Willa declared to Anna. "As finely garbed as Lady Marie herself." She dropped to one knee. "And Father Ignatius! What a marvel."

"You look well, Willa," the priest said with real pleasure.

"And you bring a stranger to us," Edgar said with disapproval, speaking quickly as if to interrupt the priest from saying more. He was a burly man and folded his arms across his chest to regard them all. His tone was filled with disdain. "A knight. A *French* knight by the look of him."

"I gather you have learned little good of knights," Bartholomew said smoothly. He offered his hand. "I am Bartholomew of Châmont-sur-Maine. I vow that I will honor the bond between guest and host in this place, if you would offer me hospitality for a short while."

Edgar blinked and stared at his outstretched hand. Anna smiled, for none of them had known a nobleman to speak to them as better than dogs. "You must not reveal us," he decreed.

"Never," Bartholomew said with conviction.

"Swear upon the pommel of your sword," Anna advised, then spoke to Edgar. "It has a shard of the true cross within it."

The eyes of the miller's son opened wide, but he accepted her word. Bartholomew pledged as bidden, the men shook hands, and Edgar eyed the pommel with astonishment. Father Ignatius beamed, and it was evident to Anna that possession of such a prize had only raised his estimation of Bartholomew.

"What has happened, Anna?" Edgar asked when all was agreed.

"Percy and I robbed this knight's company, then Percy was captured by Gaultier along with the spoils." Anna nodded at

Bartholomew. "He and his company took me into Haynesdale, in disguise, that we might retrieve both."

"What company?" asked Willa.

"They have ridden on without him. Father Ignatius aided our escape with Percy, but the stolen item is yet in the keep."

"As is one of their men," Percy contributed. "We must save them both, then the knight will leave us."

Edgar nodded. "We heard the knights ride out from Haynesdale in pursuit. They take the road to Carlisle."

"They pursue my fellows," Bartholomew agreed.

"Norton and Piers followed, to discover what they do." Edgar referred to the two older sons of the plowman, Wallace, who remained in the village with his wife. "I suspect they will ride to the boundaries of Haynesdale, then return. We must be vigilant that we are not discovered."

"You are welcome here," Anna said to Bartholomew. "But we will wait for the boys to tell us that the knights are back at the keep before there will be a fire."

"A fire is the least of my concerns." Bartholomew bowed to Edgar and then to Anna. "I thank you both."

Anna was amused to see his courtly manners in the midst of the forest, but she was more amused by his reaction when the others revealed themselves. Willa and Edgar's three children were first to erupt from their hiding places, their oldest boy—who was of an age with Percy—demanding the full tale from his friend. Esme herself came forward, surrounded by her chickens, and gave Anna a hug. Father Ignatius was dispensing blessings, and greeting those he had not seen in two years.

Lucan the cooper and his wife Bernia stepped forward, their daughter fast behind them for she was uncommonly shy. Rowe the carpenter was as hearty as ever, shaking Father Ignatius' hand, his red hair gleaming in the sun. His sister, Ceara, as fiery-haired as he, fingered the cloth of Anna's kirtle in open admiration. Aidan the merchant asked to see Bartholomew's blade after they were introduced, and it was clear that he was impressed by it. His wife, Mayda, joined Ceara and explained the merit of Anna's garb to her daughters, Edyth and Ravyn.

Bartholomew was clearly astonished as more people revealed themselves. Norton and Piers were gone, as discussed, but their younger brother Sloane came into the clearing with Stewart the alemaker and his wife Moira, and their brood of five noisy children. The new arrivals were surrounded, and the welcome was warm.

As much as she enjoyed their return, and that Father Ignatius came with them, Anna's gaze was drawn repeatedly to Bartholomew. He was clearly astonished by the number of villagers who had taken refuge in Haynesdale's forest. Any concern she might have felt that he would see them as outcasts and criminals, that he might reveal them or worse, was quickly dispelled. Not only had he given his word, but he was amiable to all who spoke with him. He indulged the curiosity of the children and shook hands with the men. They continued as one to the sheltered area where they gathered in the evenings, and Anna saw his gaze rove over the platforms in the trees. He doubtless noted the number of villagers who carried bows slung over their backs and quivers of arrows made when all was quiet in the forest.

"I will guess that you taught them to shoot," he said, his smile revealing his opinion of that.

"We must defend ourselves."

He sobered. "Against your liege lord. It is not right that he should compel you to defend yourselves thus, Anna."

She smiled that he did not insist that Sir Royce had the right to do whatsoever he desired. "Nay, it is not."

"How long have they been here? Since that fire two years ago?"

Anna nodded. "Before that, we were taxed heavily and shown little consideration, but all went awry then."

"And the villagers fled, and the forest was burned," he mused. "What changed?"

Anna dropped her gaze, not prepared to reveal her role in that. "Much."

Bartholomew considered her for a long moment, but then he helped Father Ignatius to distribute what bread he had brought. It was received with enthusiasm, and Father Ignatius professed that he would welcome an egg. There had been few at the keep or in the village since Esme had reclaimed her chickens.

"I would like to deny Sir Royce more than an egg!" the older woman declared with gusto and the villagers murmured assent.

Anna watched Bartholomew and felt a pride in how well they had survived in the forest. He returned to her side with a piece of bread and shared it with her, then turned a bright gaze upon her. "Why do they follow you?"

"Of what import is it to you?" she asked, trying to deflect his curiosity.

"A matter of curiosity. What claim do you have to lead the villagers of Haynesdale?" he murmured, his gaze roving over her. "You must have one. There are men in this company, and if you are their equal, they would choose a leader from amongst themselves."

"I am the smith's daughter," Anna said proudly. Bartholomew shook his head, but she dared not linger lest she feel compelled to tell him more.

After all, there was a deed she had to complete, and she would need Father Ignatius' aid to see it done. She should speak to him about it. She left Bartholomew without further explanation, well aware that his gaze followed her.

He was curious, to be sure, and keen of wit. She could not help but wonder how long it would take him to unveil her secrets.

❧

Royce stared at the reliquary, a little embarrassed that he had not made the connection sooner. First, a remarkable prize is discovered in the possession of the smith's youngest child, a boy known to be a troublemaker and banished to the forest as an outcast. There was no good explanation for the boy, who was a peasant, to have such a marvel in his custody. Insolent brat that he was, Percy had been disinclined to share any tidings of how he had come by the reliquary.

Undoubtedly he had stolen it.

But it had never occurred to Royce that the boy might have stolen it from the party that had arrived at his gates the day before, not until they had been caught in what had obviously been an attempt to retrieve it. They had only come to the gates of Haynesdale to fetch the reliquary.

He should have seen the truth of it sooner.

But where had it come from in the first place? Royce had never seen the like of it. Even when the mass was celebrated at the king's own chapel, there were never such magnificent pieces as this shown to the faithful. Not even in the great cathedrals were such treasures displayed.

Worse, he had never heard of this reliquary, or even the saint whose name was engraved upon it. Still, that was of less import than its presence in his abode. Royce might not be the most clever baron in Henry's kingdom, but he had a nose for trouble.

This mysterious relic brought trouble, and he had a feeling it would bring more.

He wanted very badly to be wrong about that. He wanted to keep this remarkable prize, so he demanded the prisoner be brought to him. He had the Scotsman escorted to the chapel. They were a barbaric and superstitious lot, in his experience. Perhaps the setting would loosen the Scotsman's tongue.

If not, there were other means of encouragement that could be used. In fact, Gaultier would be disappointed if the prisoner confessed too much too soon.

The door was hauled open and Gaultier appeared on the threshold. His expression was grim and the cut on his cheek was angry. He looked to be in even worse temper than usual. The Scotsman was getting a bruise on his cheek—indeed, it looked as if he would have a splendidly blackened eye—and he looked scarcely more amiable than Gaultier. Royce did not doubt that Gaultier had already tried to encourage the man to confess more.

The Captain of the Guard did have an unbridled taste for violence. Doubtless, the Scotsman had many more bruises beneath his garb.

Gaultier released the prisoner's arm, and the Scotsman gave him a disparaging look before putting a step between them.

"I would not advise you to run," Royce said smoothly.

"I do not intend to flee," the Scotsman said gruffly. "I still have sufficient wit to recognize that the gates are barred against me." His gaze flicked to the reliquary and Royce placed his hand upon it.

"Familiar?" he asked.

The Scotsman granted him a cold glance. "It is my sworn duty to deliver it safely to its destination. Of course, it is familiar."

"You tried to steal it."

"I tried to retrieve it."

"I say it was not yours to retrieve."

The Scotsman smiled. "And I say it is not yours to claim."

"By what authority do you claim possession of this prize?"

His gaze was unswerving and he spoke with conviction. "By the highest authority there is."

Royce was more unsettled than he chose to admit. He spoke mockingly as a result. "Are you saying that God granted it to your care?"

"Does God not grant all quests to all men?"

Royce frowned. "I mean, to whom did you swear that you would deliver it?"

"That truth is not mine to share."

"And where are you pledged to deliver it?"

"Again, that tale is not mine to surrender."

Royce flung out a hand. "But you must know your destination!"

"And clearly I vowed not to confide it in another. The one who dispatched it knows, and the one who awaits it knows. That is sufficient."

Royce heard the implied threat. "And if it does not arrive as intended?"

The Scotsman's smile broadened. "Then it will be sought, of course, and woe to any who have interfered in the great goodness of this plan."

There was something chilling about the Scotsman's manner. Surely he could not have had this prize granted to him by the divine.

But he could have been entrusted with the delivery of it by some man acting in the name of God. A bishop. An archbishop. The pope.

Royce licked his lips and considered the golden reliquary again. It was a prize worthy of the attention of such a great man. He could believe that it might be dispatched in secrecy, the better to protect it from theft.

Yet he had stumbled into possessing it, quite by chance. He could see no advantage to himself in letting the Scotsman continue on his quest. For all Royce knew, the Scotsman had stolen it from some other emissary!

"Saint Euphemia," Royce said, making a show of reading the inscription. "I have never even heard of this saint. Perhaps her relics have little value."

"So might a man suggest who did not believe in her powers."

"Which are?"

The Scotsman shook his head, as if in pity. "The ability to distinguish between right and wrong. Perhaps it is no mystery that she is unknown in this keep."

Gaultier glowered at him but Royce raised his hand to halt his Captain of the Guard. He closed the distance between himself and the prisoner. "I know the difference between right and wrong," he said in a low, silky voice. "Which is why I do not believe you. No man alive with the power to dictate the direction of such a treasure as this would surrender it to the custody of the likes of you." The Scotsman's eyes flashed, and Royce took satisfaction at having irked him. "I say you lie. I say you stole this yourself from its true custodian. And I say that such a man as you should be cast in darkness and abandoned until you die."

Gaultier seized the Scotsman with satisfaction and spun him around roughly, pushing him back toward the door.

"But what of the reliquary?" the Scotsman demanded. "Surely you do not imagine that you can keep it for yourself?"

"What I can or cannot imagine is of no concern to you," Royce declared. He gestured, and Gaultier shoved the Scotsman out of the chapel, even as Royce looked back into the rich gold of the reliquary.

It was a prize beyond compare.

It was a treasure that awakened every covetous urge within him.

But the Scotsman was right. Someone would seek it. Someone would kill for it. And no one could find it in Royce's treasury.

Nay, the best way to put this prize to work was to give it away. It would make a fine token of esteem for King Henry, for example, the perfect indication of obeisance from a loyal baron.

He would send it to Winchester with the tithes and his fondest regards.

But first, Gaultier and his men must ensure that the remainder of the party that had just left his gates were hunted down and silenced.

Forever.

He heard Gaultier's footstep behind him and did not turn to address him. "What of your men?"

"They are ordered to pursue the vagabonds to the borders and then return to report on their course," the Captain of the Guard replied. "I expect them before the dawn, with the party captive."

Royce drummed his fingers on the board. "I hope they succeed," he had to content himself with replying. "For your sake and that of our guest."

"They will not abandon him," Gaultier said with confidence. "Even if they outrun the knights, they will circle back for him."

"Double the sentries on watch," Royce commanded. "If we are surprised again, you will pay the price."

۶▲

"You are surprised," the old woman said when Bartholomew passed her a piece of the bread Father Ignatius had brought from Haynesdale keep. He was startled by her words, because her eyes were milky and he had assumed her to be blind. She grinned at him when he did not immediately reply, and he realized she was more perceptive than most.

"And how did you guess as much?" he asked, his tone light.

She gestured. "I smell it."

"Indeed?" He could not help but smile and was glad she could not see his expression. He did not wish to offend her, however whimsical she might be.

"When a reaction is anticipated, the subtlety of it can be felt or even smelled." She smiled. "You may trust me on this. I hope that you never have the opportunity to learn that I am right." She seemed to watch him. "So, tell me, sir, what surprises you?"

"That there are so many hidden in the forest," Bartholomew acknowledged, for that was the most obvious confession. "And that you have evaded detection for two years." He smiled. "That you have chickens. Are there not foxes in these woods?"

The old woman cackled, sounding much like one of her brood. "My son has made them a pen. They return to it each night and are hoisted high into the trees. It is some trouble, but we have eggs this way, and on occasion a fine stew."

"Ingenious," he acknowledged and she smiled.

She tapped him on the arm. "You are also surprised that we follow a woman."

He was startled that she had overheard his question. "I wondered whether I merely imagined it. Anna is most decisive."

"And yet you think it would be a marvel for so many to let a woman command them, even the smith's daughter."

"Even?"

She smiled. "Where have you been, sir, that you do not know the place that the smith holds in the hearts of the occupants of every village? His gift is akin to sorcery, and he must labor long to master it. A smith is always held in high regard, and his words carry great weight."

Bartholomew considered this and found it easy to believe. "That makes good sense. I have never lived in a village, so would not have thought of it."

"Never lived in a village? Only in a castle?"

"In a few of them."

She leaned closer. "Where else?"

"A monastery," he said, just to watch her reaction.

She giggled with glee. "Or you are one filled with surprises. I am glad that Anna saw fit to bring you here. Did she tell you that she was the daughter of the smith?"

"Aye, she did, and the Percy is her brother."

The woman nodded. "And she still carries the crossbow?"

"Not exactly." Bartholomew laid the weapon across his knees. "I hold it hostage until our wager is completed."

The woman reached out and he guided her fingers to the hilt of the crossbow so that she could not injure herself inadvertently. She stroked the wood with reverent fingertips. "And where would a woman of the woods win such a fine weapon?"

"You must know that it was her father's."

"She told you as much, did she?" The old woman raised her brows. "And yet, and yet, how curious that a smith should own such a fine crossbow. One would expect him to leave a hammer and forge to his children, or some fine metalwork of his own crafting. Not a crossbow." She arched a brow, and Bartholomew did wonder.

"Any man may learn to use a bow," he countered easily. "Although it is a noble weapon, its use is not proscribed to noblemen."

She had a good laugh at that, shaking a finger at him in her merriment. Bartholomew had an uncanny sense that she was trying to tell him something.

Was Anna not the smith's daughter?

Then why would she have told him that she was?

He knew that Anna had no capacity to lie. The truth was always clear in her eyes. Nay, this old woman must have it wrong. Perhaps she mingled two old tales together.

She might have been surveying him, by the way she seemed to look him over, but it was her hand on his forearm that told her the most, he would wager. "Chain mail," she murmured. "And you are tall and young. A knight." She seemed to peer at his face. "Are you the lost son returned?"

"You tell the same tale as Anna," he said by way of reply and she appeared to swallow a smile.

"We do not have many knights visit our abode," she said, and he was relieved she did not pursue her question. "You must have good reason to be here."

"My party merely passed through the forest," Bartholomew said, choosing to share only part of the truth with this stranger. "As you heard, we lingered because we were robbed."

The old woman cackled. "By Anna and Percy," she guessed.

Bartholomew nodded before he recalled himself. "The very same. Then Percy was captured by the baron's men, along with what he had stolen from us, and both had to be retrieved."

"I hear the boy," she said. "But you must not have your own goods?"

"How so?"

"You would have ridden on, if that were the case. Anna would not have brought you here if she had not felt some obligation to you." She leaned closer. "What else have you lost?"

"One of my comrades was captured. He carried our goods."

"So both are in Sir Royce's clutch." She nodded understanding.

"You are perceptive."

She smiled again. "One does not need eyes to see the truth, sir."

"Clearly that is true. Though I cannot imagine how you knew me to be surprised."

"Ah! You speak with authority and walk with a confident step. I believe you thus to be a man of good sense." She ran a fingertip over the back of his hand and Bartholomew would not have been surprised if she guessed more about him from that light touch. "A practical man, who solves matters with his own hands. There is a callus here, from wielding a broadsword. Your spurs are not for appearances, sir."

"Nay, they are not."

"And such an accent. Not quite French. Not quite Norman. Where have you been, sir? Where was this monastery?"

"Outremer."

The woman sat back with apparent wonder and great satisfaction. "That does explain much. There is something exotic about you, sir."

"Exotic?" Bartholomew smiled.

"Uncommon, then. The kind of man we seldom see." She lowered her voice. "The kind of man we await, whether you admit as much or nay." Before Bartholomew could encourage her to change the line of her speculation, she did, raising her voice. "A man of good sense, it is clear, and what man of good sense would not be surprised to find all of a village living as outcasts in the forest?"

"It is hard to believe that nigh every resident of a village should be a criminal, even in the most foul of places."

"'Tis indeed," the woman agreed with a sage nod. "What baron of sense would have no use for his villagers? Who tills the fields and shods the horses? Who harvests the grain and salts the fish?" She shook her head. "His life must be worse without us, but he is too much a fool to see the truth."

"He thinks us all dead, Esme," Anna said, coming to stand before the old woman.

"Only because he listens to lies. It is a foolish man and a poor judge of character who relies upon the counsel of one such as Gaultier, Captain of the Guard."

Anna stiffened at the mention of that man's name, as if to lend credence to Bartholomew's suspicions. Was she evading his gaze?

The old woman chuckled. "But then, Sir Royce has always shown undue respect for whichever man leads his forces. We each have our follies. Perhaps that is his."

Bartholomew thought it was his trust of his wife that was misplaced, but decided not to share his thoughts.

Anna propped her hands on her hips as she surveyed him, a challenge bright in her eyes. "I go with Father Ignatius to the old burn. Do you wish to come?"

"Why?" Bartholomew asked, of all the questions he might have chosen.

"We bury our dead there, for the ash is easy to dig and vermin do not sully the remains. Father Ignatius would bless those who have passed without his prayers."

"Is that the burned forest we passed?"

"Nay, another. We have the old burn and the new."

"So much fire," he mused and Anna almost smiled.

"Aye. Come and you will see."

And because he did want to see, Bartholomew rose to his feet to accompany her.

Chapter Eight

Why had she invited Bartholomew to join them on this errand?

Anna could not explain her impulse and in hindsight, she wished she had not made the offer. She supposed that she wanted to ensure that she knew where Bartholomew was, just as he had vowed that they would remain together inside Haynesdale keep until their respective ends were achieved. Those goals had not been won, so their paths remained bound together.

But this was a moment she dreaded.

Her breath was hitching in her chest, and her pulse was unsteady. Her tears were rising and threatening to spill, and this long before they reached the old burn. She felt him watching her and more than once, he offered his hand to her as they climbed over logs or crossed a stream. How much did he discern?

She was weak enough to accept his assistance, even though she did not need it. She had fended for herself for years and had no need of a man. Perhaps it was the garb that betrayed her and made her comport herself more like a lady than was her usual manner.

"I have not been to the old burn in years," Father Ignatius said, his manner so jovial that he might have been trying to lighten the mood.

"What of the place in the forest that was burned two years ago?" Bartholomew asked.

Father Ignatius exchanged a glance with Anna. "That is the new burn," he said.

"No one goes there," Anna contributed flatly. Who could go there? She was sure that she could still smell burning flesh, the residue of those lives lost for no good cause other than a nobleman's thirst for vengeance.

"When else were these woods burned?" Bartholomew asked.

"You have seen that the hall of Haynesdale is newly built,"

Father Ignatius explained. "The old burn is the lost keep, the fire that Sir Royce struck when he invaded Haynesdale and claimed it for his own."

Anna did not miss Bartholomew quick glance at the priest. "When was that?"

"In the year 1169, almost twenty years ago," Father Ignatius said. "Few of us have been on this holding since that day."

"Old Esme," Anna said. "The one you were talking to. She was the miller's wife then."

"I arrived a few years later," Father Ignatius said. "When Sir Royce wed the first time, God bless the lady's soul." He beamed at Anna. "I remember Anna's birth."

"And Percy's birth," she amended.

"Of course, I recall his birth very well." Father Ignatius smiled. "Never has a child come into the world with such a ruckus. He was both welcome and unexpected."

"How so?" Bartholomew asked.

"All knew the smith's wife was with child, naturally, for she ripened most vigorously. But smith and wife were of such an age that they did not anticipate another babe." Father Ignatius nodded with satisfaction. "Percy was a child destined to challenge expectations from the very first."

"And still he is," Anna said, even as she came to a halt.

They had stepped through the last of the trees into an area that had been burned clear. A few trees grew in the soil, which was still blackened with the ash of that fire, and a line of crosses adorned the ground. Beyond this field, the ruins of the old keep could be seen, its foundation stones washed clean in spots and stained with soot in others. The village could be discerned in the ruts in the ground and far to the left, the open fields were still rutted from furrows long left fallow. Beyond the keep was a sparkling expanse of water where the stream made a mill pond.

Bartholomew stared like a man struck to stone.

Father Ignatius crossed himself as he looked sadly at the new graves. "And still you use the consecrated ground of the old cemetery. That is most wise. Even without my blessing, they are safely in the hands of God." He beckoned to her. "Come, Anna, and tell me who lies in each grave that I might pray for their immortal souls."

Anna brushed away her tears and indicated the first grave, barely aware that Bartholomew strolled away from them. She supposed he could not be expected to grieve for strangers, and in a way, she was glad that he would not hear her own confession.

Father Ignatius, she knew, would not share it with another living soul.

è&

Against all expectation, Bartholomew was home.

Anna had set a brisk pace to this "old burn" and had not followed a clear path. She had ducked under low hanging boughs and slipped through the bracken, her route tending ever downward. The priest had not so much followed her as walked alongside her. It was evident they both knew how to find their destination. The forest seemed to be denser and darker in this place, and Bartholomew could not hear many woodland creatures.

He realized why when they burst abruptly from the undergrowth into a clearing. Vegetation was remarkably scarce, especially given the lush growth of the forest behind them. There was a body of water that shone in the distance, its surface as smooth as a looking glass. He spied a wheel on the building at one end and realized it was a millpond.

Esme. He stared at the mill and recalled the miller and his wife, a plump woman with a ready smile, then recalled the woman who had spoken to him this very day. Surely she did not recognize him. She could not see, after all.

But she might recognize something about him.

Just as he recognized this spot. Once again, he could not have described it an hour before, but now that it was before his eyes, he knew it well.

The keep had been on this spot. The bailey had been there. The stables where Whitefoot had been born, one of eight wiggling puppies, had been over there. The miller had been a kind man with a round belly and a jolly laugh. Bartholomew could see him in his mind's eye. He felt again the grain running through his fingers and the vibration of the mill stones as his mother visited the miller's wife after she bore another child.

Esme.

Aye, Esme.

Memories flooded into his mind, as if a dam had been opened. Bartholomew walked like a man in a dream to one spot on the barren land and surveyed the scene before his eyes, his memory filling in the gaps. He had played on the floor in that mill, with the miller's older boy, a child of an age with himself. Oswald. Far to the left were fields, many of which were fallow. To his right had been the village.

The window of the solar had looked this way. His mother had held him at this window to watch the sun rise, to look over his father's holding. Each and every day, he had come to her and as he grew larger and older, he had stood upon a stool for these precious moments together. Whitefoot had braced his feet on the sill, to look and apparently to listen as well.

He closed his eyes and could feel her heat by his side. He could smell the floral scent of her skin and hear her murmur in soft Norman French. "See, the miller is at his labor, Luc, for the wheel is turning even so early in the day. It is good for the miller to have too much to do, for then those in the village will eat well. The harvest has been good this year. See how the last of the wheat is touched by the sunlight. It is golden and ripe, ready for the villagers to make the harvest. We will have a fine feast in a week, to celebrate the goodness of the year. Look! Your father rides out to hunt, that there will be venison aplenty on the board."

He could see the white-haired knight on his destrier below, saw now the smile on his father's lips and the affection in his expression when he waved to his wife and son. He could remember that feast, the warmth of the hall, the sound of laughter and music, the conviviality of his father's keep.

He recalled another day, when snow touched the land before them. "Look at the smoke rising from the huts in the village," his mother had said that day. "There is comfort in the homes of those beneath your father's hand, for he is just and his holding prospers because of that. His lands extend to that far hill, the one that is touched first by the morning sun."

He felt a tear ease from the corner of his eye, for these were the memories he had desired above all others, but they had been elusive. His throat was tight and he found Cenric nuzzling his hand, beside him as Whitefoot had always been.

Bartholomew scratched the dog's ears, then he turned, filled with marvel, to see Anna weeping. He was so surprised to see her show such vulnerability that he doubted his own eyes. But there could be no doubt—her cheeks were streaked with tears and she held one hand to her lips as she stared at a grave. Father Ignatius was blessing whoever had been laid to rest there, and Bartholomew wondered who it had been.

Someone Anna had loved well, it was clear.

One of her parents? A sibling? A good friend?

It did not truly matter. This warrior maiden wept, and he would console her.

ॐ

Bartholomew came to stand silently beside Anna as Father Ignatius finished his prayer. He did not touch her, but she felt his heat close by his side.

It was odd how reassuring she found his presence. She had vowed never to rely upon a man, never to desire a partner, and yet this man, with his beguiling combination of humor and strength, struck a chord within her. She had yearned to trust him from the outset, and it was her own history that had made her distrust her own sense of what was right. Yet, as he continued to do as he had sworn to do, as he kept his word and acted with honor, Anna knew that her initial response to him had been right.

That made her want to trust him more, to share with him all the secrets that burdened her and to have one living soul know all the truths that she did.

On impulse, she slipped her hand into his, recalling how he had held her hand in that great bed the night before, as they had feigned passion.

His fingers closed resolutely around hers, giving her that enticing sense of security. Aye, a woman would be safe with this man by her side, no matter what ill fortune came upon them.

Anna found herself wanting to be that woman with a fervor that shook her with its power.

Yet was pleasing all the same.

She swallowed and stared at the grave, wanting to confide in him but not knowing where to start. It was comforting to realize that he would wait until she chose to do as much, if she did so.

The priest spared them the barest glance as he finished his prayer. He moved to the next grave.

"That is Oswald, the miller's son," Anna said quietly. She felt Bartholomew start.

"Esme's son?" he asked.

"Aye," Anna acknowledged. "And beside him, his wife Rheda and their son, Nyle."

"All of them," Father Ignatius whispered and caught his breath.

"All of them," Anna agreed, knowing that the loss had torn Esme's heart in half.

Bartholomew squeezed her hand as the priest began his prayers for Oswald.

"He cannot have been that old," he said.

Anna shook her head. "Not yet thirty summers, but older than me."

"I meant his son."

She frowned and glanced up at her companion. He had met Esme and knew she was aged. Indeed, Oswald had been the oldest of her sons. How could Bartholomew assume the age of a stranger? But the knight's expression was thoughtful, so she only replied to his query. "Aye, Nyle was of an age with Percy. They were great friends."

"And they all died in the new burn?"

Anna nodded and shook her head. "It was my fault," she whispered, her voice uneven, and found herself relieved when Bartholomew gathered her into his embrace. He was warm and strong, and he simply held her, offering solace with his heat and his presence.

"It cannot have been your fault," he chided quietly, his words a breath in her hair.

"It was," she insisted. "I had a scheme and it went badly awry. The new burn was Sir Royce's retaliation for my audacity."

He pulled back, holding her shoulders in his hands as he looked down at her. "You provoked him to burn his own forests? And yet, you had the courage to enter his hall willingly again yesterday? Did you not fear he would recognize you?"

"Of course."

Bartholomew shook his head in awe, and his eyes began to

dance. She knew he would tease her, and her mood lifted in anticipation. "You must have thought to kill me when I left you alone with him in the hall."

"I did curse you thoroughly," she admitted with a smile.

He grinned. "You should have warned me."

"I am not so quick as that to confess my secrets."

Bartholomew sobered. "Nay, you are not." He turned her around so that she faced the grave that Father Ignatius had already blessed, holding her shoulders in his hands again. Her back was against his chest, though, and he leaned down to murmur in her ear. "Tell me this, though, Anna. Who lies here?"

"A child," she admitted.

"As young as Nyle?"

"Younger yet. A mere infant." Her tears rose again and she was embarrassed to feel one splash on her cheek. Her words were thick when she continued. "She did not survive her first winter, not here in these woods." She took a shaking breath. "We dare not light a fire when the baron hunts us, for the smoke would reveal us all. That winter, he hunted ceaselessly, for he wished to rout us all, and it was cold. Cursed cold." Anna's words faded as she remembered her efforts to keep the babe warm.

Futile efforts, for she had not been warm herself.

She swallowed, the pain of loss enough to rend her heart.

"Had she a name?" Bartholomew murmured.

"Kendra," she admitted, her words thick.

"Kendra," he repeated. "I suppose you blame yourself for this, as well."

Anna could only nod. It had been too cold for one so young.

Again Bartholomew gave her a moment to compose herself, and when he continued, his tone was thoughtful. "It seems to me that you have paid little heed to the sermons of Father Ignatius. Does he not teach that our days on this earth are chosen by the great creator himself, that He alone shall choose when a babe comes into the world, and how many breaths each of us shall take?"

Anna nodded reluctant agreement. "I should have taken better care," she admitted.

Bartholomew, to her surprise, kissed her temple. "And so it might not have mattered. Her days might have been planned to be short, by some scheme we cannot discern."

"But..."

"Did you do your best to warm and defend her?"

Anna nodded.

"Then no divinity can ask for more." Without waiting for her agreement, he dropped to his knees then, in the snow at the foot of that small grave. He bowed his head as she watched him and prayed for Kendra's immortal soul.

Anna found herself powerfully affected by this gesture of respect. Her tears flowed anew, but she, too, knelt in the snow beside him. Again, her fingers found his hand, and she had the sense that their prayers together were stronger than both uttered in isolation.

She assisted Father Ignatius by naming the rest of the fallen, well aware that Bartholomew watched and waited, Cenric seated by his side. Each time she glanced his way, he gave her a small smile of encouragement. She felt less alone than she had. She felt a tentative healing begin. She wondered whether she might not be completely responsible for all the woe that had fallen upon the villagers of Haynesdale two years past.

When Father Ignatius finished blessing the graves, she found herself once again putting her hand into Bartholomew's warm grasp. She knew how she wanted to repay him for this gift he had granted to her. She did not doubt that he would soon be on his way, and that she would not see him again once he departed, but there was a memory that Anna particularly wanted to have of this knight.

That it would help her to heal yet more was only an indication that it was the right choice.

She would welcome him abed, surrender to him the pleasure that they had feigned the night before, and perhaps abandon her fear of all men. It was a bold choice, but one more characteristic of the maiden she had been, not that long ago.

And Anna wished to be that intrepid woman once again.

She might well conceive Bartholomew's child, but that would offer only more solace. She would like to have a child to remember him by, a boy with his father's dancing eyes and dark hair, a son with his father's sense of honor.

Aye, that would suit Anna well indeed.

❧

Something had changed in Anna.

She seemed softer to Bartholomew, and less wary. Perhaps her telling him of Kendra had removed a barrier between them. He did not care. He welcomed the chance to know her better.

The company was awaiting them, and he could smell the stewed meat. His belly growled as they drew closer to the camp. The fire had already been doused, although Anna strode forward with concern.

"It had been burning before you arrived," said an older man, obviously anticipating Anna's query. "It was in coals and we doused it, but used the rocks from the fire pit to heat the stew from yesterday."

"Smells like venison," Bartholomew noted.

"Naught but the baron's best for us," agreed the man with a grin.

"You will hang if caught," Bartholomew noted, for he could not help himself.

The man shook his head. "We are outcasts already. We have lost our homes, our hearths, many of our kin and neighbors. There is little more that can be taken from us."

"You would not say that if you were in the baron's dungeons," Anna noted.

"I might at that," the man countered. He passed a hand over his brow. "I weary of this life, Anna, though that is not an accusation. I would see it change, one way or the other, rather than endure more years of mere survival." He glanced up at Bartholomew. "Understand me, sir. If I had done more than protest the cruelty of an unjust baron, I would accept my punishment as due. I would rightly be outcast and criminal. But all I did was raise my fist against the imprisonment of the innocent, and in so doing, found myself accused, as well." He shook his head again. "It is a sorry excuse for justice offered by Sir Royce, and were the king not so inclined to live all his days in Normandy, an honest man might petition him for aid. As it is, I would die or see our village restored."

"Indeed," agreed another man, for there were many tending the man's words with interest.

Anna appeared to be taken aback by this, but Bartholomew did not release her hand. "You have done well for yourselves here," he acknowledged, seeing that praise was due. "For there is more comfort in this forest than I would have expected."

"Aye, there is that, thanks to Anna." The company saluted her, but Bartholomew saw that she was still troubled.

"But the true son would find a willing army in his forests, if he deigned to return," said the man and the company cheered as one.

Could Bartholomew so imperil these former villagers with a quest to reclaim his legacy? It was not the place of such men to fight, though he saw that they had the will to do as much. He feared that he found his desire mirrored in their resolve, and that to take them at their word would be unjust, for many would die.

He noted that they were thin, much like the dog, and knew the time in the forest had been hard upon them. Their garb was threadbare and their shoes worn through. They looked older than their years, even the children, and he imagined that the force of their will might not be enough to make strong opponents of them.

The man meanwhile turned to face the company. "Let us dance then, this night, as if it is to be our last. Anna and Percy are returned, and that is a matter to celebrate."

"It would be folly," Anna said. "The baron's men may hear us."

The man was dismissive. "You may rest assured that they are back in the baron's hall, feasting themselves, for they are not men to sacrifice the comfort of a warm bed."

"Or a warm wench!" cried another and the company laughed again.

"A cup of mulled wine," sighed a woman and others nodded.

"A feast at Christmas in the baron's hall," added another.

"It is our right, and one withheld these many years," grumbled another.

"But we may yet dance!" cried the first man and a ripple passed through the company.

There was a wildness about them, a recklessness that Bartholomew saw was born of desperation. He felt sympathy for them and dared to hope that he might be able to change their circumstance. On the morrow, he would try to free Duncan. In less than a fortnight, his fellows would return.

On this night, though, there was naught to be done but take the man's suggestion.

"Then let us dance," he declared and spun Anna around.

Someone had a flute and began to play a tune, the others clapping their hands to the beat. They had no ale and only a thin venison stew in their bellies. They would sleep in the forest, on platforms built in the trees, and it might well snow again this night. Many would be cold. But they would take merriment where they could find it and Bartholomew admired their spirit.

He turned Anna before them all, and many whistled at the change in her garb. She flushed a little but he liked the sparkle that lit in her eyes. Then the tune became faster and she picked up her skirts, granting him a glance of pure mischief before she began to dance the jig.

It was a challenge, and one Bartholomew was inclined to take. He gestured to the musician, who played even faster, placed his hands on his hips and danced opposite Anna, daring her to best him at this. The company hooted, bets were undoubtedly laid, hands clapped and feet stamped, but there was only the merry sparkle of Anna's eyes and the flash of her feet for Bartholomew.

Had he ever met a more beguiling woman? He was certain he had not.

❧

The sky was filled with stars, when Anna took Bartholomew by the hand. The wind was rising and she knew that clouds would come before morning. She could smell the dampness of snow in the air and felt the pending change in the weather.

They would be safe and warm in the cave, though.

She liked that he did not ask her questions or make demands. He simply let her lead him away from the company. It was that cursed confidence to be sure, and the realization made her smile.

Many had retired, and still others made preparations for the night. They had danced vigorously and would sleep well. Wooden platforms groaned overhead as the villagers rolled themselves in cloaks and blankets and furs, whatever they could find, and huddled together.

But Anna led Bartholomew away. She was warm from their dancing, but her heart raced because of the admiration in Bartholomew's eyes. The dog padded silently behind him, and she liked that he had won the beast's loyalty so quickly. Her mother had always said that dogs were the best judges of men.

That she had reminded them all of this after a hound in the village snarled at Sir Royce had not been appreciated by the baron.

The land became rocky as they approached the cavern where she and Percy often took refuge. She paused in the last cluster of trees to listen and look. There were no footprints outside the cavern's opening, and the snow gleamed in the starlight. She and Bartholomew crossed the river on the stones placed within its course, and she was impressed that the dog managed to do the same.

They ducked into the shelter of the cavern and she was glad it was high enough that Bartholomew did not have to bend. She continued alone to the hiding place at the back, locating the tinder and stolen candle. She lit it, then turned to face him, watching the golden light play over his features.

"Your own refuge?" he asked, looking about himself with curiosity.

"In a way. When Percy and I have stolen from the baron before, we have hidden here."

He arched a brow. "Do you often steal from the baron?"

Anna shook her head. "Not since the new burn. There was a time when there was more traffic upon the road to Haynesdale, and a passing merchant could be relieved of his coin or his provisions without much trouble. When there were fewer of us in the forest, sometimes one would ride to Carlisle on a stolen steed and buy more provisions with that coin." She shook her head. "But two years ago, so many more came to us. At the same time, far fewer travel to Haynesdale."

"You must have thought we offered salvation."

"I thought that fat saddlebag might contain the most food."

Bartholomew's gaze was knowing. "And Percy paused to peek, because he was hungry, and so he was both disappointed by his prize and caught."

Anna nodded.

"Was he caught here?"

Anna shook her head. "Nay. It is undisturbed. His curiosity must have compelled him to look sooner." She smiled. "He is a curious boy."

"He is that." Bartholomew took a step closer to her. She

gripped the candle, her valor slipping away now that the prospect of intimacy was upon her. "And so all went awry with our arrival." He paused directly before her, his gaze searching.

"For your company as well," she had to point out.

He smiled a little. "And yet, I cannot regret our arrival at Haynesdale." He reached out with a fingertip and touched her cheek, his light caress sending a shiver through her. "Why did you bring me here, Anna?" he asked quietly.

"Because I would challenge you to make me moan."

Bartholomew's smile flashed in his surprise. "You are a bold maiden," he said, and that admiration filled his tone.

She was no maiden, but when she opened her mouth to tell him as much, the weight of his finger fell upon her lips. His gaze was sober and locked with hers. "I know," he continued with heat. "That you have known unkindness from men."

Anna's heart fluttered.

"And I would vow to you not only that I will not injure you, but that you can halt me with a single word, at any time."

Her mouth went dry. She felt warm and flustered, yet knew that her choice was utterly right. She claimed his hand and lifted his finger away from her lips, pausing to kiss it. "I know," she whispered. "You defy my every expectation of French knights, and that is why I have brought you here." She licked her lips. "Bartholomew," she added, hearing a reverence in her own tone.

He smiled and stepped closer, framing her face in his hands. He bent, studying her for a long moment, then captured her lips beneath his own. His was a sweet hot kiss, filled with passion, yet requesting her participation, not demanding it.

That he asked, even after her invitation, was all the evidence Anna needed that she had chosen aright. She dared to put her arms around his neck to draw him closer and rose to her toes, surrendering completely to his touch.

෧

Bartholomew knew he had to take matters slowly. Though Anna gave every appearance of being her usual fearless self, he could feel the tremor within her. It betrayed the uncertainty she would clearly prefer to hide. He moved slowly, ensuring that her pleasure was served first.

She seemed to know that he was determined to see her pleased, and that appeared to feed her confidence. Her kiss became bolder the longer they embraced. He opened his mouth to her and she mimicked him, her tongue daring to tangle with his own. She pressed against him in silent demand, wanting more of what he gave, and Bartholomew caught her close.

She was intoxicating, her passion and fire heating him to his marrow. He wanted her as he had never wanted a woman before. His fingers were untying the laces of her kirtle before he realized what he was doing, then he halted and stepped back. Her cheeks were flushed and her lips reddened from his kiss, but her eyes widened in uncertainty. "What is amiss?"

He surveyed them both and grimaced. "Too much garb."

She laughed in surprise, then blushed. "You might fix that."

"Nay, I would have you do it." He lifted his hands and smiled at her, hoping to reassure her that she was in control of their union.

Her cheeks burned brighter, but as he had anticipated, she did not delay in taking his dare. She unbuckled his belt and set it aside with care, her respect for his weapons nigh as great as his own. "I still cannot believe you carry a fragment of the true cross," she whispered, her fingertips sliding over the pommel of his sword. "Your friend must be affluent."

"He is generous, to be sure."

"You have known him long?"

"Most of my life. He took me into his care when I was younger than Percy, and taught me all I know of life."

"A strange choice of companion for a knight," she mused.

Bartholomew found himself grinning. "He oft said he would have preferred to have left me behind, but I would not allow it."

She smiled up at him. "Aye, I can imagine you to be so stubborn as that."

"At least we have a trait in common."

Her smile turned knowing, then she tugged his tabard over his head. She folded it with care and laid it beside his belt. She wrinkled her nose as she surveyed his hauberk.

"Over my head," he said. "I will bend over and you must ease it to the ground. Do not attempt to catch it. Just get it off my back."

Anna nodded and he bent as he had said. As was oft the case, the hauberk caught on his padded aketon. Anna tugged it free and it fell to the ground with a clatter of steel. Bartholomew rolled his shoulders once he was relieved of its weight.

Anna, of course, tried to lift it. She swore softly but with vigor. "All day, you bear this burden?"

"It is better than a blade between the ribs." Bartholomew scooped up the hauberk, putting it alongside his belt.

Anna was frowning when he turned. "You said you came from Outremer."

"Aye. My friend was sworn to the Templars, and he was dispatched to serve in Jerusalem. I went with him as his squire, almost fifteen years ago." He turned his back on Anna that she might unlace his aketon. He felt her fingers tugging on the lace.

"But he left the order?"

"His older brother died, and he became heir to his family holding in France. It was a surprise to him, to be sure."

"Did he take a wife?"

"Aye, for he desired an heir with all haste. To be sure, he knew little of women after his years in the service of the order."

"One might not lead to the other for many men."

"True, but it did for Gaston. He is a knight of much honor and merit."

"You admire him." He heard the smile in her voice.

"How could I not? He was all I knew a knight should be, and as soon as he had the right to do so, he dubbed me a knight."

"Granting you rich gifts."

He turned and helped to tug the aketon forward.

Her gaze was assessing. "He must have thought well of you."

"I hope so."

Anna arched a brow.

"You are right," Bartholomew acknowledged with a smile. "I know so."

"Yet there was no place for you in his new household?"

"Why do you ask as much?"

"Because you are here and he is not. Further, this is not France." She propped her hands on her hips to regard him as he removed the aketon and set it aside. "Or did you lose his favor?" She shook her head. "I cannot believe it. A man such as you and a man such as he would find no points of disagreement. It would be honor and integrity on all sides."

Bartholomew smiled at this assessment of his nature and that of Gaston, not just its accuracy but that Anna thought well of him.

She snapped her fingers and turned upon him. "Fergus said aught of this," she said, evidently just recalling as much. "That there was little point in his offering you a post as you had declined Gaston's offer."

Bartholomew felt the back of his neck heat, for he neither wished to confess his secret nor deceive her. "I declined the post Gaston offered to me," he admitted.

"Why?"

"Because I would seek my own fortune. It is possible for one man to be too beholden to another." He lifted the circlet from Anna's hair, then removed her veil and wimple. It was simple to find the pins that bound her braid in place and when he had removed them, the plait fell to hang down her back.

"I suppose," she ceded as he unbound her hair and pushed his fingers through its thickness. "But where do you expect to find your fortune?" She glanced over her shoulder. "In Scotland, among the kin of Fergus? Or maybe you seek an heiress?"

"Why are you so curious?" he demanded in a teasing tone, wanting to deflect her interest.

"Because they said you had chosen this road through Haynesdale. I cannot imagine why. There is not an heiress to be found within a week's ride of here."

Bartholomew shrugged, aware that she watched him closely. "It looked more fair than the alternative, no more than that." He beckoned to her, his manner playful. "Now you are the one overdressed."

She smiled and lifted her hands, giving him access to her belt and the laces on her kirtle. Once they were unfastened, he slid one hand beneath the crimson wool, holding her gaze as his hand slid up to cup her breast. She stared at him, then licked her lips.

He bent and kissed her lightly, then teased her nipple with his finger and thumb. She could step away if she so desired, for he had one hand on her breast and one on the back of her waist, but Anna held her ground. She gasped as he tugged the cloth over her head, bending to kiss her nipple through the cloth of her chemise. She arched her back and shivered, then he caught her close and flicked his tongue across the turgid peak.

"Your boots," she whispered and he halted to look down at her with a grin.

"Truly? You were thinking of my *boots*?"

Anna laughed, her eyes sparkling in a most alluring way. He took their cloaks and made a nest on the floor of the cavern, noting that Cenric had taken position as sentry at the opening. He tugged off his own boots and unlaced his chausses, then removed his braies. He turned to Anna clad only in his chemise, and pointed. "Your shoes and stockings."

To his delight, Anna sat on the pile of cloaks and leaned back on her elbows. She lifted one foot toward him. "I think you should aid me, sir."

Bartholomew knelt before her and unlaced her shoe. He eased one hand under her chemise, trailing it up her leg. Her eyes widened and she inhaled sharply, but she did not pull away. He eased aside the chemise, baring her calf to view, and inclined his head to unfasten her garter with his teeth. She giggled and squirmed.

"Your breath tickles!" she protested.

He touched his tongue to the tender skin behind her knee and she wriggled anew. It took some time for him to see both garters untied and both stockings removed, and by then, Anna was flushed.

He stretched out alongside her, his hand upon her breast and kissed her with leisure. She rose to his touch and her nipple tightened beneath his fingers. He kissed her ear, her neck, the hollow of her throat, then closed his mouth over the sweet bud of her nipple. He kissed it and teased it, coaxing it to a tighter bead, then grazed the tender flesh with his teeth. When Anna was writhing beside him, he leisurely turned his attention to the other breast. He could feel the heat emanating from her and smell her arousal, but he wanted to be certain she was fully pleased.

His hand was beneath her chemise, moving from her knee up the smooth flesh of her thighs. She arched her back and opened her mouth, offering an invitation he could not refuse. He kissed her, even as his fingers slid into her slick heat. He swallowed her first gasp of surprise, then her quiver of delight. His fingers moved against her, conjuring more desire and he smiled into their kiss when she clutched his shoulders.

"Bartholomew!" she whispered and he grinned at her.

"You granted me a dare," he reminded her.

"But surely this is sufficient."

"Surely we have only begun." He caressed her with the end of his thumb, loving how she gasped in pleasure, and knew what he had to do. "Before I make you moan," he whispered. "I think we should explore the treacherous tickle that so surprised you."

"I but concocted a tale," she argued, clearly not understanding his intent.

"And I would show you the truth," Bartholomew vowed. He winked at her, savored her confusion, then tugged back her chemise. He slid between her thighs and granted her a more intimate kiss.

The way she gasped in astonishment was most satisfying, but Bartholomew would strive for more success than that.

The lady, after all, had yet to moan.

ò▲

Who would have guessed that a person could die of pleasure?

Anna certainly had never imagined as much, but Bartholomew's kisses—his tongue, his teeth, his caresses—made her both burn and tingle. She was aroused and desperate for some satisfaction she could not name.

He tormented her without cease—nay, he did cease, each time she thought she drew nearer to some culmination. He teased her and she knew it, but she could scarce complain. It was incredible to have such a man conjure her pleasure with such diligence, putting himself in her service, so to speak. Anna thought it could not be right, but then, she could find naught amiss with what he did.

She found herself lying back in the furs and savoring the sensations he awakened.

It was a curious balance, for while he paid homage to her with his touch, she felt that she was in his thrall. She had no notion of how to reciprocate, and he gave her no opportunity to do as much. His amorous attention was relentless.

And more than welcome.

Still, Anna fought the urge to satisfy him with that moan. She feared that when she did moan, he would halt, and she did not wish for that. She called herself selfish, then reasoned it was all part of his scheme. She could not have named how many times he ushered her to some nameless summit, then tugged her back.

She was panting and flushed from head to toe when he fed her desire to a crescendo again. She knew she could not hold out much longer, but she tried. Anna bit her lip as her heart pounded. She gripped his shoulders as the quiver began deep inside her, and she locked her thighs around his head. Bartholomew gave her no quarter, his touch feeding her need steadily, his wicked tongue making her want to roar. His hands gripped her buttocks, ensuring she could not escape the sweet torment he inflicted upon her.

She finally surrendered and moaned, feeling that the sound came from the very core of her being. It also lasted far longer than she could have expected. Bartholomew chuckled then touched his teeth to her, the sensation making her cry out as the tumult passed through her like a great wave.

Anna found herself in Bartholomew's protective embrace when the tremors passed and she opened her eyes to find his own eyes twinkling in close proximity. "So, it is a treacherous tickle that will make this lady moan," he teased. "That is worth the knowing."

"I am no lady."

He caught her chin in his hand and turned her to his solemn gaze. "This night, you are my lady," he murmured with heat and kissed her with such thoroughness that she was left breathless. She felt his erection against her hip and knew his pleasure had to be won, as well.

She might have rolled to her back and spread her thighs, bracing herself for the deed, but Bartholomew locked an arm around her waist and rolled to his own back so that she sprawled atop him. He pulled up the hem of his chemise and placed his hands on her waist. "I am yours to command," he whispered, his voice husky.

There was a lump in Anna's throat that he so understood her fears. She rose to her knees and straddled him, her concern rising anew. His hands moved to cup her buttocks and he lifted her into place, so that she could feel his heat against her.

"As slowly as you like," he murmured and Anna eased lower. She watched him inhale sharply as he was drawn within her and savored how he closed his eyes.

Did it give that much pleasure to him? There was a satisfaction for her, as well, particularly as she watched him being as tormented as she had been.

She moved steadily and slowly until he was completely within her and felt his hands flex. He whispered her name, and she felt powerful to have such a man as this in thrall to her. She moved, savoring his reactions. He was shaking beneath her, struggling to maintain control, and as soon as Anna realized as much, she knew she had to test him further.

"Perhaps I should try to make you moan," she whispered.

His smile flashed. "Temptress," he accused and Anna was emboldened.

She teased him then, moving slowly and then quickly, setting a rhythm then breaking it. His eyes opened and she liked how they glittered, how he studied her as if she were a marvel, as if she were his lady, as if they were the only two souls in all the world.

He smiled at her and she cast off her chemise and shook out her hair. She displayed herself to him, liking that his admiration was so clear, proud of her femininity as she never had been. She rode him hard, drawing him deeper with each thrust, and was surprised to find her own desire rising anew.

She knew from his sudden smile that he had more torment in store for her. She gasped when his fingertip slid between them and touched her in that most tender spot. He grinned at her gasp of delight, teasing her with that fingertip even as she rode him harder and faster.

Anna braced her hands on Bartholomew's chest, her hair spilling all around them, and smiled down at him. She saw the fire in his gaze, felt the spark within herself and moaned in truth when they found exultation together.

She tumbled into his arms then and he flicked the fur-lined cloak over them, his arms locking around her even as he kissed her temple. His fingers were in her hair, and she was both safe and warm, snared in the embrace of the finest man she had ever known.

What a gift he had given her this night, in teaching her not only to moan but to find pleasure in such intimacy.

To her own astonishment, Anna fell asleep, nude and atop Bartholomew.

Truly, in all of Christendom, there was no better place to be.

Monday, January 18, 1188

Feast Day of
Saint Volusian of Tours.

෨

Claire Delacroix

Chapter Nine

Fergus dreamed.

He was chilled to his very marrow, curled up in his cloak as Yves took the watch, but he dreamed of Jerusalem. He recalled the heat of the sun, the dust, the flies, the smell of good horses, and manure. In his mind's eye, he strolled into the stables of the Templars.

He found Bartholomew arguing with a young boy in the stall of Gaston's destrier. He had seen the young boy in the stables before and knew him to be a Saracen as well as a friend of Bartholomew's.

Fergus eavesdropped, for they were unaware of his presence. To his surprise, the young boy was, in fact, a girl, and one determined to leave Jerusalem.

Leila.

Fergus awakened suddenly with a strong sense of doom. His thoughts were so filled with his memories of the Templar stables that he was surprised to find himself in the forest in the snow. He could not smell straw or hear the horses, the swish of their tails and the sound of their hooves on the stone floor. He rolled over immediately and saw that Leila slept, wrapped tightly in her cloak. Why had she been so determined to leave? He was glad to see that she was safe this night, for that had been his first concern after the dream. His fellows were asleep, the horses dozing where they were tethered. The sky was pale, but the sun had not risen as yet. The forest was quiet, save for the call of birds.

Why had he dreamed of Jerusalem?

Or had he dreamed of Bartholomew?

A man newly knighted, with a strong moral code. A man they were to meet at the next new moon, in twelve days' time.

A man who must be in peril, or soon to be so, just as Leila had been.

They had ridden far to the north of Haynesdale to evade Royce's men and had intended to ride farther to ensure they were not detected. But Fergus' dream was a warning.

They would ride back to Haynesdale this very day and hope that they arrived in time.

Or that his dream was wrong. Fergus could not shake the sense that much was amiss, though, and knew he would sleep no longer this night.

He rose and began to pack his belongings.

❧

Anna awakened to darkness and the sound of a dog snoring.

For a moment, she was startled that she could see so little, but then she recalled where she was. The cavern was dark, and Bartholomew was curled behind her, one arm cast around her waist. The dog was at their feet.

Bartholomew's breathing was steady and his body cast a welcome heat. It was not unpleasant to be caught in such an embrace. Anna lay in the darkness and thought of all she knew of this man, this knight who challenged her expectations so much. She did not believe for a moment that he had declined his friend's offer of a place in his household with no clear plan of where to find his fortune. Indeed, she knew he was one to think far ahead.

Then what was his scheme? He must have a destination.

How curious that Bartholomew had been the one to guide their party to Haynesdale. Why?

Anna recalled that odd mark on his flesh, the one she had glimpsed in the bedchamber in Royce's hall. That Bartholomew had turned away and covered it so quickly convinced her that it was important.

It could not be.

Surely, her suspicion must be wrong.

There was but one way to be certain.

Anna eased away from Bartholomew, listening with care to his breathing. To her relief, it did not change.

She eased from the warmth of their bed, finding her chemise and drawing it on once again. Bartholomew dropped a hand to space she had vacated. To her dismay, he stirred. "Something amiss?" he asked, his tone so sleepy that she did not think he was truly awake.

"I must relieve myself," she whispered and he exhaled. He rolled to his back and his breathing deepened again.

Anna stood there and watched him for long moments, her heart thundering. She found the candle again, and the tinder. She turned her back upon him to strike the flint, wishing the sound was not so loud. She lit the candle and pivoted, pleased to see that he still slept.

Perhaps she had exhausted him with their lovemaking.

That might have made her smile if she had not been so intent on proving her suspicion right or wrong.

Anna cupped her hand around the flame and eased closer. Cenric lifted his head to give her an annoyed look, then yawned and burrowed his snout beneath his paws. He groaned a little, stretched, and began to snore again.

The candlelight played over Bartholomew as Anna drew nearer. He was on his back, his hair tousled, one hand flung out to the space she had abandoned. She smiled that his confidence was evident in his posture even when he slept. Even his lips had a slight curve, as if his dreams were merry. She could have simply stood and stared at him in the light of the candle, for he was a most alluring man.

But she wished to know.

She needed to know.

The tie of his chemise was yet undone and a generous expanse of golden flesh bare to view. Anna could see the pucker she had noted earlier. It was right over his heart, and her memory stirred with an old tale entrusted to her years before.

Surely it was but coincidence. Knights must have many scars, and surely any opponent of sense would strike at the heart. It must be a common location for a scar.

Still, her mouth was dry. Anna leaned closer, so the light played over him. Bartholomew did not stir. The mark was about the size of the last phalanx of her thumb and roughly oval. It was an old wound, to be sure, for it was not red and the hair on his chest had grown around it. She bent low and peered at the wound.

When she discerned the familiar wyvern rampant burned into his flesh, Anna was so shocked that she nearly dropped the candle.

She gasped and turned her back upon him. She tugged the lace that hung around her neck and in the candlelight, studied the token that she carried there. The same wyvern rampant graced the signet ring, save that it was the mirror image of the one impressed in Bartholomew's flesh.

He could not be the lost son returned.

But he was.

She glanced over her shoulder at him, awe flooding through her as she surveyed him anew. The rightful heir was returned to Haynesdale.

And she had been so bold as to bed him.

Anna's own audacity made her cheeks heat.

What should she say to him? What should she do?

Naught, she realized, feeling flustered as she had not been just moments before.

As much as she wished to run from the cavern and shout the truth to any who would listen, Anna knew the secret was not hers to share. She extinguished the candle and eased back into the space beside Bartholomew, a curious pleasure stealing through her when he gathered her close against his side.

She must hold his secret fast, just as she held all the others, and wait for his decision. The rightful baron must choose the path.

But she would do whatever he requested to see his rightful legacy restored. She closed her eyes and felt a tear on her cheek, relieved beyond all that the ordeal they had endured was soon to be ended.

The seed of Nicholas was returned and he was as valiant and just a man as they had all hoped he would be.

៩♠

Bartholomew awakened to find Anna nestled on his one side and Cenric on the other. It was an improvement over their sleeping arrangements at Haynesdale keep, in his view, for he liked having Anna close.

But he knew what he had to do.

The dog wagged its tail as soon as Bartholomew sat up, and he rose carefully from the nest he and Anna had made for themselves. She must have been exhausted for she did not stir, even as he dressed. He cast the hauberk over one shoulder, knowing he would have to find some soul to assist him in donning it.

He watched her sleep, not wanting to leave. His urge to take her with him was folly, though. Doubtless, they could have no future together and she would only be endangered in his company this day. He had no holding as yet, and thus no right to claim a woman's hand, and if he did manage to secure Haynesdale, it would be his destiny to make a strategic alliance. Indeed, the king might demand to make the match, as part of his agreement to bestow the holding upon Bartholomew. He thought of Lady Ysmaine's conviction that marriages were not based upon love, or even attraction, but good sense alone. Bartholomew reminded himself of all of this, and yet, he wished to linger with Anna.

He knew that if he awakened her to say farewell, he might lose himself in her charms once more.

What if she conceived his child? The notion made his chest clench, although he knew it was unlikely after just one night together. The possibility gave him more impetus to leave soon, for he could not be tempted to seduce her again. He would have to leave coin with someone who could be trusted to grant it to Anna in a way that she would not find insulting.

Bartholomew smiled, for that would be a feat.

He felt torn, but it was time to save Duncan, and thence to seek a way to earn the king's favor. Bartholomew would not achieve either by spending a day abed with Anna. He turned to leave, knowing what must be done.

Perhaps he had changed her view of knights. Perhaps he had achieved something of merit in this short interval in her company.

Perhaps it should be enough.

He left her wrapped in his cloak, tucking it around her so she would be warm. He took the crossbow and laid it on the cloak beside her.

He had promised its return when their paths parted.

He wished it had not been so soon.

Bartholomew paused at the opening of the cavern to watch Anna for another moment. It was likely he would not see her again. He was glad that she slept, for he doubted she would willingly be left behind, and he did not want their last words to be contentious.

He had to free Duncan, and he had to do it alone.

Bartholomew kissed his fingertips in silent salute, then strode into the forest with new purpose. It was snowing, fat flakes cascading from a pewter sky, and the dog loped along beside him. He smelled a fire before he saw the smoke and headed toward the villagers to request assistance. Percy appeared and smiled, then beckoned Bartholomew to join them. He led Bartholomew to Esme, who muttered over a pot set on the logs.

"Anna took you to the cavern, did she not?" the boy asked.

"Aye, she did. She sleeps this morn."

Esme nodded sagely. "'Twas the visit to the child's grave that did it." She exchanged a knowing glance with Bartholomew, then glanced pointedly at Percy.

"Percy, would you aid me with my hauberk?" Bartholomew asked. "Then I wish you would ensure Anna's safety while she sleeps."

The boy stood taller at the combination of these requests. He laced the back of Bartholomew's aketon with speed and enthusiasm, heeding the knight's quiet instruction. He faltered visibly under the weight of the hauberk, but doubtless recalled that Timothy was not much taller than he. He valiantly held it so Bartholomew could tug it over his head, and when it tumbled over the knight, the boy laced the back.

After Bartholomew donned his tabard, Percy buckled Bartholomew's belt for him, his fingers brushing the hilts of Bartholomew's blades with a kind of reverence. "I would be a knight," he murmured and Bartholomew thought it would be cruel to remind him that such a role was not his birthright.

"Then you must defend widows and orphans and treat all you know with honor."

"Even villains?"

"Especially villains. The mark of an honorable man is the respect he shows to all, whether they are worthy of his esteem or not."

Percy considered this. "But villains must be brought to justice."

"Which means they must come to a court, where judgment is made after consideration."

"That does not happen in Haynesdale's court."

"But once it did," Esme interjected.

"And once it may again," Bartholomew said. "Do not blame the court for the merit of the judge." He smiled at the boy, who was clearly thinking about this. "Now, go to Anna, please. Take Cenric with you, please."

Percy turned and ran through the forest. The dog hesitated, looking between knight and boy, until Bartholomew patted it and pointed. Cenric bounded after Percy then, and Bartholomew watched them go with satisfaction.

And a measure of regret. Would he return here after Duncan was free? He did not imagine as much. His own words haunted him, for claiming Haynesdale with violence was not the proper choice. He must appeal to the king for the restoration of his family holding, and might well be declined for lack of coin to pay an escheat. He would have liked to have kept the dog, but could not risk the creature's companionship when he ventured into Haynesdale for Duncan.

"There is porridge if you would have it," Esme said. "It is not fine, but it is warm."

"I would welcome it, thank you," Bartholomew said and sat on a log beside her. She served him a large portion of the porridge and gave him a wooden spoon. True to her word, steam rose from the contents of the wooden bowl. "You are generous," he noted. "Will this cheat another of their due?"

"You have greater need of it this day," she replied. "Unless I miss my guess."

He smiled. "You do indeed see much, Esme."

"It is the dreams," she said mildly. "I dreamed last night as I have not done in years."

"What did you dream about?" he asked, simply to be polite. He blew on a spoonful of porridge.

Esme sighed. "A fine lady. I had almost forgotten how fine she was, and kind."

"Had she a name?"

"Lady Gabriella of Haynesdale."

Bartholomew's heart skipped at the mention of his mother's name.

"She came to me when my youngest, Edgar, was born. Oswald played with her own son, a handsome dark-haired boy, right on the floor of the mill. They were of an age." She chuckled. "Amidst the grist, if you can imagine. The baron's own son."

"I can," Bartholomew admitted softly, remembering the very

day.

Esme cast grain at her chickens, which pecked the earth around them with enthusiasm. "I was yet abed after the birthing and felt it disrespectful to remain thus when the lady herself came to visit, but she insisted that I rest. She fetched the child and admired him greatly." Esme shook her head. "It was Father Ignatius blessing Oswald, his wife and son yesterday that put such old memories in my thoughts, to be sure."

"To be sure," Bartholomew agreed, wondering whether there was more to it than that.

"And now you are away, perhaps not to return," she said.

"Again, you surprise me, Esme."

"You dismissed both boy and dog, and you must know they both would follow you to Hell itself. What do you mean to do this day?"

"My comrade is yet imprisoned inside Haynesdale. If I am right, the baron's men are yet in pursuit of my fellows. The keep may be as lightly defended as it will be in the foreseeable future."

"Yet your course is not without peril," Esme said. "So, you would go alone."

Bartholomew smiled into his porridge, not feeling it was necessary to agree. They sat in silence for a few moments and the porridge warmed his belly as he ate it. The chickens continued to peck the earth and Esme continued to cast them grain.

"How do you have grain?" Bartholomew asked.

Esme smiled. "I took all that was mine from the mill when we fled. The flour is gone, and there is little seed left but the birds must eat. We cannot till the seed, but we can eat the eggs."

Her words made Bartholomew think of how much labor would be required to rebuild the village and the prosperity of the holding. Where would he find so much coin?

"Did she tell you of the child?"

There was no doubt who Esme meant, and Bartholomew chose to be as direct as Anna. "Only that she felt responsible for Kendra's demise, for she believed the infant consigned to the forest because of her deeds."

Esme snorted. "And there is but a part of the tale, to be sure. Not even half, by my measure."

Bartholomew was intrigued. "How so?"

"Did she tell you of Kendra's father?"

He shook his head before he recalled her blindness. "Nay."

Esme sighed anew. "He was a boy of an age with Anna. I call him a boy, although of course, he grew to manhood and it was a man's deed that put that babe in Anna's belly. They were as thick as thieves, they two, always together, always in mischief as children, always daring each other to new feats. They fairly ran wild, but their hearts were good. He was the eldest of Wallace the plowman and his wife, Erna."

"Are they here?"

"Nay, they sent the boys but stayed in the village. Wallace wished to see the fields tilled, but he no longer has either horse or ox to pull the plow. Royce sold them a year ago, as if Wallace had not enough to bear."

"How so?"

"Kendrick and Anna resolved between them to see Anna's mother freed when she was arrested by the baron."

"Just over two years ago?"

"Aye. I do not know what they planned or how much havoc they managed to wreak, but they were captured instead." Esme frowned. "Kendrick was executed, his head hung upon the gates of Haynesdale as an example to us all of the price of treachery." She shook her head. "He was but a boy to me yet, though he had seen twenty summers."

Bartholomew set aside the remainder of his porridge.

"It was a month before Anna returned to us, bruised and filthy. She escaped that foul keep, naked, in the midst of the night. Perhaps they left her untended for they believed her near death. Perhaps another would have died or fallen broken in the road, but she is not one to surrender."

"Nay, not Anna," Bartholomew murmured.

"She crawled to the village, without being detected, and truly the elements were with her, for it was a foul and stormy night. She knocked and then collapsed outside my door. Oswald gathered her up, then declared that he could tolerate the cruelty no longer. We were all so fond of her, you know, and to see her in such a state was more than we could bear."

"I can well imagine."

"We fled that night, all of us, in the midst of that tempest, and made to take refuge in the forest. We were outlaws then, for we defied the will of the baron." She swallowed. "Oswald thought Sir Royce would see reason when the mill wheel ceased to turn and there was no flour for his bread. He thought we might be able to negotiate, for the baron needs his villeins as much as the peasants need their baron."

Bartholomew guessed that had not been the case. He waited, watching the play of emotion on the older woman's features.

"The others came soon after us, a tide of villagers fleeing the baron's wrath. The number of us in the forest was swelled beyond all expectation. We knew there had been those taking refuge in the forest already, but we did not find them before the baron's men were upon us. The knights encircled us, trapping us in a small space. They rode their steeds around us until the storm stopped and the stars came out overhead. We were wet and cold, fearful, even before they set the trees afire. I thought they would not burn after the fire, but the knights persisted until they did. Oswald saw that we would be killed. He made us flee before the circle was fully closed. I feared I would slow them too much. They would not leave me behind, my good sons." She halted then, her words turning husky. "Oswald on one side and Edgar on the other, then Willa stumbled and Oswald lifted me in his arms."

Bartholomew reached out and took her shaking hand. She clutched at his fingers and he felt her shaking. "You do not need to tell me of it."

"I do," Esme insisted. "I *do*. For Oswald lives only when his valor is remembered." She took a shaking breath. "He carried me, even as Rheda carried Anna and urged Nyle to speed. Edgar aided Willa, but they fell behind with their two young ones. Willa was with child and very near her time."

"Yet Rheda managed to carry Anna herself?"

"Anna was so thin, she might have been a child. We fled into the darkness, away from the fire, having no good sense of direction. A horse and rider appeared before us. I can see them yet. We turned and fled into the undergrowth, but were not fast enough. I was looking over my son's shoulder. I saw the warrior lift the crossbow. I saw him take aim and I closed my eyes to pray. But Oswald was struck. He stumbled once, then fell over me. Rheda was felled a moment later, Anna crushed beneath her. Nyle cried out and ran, though I reached for him. I know he did not get far for I heard his shout of pain." She shook her head and her tears fell. "I could not move. I did not want to move. Those I loved had been stolen from me, and there was only fire and death on all sides. Indeed, I wished only to die myself."

Bartholomew watched and listened, wishing he could change what had occurred.

"It is an evil thing for a mother to see her child die before she breathes her last," Esme said. "And her grandchild as well. That was a dark night, darker than any I have ever known, for I had no wish to survive. And so it was that Oswald protected me even in his death. I was overlooked by the marauding knights, for we were just another pair of corpses in the mire. A great burning ring of fire lit the sky that night, one that I shall never forget—for its heat, for its brilliance, for the sounds of those dying within its blaze."

"The new burn," Bartholomew murmured.

"It was uncommonly cold when I awakened, the sunlight so bright that it hurt my old eyes. The trees were blackened all around me, and smoke rose from the ashes. I thought I dreamed when I heard movement near me, for it seemed that all the world was dead and gone. It was Anna, her fingers grappling against the ground. I found my strength then, and moved from beneath Oswald. I cried out and Edgar found us, for he had been seeking us. He rolled Rheda away and found Anna alive. We stumbled away from there together, and soon those who lived as outlaws in the forest found us. They took us to their haven, clothed and fed us, and it was not long before Anna rounded with child. She named her Kendra."

"After the father."

Esme nodded. "Anna was not the sole one to see hope in that babe's birth, but I knew from the first that Kendra would not thrive. She was small and sickly, too thin and too pale." Esme bit her lip. "I was not surprised that the sweet babe did not survive her first winter, but I wept all the same."

Bartholomew held Esme's hand while she mastered her tears, hoping that his presence gave her strength. "I thank you for trusting me with the tale of Oswald," he said quietly, aware that others began to stir. "I would have liked to have known such a brave and good man." It was not a lie, for he had only a vague recollection of the miller's son. They had not known each other in truth, though they had met, that long ago morning on the floor of the mill.

"I thank you for your kindness, sir," Esme said, her words yet uneven.

Bartholomew was resolved then that although he could not change the past, he would affect the future of these people. How could the king be persuaded to take his cause? He did not know, but his first task was to free Duncan.

"And now you would leave us," she said, a hint of accusation in her tone.

"And now I would do what must be done," Bartholomew corrected.

"It will be dangerous."

"No man of merit shirks a dangerous obligation." Bartholomew took the purse from his belt and put it into the older woman's hands. "Please give this to Anna for me."

"Because you leave," Esme accused.

"She will want to spurn the gift, but I trust you to convince her otherwise." He heard his voice drop deeper. "There might be a child."

Esme caught her breath. "Coin will not be what she needs."

"But it is what I can give." Bartholomew lifted the older woman's hand and kissed her knuckles. "Be well, Esme. I hope our paths do cross again."

"As do I, sir. As do I."

Bartholomew stood and turned to stride away, but Esme cleared her throat so loudly that he glanced back.

"Ask Father Ignatius for his keys," she advised. "I have no doubt that he will entrust them to you, and your quest may be simpler."

Bartholomew smiled, for he had forgotten the priest's ring of keys. He had the key to the dungeon and had thought it sufficient. There had been others on that ring, though. "Indeed, it will, Esme. I thank you."

≈&

Anna awakened and stretched with leisure. She felt wondrous, both satisfied and desirous of more, both at ease and filled with anticipation.

Because of Bartholomew.

She smiled and reached for him, only to find herself alone.

Anna sat up with haste, her hair tumbling over her shoulders. She wore only her chemise though the fur-lined fullness of Bartholomew's cloak was wrapped around her. It was light at the mouth of the cavern and she could see fresh snow falling. She heard Percy playing with the dog and pulled the cloak over her shoulders. It was when she gave the cloth a tug that she discerned the weight upon it.

Her crossbow.

The pale wood shone on the dark wool cloth and she stared at it for a moment, wondering that Bartholomew had left it by her side. The quiver of bolts was beside the candle and tinderbox.

Where was his armor?

Why could she not hear his voice?

Filled with dread, Anna swept to her feet. She was not reassured to discover that every piece of Bartholomew's garb was gone, save the cloak, as well as every weapon, save the crossbow. She hastened to the opening of the cave in time to see Percy cast a stick for Cenric, who raced after it, tail wagging.

There was no knight watching them.

There were no other footprints in the snow.

Bartholomew was gone and had been gone for some time.

Worse, he had no intention of returning. The crossbow made that most clear—he had vowed to give it to her when he left Haynesdale for good.

But he was the rightful heir! He could not abandon them now.

"Anna!" Percy cried and raced toward her, his eyes glowing. The dog ran right behind him, still carrying the stick. "Bartholomew bade me stand guard while you slept."

Cenric came to lean on Anna, his tail wagging in welcome.

"He is gone then?"

"Aye, at the dawn."

"Do you know where?"

Her brother gave her a disparaging glance. "To save his friend, of course. That is what good knights do."

He had gone to Haynesdale keep. And once he had freed Duncan—if he succeeded in doing so—he would leave.

Anna's lips set and she turned back to the cavern to dress in haste. Bartholomew would not follow his scheme without hearing her thoughts on the matter first. The rightful heir could not simply ride away. It was his obligation to help the villagers of Haynesdale.

If Bartholomew had forgotten as much, Anna would be more than glad to remind him.

❧

Haynesdale keep was even more quiet than Bartholomew had expected.

There was only one guard at the gate and that man seemed to doze at his post. Two men walked the summit of the wall, but their manner was desultory. The snow was beginning to fall more thickly and he wondered whether they were cold. He would have been, if his heart had not been beating with such vigor.

How many more were there? He knew four had ridden out in pursuit of their party the day before. Had those men returned? Had the Captain of the Guard ridden out, or did he remain at the keep? Bartholomew did not have a full tally of how many warriors labored beneath Royce's hand. He could not hear horses at all and the village could have been a graveyard.

There would be Lady Marie and her maids, of course, but surely she lingered abed on a winter morn like this one. He had to assume that some servants were in the kitchens, so he would avoid that area as well as the great hall itself.

He eyed the keys Father Ignatius had given him. The smallest one was for the chapel in the village, though the priest had confessed it was not locked. There were no valuables there any longer and Father Ignatius did not wish to deny those remaining villagers the solace of prayer in a sacred space.

The next, which was nigh the same size but more ornate, was for the treasury in the keep's chapel, where the reliquary had been secured.

The next largest was for the chapel within the keep.

The fourth opened a portal in the curtain wall near the chapel.

The final key in his possession was the large plain key to the dungeon that Father Ignatius had given him earlier. Bartholomew considered the fourth key and recalled the layout of the keep.

The chapel was on the far side of the bailey. Bartholomew had not noticed the door in the wall near it, but he had not been seeking it. It might be the easiest way into the keep.

He eased around the perimeter of the keep, remaining in the shadows of the forest. He moved only when the sentries were turned away, for he could not rely upon the bare trees to hide him completely. The snow fell more quickly, making the world seem silent.

That only meant that sound carried farther. He could hear the footfalls of the sentries, for example.

On the far side of the keep, Bartholomew hid behind a tree, waiting for the sentries to turn their course toward the front gate. If he made any sound on this flight to the wall, they would discern him and raise their bows. Once against the wall, he would be out of their view again. He peered around the tree and eyed the distance. It was a good hundred paces, all devoid of cover. Snow covered it all like a blanket of white, disguising any small obstacles. There was a depression before the sides of the motte rose to the curtain wall, and he wondered how deep the moat was on this side. He had to believe it was frozen.

The guards paused to chat directly over the door. One gestured to the forest and Bartholomew slipped behind the tree again, fearing he had been discovered. He heard the other laugh, then the grind of heels on the walkway. They had parted ways and each paced a solitary circuit back toward the gates.

Bartholomew took a deep breath and ran.

He eyed the parapet as he reached the moat, then said a prayer as he took the first step. He slipped down quickly and feared that he would be plunged into icy water—then his boots slid on ice. He was up to his knees in snow, but at least the moat was frozen. He slid across it, unable to keep from disturbing the snow, scrambled on to the opposite bank, and slipped. He slammed one knee on the lip of stone that confined the moat and closed his eyes at the pain. There was no time to linger, though. He limped onward, wincing as he barreled up the steep slope and fairly tossing himself against the curtain wall.

He was panting, and sweat ran down his back. He stood there for a long moment, but there was no cry of discovery.

To Bartholomew's dismay, his path from the forest was abundantly clear. The sentries would not fail to see it when they reached this point on the curtain wall again. That was sufficient to send him hastening on. He eased along the wall to the door, fitted the key into the lock and turned it, wondering what he would find on the other side. He kicked the snow away from the bottom of the door, drew his knife and opened the door cautiously.

It gave into a corner beside the chapel, one tucked into the shadows beside the armory. In truth, Royce's armory was no more than a lean-to, with the only closed wall being that of the curtain wall behind it. It was hung thickly with armor and weapons, and he guessed that a smith might set up a forge just outside it when necessary. The array of armament cast many shadows, though, and gave him places to hide. The stable had a wall on this side with a door, so the steeds could not reveal his presence. The bailey was beyond, empty and wide, a space he had to cross to reach the entry to the dungeon. He closed the door behind himself and eased into the armory to consider his course.

A warrior stood at the portal on the far side of the armory and clearly was not vigilant about his duties. The man yawned as he tugged up his gloves. This one was sturdy in build, though it was unclear whether sloth or indulgence was at root. Bartholomew wondered how loyal the men employed by Royce were to their lord baron. He certainly did not discern many signs of enthusiasm or dedication. He considered the man's helm, which disguised his face, and his tabard, marked with Royce's insignia.

The wyvern rampant of Haynesdale.

Bartholomew picked up a length of rope as he moved stealthily through the shadows of the armory, and then a bolt for a crossbow. He crept up behind the other man, then flung the bolt into the armor at the left. The man spun at the sound, his blade at the ready, but Bartholomew jumped him from the other side. They scuffled but Bartholomew had surprise on his side. He knocked the warrior hard on the head so that he lost consciousness, then stole his helm, his knife and his tabard. He left the warrior trussed in the armory, a length of his own tabard knotted over the man to silence him.

He took the man's cloak and fastened it over his shoulders, holding it closed to disguise that he was more trim than his victim. Garbed as a knight of the household, Bartholomew crossed the bailey openly. He ensured that his pace was steady, as if all was routine. One sentry hailed him by name—Hermann—and he waved a greeting in reply, for the sound of his voice might reveal him. He was glad to step into the shadow of the hall, but scarce took the time for a reassuring breath.

Bartholomew went directly to the dungeon. He unlocked the portal and kicked the rope ladder into the space. "Hurry yourself, varmint," he growled. "You are given one last chance to say your prayers, but any protest will see the baron's mercy withdrawn."

"Mercy," Duncan repeated, his disgust clear. "What does this man know of mercy, much less justice? I decline to be dragged to a priest to ease his fears!"

Bartholomew strove to keep his frustration from his voice. "I command you, prisoner, to hasten yourself." He peered into the shadows below, only to find Duncan glaring up at him, the other man's expression most stubborn.

"And I command all of you to hasten yourselves to Hell," Duncan retorted.

Bartholomew gritted his teeth. He glanced about himself, but there was no one else in view. "Duncan," he muttered. "Hurry!"

Duncan took a step back, then peered at him with suspicion. "Who are you to call me by name?"

Bartholomew swore. He hauled off the helmet and savored Duncan's surprise. "Hasten yourself, worm!" he muttered, glad to see that the other man finally heeded his command. Duncan climbed the ladder, and Bartholomew found it somewhat satisfying to push him into the wall and bind his hands behind his back.

"Temper, lad," Duncan murmured.

"I should leave you behind," Bartholomew retorted in an undertone, though he would not do as much. "When last did a prisoner refuse to be saved?" He dropped the trap door in place again and turned the key in the lock. He raised his voice as he pushed Duncan forward. "Do not be so fool as to test me again, knave," he said in a louder voice and shoved Duncan into the bailey.

As he had anticipated, the sentries on the parapet turned to watch. Bartholomew continued to push Duncan or drag him by the rope, and Duncan stumbled repeatedly in the snow, as if weakened by his ordeal.

Bartholomew hoped the other warrior pretended to be in worse shape than he was. If Duncan could not run, they would not manage to flee the gates. The other man certainly smelled foul, and his plaid was stained. There was a mighty bruise upon his cheek, but Bartholomew was encouraged by the glint of resolve in Duncan's eyes.

The sentries jested and pointed, enjoying Duncan's situation more than could be admired. One crowed that he would see Duncan at his execution.

"Did you have the chance to defend yourself in his court?" Bartholomew demanded quietly, for he did not see how it could have been done so quickly.

"What court?" Duncan muttered and spat in the snow. "This one knows naught of justice. You can see the mark of it on all his holding. Pity the poor wretches condemned to live beneath his hand."

Bartholomew said naught to that, but unlocked the door to the chapel and cast Duncan through it. The other man contrived to fall through the portal and land on his knees, which amused the sentries greatly.

Bartholomew shut the portal behind them and abandoned Duncan, making haste for the hidden reliquary.

"Where do you mean to hide it?" Duncan asked. He did not move from his spot inside the door, as if conserving his strength. Bartholomew tried to not think overmuch about it.

"I will suddenly develop a paunch, the better to resemble the knight whose tabard I claimed," he said.

Duncan grinned but he looked most tired.

"Are you sufficiently hale?" Bartholomew had to ask.

"I have been better, lad, that much is certain. Fear not. I will not slow you down."

Bartholomew nodded and struggled to fit the key into the lock. The helm would provide an admirable defense against arrows, but he could not see clearly. How backward was this realm that the knight's visors were not hinged? He cast off the helm and fitted the key into the lock with ease. He turned it, opened the sanctuary and stared at its emptiness with shock.

"What is amiss?" Duncan asked.

"It is gone!" Bartholomew turned to face his companion, uncertain what to do. The portal to the bailey opened in that moment, and Duncan gasped. There was not time to shut the cupboard and don his helm both, and Bartholomew managed neither before Lady Marie swept into the chapel.

She took one look at him, then gestured to the maid who must be following her but as yet out of sight. "I will pray alone this morn," she commanded, shut the portal, and leaned back against it.

Silence crackled in the chapel. Bartholomew returned Marie's gaze, and Duncan looked between them, clearly uncertain what to expect.

Then Marie smiled and strolled toward Bartholomew. "Now here is a tale," she said softly, and not without satisfaction.

Did she know about the reliquary at all?

Did she know its location?

Would she reveal them?

A thousand possible lies flicked through his thoughts, not a one of them convincing, and his heart stopped cold. Duncan remained on his knees and perhaps he prayed in truth.

The lady swept past the older man, her confidence clear as she approached Bartholomew. "I believe you might find my offer of assistance more savory on this day, sir," she purred and offered her hand to him.

Bartholomew hesitated only for a moment before he took her hand and kissed it. Would she truly help them escape?

Could he truly give her what she desired?

His moral code fought against his awareness of what he knew she wanted of him, but survival had to be worth some sacrifice.

Lady Marie's could have been higher, to be sure.

Chapter Ten

Duncan was tired and he was sore, he was hungry and more than impatient with the hospitality of Haynesdale. Still, those were not the sole reasons he found the lady's solution unsavory.

He stared at the black hole of the sewer and sighed. "No other way?" he muttered.

Lady Marie had ushered them to the back of the stables, one at a time, using her cloak to disguise them from view. Bartholomew had already cast aside his stolen helm and had opened the wooden trap placed over the hole. The smell was pungent and strong enough to bring a tear to Duncan's eye. The mingling stink of kitchen waste, dung from the horses, and slops less than inviting.

"No other way," Lady Marie insisted. "Be quick!" She stretched to kiss Bartholomew's cheek. "On the first day that the sky is clear after the snow," she whispered. "Meet me at the old mill after midday."

The younger knight nodded once, his expression grim. The lady strolled through the stables to her waiting maids.

Duncan looked at the open square of the front gate, yearning for a cleaner solution. "Could we not detain another guard, lad?" he asked, even as Bartholomew shed the borrowed tabard. "Or one of us walk out the gates?"

"We would not get far," the knight replied. "Or travel quickly enough to evade pursuit once they lent chase." He gave Duncan a look. "It cannot be that deep."

Duncan thought of the height of the motte and was not so certain of that. The conduit might narrow too much for them at some lower point, and they could be trapped within a sewer for good. He might have argued more but one of the sentries shouted from the curtain wall.

"Hoy!" that man cried. "An intruder has entered the keep from the back portal! I see his tracks in the snow."

"Drop the portcullis!" shouted another. "He will not leave this place alive."

The gate could be heard to creak, then the iron spires fell to the ground to secure the bailey.

Marie strode to the bailey and raised her voice imperiously. "An intruder? In our keep? Find him immediately!" The guards and sentries scurried to do her will, even as she barricaded the view of the stable's interior. The horses nickered and tossed their heads, sensing the agitation of the men.

"No other way," Bartholomew said quietly, then arched a brow. "After you."

Duncan growled disapproval, but lowered himself into the hole. It was not that tight a fit, being almost arm's length in diameter. It was wrought of a column of fitted stone, and he was reassured that the walls would be more stable that way. Duncan could not discern the bottom beyond a glimmer in the distance and was unsure of its depth. Bartholomew knotted a rope around the end post of a stall, then cast it down into the hole. Duncan gripped the rope, braced his feet on the walls of the sewer and rappelled himself down into the darkness.

Zounds, but the stink only grew stronger.

Darkness closed around him, the circle of light above him blocked by Bartholomew's figure. He heard the knight drag the wooden trap over the top, then the scrape of the knight's boots on the stone walls above. There was muffled shouting from the bailey, and he moved more quickly.

They had to reach the bottom before the rope was discovered.

Nay, they had to be through the sewer and in the forest before the rope was discovered. He hoped Lady Marie could keep her husband's men at bay.

Then his boots splashed into muck. To his relief, it came only as high as his knees.

Which meant the outward passage must be higher than that. He flattened himself against the wall as Bartholomew dropped into the mire beside him, then slid his hands over the wet walls.

Oh, they were thickly coated with a substance he did not wish to feel on his hands. Perhaps there was a blessing in the darkness, for he could not see what surrounded them.

Though the smell was sufficient to leave no mystery.

"Here," Bartholomew whispered, then guided Duncan's hand to the gap in the wall. It was of similar diameter, but a horizontal bore, with a slight downward slant. At the far end of it, he could see light again.

He grimaced, then climbed into the tunnel, crawling forward on his hands and knees. At least there was only a handspan of filth in the tunnel, but Duncan hastened on, fully anticipating that some soul would cast some mess down the sewer. The last thing he wanted was that tide rising beneath his plaid.

He swore when he reached the grid hammered over the end of the sewer, and gave the metal bars a hard shake. Bartholomew joined him but a moment later and peered through the bars.

"We are on the other side of the keep," he murmured. "See how this drains into the river?" He nodded with satisfaction. "My tracks in the snow are on the other side."

Duncan gave the bars another shake. "We are not away yet, lad."

"Nay, we are not." Bartholomew peered at the bolts that secured the iron grid in the stone. "The mortar is chipping," he noted, picking at it with a finger. It crumbled beneath his touch, but not enough to loose the grid.

Duncan pulled his dagger from its scabbard and stabbed it into the crumbling mortar surrounding the bolt closest to him.

"That is fine steel!" Bartholomew protested in shock.

"And my life is well worth losing the hone of the blade," Duncan muttered.

"True enough." Bartholomew pulled his own dagger and hacked at the mortar on his side. It was not long before they had loosened two of the four bolts. Bartholomew gestured for Duncan to move aside, then he kicked at the grill with his legs. Duncan did the same, the pair of them alternating until the grid broke free and tumbled down the slope to the snow-covered moat.

They waited a moment, fearing it might have been seen, but no alarm was cried. Without further ado, they climbed out the hole, each helping the other. Again, they waited against the wall for a sign of discovery, and when there was none, they bolted toward the forest.

One of Duncan's boots crashed through the ice on the moat,

and he bit back his cry of dismay. Bartholomew seized his arm and fairly dragged him to the opposite side. They crawled on to the bank but did not dare to linger. Duncan refused to consider how readily the hounds would track them, much less when he might be cleanly garbed again.

First, they had to escape.

He only breathed a sigh of relief when they had taken fifty paces into the forest, but Bartholomew did not slow his pace even then. Duncan was aching from head to toe, but he would not delay their retreat.

Indeed, he did not doubt that if they were captured again, neither of them would survive the day.

&

Bartholomew was not certain how far they had run, but he did not think it was enough. Duncan was limping, though that man struggled on, and he wished he had Anna's knowledge of the forests. Which was the best direction to flee? Where might they find a haven? It was clear that Duncan could not travel much farther. Bartholomew might have led the other man back to the refuge of the villagers, but he was uncertain of his direction in the snow, as well as aware of Anna's protectiveness of her fellow outcasts. He did not doubt that Royce would hunt him and Duncan and did not want to bring danger to those who had shown him hospitality. Were there more hidden caves? Could he find one?

They reached a stream that looked familiar, though he would wager that all streams looked much the same. Some slight sound prompted him to glance over his shoulder at the surrounding forest.

Then he froze in place, for in the shadows behind them, he could discern Anna. She had loaded the crossbow and aimed it at his chest. She was dressed again in man's garb, her chausses and tabard simple and dark of hue. Her hair hung down her back in a dark braid and her expression was accusatory.

He recalled all the warnings he had ever heard of the wrath of a woman scorned and took a step back.

"Come, lad," Duncan said, with a glance at the sky. "If we hasten, we can put good distance between us and the keep before they can lend chase."

"Nay, Duncan," Bartholomew said quietly.

The older man turned and followed his gaze. He whistled through his teeth even as Anna took measured steps toward them. Her gaze was steely and her aim unwavering.

Bartholomew licked his lips. "I did not wish to awaken you this morning."

"Because you will leave," she charged. "You pause only for your comrade and now would leave forever."

Bartholomew had no argument to make against that.

"Surely, you did not imagine he would stay," Duncan said, looking between the pair of them. "Come, lass, his fortune lies away from this place."

"Does it?" Anna challenged, which puzzled Bartholomew. "You did not tell them," she said to him, fury in her tone.

Duncan sat down heavily. "Tell who what?" he demanded with impatience.

"He is the lost son of the last Baron of Haynesdale," Anna declared.

Duncan regarded her. "How do you know?"

"He bears the mark of the true son."

Bartholomew's blood went cold. "You cannot know..."

"I do." She glared at him.

Duncan rubbed his brow. "How do you know, lass?"

"He was marked by the smith, my father, so that he could be identified no matter how much he changed or how many died." She glared at Bartholomew, her vexation with him clear. "You mean to abandon your legacy!"

Bartholomew was well aware of how Duncan looked at him in curiosity. "So this is why you insisted upon the Haynesdale road," the Scotsman mused. He considered Anna anew. "And this is why Fergus says you are bound to his fate."

"I am?" Anna asked in surprise.

Duncan smiled. "It was why he bought the kirtle, he said, for he saw you in his dreams."

This appeared to fluster Anna. "I do not believe it. No one can see the future."

"Fergus can," Duncan insisted. He eyed Bartholomew, then spoke to Anna again. "What is this tale you tell of my companion?"

"It is no tale. It is truth. Haynesdale is his rightful legacy."

"What do you know about it?" Bartholomew demanded.

"Everything! You are the lost son returned. You are the hope of all those people, who begin to despair that justice will ever be restored."

"It is not that simple..."

"It is cursed simple. You are the rightful baron!" she cried, interrupting him. "You bear the mark of the signet ring, impressed into your flesh by the smith when you were but a boy, at your mother's command." Duncan blinked at this revelation and Bartholomew's neck heated. Anna took another step closer. "How dare you abandon us to this tyrant and evade your responsibility?"

Bartholomew ground his teeth. "I have no choice, Anna."

"You have every choice, and you make the sole bad one!" She lifted the crossbow higher.

"Anna, you must understand." He exhaled when it was clear she did not. "I make the sole *possible* choice. I must appeal to the king and the king's justice to see this matter changed."

She did not relent. "You should take Haynesdale for your own first."

Bartholomew flung out a hand, his temper expired. "And what merit of a deed would that be? What would be the difference between me then and every other villain who simply steals what he desires for his own?"

"Might makes right," Anna argued.

"Nay, never that." He marched toward her, ignoring the crossbow in his anger. Indeed, he pushed it aside with a fingertip. "Do you not think I have seen the effect of such choices? Do you not think I have seen grown men steal food from children to sate their own needs? To steal whatever gold they lust to hold as their own, regardless of who rightly claims it? To savor a woman, whether she wills it or nay, simply for the sake of their own lust?" He flung out his hands and his voice rose. "What is the difference between us and barbarians, if our word has no value, if we cannot be relied upon to do what is right, if we do not cede to a higher justice?" He shook a finger at her. "What then is the point? I will not be as those fiends I have seen in Outremer. I will not take simply for my own desire. I will not disregard law and order and justice and truth, simply because it is not convenient for me to do as I have pledged."

"Amen," Duncan said quietly, but Bartholomew ignored him.

"And if it means that I shall die without the seal of my father's holding in my hand, so be it. I shall die an honorable man."

Duncan nodded approval of this sentiment.

Anna was less convinced. "Is it not just as foul to turn one's back upon wickedness?" she insisted. "Or to abandon those in need of your aid?"

"I do not abandon you. I seek recourse by the only honorable means."

"Kill Royce before you go, then!"

"I will not do as he has done." Bartholomew glared at Anna, furious that she could not see the merit of his choice.

She glared back at him, evidently just as angry that he refused to do as she desired.

Suddenly she lifted the bow again and aimed once more at his heart. Bartholomew reached for his knife, though he knew he could not draw it in time. Indeed, her bolt was loosed before the blade was clear of the scabbard. It sailed over his shoulder, fairly nicking his ear as it flew past him.

He had a heartbeat to believe that she had missed.

Then he heard it sink home.

Bartholomew spun in time to see the victim raise a hand to his wound.

The assailant wore the baron's colors. The bolt had caught him at the base of the throat and he bled profusely. His eyes were wide and he fell slowly, first to his knees and then fully to the ground. His loaded crossbow dropped to one side, released from his loosened grip.

His companion fled through the forest, no more than a flickering shape in the distance. His boot falls faded from earshot with all speed.

Anna strode past Bartholomew, another bolt loaded and trained on the bowman. She reached the man's side and kicked his crossbow out of his reach, then rolled him to his back with a nudge of her foot. His hand slid limply to the earth beside him and his blood stained the snow. He stared at the sky, unseeing, and his chest did not rise again.

Anna waited a long moment, watching for some sign of life. She then removed the bolt from her own crossbow and slung it over her back. She claimed the fallen man's crossbow, removed its bolt, then returned to Bartholomew.

She dropped to one knee before him and offered the weapon on the flats of her hands. "My lord," she said and bowed her head.

She paid homage to him.

"You have killed one of the baron's men," Bartholomew said, when he had recovered his speech. "You have made yourself an outlaw in truth."

"I have saved the true baron's life," Anna corrected, that familiar fire in her eyes as she looked up at him. "And I have ensured that he is armed."

"And I wager that Sir Royce will know the truth of your identity soon enough," said Duncan, his eyes gleaming as he watched. "You will be hunted to the ground, lad, sure enough."

ᘓᗑ

Bartholomew could not leave Haynesdale, not without seeing justice served first!

Anna was aware of his resolve, though, and knew he would do as much if she did not intervene. She admired his respect for the law — indeed, that would make him a good baron and overlord — but she disagreed with his conviction that justice would prevail. Anna had learned to expect the opposite. Justice was won when those who could dispense it had little choice in the matter.

Particularly when it came to righting a wrong. In her view, Bartholomew's appeal to the king would be vastly improved if he had already claimed the barony from Royce.

Even if that required Royce's demise.

How could she change Bartholomew's thinking?

He took the crossbow from her, and she noted how he admired its craftsmanship. It was a finely made weapon, and a baron — in her view — should be a warrior, as well. He had an archer's hook on his belt, so she knew he could use the weapon and well. Anna gave him the fallen man's quiver of bolts, as well.

Though he accepted both, he made no acknowledgment of her obeisance, much less Duncan's comment.

"You are too weakened to go far this day," he said to Duncan instead. "I would not have come to your sanctuary while the baron's men pursued us, Anna, for I would not have put the villagers at risk. I would ask you for shelter, though."

It was not what Anna truly desired of him, but it was better than him leaving immediately.

Perhaps she would have a chance to persuade him.

"Of course." Anna rose to her feet and gestured for them to follow.

Duncan stood with a small groan, but kept a good pace when Bartholomew took his arm. "That bastard beat me truly," he said through his teeth. "Though it was not a fair fight."

"His kind does not fight fair, Duncan," Bartholomew agreed, and Anna was glad that he had some understanding of the nature of the men beneath Royce's command.

To her relief, both men moved quietly through the forest. It made no sense to blindfold them, since Bartholomew had come from the refuge earlier that day, and she thought it might be a good sign of trust not to suggest the blindfold for Duncan. She still guided them on a circuitous path to ensure they were not followed. The snow was falling with greater volume which meant it would quickly disguise their tracks.

When they reached the edge of the haven, she heard a whistle, like that of an owl.

Moments later, they were seated beneath a lean-to, where soup simmered on a low fire. If Duncan was surprised to find so many people hidden in the forest and living as outlaws, he hid his reaction well.

"You are saved!" Percy cried and flung himself so hard at Duncan that the Scotsman near lost his balance. "He saved me!" he declared to the others and Duncan ruffled his hair.

"It is likely too much to hope that you will give up thieving," he said gruffly and Percy laughed.

That Duncan was Bartholomew's friend and had been brought by Anna would have been sufficient to see him welcomed, but Percy's greeting ensured his welcome was even warmer. Edgar found him a seat by the fire, and Willa served him a brimming bowl of soup. There was yet a bit of bread left and it was given to Duncan without discussion. The soup was thin but warm, and Anna saw Duncan's surprise when he tasted it.

"Chicken?" he asked, looking about himself. The company

laughed.

"Esme brought her hens from the village two years ago," Anna said. "She refused to leave the flock behind, so we have eggs instead of the keep."

Duncan bit back a smile and clearly savored the soup. It seemed to restore him greatly, though the bruise on his face looked sore. She wondered how many other bruises he sported, for Royce's men could be cruel.

Willa refilled the bowl with a smile. "I wish we had better, since you have been in Haynesdale's dungeon."

"It is the finest meal I have eaten in a long while, lass. I thank you for it."

Percy demanded the tale of Duncan's escape and Bartholomew told some of it, though Anna expected he was unduly modest. Duncan's quick sidelong glances confirmed her suspicions. He gave her great credit for saving him from the archer and showed the bow to the others. Duncan asked if any man had a steel, and set to honing their daggers while the boys watched with interest.

The snow fell thickly, blanketing the world in white and bringing a peaceful quiet to the forest. All the while, Anna puzzled over the question of how to convince Bartholomew to stay, or to overthrow Royce before he departed to the king's court. He could be gone months once he left, for the king was likely in Anjou, and crossing to France in winter could be precarious. He might not return at all. The very notion chilled her, like a hand of ice closing around her heart.

Her dismay was not entirely for fear of the future of Haynesdale.

Nay, she would miss him.

And she would miss the conviction that the true son would return, no less the hope that such a belief gave her. She surveyed the tired group of villagers and feared that many of them would lose hope, as well. She could not bear to see them suffer more than they had.

Which meant that she had to make use of the time that Duncan rested to try to persuade Bartholomew of her chosen course.

In addition, she should seduce him as oft as possible before he departed, the better that she might conceive his heir. There could still be a true son. Though Anna put little stock in her sensual allure, her night with Bartholomew had been wondrous. Perhaps he found her enticing despite her inexperience. Her heart skipped a beat.

Perhaps she should put the gathering of the villagers to use in pursuing her first goal.

"I have a tale to entertain you on this cold day," she said, raising her voice to the company. They nodded and gathered closer, more than amenable to her suggestion. "It is a tale of which many of you know parts, but I know the whole of it. On this day, perhaps we will learn the ending."

"Anna," Bartholomew warned in a growl, obviously anticipating which tale she would tell, but she ignored him.

"Once upon a time," Anna began. "There was a baron who held the seal of Haynesdale. He came from a long line of noblemen who had been lords of the same holding, son after father, father after son. Their lineage was Saxon, though they had taken Danish brides when Knut held thrall in England. When the conqueror came and all old rights were swept aside, the baron of that time saw the course of change. He surrendered his seal to the new king, in exchange for the welfare of his people."

"A wise choice," murmured Duncan. "It is a rare man who can see his way through war with his holdings intact."

The company nodded agreement with this before Anna continued.

"William admired the baron's bravery and his repute. Though the holding was claimed by the crown, the crown granted it anew to the baron in exchange for his faithful service in future. The baron not only served William but took a Norman bride, at the king's suggestion."

"A tradition at Haynesdale, evidently," Bartholomew said but again, Anna ignored him.

If he meant to warn her that he could not ask for her hand, he wasted his breath. She knew he was born higher than she, and she understood how such matches were arranged. She was not some witless village girl. She lifted her chin, granted him a look, and continued.

"And so it always has been with the Barons of Haynesdale: they honored the past but defended the future. They upheld the law but were unafraid to fight in defense of what they called their own.

They blended the old ways with the new, just as they blended their bloodlines, to ensure the safety and prosperity of those beneath their hand. Perhaps because of their reputation for honor and justice, perhaps because their holding was not so rich as that, and perhaps because Haynesdale was a little too far from the king's court, they were trusted by the crown."

"Perhaps it was that they never defied a king's will outright," contributed Father Ignatius. "Or rose in rebellion against the crown."

Anna smiled. "Or perhaps it was because they paid their tithes on time, and sent gifts to the king with regularity. The Barons of Haynesdale were able to pass their holding and title down through their own blood sons."

"That is as it should be," protested one of the company.

"With the payment of coin for the escheat, to be sure," Duncan muttered.

"When William the Conqueror claimed this land, he took suzerainty of it all himself," Bartholomew contributed. "He granted titles to his favored barons, but on the death of the baron, the title and holding reverted by law to the crown. So it has been these hundred years in England. When a baron dies, the assignment of his holding remains the king's own right."

"Some were more vigorous about this than others," Duncan provided. "The current king, Henry, is less concerned with England than with Normandy, and prefers not to trouble himself with the assignment of holdings he deems petty."

"Then they can pass from father to son," said Percy.

Bartholomew smiled. "With the payment of coin to the crown, the escheat can be passed, it is true. Without one, who can say?"

Father Ignatius shook his head. "It is no better than a bribe."

"And so it is not, but that is how suzerainty passes in England," Bartholomew agreed.

Anna cleared her throat, disliking this evidence of his resolve. "And so it was that there was a Baron of Haynesdale who was much loved by his people, and not that long ago. He was wedded as soon as he came to hold the seal, as is right and good. His wife was chosen for him by the king himself, and it is said that he was much smitten with her charms. They wed and returned to Haynesdale, where she quickly rounded with child. It was said that the Baron

Nicholas was blessed beyond all—until his wife died in the bearing of their child, and the babe was lost as well."

Many in the company shook their heads, for they had seen women lost in childbirth. Esme listened avidly, and Anna knew she recognized the tale.

"There is a stone in the chapel by the old keep where she was laid to rest. Perhaps it has survived the burn. My mother said a thousand masses were said for the lady, and a thousand candles burned for a year in her memory. She said Baron Nicholas was broken by his loss and that he could oft be found, praying at his wife's tomb. The loss changed him, my mother said, for he refused to consider any suggestion that he might wed again. His heart was buried with his bride. That was his conviction."

Esme nodded sadly in recollection.

"Baron Nicholas ruled for many years without a wife, and the prosperity of Haynesdale grew beneath his care. Our markets abounded with goodness. Our granaries were filled every winter. Our sheep were fat, and our cows gave plentiful milk. The years passed and the baron grew aged. And though this is the nature of all things, there were those who began to be concerned with the future. What would happen to Haynesdale when the beloved baron died? He had no son or heir, not even a brother. Who would ensure the protection of all those who lived beneath his hand?"

A murmur passed through the company as all considered the merit of this question. More than one noted that Royce had no son and grew older, as well.

"There was a meeting in the village, for a conviction was dawning that the baron's advisors were leading him astray. Did one of them wish to take the seal himself? It could not be borne. My father was the smith of Haynesdale village, a quiet man who considered long before making his choices. He was much respected, and so it was that he was chosen to take the concerns of the village to the baron's next court. You can be sure that many came to listen."

"I was there!" called an older alemaker from the group, and Esme nodded agreement. More than one in the company appeared to realize then that this was not a tale of wonder, but one of Haynesdale's recent history. They leaned closer to listen.

"My father was no orator. He could not beguile another with

fine words and clever phrases, but he spoke always from his heart. He appealed to the baron as a villein who loved his lord dearly and did not wish to see all lost upon that man's inevitable demise. Baron Nicholas listened to him, his fingers toying with his own beard as he sat on his great chair in silence. There were those who feared there might be retribution for my father's audacity, and perhaps my father shared that concern. But when he had said all he had come to the court to say, and I doubt it was lengthy, Baron Nicholas thanked him, then left the court."

The company was silent, their interest clear.

"There was no word from the baron for a week, though once again, he was seen in the chapel, praying at his wife's tomb. The candles were lit once more and burned through the night, and masses were sung in her honor again. And at the end of the week, the baron strode into his bailey and called for his horse. He rode out that very day with a retinue of courtiers, journeying south to the king's court with a speed that would have done a younger man proud. It was said later that he strode directly to the king in his chambers, then dropped to one knee and asked his sovereign to suggest a bride for him to wed."

There were nods of approval at the baron's decisive choice.

"The year was 1163, and King Henry II had just returned to England. He was intent upon putting his kingdom in order, and he liked that Baron Nicholas had remained loyal to him when Stephen and Matilda had challenged his claim. He also was impressed by the purpose shown by this older knight in his determination to do what was right. He vowed to ponder the question, then invited the baron to the board. A lady in the queen's service ensured that she sat near Baron Nicholas, for she was intrigued by him. Gabriella was a beauty and a widow. Her nature was as different from the baron's beloved wife as could be. She was said to be stubborn and outspoken. Her first husband had jested that she was better suited to lead an army than to ply her needle at embroidery."

There was a chuckle in the company at this, and Anna saw Bartholomew glance her way. "Many a man would prefer such a woman as his partner," he said quietly and Anna blushed. The company nudged each other at that and her face burned as she continued.

"Gabriella and the baron discovered that evening that they were both equally forthright. Baron Nicholas said he would never love another as he had loved his wife. Gabriella assured him that she would never love a man as she had loved her lord husband, and here, too, they found common ground. They were both practical, as well, and spoke of finances and expectations, their notions of justice, their taste for luxury, and a hundred other matters that first night. By the time the court retired for the night, each was convinced of the merit of the other."

Anna continued. "It was said that Baron Nicholas prayed that night for his wife's blessing for him to wed this lady, in order to ensure the security of his holding. He was granted a sign, in the sudden leap of the flames on the candles in the chapel and took this as her agreement. The king had witnessed the felicity between the pair at his board the night before and pronounced that Baron Nicholas should wed the lady Gabriella. They exchanged their vows before the court the next day and returned the Haynesdale."

"I wager she was welcomed," said one of the men in the company.

"Aye, she was. The lady won the hearts of the villagers quickly, for she was kind yet firm. She gave alms and she granted good counsel and had an unerring sense of what was right. Those in service in her hall were treated well, and she suggested new possibilities to the baron. Their match appeared to be amiable, and indeed, she rounded with child within the year. The baron was seen to be concerned, but the lady might have been fearless. One the anniversary of their nuptial vows, Lady Gabriella delivered onto him a healthy son. The babe came quickly, as if she wanted to see her husband's fears set to rest as quickly as possible, and there was much merriment in Haynesdale." There was applause at this and Anna turned to the priest. "Father Ignatius, did you baptize the boy?"

"Indeed I did. He was named Luc, which was the name of Baron Nicholas' father, and Bartholomew, in memory of Lady Gabriella's first husband. In the tradition of Haynesdale, his names blended two strains, just as the alliance of the marriage had done. He was a most robust child. Handsome and well wrought."

Anna saw Bartholomew start at the mention of the boy's name.

"He had a valiant heart," Esme contributed. "It could be seen even when he was a boy, and he possessed a generous nature. He played with my Oswald when the lady Gabriella came to visit me."

"There was the day," sighed a woman. "We did not appreciate our good fortune in our baron and his wife until they were gone."

Anna saw how Bartholomew observed the company. "It seemed all went well at Haynesdale but in truth, there was trouble brewing," she said. "The baron battled a neighbor on his northern borders, one whose holding was not so prosperous and who had an avarice for what was not his own. His name was Royce, and it is said that once he saw the lady Gabriella, his attacks grew in ferocity. The two barons treated and it was believed that all might be at peace, for a few years at least. The boy was four summers of age when Royce's men came in stealth. It was Christmas and Baron Nicholas had invited those on his holding to feast in his hall. The ale was tainted, by command of Royce, and all slept too soundly that night. The villains crept into the keep at Haynesdale, slaughtering any who awakened to challenge them, and murdered Baron Nicholas in his own bed. His wife would have been taken captive, for Royce desired her for his own, but she fled the hall, disguised as a servant."

Esme crossed herself. "God in Heaven, but I remember that night," she said softly.

Anna swallowed. "In truth, my mother gave the lady her own garb and aided in her escape. She came to our home, which must have been humble to her, but my mother said she was gracious and grateful. When the keep was set ablaze by the attackers, my father kept the lady from trying to aid those who were surely lost. They said the keep of Haynesdale became the old baron's funeral pyre."

More than one crossed themselves. "The old burn is still haunted," muttered someone. "You can hear their cries of pain when the wind rises."

"At Christmas," added another grimly.

"Fiend," said a third and spat at the ground.

"By morning, the fire was spent, the keep reduced to ash and the air filled with lingering smoke," Anna continued. "Villagers had been gathered up by the attackers and imprisoned. My parents had retreated to the forest with the lady and her son and watched in horror as Royce's men strode through the remains of the village, setting fire to homes and routing those who were hidden away. It was declared repeatedly that Royce would show mercy if the lady

Gabriella surrendered herself to him."

There was silence at this, and more than one woman eyed Anna with compassion, for her own ordeal was not as secret as she might have preferred. Again, she saw Bartholomew take note of the reaction and felt his gaze upon her.

Her cheeks were hot, but she continued. "My mother said the lady Gabriella seemed to be filled with new resolve by this sight. There were three men loyal to her husband beyond doubt. My father found them, at her request, and they stood witness as she declared the plan. She knew there could be no triumph for her son on this day, not when he was such a young boy. She charged the knights to take her son to the queen, whose court was in Aquitaine, and surrender him to her safekeeping. She wished for him to come of age in that court, to train as a knight, then return to avenge his father."

She took a deep breath. "To ensure that he would be known as the rightful heir, Lady Gabriella had my father heat the signet ring of the Baron of Haynesdale and press its mark into the flesh of the boy, right over his heart. He was branded with the evidence of who he was, that none could doubt him on his return."

More than one villager grimaced in sympathy and Bartholomew looked at the ground.

Anna paused. "My mother said he was born valiant, for though the flesh was seared and the pain must have been considerable, the son of Baron Nicholas did not make a sound."

There was a murmur of approval at this.

"The lady then kissed her son's brow and bade him be good, and she did not watch as the knights disappeared into the woods with the boy. My mother said she wept silent tears. Then she strode back into the village, challenging Royce to show the mercy he had promised. She said she would come to his bed if he released the villagers. He did, and they watched in awe as she mounted behind him on his steed and went to his holding to become his new wife."

"Poor lamb," Esme said.

"There were those who thought the lady had been disloyal to her husband's memory, and still others who believed she had seen only to her own advantage. My mother said she had seen the love blossom unexpectedly between the baron and his wife, and she advised all to wait and see. And so the tidings of the truth came within days. The lady Gabriella had hidden a knife and attacked the new baron when he came to her bed. She had stabbed him in the eye before he realized her intent, then when his men were summoned to his aid, she plunged the dagger into her own heart. She killed herself before them all, rather than pledge herself to him, and avenged her lord husband. Royce bears the mark of her rejection still."

Anna heard the outrage in her own voice. "Royce paid the escheat on Haynesdale with Baron Nicholas' treasury, and there was none who dared to raise a protest against him. None who would be heeded, at least. He sought the signet ring with fervor but never found it. He learned bits and pieces of the truth, sufficient that he sent knights in pursuit of the missing boy, but we heard naught of what transpired. In the meantime, he built a new keep for Haynesdale, funded by the taxes he imposed upon us."

"It grew larger with the dowry of his second wife," noted Edgar.

"Aye, it did. My father was one of the first to become an outcast, but he was not the last, and now the forests of Haynesdale are home to more of us than the village."

Anna turned to Bartholomew. "And since that day of Haynesdale's loss, we have waited. We have told the story of Baron Nicholas and Lady Gabriella to our children and our brothers. We have endured the tyranny of Sir Royce and we have prayed for the return of Luc Bartholomew, the son of Baron Nicholas, and the rightful Baron of Haynesdale."

Anna reached into her chemise and tugged out the ring that hung there on a lace. "What no soul knew was that the lady Gabriella surrendered her husband's signet ring to the care of my father, that it might be hidden until her son's return. I am the daughter of the smith and this is the signet ring of Baron Nicholas." She held it up so that it caught the light. "My father held it in trust until he was taken to Royce's dungeon to confess what he knew. My mother kept it hidden until she, too, was taken to the dungeon to surrender what she knew. I know that neither of them admitted the truth, for I yet have the ring."

The entire company was silent.

"And on this day, against all expectation, I have found the mark made by my father, burned into the flesh above the heart of her son at the command of Lady Gabriella. I have seen the scar that fits this ring." She turned to Bartholomew and offered him the ring, dropping to one knee as she did so. "The mark of your legacy is returned, sir, as your mother decreed it should be."

Chapter Eleven

Anna endeavored to make it impossible for Bartholomew to leave.

And indeed, her strategy was a good one. He felt the hope surge through the bedraggled company of villagers, so weakened by their history in this place, and he was not immune to the power of their desire. They looked at him with relief in their eyes, and he knew they had endured much. He knew they deserved to return to their village and live in peace.

Truly, their welfare was his responsibility.

He could not blame her for trying to force his hand. She felt strongly about the future of these people and believed that he erred. She had had no opportunity to learn a respect for justice, not beneath Royce's hand, but Bartholomew could not undermine the law before he even claimed his holding.

He felt the urge of the entire company to ride forth and claim Haynesdale, to slice down Royce and restore his father's line to the barony. But it was not that simple. And he feared that these people would face much more hardship if he acted with such folly.

It was his task to act with prudence and protect these people, to uphold the legacy of his forebears.

To convince the villagers of Haynesdale of the merit of justice once more.

Bartholomew had been composing his argument when Anna had reached into her chemise. When she withdrew the lace that had so intrigued him, her hand had been closed over the prize that had been trapped between her breasts. She tugged the lace over her head, holding his gaze. When she opened her hand, he was astonished to see what rested on her palm.

It was his father's signet ring.

"Praise be that the true son is returned," she said softly.

Duncan whistled quietly through his teeth.

"So, this was how you knew," Bartholomew murmured.

"It matches perfectly," she said with conviction and those attending her words exchanged glances. "The seed of Baron Nicholas is returned."

The company cheered.

Bartholomew knew what Anna desired of him. He wanted to claim the ring more than anything else in the world, but he knew he could not do it. It looked so small, but the responsibility it carried was a heavier burden than its actual weight.

He stood and took a step back. "Only the king can make a baron of the realm, Anna," he said with quiet heat.

The villagers stared at him in shocked silence.

"But will you not reclaim your legacy?" demanded a tall man, perhaps the cooper.

"You do not realize what you ask," Bartholomew said. "I would not imperil you more."

"We want to go home!" cried the tall man's wife.

"We want to live in the village and tend our gardens," insisted Willa.

"And plow the fields as they should be," declared the alemaker. "Grow grain for bread and for ale."

"How long it has been since we have tasted your ale?" murmured his wife.

Edgar dropped to one knee before Bartholomew. "Take us home, my lord. I would follow you to do whatever needed to be done."

"Aye!" came the chorus of assent.

Bartholomew sighed. "And what would I be asking of any who followed me? To offer themselves for slaughter against trained and armed knights?" The villagers exchanged glances as he counted off Royce's forces on his fingers. "There is Royce, there is Gaultier, there are four more knights and at least a half a dozen men-at-arms."

"Eight," the red-haired man affirmed.

"Eight then, plus the others means thirteen armed and trained warriors, prepared to kill in their liege lord's defense." A ripple of unease passed through the company. "We have few swords, few daggers, no armament and solely two men who have tasted the kind of battle we would face."

"One at less than his full capacity," Duncan added.

"But..." Anna protested, but Bartholomew held up a finger.

"Add to those fourteen the squires, most of whom are training for battle as part of their service. I saw at least a dozen of them, and they are armed, as well."

"We are outnumbered," murmured the red-haired woman to the man beside her. He nodded grim agreement and Bartholomew saw hope die in many a face.

"Add to that the fortification of the keep itself. It is tall and well-wrought, designed to keep attackers at bay. We have no siege engines or horses. We cannot besiege a fortified keep with loose stones and bare hands, not if we mean to triumph."

"We have our fury," Anna said. "That is not to be overlooked."

A few villagers agreed, but Bartholomew heard his own tone grow impatient. "There is passion and there is folly. I have seen enough to know the difference, and I have seen enough of futile death to suffice for all my days and nights." He shook his head. "Nay, I would be no better than what you have known if I were to lead you all in such an assault. It would be irresponsible and wrong."

Father Ignatius nodded quietly, his expression approving. "He is his father's son indeed," he murmured but Bartholomew did not reply.

Anna challenged him anew. "You could have attacked from inside, while we were all there. He would not have suspected such a feat."

"Sir Royce was my host," Bartholomew countered. "I could not betray his hospitality with treachery."

Anna gasped. "But you endeavored to steal from him!"

"I tried to retrieve what had been entrusted to our party," Bartholomew corrected. "And I ensured your brother's freedom. To take more than our due when we were guests would have been wrong."

"Surely Haynesdale is your due!" cried Edgar.

"It might well be, if I can claim it and if I can pay the escheat. We like to believe that holdings should pass from father to son, but since the Angevin kings claimed England, that is no longer the law. I will not kill Royce to make this claim." He bit off his next words.

"I will not ignore the law for my own convenience."

They stared at him in silence.

Bartholomew turned to Duncan, well aware that he had disappointed the villagers, but he saw no reason to lie. "Give me your boots, Duncan, and I will clean them along with mine."

Chatter broke out amongst the villagers, whispers he could not hear clearly but doubtless filled with speculation. He imagined they blamed him or thought him a coward, but he knew the limits of what he could do. Bartholomew was aware that Father Ignatius followed him, but did not see the glance that the priest fired at Anna.

He heard her footsteps behind them, though, and shook his head. How like Anna to refuse to accept any answer other than the one she desired. In a way, her passion was inspiring, but he would not be reckless with the lives of others.

He could not simply seize what he desired, as Royce had done.

Still, there had to be a solution. In this moment, Bartholomew was glad beyond belief that he had known Gaston and learned from that man's experience.

For it would take a diplomat and a man of integrity to see this victory won.

ॐ

Father Ignatius found himself liking this knight more than he had liked any new acquaintance in a while. He followed Bartholomew to the stream, where the younger man squatted and scooped up a handful of snow. Father Ignatius watched him scrub his boots with fresh snow, then cast the mired snow into the stream before taking another handful. He was not afraid to work, this knight, or to perform tasks beneath his station when they needed to be done. And Father Ignatius respected the care Bartholomew showed for the villagers of Haynesdale.

He had not made a jest when he had called the young knight his father's son.

Bartholomew did not acknowledge his presence, even when the priest took one of Duncan's boots and began to clean it with the snow in the same way. The pair of them worked in silence together while Father Ignatius chose his words. Anna remained out of sight and behind them, doubtless both vexed and listening.

"You startle them all," he finally said, his tone mild.

Bartholomew glanced up. "How so?"

Father Ignatius smiled. "They have not known so many knights of merit in recent years, nor come to expect a man to act upon principle."

"I know of no other way to be."

"But you recognize why they have the expectation they do."

"Of course." Bartholomew straightened. "But the fact remains that the king must create a baron by his own will. And in order for that to even be a possibility in the case of Haynesdale, Royce Montclair would have to be dead and the man who wished to be baron in his place would need coin to pay the escheat." He shrugged. "Royce is not dead and I am not going to kill him."

"Because you do not have the coin for the escheat."

"Even if I did, it would be wrong to murder the man who held my desire, regardless of what he has done in the past. Surely I do not have to argue that with you."

Father Ignatius let the silence grow between them before he continued. "Do you remember the events of those days?"

Bartholomew shook his head. "I remember fire. I remember my mother's voice." He cast a smile at the dog that had come to sit beside him. "I remember a dog much like this one but named Whitefoot."

Father Ignatius smiled. "I remember that dog. This one would be his great grandson, at least."

"Then he is related!"

"Aye. Those of your father's dogs that survived went to the miller's abode." The priest rubbed the dog's ears. "But you must not have ever reached the king's court in Anjou."

Bartholomew shook his head. "Nay. I suppose we were followed and the knights who had me in their care were betrayed and assaulted. I know only that I was awakened one night by one of them and bidden to run. He told me to go to the church where we had prayed that day and that he would meet me there. He never came." The younger man frowned. "We were in Paris."

"You must have been frightened."

"I do not think I fully understood what had transpired. I was hungry, to be sure, and I knew that knights had defended me. My father had been a knight, after all, and my mother had entrusted me to the care of these knights. So, when I saw a knight come to that church to pray, I followed him. He wore the red cross of the Temple and I had never seen a surplice so fine." Bartholomew smiled. "He could not be rid of me, for I saw him as my sole chance of survival."

"There must have been other knights in Paris."

"I had eyes only for him. I followed him. I vowed to be of assistance to him. I swore to do whatever he desired so long as he took me with him." Bartholomew shrugged. "Who knows how much Gaston saw of the truth? But after I made my case and struggled to prove myself by trying to help him, he surrendered. He lifted me to his saddle and took me with him, calling me his squire, though I was too small to be of much use."

"You grew."

Bartholomew smiled. "Aye, I grew. And he was destined for Outremer, I came of age in Jerusalem."

"You have been there all these years?"

The knight nodded. "Most of them. We only left because Gaston became heir to his family holding and returned to France. He chose to dub me a knight once there, for he is both good and generous."

"A man of principle," Father Ignatius said, guessing where Bartholomew had learned his code of honor.

"Indeed."

"You could have come into the power of another less honorable."

Bartholomew nodded. "I could have, quite easily."

"It seems that God has held you in the palm of His hand."

"Perhaps so. Perhaps it was all Gaston's doing." They shared a smile. "I would not disgrace the honor Gaston has shown to me by doing any deed that would cause him displeasure. He used to negotiate for the Templars in Palestine, seeking compromise and balance."

"A temperate man, too, then," the priest guessed. "You must have come to Haynesdale apurpose."

"I journeyed to Scotland with Fergus and Duncan, for Fergus will claim Killairic and wed his betrothed this coming spring. I thought it an opportunity to see what had happened at Haynesdale."

"Did they know of your intent?"

Bartholomew shook his head. "I did not know what I would find. In a way, I hoped that all would be well here and there would be no need to avenge my parents. In another, I yearned to set matters to rights. Either way, I had to discover the truth before I could try to make a change." The younger man finished cleaning his boots and cast a glance over the forest. "I did not truly remember it, not until we were here. Cenric reminded me of Whitefoot. When Anna took us to the old burn, I remembered the keep and my mother. I have always had nightmares of fire and pain, but her tale fills the gaps."

"What will you do now?"

Bartholomew met his gaze. "I will petition the king. I expect Henry has gone back to Anjou, which is near Gaston's holding."

"Perhaps your friend will vouch for your character."

"Perhaps he will, but there remains the fact that Royce yet lives."

"And the need for coin. Will your friend be of aid in that?"

Bartholomew smiled and shook his head. "He has been very kind to me, Father Ignatius. From Gaston, I have my spurs, my blade, my armor, my destrier."

"Your understanding of how a knight should be and your code of honor."

"Aye. He has given me the wealth of a king in that, and he is not as wealthy as a king."

Father Ignatius braced his elbows upon his knees and put the tips of his fingers together. "What if the coin for the escheat could be found?"

"Found?" Bartholomew echoed.

"I know that Sir Royce will dispatch his taxes to the exchequer of the king in the next few days."

"Surely you do not suggest a theft, Father Ignatius."

"I am not certain I would call it a theft, if indeed his messengers were divested of their burden."

"Indeed?"

"Indeed." Father Ignatius held Bartholomew's gaze. "Taxes are gathered from the villagers and those dependent upon the baron."

"Once paid, they no longer belong to the one who surrendered them."

"But they are paid for services due from the baron. We pay for the right of security in our homes, for the keeping of knights to defend us, for the establishment of courts to ensure that justice is served in the holding, for a Christmas feast at the baron's table in reciprocity. The knights of Haynesdale do not defend the villagers. Truly, they prey upon them. And I cannot recall when last Sir Royce held a court. He has welcomed no villager within his walls since wedding his lady wife." The priest shrugged. "It could be said that the villagers have not received their due for their taxes."

"You know they do not have the right to reclaim the coin."

"Perhaps they should."

Bartholomew shook his head. "I call it sophistry. You cannot declare it just to steal from another, even to serve what you perceive to be a good end. There is right and there is wrong, and a wrong can never repair another wrong." He shook a finger at the priest. "Were I the baron of a holding and my villeins thought it fitting to rob from me for their own ends, I should scarce call that justice."

Anna exhaled in audible frustration and Father Ignatius smiled.

"You find my view amusing?" the knight asked.

"I find it refreshing," the priest replied. "And it only adds to my conviction that the true heir is returned and must be restored." He laid a hand on Bartholomew's arm before that man could protest. "You think it wrong that any should kill Sir Royce, even after what he has done to your own family."

Bartholomew winced. "I have no evidence of what he has done. I have a tale, and it is a compelling one, but there is no proof of his villainy."

"Aye, there is," the priest insisted. "But it is not mine to share."

"I do not understand."

"Let Anna tell you why she would be willing to strike the fatal blow against Royce Montclair. This is not a court, but her testimony might change your view."

&♥

Anna did not welcome Father Ignatius' suggestion, but she feared he was right. She emerged from the forest, having realized only when he spoke of her that both men knew of her presence. Bartholomew studied her, but she could not guess his thoughts.

Was he irked with her for sharing his tale?

She was irked with him for denying his responsibility.

But all the same, she knew that if he had leaped to his feet and set off to kill Royce, then claimed Haynesdale without regard for another, she would have thought less of him.

She took the seat abandoned by the priest and watched that man stride back to the others, his confidence that he had done aright more than clear. She did not know how to begin, for she could not simply blurt out her confession. She took a breath. "I have never seen you so irked as you were before the company."

Bartholomew shrugged. "I felt there was cause."

"Because I challenged you?"

"And not for the first time," he noted. "But not simply that." He fell silent, frowning as he worked the snow into his boots.

"What then?"

He exhaled noisily. "I had a plan. I intended to ride through Haynesdale and ascertain its state. I wished to see if it had a baron who treated the villeins well. I wished to see if all were as it should be."

"Or better, find cause to challenge any baron."

"Perhaps so. Either way, my plan was soon shredded by a pair of thieves."

Anna bit her lip.

"We were robbed, as you well know, and in retrieving our possessions and the captured thief, Duncan was captured in Percy's stead. Now my companion is wounded, the reliquary is yet lost, my steed and squire have ridden on with my fellows, I have made a vow that I dare not break yet will demand I act ignobly—"

"What is this?" Anna asked, but he did not pause for breath.

"Worst of all, I find myself falling in love with the most vexing maiden I have ever met in all my days, and there is naught I can do about it."

Anna found herself blushing as she had no doubt who that maiden might be. "Naught?"

He cast her a simmering glance. "Naught honorable. Indeed, I have already taken too much from her, because the matter remains that if ever I manage to plead my case before the king, even if I have the coin for the escheat, he will likely desire to ensure my loyalty."

"By naming your bride."

Bartholomew nodded, then turned his attention to the other boot. "And she will not be a smith's daughter. She will be the daughter or the widow of a man already allied strongly to the king."

They sat in silence for a long moment. "What vexes you most?" Anna asked finally. When he glanced at her, she smiled, hoping to improve his mood. "It is an impressive list for its length."

Bartholomew's smile came slowly, as if summoned against his will. "The maiden," he said. "Definitely, the maiden."

"Because she is vexing?"

He turned to look at her, wonder in his eyes. "Because she is bold and fearless, because she challenges me and she confounds me, because she is alluring and because she is like no other maiden I have ever known."

Anna found her cheeks burning. "She is not truly a maiden," she said and his expression turned rueful.

"Yet she has such an honesty about her that I shall always think of her as one." He glanced at her. "No matter the state of her innocence."

Heat flared in Anna's heart and she realized that she loved Bartholomew as well. She would not confess as much, though, for she saw that he was already conflicted about his path.

She gripped his hand and appealed to him anew. "You cannot surrender the quest for Haynesdale. Royce is not a good baron, and I will tell you why."

"Father Ignatius said you had reason to wish him dead."

"Aye. There were rumors always that you would return and tales of the ring entrusted to my father's care. I don't know when Royce heard them, but he waited until my mother was rounding with Percy before he acted upon them. My father was seized in the night, dragged away by Gaultier and his men. Perhaps they thought my father would be more likely to confess what he knew because of my mother's state, but he did not." She swallowed, recalling her mother's terror well enough. "He never returned home. We next saw him when his head was hung from the gates, as a lesson to all who chose to defy Sir Royce's requests for information. I was nine summers of age and will never forget the sight." She shuddered. "He was left there to rot all the winter long, denied even a decent burial."

"I am sorry, Anna..."

She did not give him the time to complete whatever he might have said. "Royce then taunted my mother. Perhaps he feared to meddle with a woman so close to her time. Perhaps he has some conscience. The fact was that Percy was unanticipated. My mother thought herself past the time of bearing children, but she ripened all the same. My father was so happy when she shared the news. He wanted a son, to carry on the tradition of smith in the village, but he never saw Percy." Bartholomew closed his hand around hers. "Royce used to comment as he passed through the village, insinuating that my mother did not carry my father's child. She knew he was not done with her. He came one night and vowed to leave her to raise her children if she surrendered the ring to him, but she knew it was a lie." She flicked a look at Bartholomew. "She knew he was not a man to keep his word."

He frowned, considering that.

"She made those months count. She told me every tale she knew, over and over again, and before her labor began, she gave me the ring and bade me hide it where no one could find it." She swallowed. "Gaultier came for my mother as soon as the babe cried. He dragged her to the keep and his men cut down all who protested. My mother was sobbing when last I saw her alive. Sobbing and still bleeding. I was left with Percy, still wet from her womb and wailing for her milk."

She could feel Bartholomew's anger rising and carried on. "And so this is the justice offered by this baron. He had my mother's head displayed, on the post opposite that of my father, leaving it there until the crows had picked the flesh clean. He said they were together in Hell. He taunted me, as he had taunted my mother, biding his time, watching. The tanner's wife nursed Percy and I might as well have been his mother." Anna kept her head bowed. "Until two years ago, when Royce decided my time had come."

Bartholomew caught his breath. "You should have given him the ring and saved yourself."

"But it would not have saved me!" Anna protested. "He is wicked and filled with greed. He is not a man who upholds his vows. He would have taken it and destroyed the chance of you ever being able to prove your identity. I would have suffered the same fate, if not worse. The villagers would have lost hope forever. Nay, there was naught to be won by capitulation." She took a breath. "Truly, his conviction that I knew the location of the ring might have been the sole thing that saved me."

"Because it was required to challenge him," Bartholomew mused. He squeezed her fingers. "And what of Kendrick? Does he enter this tale?"

"He does." Anna smiled, though it was a sad smile. "He crept into the keep, intent upon saving me. He confronted Gaultier and was slaughtered for his audacity. Right before my eyes, they cut him down, then cast him aside like so much offal. He was so good!" She shuddered, welcoming the tension that she felt within Bartholomew. "But I had the key, for Kendrick had given it to me before he was caught. When they finally left me, I managed to flee."

"And they pursued you." His voice was grim.

"And burned the forest in vengeance. It was my fault that all suffered so badly, for I defied Sir Royce and he did not approve."

"But he thought you dead? Until yesterday?"

Anna nodded. "I believe so. I hid in the forest, joining the other outcasts after my escape. I retrieved the ring and began to wear it, for no one would seek it from me."

Bartholomew stared down at her, concern in his eyes. "But then you lost the babe Kendrick had given you, the one that would have been his living memory. Truly, Anna, your determination is fierce."

Anna took a deep breath, knowing she had to tell him all of the truth. "Perhaps so, but maybe less than you think."

He arched a brow.

"Kendra was not Kendrick's child," she admitted, her words husky. "We were friends and comrades, but never lovers."

He frowned at her, not comprehending.

"Royce gave me to Gaultier, in a last effort to compel me to talk. I was a maiden when captured, but not for long after that." She swallowed at the fury in Bartholomew's expression. "Kendra was Gaultier's child." Her throat was tight. "It was not her fault that she had been wrought in violence, and I did not want the others to know of my shame. I gave her that name apurpose. Only Father Ignatius knows the truth, and now you."

Bartholomew stood up and paced the bank of the stream,

222

agitated anew. He grimaced and crouched down before her to capture her hand once again in his. "I think Percy knows it."

"He knows I despise Gaultier, but not why." She shook her head. "He is only a boy. He does not need to know all of the wickedness of which men are capable." Anna swallowed. "Not yet." She tightened her grip upon his hand. "Bartholomew, you and your company already show him what it means to be a knight and a man of merit as well. I would have him learn more of your kind. You must reclaim Haynesdale, and I will help you to do it. I consider you my rightful baron. Command me to kill Royce and I will do it, regardless of the price to myself."

Bartholomew reached out and wiped the tears from her cheeks with his fingertips. "I never thought to see you cry, much less twice in as many days," he whispered with a smile. "Fierce Anna."

Her throat was tight, but she could not ask him again.

He eyed her solemnly. "You know that I cannot do what you ask of me. I cannot command such a deed of any person, especially not you."

"I know that you will not ride into Haynesdale and slaughter Sir Royce, though he roundly deserves as much, and I know that you will not take the ring and seize the holding as your own. I suppose that is the price of being a man of honor." She lifted her gaze to his. "Do you not desire the holding?"

"I do want it," Bartholomew spoke with passion. "I want to be baron more than anything else in all the world. But I cannot be the same as Royce, Anna. I cannot let my desire dismiss my morality. There must be a way, and I pledge to you that I will spend all my days and nights endeavoring to find it, but villainy is not the solution."

"I said I would kill him for you," she reminded him.

"Aye, I have no doubt that you would." He touched her cheek with a fingertip and she was surprised to see a twinkle light his eyes. "Your valor is one of the traits I most admire about you, Anna."

She found herself smiling in turn. "And truth be told, your honor is the trait I most admire about you."

"But I would not see you commit such a crime, even for me."

Their gazes held for a long moment, and Anna's mouth went dry.

Then she recalled something Bartholomew had said. "What pledge do you dare not break that will ensure you act ignobly?" she asked, knowing when Bartholomew winced that there was a detail of import she did not know. "I cannot think of any vow that would compel you to do as much."

He sat down heavily beside her. "That is because I have not told you all about our escape from Haynesdale."

What else had happened within those walls?

ॐ

Trust Anna to ask the question he least desired to answer.

Bartholomew was confounded by his promise to Marie. He was caught between his word of honor and his commitment to good conduct. He knew Gaston would not have sympathized with his situation, and then realized the truth of it.

While he had learned much from Gaston, he had learned even more of Ysmaine. The notion of seeking Anna's counsel filled him with new optimism, though he saw her surprise when he smiled at her.

"Suddenly this obligation gives you joy?" she asked.

"Nay, it is an idea that fills me with new hope. I have spoken to you of Gaston."

"The knight of honor and Templar, the one who saved you from the streets of Paris and granted you both spurs and sword."

"The very same. When Gaston heard that he was to be a baron, he found himself a wife, quickly, for he knew he would have need of a son."

"A man can expect more than that from his wife."

"As he learned from Lady Ysmaine, his chosen bride. We knew little of women after so much time with the Templars, but she was inspired by her parents' match, and how they conferred together. Gaston did not dare to trust her, but in the end, she was the one who ensured that his task to deliver the reliquary to Paris was successful." He took Anna's hand again. "And so, I would take from Lady Ysmaine's example and ask for your assistance in solving this riddle. Better, I would do so before it is too late."

"You and your word of honor! To whom have you made a pledge now?"

224

"Lady Marie." He sat back, awaiting the tempest, and was not disappointed. "I promised to aid her in conceiving a son."

Anna was clearly shocked. "What madness is this? You would aid such a viper and give her the means to dismiss your claim?"

"I declined to reply the first time—"

"That night we were at the keep!" Anna guessed, eyes flashing. "I knew she meant to seduce you!"

"But then, she aided our escape this day." He arched a brow. "And I pledged to pay her price."

Anna's eyes narrowed and she folded her arms across her chest. "She wants you to bed her?" Her expression revealed her opinion of that.

"She yearns for a child, and Sir Royce has not given her one."

Anna's lips parted in outrage. "She would conceive a bastard and deceive her lord husband?"

"I had need of her aid." Bartholomew flung out a hand. "She named the terms."

"But she is wed! Surely there is no honor in adultery?"

He gritted his teeth, for he had already turned this question in his thoughts. "None," he acknowledged. "Yet I am caught by my vow."

"You do not have to do it. She cannot come after you in this place. She will never reach you." Anna glared at him. "You could forget your pledge."

"I gave my word," Bartholomew insisted. "If I break my vow because it no longer suits me to keep it, what manner of man would I be?"

Anna audibly ground her teeth. "Yet if she does conceive, that child might be a boy." She shook her head. "A boy who could challenge your claim to Haynesdale!"

Bartholomew grimaced, for he had not considered that possibility.

"You might ensure that Royce's heir can make a competing claim to your own after Royce is dead."

"I promised, Anna."

Anna turned away. "It is a wicked bargain, to be sure," she murmured. "And one that cannot end well." She appealed to him again. "Do you not see that she will see her husband rid of the threat of the true heir? She saw you saved, but the price is your sacrifice!"

Bartholomew shook his head. "Nay, she cares naught for such detail. I believe she seeks only to leave Haynesdale..."

"No matter who bears the cost! What a selfish fiend of a woman!" Anna began to pace the riverbank in his stead, periodically kicking ice into the river. "And you!" She spun to fling out a hand toward him. "You believe all the people in Christendom to be as noble as you. What innocence is this? What folly! You are fool enough to trust *her*!"

"I gave my word. To break it would make me one of those people you condemn."

"You will step into a trap!"

"Indeed, I might." He arched a brow. "You could grant me some credit. I ask your assistance in finding a way to evade this obligation."

"With your honor yet intact?" He nodded and Anna growled. "Understand that Lady Marie is a fair match for Sir Royce, which means that she sees solely to her own advantage. She might be lovely and she might have fine manners, but her heart is as a stone. She might seduce you to conceive that son, but cares little if you are captured or killed for so doing." She seized a fistful of his chemise and gave him a shake. "Do you not see that she will betray you? She could not suffer to let a man who had claimed her live, for he might tell of it. If she were charged as an adulteress, she could lose all!"

"She might lose all if the king agreed to grant Haynesdale to me."

"Exactly! And this is why both she and Royce would see you dead." She shook her head and leaned toward him. "Do not go. Do not put yourself in such peril."

Bartholomew shook his head. "I must go, but I would find a way to survive the interval."

Anna's gaze simmering and she paced the riverbank again. "When do you meet her?"

"After midday on the first day without snow. At the old mill."

"Vexing man," Anna muttered. She tipped her head back and considered the pale hue of the sky. The snow fell thickly and it seemed that there was only snow as far as the eye could see. "But the truth is that otherwise, I should not admire you so."

Bartholomew chuckled. "I could say much the same of you."

"It appears you have some time," she mused, then turned a sparkling glance upon him. "However do you mean to pass it?"

He smiled and rose to his feet, seeing the anticipation in her eyes as he came to her side. "I hoped you might also have a suggestion about that." He dropped his hands to her shoulders and smiled down at her. "I love you, Anna."

"You do?"

"I do." He smiled as he watched her eyes light with pleasure. "I want all of this to come right, but cannot yet see a way for it to be so."

"Nor can I," she admitted, tangling her fingers with his own. "But there is one deed I would ask of you."

"What is that?"

"To give me a memory, one to warm me all the winters of my life that I will be without you." Her eyes shone with her conviction and Bartholomew's throat tightened. "I understand what you can promise and what you cannot, and why it must be so, but I love you as well." She sighed. "Let me have you so long as it snows, for that is better than not at all."

It was an invitation he could not refuse. Bartholomew framed her face in his hands and claimed her lips with his own, savoring all the passion that Anna had to give.

He would grant her memories and to spare.

When he broke their kiss, she smiled up at him, her ardor clear in her gaze. "Perhaps we might discover exactly how much a mortal man can endure of love play," she suggested, her tone teasing, and he could think of no better way to spend this time, however long it might be.

"Once again, I take your challenge, Anna." Bartholomew declared, and kissed her anew. He loved the passion of her response, that she was both honest and intrepid, and wished they could be together for all time.

He swung her into his arms and strode for the cavern, not caring who saw them or what was said. There was only Anna, Anna and the sweet fury of her kiss, and all the joy they could summon together.

ॐ

Royce was pacing the hall when Gaultier answered his summons. He fully expected an outbreak of temper from his overlord, since the prisoner had escaped and one of the finest archers was dead.

"I have heard the testimony of Roger," he said, gesturing to the one bowman who had returned from pursuit of the prisoner. "He brings most curious tidings."

"Indeed, sir?" Gaultier had not questioned Roger, but sent him immediately to Royce to make his report, as the body of his companion had to be retrieved. He braced himself for Royce's reaction to more bad news. "The other men have returned, sir, for they could not discern the trail of the escaped prisoner and his comrade."

"It does not matter," Royce said, to Gaultier's surprise. "This Bartholomew will return here to the keep. He can do naught else."

"Sir?"

"Have you not heard the tales of the one true son doomed to reclaim Haynesdale, Gaultier? I thought them nonsense, or willful thinking, and perhaps it is nonsense, but this knight, Bartholomew, believes himself to be the son of my predecessor, Baron Nicholas." Royce paced more quickly. "He will meet his father's end, to be sure."

Gaultier glanced at Roger and held his tongue.

"Sooner or later, I will be rid of him." Royce straightened suddenly, then smiled. Evidently, some detail had occurred to him. "Perhaps sooner than he anticipates."

"Sir?"

Royce dismissed Roger then seated himself. He smirked at the Captain of the Guard. "How could it be, Gaultier, that my wife left this hall to say her prayers in the chapel, yet did not see the thieves when they entered the same chapel?"

Gaultier blinked. "How do you know they were in the chapel, my lord?"

"The cabinet by the altar, the one for the prizes of the chapel, was unlocked. It is never left so." Royce lifted his gaze to Gaultier. "They were there, likely in the same moment as my lady wife."

If the cabinet had been open, Gaultier had to agree. He had seen Lady Marie that morning, walking toward the stable, before the hue and cry had been raised about an intruder. "Did they claim the prize, my lord?"

Royce raised a finger. "Fortunately, I had the foresight to move it to a more secure location."

Gaultier assumed that was in his lord's own chamber.

"But consider the course of my lady wife. Not only was she in the chapel, but she chose to visit her mare in the stables, immediately after her prayers," Royce continued. "Where not only another sentry had been left bound and silenced, but a rope had been lowered into the sewer."

"The sewer was their means of escape, my lord. The grill on the other end had been removed."

Royce nodded. "But what of my lady wife? Does she truly know naught?"

Gaultier was not such a fool as to accuse his baron's wife of any crime. "Women do not always observe keenly as men, sir...."

Royce interrupted him with a short laugh. "Or perhaps she *lies*, Gaultier." He rose to his feet anew, paced the chamber quickly, then spun to face him. "Where was my lady wife when the intruders were discovered?"

"Before the stables, sir."

"Exactly. And how many times was she said to have gone from chapel to stables?"

"Twice, sir, for she forgot her psalter the first time."

"And one has dire need of a psalter when visiting a mare." Royce strolled toward Gaultier. "How often does my wife visit her mare?"

"I cannot think of the last time, sir."

"Exactly! What if my lady wife did see the intruders in the chapel? What if she spoke to them there?" He halted before the Captain of the Guard, his expression exultant. "What if she made a wager with them, that she would aid in their escape?"

Gaultier could not imagine what a thief could offer to the lady of Haynesdale. "To what purpose, sir? Does she know that this villain believes himself to be destined to take your place?" It seemed folly for Lady Marie to ally herself with such a man while her own husband was yet in command of the keep, but Gaultier had never troubled himself to understand the thinking of women. They had but one purpose in his view, and it was not conversation.

Royce clapped him on the shoulder, his manner amiable. "I like that your thoughts do not readily travel the same path as mine, Gaultier. It is a good sign for our shared future."

"Sir?"

"I do not know what my wife schemes, Gaultier, but I would find out. Ensure that Lady Marie is followed whenever she leaves the keep and do as much without detection."

"She does not leave the keep often, sir."

"I think she will find an excuse to do as much and soon."

Understanding dawned in Gaultier's thoughts. "You think she will meet with the young knight."

"I think she has made an agreement and must collect her price. We shall see whether he is fool enough to pay it." Royce drained his cup of ale. "I wonder whether he is bold enough to enter this keep willingly again," he mused. "Be sure you post a sentry to watch the windows of her chamber."

"Of course, my lord."

Friday, January 22, 1188

Feast Day of the martyr Saint Anastasius.

Chapter Twelve

Finally, the snow had stopped.

And not an hour too soon. It was morning still. As the sky cleared, Marie's hope rose that her goal would be achieved within hours. She stood at the window of her chamber and surveyed the village outside the gates of the keep. Smoke rose from the roofs of the houses that were still occupied, and she was relieved that the population of the village had not been diminished yet again.

Her relief was not selfless. She had need of the elderly apothecary. It would have been most inconvenient if he had not survived the storm.

She called for her heaviest boots and her thickest cloak, insisting that her maid Agnes search for the fur-lined gloves she had not worn yet this winter. The maids dressed quickly once Marie was garbed, knowing full well that she might leave them behind.

The trio descended the stairs, and Marie felt rather than saw that they were watched.

Of course, Royce was absurdly suspicious. She pivoted and sought him out deliberately, as if she was required to ask his permission for every step she took.

"My lord," she murmured when she found him at his books. "I would beg your leave to visit the village this morn."

She saw the gleam in his eye when he glanced up, though he quickly hid his satisfaction. "Why would you venture into the cold, my lady?"

"No ordeal is too much for me to bear, sir, in the pursuit of our common goal."

He leaned back, surveying her. "Which goal might that be?"

"The conception of a son and heir, of course!" She gestured to the maids who stood demurely behind her. "Emma reminds me that an apothecary in her mother's village had a potion to hasten conception, and I recalled that there is an old apothecary in your own village. I would beg his assistance this day, sir."

"How strange that Emma recalls this incident only now."

Marie laughed lightly. "Memory is a strange thing, my lord. We were talking during the storm of other such foul weather we had known, and Agnes recalled her aunt laboring to deliver a child in a snowstorm, when all feared the midwife would not arrive in time." She stepped forward and lowered her voice, as if her words were for Royce alone. "Indeed, sir, that prompted me to confide my disappointment in my maids for the first time. It is not fitting for them to realize that we have any weaknesses, but in this instance, I think the confession may lead to good result."

Royce sensed the deception, to be sure. He considered her for a long moment. "I thought you shared all with Agnes and Emma," he murmured, speaking in English obviously in the hope that they might not understand.

More fool he, for both maids were fluent in French, English, and German. Marie was glad once again to have her assets underappreciated.

"Only what is fitting, sir," Marie lied. She pouted a little. "Surely you, too, would like to see this quest achieved."

He smiled and waved at her. "Of course, my lady. I hope only that you will grace the board at midday."

"Of course," she agreed, smiling so that he would not note how she gritted her teeth. She turned back to her maids at his dismissal and marched to the hall, with them in quick pursuit. "After all," she murmured under her breath. "Who would miss yet another meal of venison stew? Oh, what I would do for a measure of butter and honey spread on fresh bread!"

Butter and honey were the least of Marie's ordeals at Haynesdale, however. There was but one way to secure her freedom, and that was with the son. She had not lied about her intention of seeking that particular potion from the apothecary.

But she planned to seek another, as well.

They were followed by Gaultier—discreetly, but not so discreetly that she was unaware of his presence—which proved the merit of her foresight.

Aye, she would have the encouragement to conception and the sleeping potion, too.

Perhaps double of it, just to be sure that both Royce and his Captain of the Guard dreamed sweetly this afternoon.

૨ક

Bartholomew could not evade his obligation. The sunlight filled the opening to the cavern with a radiance that could not be ignored. The fresh snow glittered in the forest, inviting him to keep his vow. He wanted to linger with Anna but this task must be behind him. She was awake, nestled against him, her fingertips tracing circles around the mark upon his chest.

How would he keep his word to Marie without sullying them both with an adulterous act? It was a riddle, and consideration had not revealed a solution.

Perhaps there was not one.

He rose from the bed with a heavy heart and began to dress. Anna was watching him, her expression wary, and he knew she would not be silent for long.

That she was so forthright was part of what he loved most about her. He wanted her to be happy, even in his absence, but wondered whether he had erred in being honest. Had he destroyed her future happiness by confessing his love to her? All the same, he could not regret the sweetness they had found in each other's touch.

It seemed he could do naught right since coming to Haynesdale.

"Will you assist me with the aketon?" Bartholomew asked, marveling that she had not spoken so far. Anna rose and came to him, splendid in her nudity and as bold now in intimacy as she was in all other matters.

Perhaps he had achieved something.

"Why do you smile?"

"Because you are beautiful." He caught her nape in his hand and kissed her, lifting his lips from hers with such reluctance that she smiled in her turn.

"Turn around," she murmured, bending to pick up the aketon. He did not immediately follow her instruction, but savored the sight of her instead. Her hair fell over her shoulder in a dark curtain, and he yearned to kiss her fair skin again and conjure her passion once more.

But there was no time.

Bartholomew donned the aketon, turning his back upon her. Anna laced it with care, and he guessed that she lingered over the task to delay his departure. Her hands landed on the back of his shoulders and he wondered why she stopped.

"What if," she began softly and he glanced over his shoulder to find her frowning. "What if Royce died?"

"I told you..."

"Nay, I know you will not kill him outright, but what if he died in a battle of honor?"

"I do not understand."

Anna knotted the lace. "If Royce died and you wed Marie, would the king look more favorably upon your request to hold Haynesdale's seal?"

Bartholomew did not wish to think about wedding a woman like Marie. He imagined her charm would flee quickly once nuptial vows were exchanged, but Anna was so intent that he considered the question. "He might." He shrugged. "It might be seen as continuity in the administration of the holding. It is difficult to say."

Anna nodded. "But the treasury of Haynesdale would become your possession then, as Baron of Haynesdale by her, so you would then be able to pay the escheat."

"But Royce would still have to die." Bartholomew frowned. "Plus the problem remains that I must keep my word, but would prefer not to commit an indiscretion with another man's wife."

She met his gaze. "So meet her, but be discovered before any such indiscretion is committed. Be challenged by Royce and fight him, man to man."

Bartholomew lifted his hauberk, considering this. He tugged it over his head and Anna laced the back for him, then helped him to don his tabard.

"It might work," he mused.

She brushed off his tabard and granted him a smile. "Only if you win."

Bartholomew suspected victory would not be readily won. "He will cheat," he said with a smile.

Anna laughed and caught his face in her hands. "Finally, you learn some distrust of others," she said, then kissed him.

It was a sweet yet fiery kiss, one that sent both heat and purpose through his veins, and one that ended all too soon.

He smiled as he looked down at Anna in his embrace. Her pride in her notion shone in her eyes. "It is a devious scheme."

"And one that no one would expect from a man of your ilk," she agreed. "But you might be able to use Marie for your ends, just as she would use you for hers. I think that would be fitting."

He grimaced. "And what shall we do, you and I, when I am baron and wedded to Marie and you yet live in the village?"

Anna swallowed and her eyes shone with unshed tears. "We shall wish each other well and conduct ourselves with honor," she replied, her words husky. "You can have no future with the smith's daughter, and I know it as well as you do."

Bartholomew kissed her again, more lingeringly, for he feared it would be the last time. He would not sully any marriage he made with infidelity, even if it was to a woman like Marie. He wished it might be otherwise. When he broke their kiss, he filled his gaze with the sight of Anna, his heart pounding fit to burst. "Be well," he murmured, and brushed a tendril of hair from her cheek. "I shall never forget you, Anna, and my heart will always be yours."

"And mine yours, to be sure," she replied, then bowed as if he were a fine lord already. "Godspeed to you, my lord," she added, and he saw her blink back her tears. "May every good fortune come to your hand."

Bartholomew heard the quiver in Anna's voice and wanted to reassure her, but he knew that if he touched her, his resolve would be lost.

"Keep the dog with you," he said quietly. When she nodded, he turned and strode out of the cavern, bracing himself for whatever the day might bring.

He would endeavor to follow her plan and hoped it might succeed, for it offered the best possibility for their future.

As much as he might have wished otherwise.

Though the barony might be close to his grasp, Bartholomew was surprised to realize that he would surrender it all to be with the smith's daughter forever.

His personal desire did not matter. He had to keep his word.

This was the price of being his father's son, a knight and a man aspiring to hold the seal of Haynesdale in his own hand. Bartholomew had never before considered that the cost might be too high.

Claire Delacroix

è▲

Anna knew Bartholomew could not have chosen differently. He was a man of merit, which was why she feared for his fate in the company of those who showed no regard for honor, justice or the welfare of others. It was not that he failed to realize there was wickedness, but that he could not participate in it. He would not become like them, and the fact of it made her heart ache.

If he died, she would mourn him all her days.

If he did not die, she would yearn for him all her days.

It was a poor reward, and Anna was saddened that love's result was so meager.

She sat and watched Esme's chickens, more despondent than ever she had been. If there was no son destined to return and no Bartholomew to challenge her, Anna could not imagine a good reason to awaken each day. If he succeeded and wedded Marie and she had to see him every day in that woman's company, that too was reason to linger abed.

Anna much preferred the reason she had had to linger abed during the storm.

Cenric leaned on her leg and she rubbed his ears, smiling despite herself at his interest in the chickens. They ignored the hound, already confident that he would not touch them.

"So, he is gone," Esme murmured, then came to sat beside Anna. "I doubted he would linger at Haynesdale once the snow ceased to fall."

"He does linger at Haynesdale," Anna replied. "For he keeps a pledge to Lady Marie."

"That one!" Esme shook her head. "Lady Marie is not the measure of Sir Royce's first wife, to be certain."

"His first wife?" Anna was happy to seize on any topic that made her forget her woes—or Bartholomew's quest.

"Aye, the one he brought first to Haynesdale, after Lady Gabriella's death. She was a beauty, though she thought little of her husband's abode."

Anna had little recollection of that woman, though she knew that Royce had been wed before. "Was that why he had no son by her either? Did she refuse his attentions?"

Esme cackled. "There were tales, of course."

"What manner of tales?"

The old woman smiled at Anna. "Did you never wonder that your father, the smith, was in possession of such a fine crossbow?"

"Of course, but it was only entrusted to me after his death. My mother saved it for me." Anna shrugged. "There was little time for questions, for she granted it to me just before her labor began."

"Your mother." Esme nodded. "I might have said that you had your boldness from her blood, but that is not possible."

Anna frowned. "What do you mean?"

"It never mattered, Anna, which was why you were not told the truth."

"What truth?"

"But now I hear your admiration for that knight, and I fear it does matter. Does he have any regard for you?"

"Esme, you speak in riddles, and this day, I cannot bear it."

"Does he?" the older woman repeated.

"It does not matter. He is a knight and may claim the title of Haynesdale. I am but the daughter of the village smith."

The older woman leaned closer. "But you are not the smith's daughter."

Anna's heart clenched.

"Your father was the Captain of the Guard at Haynesdale, and that crossbow was his own. He was the youngest son of the Duke of Arsent, with no birthright save his lineage and his spurs."

Anna shook her head, unable to accept this tale. "My mother would never have been so disloyal to my father..."

"Nay, she would not and she was not. She was, however, loyal to the lady of Haynesdale."

"I do not understand."

Esme tapped Anna's arm. "Your mother served the lady who was Royce's first wife. She labored in the hall as a chambermaid in those days and she knew the lady's secrets. She knew, for example, that the lady trysted with the Captain of the Guard."

Anna caught her breath.

"Someone else knew, as well, for they were betrayed. The lady was confined to her chambers and the Captain of the Guard was executed."

Anna raised her hand to her lips.

"The lady relied greatly upon your mother and they found

much conviviality when they both rounded with child at the same time. A first child for both of them. They even labored on the same night, under the same full moon. Your mother's labor was troubled from the outset. I remember it well, as well as the smith's agitation." Esme paused for a moment. "The smith's daughter died without making a first cry."

Anna shook her head. "But I am here."

Esme smiled. "The lady of Haynesdale bore a girl, as well, a child who showed her determination early. She was a robust babe and one who yelled mightily to announce her arrival. She was her father's daughter, for the Captain of the Guard had been both bold and valiant, if not fearless."

Anna gasped.

"And so it was that the lady of Haynesdale feared for her daughter's life, guessing that Royce would not tolerate a bastard in his abode. She no longer trusted her husband, and when your mother confessed her loss, they two concocted a scheme. They traded their children in the night, the lady claiming the corpse as her own and the smith telling all that his wife had born a robust girl."

"Nay," Anna whispered, her heart thundering.

"The lady gave the crossbow to the smith, that you might know your legacy. None knew what would happen later, and once the smith and his wife died, there seemed little merit in telling you the tale."

"Does anyone else know it?"

"I do," Father Ignatius said from behind Anna. "And others suspect it. You have your father's air of command and his audacity."

Esme leaned closer to whisper. "You are nobly born, Anna, the daughter of a duke's youngest son and a baroness."

Anna looked between the two of them with astonishment, then spun to her feet. She could wed Bartholomew. Perhaps they could triumph together.

Perhaps she *would* kill Royce for him.

"I have to find Bartholomew. Where did he go?"

"He asked for direction to the old mill from here," Father Ignatius confided.

è♠

"There are women I would trust in such a situation, lad, but this Lady of Haynesdale is not one of them."

Bartholomew lay in the snow alongside Duncan, his chin on his gloved fist, watching the old mill. The sun was just past its zenith and naught moved in the old village save a herd of goats that wandered across the snow. A pair of villagers tended them without much interest, and they bleated as they dug beneath the fresh snow for fodder.

"I do not need to trust her, not if I follow Anna's scheme."

Duncan grimaced. "I think it risky to trust her even so far as that. She might be in alliance with her husband, for truly, she has as much to lose as he."

"There are many barriers between me and the barony."

"And the simplest solution for Sir Royce would be to see you dead now, before any of those obstacles are conquered."

Bartholomew granted his companion a glance. "Do not suggest that I break my word."

The older man shook his head. "You have no argument from me over the keeping of a pledge, lad. What other man of your acquaintance has spent years keeping his word, and traveled the breadth of Christendom to do it?"

"You have?"

"If Fergus has found trouble in my absence, my life is over as I know it," Duncan growled. "I swore to repay his father for saving my life, and so his father dispatched me to ensure his son returned from Outremer." Duncan glowered at the village before them. "If he has found some mischief to make it otherwise, when I could do naught about it, I will be vexed indeed."

"Fergus will return soon enough."

Duncan's brows rose. "And so I pray that it will be."

"Years keeping your word," Bartholomew echoed.

"And I did not regret a moment of it, not until we reached Paris."

"Why was that?"

"Because I found something I cared about other than my word, lad, but one commitment must be fulfilled before another can be made. You do not have to argue the matter with me."

Bartholomew considered the older man, wondering what he had found of greater import. "What did you find?"

"Who, lad. The question is who." Duncan smiled. "A wee lass with fire in her eyes." He sighed.

"Radegunde," Bartholomew guessed.

Duncan's eyes narrowed as he peered at the mill. "One pledge fulfilled before making another. That is all a man can do."

It startled Bartholomew to realize that he and Anna were not the sole lovers kept apart by circumstance. "When Fergus returns, I will ride to Killairic with you, and threaten his life that you might fulfill your pledge."

Duncan smiled. "I appreciate the offer, lad, but you have more than sufficient challenge before you."

That was true enough.

"Look," the Scotsman murmured. "She comes."

Bartholomew watched as Lady Marie arrived before the mill. She rode a fine mare, and her maids were on smaller palfreys. All glanced about themselves furtively. One seized the reins of her lady's horse, and the other dismounted, hastening into the mill with her lady. The second maid led the three horses away, taking cover in the forest.

"She guards the road to the new keep," Duncan murmured and cast Bartholomew a knowing glance. "The lady is well prepared for her assignation."

Bartholomew was studying the scene, wondering how best to ensure he was discovered. Anna's plan was a good one, but it relied upon the presence of someone trusted by the baron. "There," he murmured, pointing to a man who stepped out of the burned remnant of the old hall. He handed his crossbow to Duncan. "Let him follow me."

Duncan nodded. "If he does not enter the mill after I have counted to a hundred, I will drive him inside." He settled a bolt into the crossbow and cocked it.

Bartholomew recalled that he yet had the keys of Father Ignatius. If he was captured, they would be taken from him. He granted the ring to Duncan, who tucked it into his purse.

They exchanged a glance, then Bartholomew headed for the mill. He remained in the shelter of the forest, heading toward the maid who lingered on the road. He stepped into the clearing of the old village before reaching her, then hastened to the mill. He paused at the portal, ensuring that he was visible and was reassured to not be struck down. He took a deep breath, then entered the mill.

One way or the other, much would be resolved by the time Duncan counted to one hundred.

&

The mill might not have been the finest place for an assignation, but it was not all bad. Marie had chosen it with care. The mill was, first and foremost, sufficiently distant from the hall that Royce would not hear any evidence of what she did. It boasted several hiding spots large enough for a man, for the old granaries were intact. It was cold, but the roof was whole, and the great millstone was of the perfect height, in Marie's experience, for intercourse. She cast off her cloak and laid it on the millstone, even as Agnes watched the portal.

"He comes," the maid said softly.

Marie wrapped her arms about herself in the cold. The encounter would have to be quick. While she had consumed the potion that was said to aid in conception, Royce had declined to take more than a taste of the wine she had tainted at the board. He said he had much labor to do on his books, for the taxes would be sent to the crown soon, and had left the board early.

While that had solved the question of her leaving the keep without arousing his suspicion, he would not be asleep as she had schemed. There had been a time when she might have savored the risk, but not on this day.

Bartholomew stepped through the portal, narrowing his eyes against the comparative darkness of the mill. His gaze flicked past her, which did not please her overmuch, to the large chamber of the miller's house. He looked most intently at the floor, then at a distant window, which made no sense at all.

"Hasten yourself!" she said, stepped forward to seize his hand. "In here and it must be quickly done." She reached beneath his tabard but he caught her hand before she could unlace his chausses.

"There must be some romance," he protested, then smiled down at her. He raised his other hand to her cheek. "I would see you pleased, Lady Marie."

"There is no time for such pleasure," she insisted, reaching again for the front of his chausses. He backed her into the millstone, which was progress of a kind, and trapped her against him with his hips. All she could feel was his chain mail and it was cold enough to make her shiver anew.

He cupped her chin in his hand. "Beguile me," he invited, his voice low, and Marie ground her teeth.

"Take me," she retorted, tugging at the hem of her kirtle. "Before we are discovered."

He considered her, still holding her captive against the millstone, then removed his gloves, one finger at a time. Marie wriggled against him with impatience, but he took an age to cast them aside. He then eased the flat of his hand over her thigh, smiling as he pushed up her chemise and kirtle, baring the top of her stocking to view. He granted her a glittering glance, and she caught her breath at his allure. He caught her nape in his other hand, then bent to kiss her beneath the ear. Marie sighed and closed her eyes for a moment, wishing there could be more time for this encounter. She sensed a shadow and her eyes flew open.

"Nay!" she cried when she saw the man silhouetted in the portal. It was Gaultier, to be sure. He lifted a knife to throw it. She kicked Bartholomew aside and he scooped her up, just as the knife buried itself in the wall behind them. Agnes leaped for Gaultier, but he struck her in the face with his mailed fist.

Agnes fell to the floor, bleeding, and did not move again.

Marie's heart thundered in terror. Gaultier aimed to kill, not to maim. He unsheathed his sword and strode into the mill, his gaze fixed upon Bartholomew.

"You would take what is not your own," he growled.

Bartholomew drew his own sword, the blade glinting in the light. "I defend the lady's right to make a choice."

"She has no right to give her lord's property away," Gaultier replied. "And I have every right to defend what is his." The two men charged each other, their blades clashing with fury. Marie fell back and scrambled toward the portal. She fell beside her maid and felt for her pulse.

There was none, and the pool of blood grew ever larger.

Agnes was dead, dead for her loyalty to Marie.

What had she done?

The two knights fought fiercely, moving back and forth across the floor and striking savagely at each other. Marie watched in horror as Gaultier moved suddenly, tripping Bartholomew and flinging him against a wall. His blade was at Bartholomew's throat, and she knew he would kill the other knight. She could not believe that Bartholomew had been bested so readily, but she would not see him die as well.

"Nay!" Marie cried again, and Gaultier hesitated for a precious moment. "My lord husband will be vexed if you cheat him of his justice."

Gaultier smiled. He pressed his blade against Bartholomew's throat and Marie feared her protest had been in vain. She could see red blood running down the blade. "Drop your weapons, and the baron may decide your fate."

Bartholomew set down his sword, moving slowly and placing it on the floor. He removed his belt with his sheathed dagger, set it down as well, then straightened with his hands held high.

Gaultier chuckled, then prodded him to leave the mill, the tip of his blade at Bartholomew's back.

"My maid!" Marie protested.

"Someone will fetch her," the Captain of the Guard said with indifference. "Hasten yourself back to the keep, my lady, if you mean to survive this day."

"I would take his counsel," Bartholomew added and Gaultier struck him in the back of the head.

"You may give your opinion when you are asked for it," he snarled and Marie seized the opportunity to flee.

ॐ

Anna flung herself down into the snow beside Duncan.

The older man spared her a glance. "He follows your scheme, though I counseled against it. Did you come to see the outcome?"

"I came to help." She watched as Bartholomew stepped into the mill and heard Duncan begin to count beneath his breath. He lifted his bow and aimed it toward the old keep. Anna saw a man loitering there.

She loaded her own crossbow.

"I will not miss," Duncan said tightly.

245

"You cannot hit three," Anna replied.

"There is no one else in the clearing."

"Save the two goatherds, neither of whom is either Herve or Regan."

"Are you sure?"

"Herve is old and walks with a staff. I doubt he has suddenly had such a remarkable recovery from his rheumatism."

Duncan pursed his lips. "Not in this weather, to be sure."

"While his sister Regan is tiny, only as tall as my shoulder."

The Scotsman nodded. "And no one else tends the goats?"

"No one else wrought like a man-at-arms."

"Who shall we take first?"

"Leave the one in the ruined keep. He is of a size with Bartholomew and must be Gaultier."

"There would be repercussions from his demise, to be sure."

She nodded. "And no voice of reason to halt the others. Once he enters the mill, I will take the left one posing as a goatherd, and you the right. If others reveal themselves, we shall take them as we can."

"One maid is on the road with the horses, just in the cover of the forest."

"Aye, I could hear her. She must have been fearful for she talked to the steeds."

"The other is with Marie."

"I would not see either of them injured, nor even Marie," Anna said, even as Gaultier stepped away from the ruined keep. He moved quickly toward the mill, drawing a knife from his belt. He flattened himself against the wall outside the portal, surveyed the clearing, then abruptly ducked inside.

Marie screamed.

Duncan and Anna fired their crossbows as one. The two goatherds fell silently, then there was a roar from the direction of the road. The goats bleated and ran for the distant fields.

Three more warriors burst from the forest and raced for the mill. They looked smaller than the others, or perhaps younger, but it mattered little. They were armed.

Anna leaped to her feet and loaded another bolt. "Left," she muttered.

"Right," Duncan replied.

Again, two bolts flew through the air. Duncan's target moved suddenly and his bolt missed. Anna's sank into the chest of the assailant she had targeted. The two surviving men pivoted and raced toward them.

"After you," Duncan said, and Anna took her shot.

The one on the left fell with a cry after her bolt sank into his eye.

The one on the right tumbled to the ground a moment later, Duncan's bolt in his throat.

They both loaded their bows again and stood silent, listening.

They could hear swordplay coming from the mill, then it suddenly ceased. Marie screamed again, then there was silence.

Had Bartholomew succeeded in their plan?

Surely Marie would weep more loudly if her intended lover had been killed?

Surely Bartholomew would shout in triumph if he had killed Gaultier?

"Back," Duncan advised and they retreated to the forest. They had barely reached the undergrowth when Marie ran out of the mill. She fled up the road, undoubtedly toward the point where her maid waited. She was weeping.

But for whom?

Anna might have gone to find out but Duncan laid a hand on her arm. To her relief, Bartholomew appeared next, his hands held high. He had been divested of his belt and weapons, and Gaultier urged him forward at the point of a sword. The Captain of the Guard immediately spied his fallen troops and gave a shout. Four more men galloped out of the forest to encircle their commander. They led a fifth steed, though it was merely a palfrey. Gaultier bound Bartholomew's hands behind his back and mounted the horse with the empty saddle, then they cantered back toward the point where the road disappeared into the forest. Marie's wails could be heard, then the sound of the party moved toward the new keep.

"The shard of the true cross," Anna whispered to Duncan. "They cannot have that blade."

He grimaced, for he evidently had guessed what she would do. "Run, lass, for they will be back for their dead."

"Whistle if you see them," she said.

"Twice," Duncan agreed and gave her a sample. Anna nodded and raced toward the mill. She looked left and right before approaching the portal, then glanced back toward Duncan from the threshold. She could see no sign of him. She hastened into the shadowed interior, then halted in dismay at the sight of the fallen maid.

She bent and touched the other woman's throat, but she was dead.

Anna crossed herself, then surveyed the interior. She could see the glimmer of a scabbard on the far side of the common room. She hastened toward it, well aware that she might not have long, and recognized Bartholomew's belt and scabbard. His dagger was still in its scabbard but his sword was on the floor. She slid it into the scabbard, astonished by its weight, then heard a double whistle.

She stood and heard the approach of hoof beats.

The granary!

Anna leaped up the stairs, wincing when a step creaked in protest. She flung herself into one of the large lidded storage bins and lowered the lid. She laid Bartholomew's belt on the floor before herself and loaded her crossbow, pointing the tip of the bolt at the rim of the bin.

If any soul were fool enough to open it, he would have a bolt in his eye as reward. From such close range, it might well pass right through his skull.

She hoped it was Gaultier.

Anna held her breath and waited.

The hoof beats halted outside the door and she heard the scuffle of boots on the stone threshold. "Aye, she is dead enough, to be sure," a man said, then raised his voice. "Fetch the wagon from the keep. I see three fallen near the road and there must be another two men."

"Aye, sir!" Hoof beats raced away.

Anna listened. How many had come into the mill? What did they do while they waited? She heard boots on the floor, and thought there was more than one man nearby.

"Three squires and two knights dead this day," grumbled one man. "There will be a price to pay for that, mark my words."

"Do not forget the maid. She was a fetching one," a man said with regret.

"Aye, you always fancy the ones you cannot have," said the other.

One pair of footsteps drew closer.

"Why would she come to this place? It is primitive and cold."

"But no one would hear her cry in pleasure."

"She will cry on this night, you may be certain. He will beat her black and blue."

"He might give her to us."

"Nay, not his legal wife." The man's voice brightened. "But maybe her other maid, as a lesson."

"If so, Gaultier will take her first, and what he leaves will not be worth the sharing."

Anna shuddered at the truth of that.

"I suppose I will have to go with the taxes now," said one man without real pleasure. The other man murmured something and though Anna strained her ears, she could not discern his words. She lifted the lid of the granary with the top of her head, just slightly, so she could hear better.

One man laughed. "Aye, you are right. Whether it is Winchester or London, there will be more whores there than here."

"What if we have to take it to Anjou?"

"You should be so lucky as to have a French whore for one night in your life."

"Maybe I should seduce Lady Marie."

"This is a gamble not worth the taking." Their voices grew louder and Anna ducked lower, easing the lid down.

"What is this?" the man asked in closer proximity. "Someone climbed these stairs this day. Look at the dust!"

"Small footsteps," agreed the other man. "Not the knight."

"Maybe the lady thought to have him there."

"Maybe she sought a fine bed."

They laughed as one, even as Anna sat like a woman struck to stone. She scarce dared to breathe. She closed one hand around the cold pommel of Bartholomew's sword, and prayed with all her heart that they not find her.

"What is up there, anyway?"

There was the creak of a boot on the stair, then the clatter of hoof beats. Anna heard the groan of a wagon's wheels, then the sound of a body being cast into it.

"Well?" shouted a man outside the mill. "Is there another in here?"

"Aye, there is," agreed one of the men in the mill and the pair of them departed. Anna closed her eyes in relief. When she heard the party ride away, she bent and kissed the pommel in gratitude.

Though she did not leave her hiding place until she heard Duncan's voice an eternity later. "Lass?" he demanded in a hoarse whisper. "We can be away now, if you move with haste."

Anna did not need a second invitation.

۶

Marie was seething.

How dare Royce interfere with her scheme and deny her any opportunity for escape from this foul hole?

She retreated to her chamber as if retiring for the night, well aware that Royce expected her to weep for her lost lover. He came to her, of course, intent upon proving his ownership and sated himself with tedious speed.

She pretended to sleep when he was done, and was glad to hear him leave. She smiled when he locked the portal to her chamber from the outside.

There were moments when it was good fortune to be wedded to a stupid man. Marie waited until the stairs had finished their creaking, until the floor overhead groaned beneath Royce's bed. She waited until the squires had finished their scampering, and the tower had grown quiet.

Then she rose and retrieved the key she had stolen years before. It fit perfectly into the lock and the portal was opened with nary a sound. Emma followed her, keeping her distance at Marie's gesture.

They reached the great hall, which had fallen into shadows. Only one candle burned at the high table. Gaultier stood there alone, his tabard mired and his hair disheveled. He lifted the cup that she had not deigned to empty at midday and drained it. Marie drew back into the shadows, unable to believe her good fortune.

Or her husband's frugality.

Gaultier loved his wine, but Royce seldom shared with his men.

The Captain of the Guard cast a furtive glance over his shoulder, then drank the rest of the wine from the other abandoned cup on the board. He smiled when he lifted the small pitcher that had been poured for Royce and Marie, the one she had treated with the sleeping potion. He poured its contents into Royce's cup and downed it, scarcely savoring it at all.

He had consumed two doses of the sleeping draught, perhaps on an empty belly. Marie hovered in the shadows, watching and hoping.

She did not have to wait long to learn that Finan's concoction was potent.

Saturday, January 23, 1188

Feast Day of virgin martyr Saint Emerentiana.

಄

Chapter Thirteen

Bartholomew ached in places he had not known he possessed. He would have sworn that his fingernails hurt, that his hair was bruised, that his very marrow had been smashed. Gaultier had been thorough in his beating, and Bartholomew had been tied down to ensure he could not defend himself.

Had he lost a tooth? All he could taste was blood and his lips were so swollen that he could not tell.

He understood now why Duncan had not been quick on his feet in their departure from Haynesdale. The dungeon was damp and dark, but his one eye was nigh swollen shut. Worst of all, Gaultier had discovered the mark on his chest. If he had not been condemned before, the mark sealed it.

The seed of Nicholas must die.

Bartholomew had been divested of his mail hauberk and aketon, then flung down into the dungeon. He lay on the dirt floor. He fought the desire to moan and could not help wishing that he did not awaken in the morning.

All was lost.

He had failed to fulfill Anna's scheme. He had betrayed his parents' memory. The people of Haynesdale would suffer for his arrival here, and it seemed there was naught of merit to result from his days.

He had many hours to consider his folly in the night, but in the end, he feared the night would be too short. He was to be hung at dawn. This was Royce's justice and his heart ached that the people of Haynesdale would have to endure it forever.

The trap door overhead opened suddenly, loosing a beam of light into the dungeon that stabbed him in the eye. Bartholomew did moan then and rolled toward the darkness. It could not be morning yet, could it?

He moved just in time, for another man was cast down into the dungeon. The body hit the dirt floor hard, but his new companion made no sound of protest.

Was it a corpse?

Bartholomew drew back in disgust, but the rope ladder was suddenly cast down from the opening. He could see a woman descending with purpose and in silence. She gestured to him with a stern finger for silence.

It was Marie's maid.

"Hasten yourselves!" the lady herself hissed from the floor above. She held a lantern so its light shone down into the pit.

Bartholomew sat up with interest. He saw that the other man was Gaultier and no longer regretted his fate. That man rolled to his back and stirred, grumbling as he made to open his eyes.

The maid punched him in the face, showing unexpected strength. Her lips were tight and her expression furious. Gaultier fell back with a low moan and she struck him again. Bartholomew heard a bone crack. She then came to Bartholomew and untied his hands. She tugged at the hem of his tabard.

"Take all of it off," she commanded in French. "You will leave this hole as Gaultier."

The ruse was enough to have Bartholomew on his feet, filled with new purpose. He stripped off his tabard and chemise. "But we do not resemble each other that much," he argued quietly.

"You will when we are done," replied the maid. "It has been commanded at the lady's request that the prisoner will be hooded for his execution so none will know until it is too late." She took a steadying breath as she offered him Gaultier's tabard. "And Agnes will be avenged."

Bartholomew was astonished. Gaultier would die instead of him? He did find the notion of Royce executing his own Captain of the Guard most fitting. He would not weep for this man who had so abused Anna and killed Agnes.

In moments, he and Gaultier wore each other's garb. They were of a size, fortunately, for the maid insisted that even their boots be exchanged.

She then seized his chin, turning it toward the light. "His left eye must be pummeled so that it swells like yours. He needs a bruise on his jaw, just so. I would do it myself if I had the strength," she added and Bartholomew did not doubt it. She lifted his hands. "Break these two fingers, as well."

"But he did not break mine, not quite."

"He tried and it will be remembered." The maid was grim. "They document injuries in this place."

"He may protest," Bartholomew noted. "Or cry out for aid."

She chuckled. "He will sleep at least two days, thanks to the potion. It was made for two men, but he drank nigh all of it." Indeed, his tabard smelled of spilled wine. He must have fallen under the influence of the potion when there was still a measure in the cup. His revival in the dungeon must have been his body's last protest against the brew.

Bartholomew nodded, well content with this plan. Indeed, he found it most satisfying to ensure that Gaultier's injuries matched his own.

It was not long before he had climbed the rope ladder to the keep. Lady Marie met him there, her eyes glowing. "So you are the true son of Nicholas!" she breathed. "And rightful Baron of Haynesdale!"

Bartholomew glanced left and right, not wanting to discuss the matter when another might overhear them.

Marie kissed his cheek with undisguised satisfaction. "The future is ours, sir. I will ensure it."

Anna's plan came to rights, but Bartholomew felt little joy in the achievement. A future bound to Marie was not one he yearned to have, but it seemed to be the sole way he might survive. He recalled Gaston's diplomacy and said little, making no promises.

This did not seem to trouble Marie.

He was soon in Gaultier's own bed, with that man's cloak wrapped around him and his hood pulled over his face. He rolled to face the wall, far more comfortable than he had been in the dungeon. Marie kissed his cheek again, her anticipation clear, and he thanked her gruffly for her aid.

The women swept away, the patter of their footfalls fading quickly. The night watch called the hour, and the sentry's voice echoed through the hall.

Otherwise, all was silent.

Yet Bartholomew was wide awake. The tide was changing and he dared not sleep until all was won.

ða

"We have to save him," Anna insisted yet again. She was vexed beyond belief, fearful of Bartholomew's condition and unhappy that there was evidently naught she could do to help him.

"And how do you suggest the feat be accomplished?" Duncan asked one more time, his impatience clear. He reiterated his objections, and it helped little that Anna agreed with all of them. "There is no way into the keep save through the gate. The sewer can only be used for an escape. And no living soul will pass through that gate unseen." He shook his head. "Even with two knights dead and three squires, the keep is yet well armed."

Those in the forest had gathered to confer as soon as Duncan and Anna had returned. They had remained awake all of the night, debating their course. The young boys had immediately gone to the old village to ensure that both Herve and Regan were uninjured, and had helped them to collect the herd of goats again before night had fallen.

"Royce baits a trap for us," Edgar says with surety and not for the first time. "He anticipates that we will try to save the true son and will kill us all for it."

"He will kill Bartholomew first," added Stewart grimly. "Mark my words."

"Unless he kills him slowly," added Edgar, which did little to improve the mood of the company.

Anna swore softly and paced. The snow had melted away in her established path, but still she walked restlessly. "There *must* be a way. Royce will send the taxes to the king soon, by the word of the guards, and we can ensure that wagon never leaves the forest." She turned to face the others, flinging out her hands. "That coin could pay the escheat!"

"But Bartholomew will be dead by then, unless we contrive a way to save him," Lucan said, his manner sober.

"He might escape!" Percy suggested.

The entire company shook their heads as one. "There is no way out of that dungeon alone, lad," Duncan said, then ruffled the boy's hair. "It is a well-designed prison, to be sure."

"But someone might have aided him," the boy insisted.

"Who in that place would aspire to see justice served?" Edgar demanded. "If there was a man who believed in any thing other than his own survival in that place, he would have defied Sir Royce already."

"And been slaughtered for it already," agreed Stewart.

Anna paced anew, then turned to confront them. "What if one of the guards left the hall? What if he could be captured, and one of us take his place? Then we could aid Bartholomew."

Duncan frowned. "He would not only have to leave the hall, but be out of sight of the sentries." He shook his head. "They will not leave the keep."

"We could draw them out," Anna insisted. "We could set fire to something Royce values."

"The mill?" Stewart suggested.

Edgar winced. "He will not see the blaze until the building is nigh destroyed, for the old village is too far away. I say it is not worth the sacrifice." He raised a finger. "One day, we may have a good baron and be restored to our village, and then we will need the mill." His words fell into silence, for with Bartholomew captive, none had much hope of that good baron appearing.

Anna sat down hard. "We cannot fail. Not now that the true son is returned." The ring on the lace around her neck seemed heavier on this morning.

Father Ignatius cleared his throat. "Where are my keys?"

Duncan reached into his belt and offered them to the priest, his expression revealing that he had forgotten they were in his possession. Bartholomew must have granted them to him.

The priest fingered them, then held up one of the smaller ones. "This unlocks the portal near the chapel."

The others straightened with interest. Perhaps they, like Anna, had forgotten about it.

"But Bartholomew used it. They will watch that path," Anna protested.

The priest squared his shoulders. "I will wager that they will not kill a priest come alone to offer last rites to a condemned prisoner."

All gazes turned to him. Anna bit her lip. "They might only hesitate."

"It might be long enough." Father Ignatius then removed two other keys and tucked them into the small purse that hung from his belt. The ring of keys he carried openly. He glanced down at the ring then blinked with feigned surprise. "The key to the chapel and its treasury appear to have been lost."

Anna bit back a smile. She had not realized the priest could be deceptive.

Nor that he would take such a risk.

"Yours is a doughty wager," Duncan murmured. "I am not certain I would take it."

"But I will," Father Ignatius said with conviction. He straightened, his eyes filled with fire. "I will."

❧

The guards tried to rouse Bartholomew, but he grunted in protest and remained rolled in Gaultier's cloak. His face was well hidden, but evidently, they were convinced by his garb that he was the other man. There were many jibes and jests, but finally, they left him alone.

"He will regret that he does not see this one swing," said one warrior.

"I wager that he regrets the wine yet more," countered another. "Do you not smell it on him?" They laughed together and went to the dungeon to gather the prisoner.

Bartholomew waited until he was alone, then marched to the armory, keeping his hood high. It was just past dawn, the sky growing light with the promise of another fine day. The man on duty at the armory bowed, but did not turn from his post. Bartholomew nodded then strode past him, as if fetching a weapon.

He pivoted in the shadows to watch.

The guard's interest was captured by the sight of the prisoner being urged to the summit of the curtain wall. Gaultier was hooded and staggered, making incoherent protests as they pushed him onward. Evidently, the potion still held him in thrall. The guards were rough with him and he was struck repeatedly as he was led to his demise. They mocked him as the son of the true baron and tripped him more than once.

The sentry outside the armory chuckled.

It was almost too easy to assault him from behind when all eyes were on Gaultier. Bartholomew had him trussed and silenced in a heartbeat, then stole his helm and left him hidden in the back of the armory. He took the other man's place and watched with satisfaction as the rope was fitted around Gaultier's neck.

He had taken the man's place not a moment too soon.

Royce appeared in the portal to the hall, sipping from his chalice as he crossed the bailey. Three men were loading a wagon with trunks that appeared to be heavy despite their small size. Royce paused to offer advice to the knights wearing his colors, who evidently were going to escort the wagon.

What was it?

Where was it going?

When all was evidently as he desired, Royce strolled to the middle of the bailey. He ensured that he had a fine view when Gaultier was dragged to the summit. That man cried out incoherently, but the baron simply waved a hand. It was a signal, for Gaultier was immediately shoved from the parapet. There was a thump as the Captain of the Guard's body collided with the inside of the curtain wall, and he thrashed at the end of the rope for horrifying moments.

Then he went limp.

Bartholomew saw a trail of blood drip down the wall but could not regret the passing of that villain.

"Display his corpse!" Royce cried. "Be sure the renegades in the forest know that their leader is dead!" He spat into the bailey. "And there is the last of Nicholas' seed."

Royce returned to supervise the loading of the wagon. The body was hauled up again, then cast over the outside of the curtain wall beside the gate, still hanging from that rope. Bartholomew supposed the hanging had been on the inside of the bailey so Royce could witness it.

He was pondering his path when he heard a slight sound behind him. He was alert when someone tried to seize him from behind.

Bartholomew spun and had his blade at the assailant's throat before he realized it was Father Ignatius. The priest had seized a knife in the armory, but he knew little of such fighting. Bartholomew flung the priest aside and out of harm's way, then flipped up the visor of the helm. The priest had made to attack him again, but halted in sudden recognition.

"I thought I had come too late!" he said with pleasure.

Bartholomew had no chance to reply.

"What is amiss there?" Royce cried, having heard the scuffle.

"I must remain hidden," Bartholomew murmured.

"Of course," the priest agreed.

Bartholomew seized Father Ignatius and shoved him into the bailey. "The priest, my lord," he said, trying to imitate Gaultier's voice. He hoped the helm helped disguise the truth.

"How diligent you are, Gaultier," Royce said. "I had thought you would be on the parapet this morn."

"The armory was undefended, my lord," he replied gruffly. He shoved Father Ignatius forward. "Doubtless, he came to offer last rites."

"But is too late for such a ritual." The baron strolled closer, still sipping from his chalice, his eyes narrowed with suspicion. "I thought you had abandoned us, Father."

"I have been ill, no more than that," the priest said. "I would not have put the health of you or Lady Marie in peril."

Royce pursed his lips, his skepticism clear. "Then you know naught of the attempted theft of the reliquary from the chapel?"

"I know that my keys are missing," Father Ignatius said. He lifted the ring hanging now from his belt, and Bartholomew saw that it had only three keys. "I thought I had misplaced them but when I found them again, the keys to both chapel and chapel treasury were missing."

Royce considered this for such a long moment that Bartholomew feared he would not accept the explanation.

What of the key to the portal in the wall?

He held his breath, fearing Father Ignatius would be caught in his lie, but Royce only frowned.

"Let him go, Gaultier," he commanded, then addressed the priest. "My lady wife's maid died yesterday and I am certain she would appreciate your solace. Perhaps you might say a prayer for Agnes."

"It would be my pleasure, sir. If you could unlock the chapel, we might celebrate a mass for her."

Royce nodded and indicated that Father Ignatius should precede him to the chapel. "Watch him," he commanded Bartholomew. "I believe he lies, but it is unwise to be quick to kill a priest."

"True enough, my lord."

"But if he gives you any cause for further suspicion, do not hesitate to act."

Bartholomew bowed agreement. He eyed the men who milled around the cart, waiting while the squires harnessed the horses that would pull it forth.

He had to go with the wagon.

He had to take the place of one of those men.

Royce cleared his throat. "Gaultier?" he said, then gestured to the interior. "I granted you a command! First, you sleep late, then you ignore an order!"

Bartholomew mumbled an apology.

There was naught for it. If he revealed himself in this moment, there were too many men who could defend Royce.

"Of course, my lord." Bartholomew bowed and headed for the chapel. He turned at the threshold to find Royce still watching him, then entered and pulled the door closed behind him.

Father Ignatius began to pray loudly over the coffin at the altar. Bartholomew waited only a moment before he opened the door an increment.

The gates were being opened and Royce stood peering out at the forest beyond. One of the knights by the wagon laughed with his fellows, then strode toward the sewer at the back of the stables, lifting the hem of his tabard as he walked.

Here was his chance.

ào

"Nay," Anna whispered when she saw the corpse hanging from Haynesdale's curtain wall. Her throat tightened and her tears rose, for she would have recognized Bartholomew's tabard in any place. He could not be dead!

They could not have arrived too late.

Her heart struggled against the notion that Bartholomew breathed no more. Would she not have known instinctively that he was gone? It seemed impossible that he was no longer of this earth.

Yet the corpse could be naught other than what it was. His tabard and boots were unmistakably his own. She might be a coward but she was glad of the hood, for she did not want to see his face after he had been hanged.

"Aye," Duncan murmured and dropped his brow to his gloved hand.

They were hidden in the undergrowth of the forest opposite the gate of Haynesdale. The sun had barely risen from the horizon, yet Bartholomew had already been executed.

Anna felt the despair of the other villagers behind her and heard Percy sniffle.

The portcullis opened slowly, the rope creaking as the iron gate was drawn up. Anna nestled lower in the snow, wondering what transpired. Royce strode out of the gate and propped his hands upon his hips. He shouted in a booming voice. "Behold Luc Bartholomew, the only son of Baron Nicholas, hung until he was dead for possessing the audacity to assault my lady wife." His voice became louder. "There will be no other Baron of Haynesdale, save me, from this day forward. Do not defy me again, or your lives will become worse than they already are. There will be no more mercy shown to vagabonds and outlaws. Return to the village this day and become loyal villeins—or die!"

He pivoted and returned to the keep as the villagers muttered to each other. "He never had any mercy," Stewart grumbled.

"So, naught has changed," agreed Edgar.

When Anna expected the portcullis to close again, a pair of horses rode beneath it. Knights in Royce's colors rode the two stallions. A pair of palfreys pulled a wagon, one man-at-arms at the reins and two more riding at the back of the wagon. One of them might have been a squire, for he was smaller. Another pair of horses rode behind, warriors mounted on their saddles.

"The taxes," Anna whispered.

Duncan rubbed his mouth. "Is the reliquary dispatched to the king or yet within the walls?" he murmured.

"Father Ignatius will claim it, I am certain." Anna eased back into the undergrowth, edging away from the road. She knew what she had to do.

"Where do you go?" Edgar asked in an undertone.

She cast him a grim look. "To the bend in the road. That wagon will not arrive at its destination."

"But without Bartholomew, we have no need of coin for the escheat," Duncan protested. "We must find the reliquary."

Anna shook her head. "Royce cares solely for his gold and his taxes. He has taken the one person I loved most, so I shall take what he loves most."

"It would be fitting vengeance," Edgar agreed, then followed Anna.

"I would see him cheated of his desire," Stewart added.

"I would see him discredited before the king," added Lucan. "A baron who does not pay his taxes will not remain baron long."

"It might be our best hope for change!" said Rowe and there was a chorus of assent.

They gathered around Anna, murmuring to each other of their enthusiasm for her ploy. Only Duncan did not move.

"Will you not join us?" Anna asked.

The Scotsman shook his head. "He taunted us," he said softly and the company sobered. "What if it is a trap?"

"Or a feint," Anna agreed, seeing his logic. She crouched down beside the older man. "Let us divide our ranks. Half shall go with me to attack the wagon. The rest shall remain with you, in case there is a second wagon to depart or some opportunity created by Father Ignatius to see Bartholomew avenged."

"I must reclaim the reliquary," Duncan insisted. "It was my responsibility to defend it."

"So, we are agreed, then," Anna said to the others. "The first priority must be to save the reliquary. Beyond that, all damage we can do to Royce is welcome. It will be our vengeance for the death of Bartholomew."

They nodded with resolve, and it was only moments later that she led one band through the forest. Percy remained in Duncan's care. Her company flitted like shadows through the forest, taking a shorter and more direct path, toward the bend in the road.

Anna fully intended that the blow they dealt to Royce was severe.

❧

The smell of cedar rose to Father Ignatius' nostrils from the coffin in the chapel. A candle burned on the altar, as if to keep the fallen in the light. He lifted the lid and winced at the injury that had been dealt to the maid who lay there. Even though she had been cleaned for burial, the savagery of the wound could not be disguised.

He felt Lady Marie come to stand beside him. Her maid came to stand on his other side and bumped against him as if she stumbled. He caught her elbow and she bowed her head, weeping. He supposed the two maids must have been close and the death of one would be difficult for the other to bear.

"I tire of living with barbarians," Lady Marie said through her teeth and he saw the tears in her eyes as she surveyed the dead maid. The other maid fell to her knees before the altar. "I will linger in this hole no longer."

The lady was resolute, hatred for her husband shining in her eyes.

"How will you depart? How will you see yourself defended?" Father Ignatius asked and Lady Marie smiled.

"It is best you do not know, Father, for you might be compelled to speak the truth when it is not convenient."

There was merit in that argument.

"Where is the reliquary?" he murmured, his glance darting to the treasury beside the altar. The door to the cabinet hung askew, revealing that the space was empty.

"He means to send it to the king as a gift," she said through her teeth.

The priest took a step toward the portal. "But the taxes are being dispatched to the king. We must hasten to intervene!"

Would Bartholomew discover its presence in time?

Was that why he had left the chapel?

Marie shook her head. "Nay, that wagon is a trick, intended to lure the rebels in the forest so they can be captured. Those trunks are filled with stones. Both taxes and gift will be dispatched only when the road is deemed to be safe."

Father Ignatius feared then for Anna and her fellows.

"But where is the reliquary?"

"He keeps his treasury close, stored in his chamber at the summit of the tower. No man can enter that place without Royce's express permission."

How could Father Ignatius retrieve the reliquary then?

Lady Marie leaned closer. "I would see Royce cheated of all he has stolen and cast out naked in the night, if it is the last deed I do." She raised her gaze to that of Father Ignatius. "This keep was built with my inheritance, a prison wrought for me of my father's coin! I will reclaim my dowry that I might wed the man I desire to father my sons."

"I would ask, my lady, for your aid in ensuring that the reliquary is returned to its custodians. It is not an item that would be wise to mislay."

The lady smiled and parted her robe. Around her waist was slung a round bundle that could only be what he most desired. "Our thoughts are as one, Father. I meant to offer this to you as a gift, in thanks for your silence about my choice."

"You have it, my lady."

She surrendered the reliquary to him, pausing to kiss the edge of the bundle. "Perhaps you might request the aid of Saint Euphemia in ensuring the cause of righteousness is served."

"But how shall it be taken from this keep without any noting it?"

Lady Marie dropped her hand to the coffin, her gaze knowing. Father Ignatius might have simply set the prize inside the box, but the lady lifted her dead maid's skirts. She placed the bundle on Agnes' belly, beneath her folded hands. It looked as if she had been with child when she passed away, yet not so far along that the fullness of her kirtle might not have hidden it. "No one truly looks at a maid," Marie murmured and gathered the fabric around Agnes' hips to disguise the bump yet more.

Father Ignatius heard the other maid inhale sharply and guessed that she was offended. The lady did not appear to notice.

She bent and kissed the dead maid's brow. "Still, you serve me," she murmured. "Godspeed to you, Agnes."

Father Ignatius gave a blessing and the lid was closed again.

The lady spoke more loudly then. "Emma, we must see that Agnes is laid to her eternal rest. I know that my lord husband has other concerns this day, but would not delay in fulfilling my duty to Agnes. Would you aid me in retrieving her belongings, that they might be distributed to the poor?" She met Father Ignatius' gaze steadily. "Could you give the final blessing at the old cemetery, Father? Perhaps at midday?"

"Of course, my lady." He understood that he was to take the responsibility for smuggling the prize through the gates. The ruse was a good one, and the risk well worth the prize. He had to remind himself of such in an effort to steady the flutter of his heart. Father Ignatius had never been a bold man, but the cause of righteousness demanded that he do as much this time. He prayed for boldness as well as Agnes' soul while the lady turned to leave left the chapel.

"Oh! Have you a key to the chapel, Father?" the lady asked sweetly, turning to face him. "I would see it locked after your departure, the better to ensure that Royce is confounded in his search for it."

"Surely Sir Royce also has a key."

"I will claim that, as well." The lady put out her hand, her manner imperious.

Father Ignatius could only trust her in the details of her scheme. He retrieved the hidden key and granted it to her. She smiled and pivoted, quickly leaving the chapel.

He took a deep breath and eyed the coffin, preparing himself for the bold deed he must do.

But it proved that Father Ignatius had misunderstood the lady's intent.

He heard the key turn in the lock of the portal and spun in dismay. He knocked on the portal, but the lady laughed softly. "No one will ever again cheat me of my due, Father. I may need this prize to negotiate all that I would make my own, and you will not have the chance to take it from me."

Father Ignatius' hand dropped to the ring of keys on his belt out of habit, but it was gone. Too late he recalled that the maid had collided with him. She had stolen his keys!

And Lady Marie had requested the one that was missing from the ring.

He had only the key to the empty sanctuary by the altar.

"My lady!" he protested and tried to force the door. It was of considerable weight and the lock was good.

Father Ignatius bent and peered through the keyhole. He could discern Lady Marie striding away. The maid cast an impish smile over her shoulder and Father Ignatius felt a shadow of dread slide over his heart.

Did Lady Marie mean to betray him?

What was her intent?

He saw the wagon leave the bailey, accompanied by Royce's men. Was Bartholomew amongst them?

He pivoted and leaned against the door, surveying the small windowless chapel with dissatisfaction. What could he do to help?

For once in all his days, Father Ignatius found prayer to be a less than compelling choice.

ەۈ

The wagon came around the bend of the road, just as Anna had anticipated. The party did not ride as tightly together as they should have done, which would make matters simpler.

They would be easy to divide. She eased from behind the tree with her loaded crossbow. Edgar did the same, though he was not so good a shot as she. She saw his nod, then Norton and Piers erupted from the forest. The boys leaped for the backs of the horses pulling the wagon even as the men guarding the load cried out.

She and Edgar both let their bolts fly.

Anna's hit the lead knight in the throat. He fell from his steed to bleed in the road and did not rise again. His destrier reared, whinnied in fear, and galloped down the road, his reins trailing. The steed of the other knight ahead of the wagon bolted in terror, despite his rider's efforts to hold him back.

Edgar's bolt struck the driver of the wagon in the shoulder. That man had moved in the last moment, startled by boys' appearance, and he wrestled with the shaft of the bolt even as he tried to hold back the horses. The boys beat the rumps of the horses pulling the wagon and they were only too glad to gallop after their fellows.

Anna saw the larger man from the back of the wagon move forward, undoubtedly to help his companion, just as the remaining warriors charged the forest. Stewart sliced down the first of them with his blade, the other village men dropping from trees and throwing rocks to halt their attack.

Anna fled through the forest, intending to cut off the wagon at the next curve. She burst from the trees just as it was rolling past and leaped on to the wagon. She struck the smaller guard in the back, who was a squire, then kicked him off the wagon. The boy scrambled to his feet and ran back toward the keep, and Anna swore that he was out of her range. She hoped Edgar would stop him.

The guard from the back of the wagon had reached the front. To her astonishment, he seized the reins from the driver, then punched that man in the face.

The driver tumbled into the road.

Anna shot him in the throat before he could get to his feet. She then leaped for the guard who now held the reins and got one arm around his throat.

"Norton and Piers!" he bellowed. "Slow the horses!"

The fiend knew the boys' names! She tipped up his helmet to better slit his throat and he swore when his vision was obscured. The cart began to lurch toward the ditch. She held fast to his neck and reached for her knife. He jabbed her in the ribs, twisting in her grip as he swore with greater vehemence.

"This is not the time, Anna!" he growled and she froze at the familiarity of his voice.

"Bartholomew?" she asked in astonishment. "But you are dead!"

"Not quite yet," that knight muttered. "Though it appears you would see the matter changed." He pulled hard on the reins even as Anna tried to accept this happy news. The horses slowed, but the wagon was too close to the side of the road. It rolled to a halt but one wheel went into the ditch. The wagon tipped so that the trunks in the back slid to one side. The shifting weight made the cart tumble to one side and Anna leaped from it with Bartholomew as the trunks spilled into the dirt.

The others were gone, and she did not doubt that lead knight would return. "Tell me, Anna, what did I do to earn such a greeting?" Bartholomew demanded, that familiar thread of humor in his tone, when they stood in the forest. "I thought you liked me." He winked and soothed the horses.

Anna laughed in her relief, unable to believe her ears. He cast off the helm and smiled at her, his eyes twinkling, and she flung herself into his embrace with relief. "I thought you dead!"

"I have felt more hale in my time, to be sure," he said and kissed her quickly. His eye was blackened and his face was cut, but she thought he looked as rakish and handsome as ever. He broke their kiss all too soon and flicked a glance at the forest. "Where are the others? There were two guards behind and one yet ahead..."

A growl emitted from the undergrowth and they turned as one

to see Cenric, his teeth bared and his hackles raised. He looked down the road and Anna spun to see that other lead knight approaching.

She had no more bolts.

Bartholomew had seized the driver's crossbow from the wagon, though, and loaded a bolt from the quiver there. He fired, then pushed her head down. Anna smiled at the sound of the knight falling from his stallion's saddle. The horse trotted toward them, its ears flicking, and at Bartholomew's glance, the boys seized its reins and soothed it to a walk.

"What about the gold?" Norton demanded, reaching for the trunks that had fallen into the dirt.

"There is none, not on this wagon," Bartholomew said. Norton had opened a trunk as Bartholomew replied, revealing a collection of rocks inside. Anna gasped. "Let us find the others before I explain."

With some effort, they got the wagon back on the road. They stacked the trunks much as they had been. Bartholomew turned the wagon around and they soon came upon Edgar and the others. One of Royce's warriors was dead and the surviving man-at-arms was bound. The squire, it seemed, had seized a horse and evaded them all. The group milled around the cart, disappointed at the sight of all the stones.

"Royce sends us an arsenal," Bartholomew said. "And a means to return to the keep."

"Your bold ploy is for naught," the man-at-arms said with a sneer. "Sir Royce is not the fool you believe him to be. He fully expects you to return."

"I have been there already and evaded him," Bartholomew said. "I even spoke to him directly. I think you over-estimate the wit of your lord baron."

"The boy will warn him," Edgar said, his manner dour.

"What of the reliquary?" Anna demanded of the man-at-arms.

"Safe from your kind," that warrior replied and spat on the ground.

Edgar pulled his knife and slit the man's throat, casting his body aside. "Safe from your kind, more like." He shoved the man into the ditch, then granted Bartholomew a rueful glance. "Such men do not deserve to live."

"Nay," Bartholomew agreed. "But our task is only half complete."

"We need the gold!"

"We need the reliquary!"

"Strip them of their tabards?" Anna asked, fully anticipating his reply.

"Hide the bodies and take their places," Bartholomew agreed, then gestured to them all. "Then bind these prisoners, these outcasts from the village who live in the forest."

Edgar looked between them in confusion. "We are going into the keep? As prisoners? Have you changed your thinking, sir?"

"It is the best way to see this matter resolved," Bartholomew said. "Royce expects his men to return from this feint with prisoners. We shall give every appearance of taking him some." Then he smiled, the twinkle in his eye reassuring Anna that it would be Royce who was surprised.

"They do not know the tale," Anna reminded him and he nodded.

"This cart is a trick," Bartholomew informed the villagers. "I had thought it carried the taxes to the king, so ensured I was among its guards, but they talked on the way of their true quest. The plan was that they would draw you out of the forest, capture you all and return to the keep. The real treasure will leave after this wagon arrives at the keep."

"With prisoners," Edgar said with understanding.

"And what of the reliquary?" Stewart demanded.

"It must be in Royce's treasury or his chambers." Bartholomew paused and Anna knew he did not want to endanger the group unnecessarily. "I would suggest we return to the keep, with all of you apparently taken captive, then reclaim the treasure from inside. We will overwhelm them and seize as much as we can of Royce's prizes."

"It will be risky," Stewart said.

"But it is the sole way to see our ends achieved," Anna replied.

Bartholomew surveyed the villagers. "I would not compel you to take such a risk. If you wish to forgo this quest, the choice is yours."

Anna looked over the company and saw that there was no doubt.

"We are with you!" she declared, smiling at the chorus of agreement that followed her words.

"We should make haste, for the squire did manage to ride back that way," Edgar noted. "He might well warn them."

"Or Duncan might ensure he does not arrive," Anna said, telling Bartholomew how they had divided their forces.

"A fine scheme," Bartholomew said with approval. "Hide the fallen men in the forest, but bring their tabards. Make haste!"

Edgar pulled one such over his head, then donned that man's helm. He cast an eye over the company and granted tabards to those villagers who looked to be of similar size to the fallen men. Meanwhile, Bartholomew bade the boys to tether the horses to the back of the wagon. He unfurled a length of rope, and Lucan showed the villagers a knot that looked doughty but could easily be slipped. Within moments, a trail of villagers was apparently bound to the back of the wagon, but they could easily free themselves. Anna had ensured that there were no signs of the scuffle remaining on the road, and had gathered a few bolts to be re-used.

"I count four knights yet at the keep," Bartholomew said tersely. "Six men-at-arms, though I left two bound in the armory."

"They might have been freed," Anna said and he nodded.

"Then there is the one squire that fled back from here."

"As well as the other squires," Anna reminded him. "The place is thick with them."

"They will be armed and trained," Bartholomew said to the villagers who nodded understanding. "And there will be servants in the hall, as well. We cannot guess their alliances."

"Send one of the boys to the old village," Edgar suggested. "Herve will be glad to take vengeance upon those who stole his goats, and the others will try to be of aid."

Bartholomew agreed and Piers was dispatched on that errand. The boy disappeared quickly into the shadows of the forest.

"Father Ignatius might yet be in the keep," Anna reminded to Bartholomew. "He went in search of the reliquary. We cannot abandon him."

"And we will not," he said, placing her crossbow on the back of the wagon, where she could readily grab it. "Once inside, all of you will contrive to steal the other wagon and get clear of the keep as soon as possible. Anna will fetch Father Ignatius from the chapel if we do not see him. Duncan and I will climb to Royce's chamber, as if to report on our mission, and not leave without the reliquary."

Anna was more than ready to see this matter resolved.

Chapter Fourteen

Royce was rather proud of himself.

His scheme was so brilliant that it could not fail to succeed. The first cart, loaded with trunks of rocks, had to be reaching the most treacherous part of the road through his abode. The rebels in the forest would attack, but they would be the ones to be surprised.

And pay the price of their treachery. He would be rid of them all by sunset!

Boys ran up and down the stairs of the tower, carrying the chests of silver pennies to the second cart in the bailey, then racing to retrieve more from his treasury. Royce supervised the efforts in his chamber, ensuring that they took the right trunks.

There would still be a measure of coin left for his own comfort. It was only three small trunks, but one was filled with gold coin. This was a clever choice on his part, for the fewer the villeins and the less trade within his borders, the lower the taxes. Goods for his table were less readily confiscated from the peasants or taxed out of them in these times. Indeed, the castellan had confided that they would have to buy flour in York by the spring to make bread in the hall.

What need had he of peasants too lazy to till the fields?

Nay, he was better without them, and this measure of coin would ensure his comfort for a good while, even with the king receiving his due. Let them all die. He would survive on venison and other game.

Who knew what good fortune might come to him from his plan? The gift of the reliquary might so impress the king that he might give Royce a fine gift.

Another holding, perhaps.

A richer one.

Royce nigh rubbed his hands together in glee.

He heard his wife weeping noisily in her chambers below his own and rolled his eyes at the fuss she had made over a dead maid. It was one less mouth to feed, as far as Royce was concerned.

Marie wailed in anguish and he gritted his teeth. Even his wife began to be a burden. She had never given him a son. He had long ago bored of her charms, and she had dared to tryst with the knight who aspired to replace him. If she could not be trusted, why should he feed her?

Did she mourn her maid, or the man who hung from the parapet, dead as he deserved?

Royce believed he knew the truth, and it gave him great pleasure.

It also fed his resolve to be rid of Marie.

First matters first, though. The last of the trunks were carried from the chamber and he realized what had been missed. "Gaultier!" he bellowed, believing that the Captain of the Guard must have taken the reliquary into his care. Gaultier knew he was to command the second cart, to ensure that the taxes arrived safely at the king's court. They had arranged all the previous afternoon.

Royce strode out of the chamber and shouted again from the top of the stairs. "Gaultier!"

There was no reply. Where was the man? He had never known Gaultier to be as vexing as he had been this day, and it was not even noon.

Royce marched down a flight of stairs, catching the sleeve of a passing squire. "Where is Gaultier? Have you seen him this morn?"

"Not since daybreak, my lord, when he could not be roused from sleep."

What was this? Royce had seen him in the bailey, when the priest had arrived. He hammered on the door of Marie's chambers, entering without awaiting an invitation. She was packing bundles and froze at the sight of him. "I would give the possessions of Agnes to the poor," she said with a proud lift of her chin.

Royce continued into the chamber with a frown. There were far too many bundles and trunks, to his view. "Agnes did not own so much as this," he protested. He lifted a kirtle from one bag. "And this is the kirtle I gave to you two years ago, at Easter."

"I gave it to Agnes."

"You did not. You would depart yourself! And without my

permission."

Marie's eyes narrowed. "I do not need your permission," she began and he struck her hard, across the face.

"You most certainly do," he retorted. "As my wife, you are my chattel, and you will do as I instruct. You will not leave until I bid you do so." He smiled. "Fear not, it may be soon."

Her lip curled. "And you would remain here, in this keep built with my father's coin, spending the dowry that should see to my comfort for all the days of my life."

"I can make those days shorter, if you would prefer. Indeed, I wonder if I might have need of a younger wife, the better to ensure I have a son."

Marie's outrage was clear. "You would not dare to put me aside. The king chose me as your spouse..."

"And the king is said to be in Anjou, mustering for a crusade. His gaze turns east not north. I doubt he would even notice any tidings of your demise."

"Fiend!" Marie cried and Royce smiled as he turned to leave.

"Lock the portal," he instructed the man in the corridor. "And do not permit my wife to leave her chambers."

"Scoundrel!" Marie shouted and Royce glanced back in time to see the crockery cup she cast at him. He ducked and it shattered on the opposite wall.

Royce descended several steps so she would not have a clear shot, and the sentry slammed the door. Another crockery cup smashed against it as he turned the key in the lock. "Have you seen Gaultier?" he asked the sentry when their gazes met.

"Not since the dawn, sir."

Marie began to laugh.

Royce eyed the door. Her laughter was filled with malice and satisfaction, much as it had been once when she had played a practical joke on a villager.

What did she know?

Surely Gaultier was not in her chamber? Surely he had not so misplaced his trust?

᪣

Marie waited, more than ready to gloat. She could hear Royce breathing on the other side of the portal and exchanged a triumphant glance with Emma.

Her lord husband cleared his throat.

"Have you seen Gaultier, wife of mine?" He spoke sweetly.

Her smile broadened. "Of course. I know exactly where he is."

"Then tell me."

Marie laughed again.

"I command that you tell me!" Royce thundered.

"And I have no reason to do as much as long as this portal is locked."

She could fairly hear him seething. She knew his eyes would be flashing and in a way, she wished he would open the portal and have his way with her. But nay, she heard his boots on the stairs as he rapidly descended.

"Pack it all," she bade Emma. "I will not leave so much as a needle behind."

Doubtless, Royce checked the hall, the kitchens, the stables, the armory, perhaps even the chapel. He would not find Gaultier in any of those places. Marie opened a trunk, removed a thin sharp blade of Venetian manufacture, and slid it into her girdle. It pressed against her hip bone and from this angle, disappeared in the folds of her kirtle. She turned to Emma and raised her hands, turning in silent query.

Emma shook her head. It could not be discerned.

Boots hammered on the stairs and the two women faced the portal as a man—Royce by the odds—halted on the other side.

"Where is he?" he demanded.

"You are surly, Royce," Marie chided. "No woman would reply to such a query."

"Marie," he growled. "I beg of you to confide in me."

It was an improvement.

"Unlock the portal first."

There was a long pause, then the key rattled in the lock.

He kicked open the door. Marie stood before the bed, knowing that her confident smile and demure manner only fed his fury. Emma continued to pack satchels and bags. Royce surveyed the chamber and she guessed that he believed she had hidden Gaultier in her chamber.

She smiled, just to vex him.

It worked. His nostrils flared and his color rose. He tore open the curtains that surrounded the bed, looked in trunks and peered behind screens. Finally, he halted in the middle of the chamber, still seeking some sign of his Captain of the Guard.

Marie stifled the urge to giggle, but only just.

"Where?" he demanded, more wildly this time.

"I will show you, husband," Marie said mildly. She took his hand and led him from the chamber. She felt his astonishment as she climbed the stairs to his own solar.

"This is madness. Gaultier is not here..."

"Nay, my lord, but you can see him from here."

"This is a jest," he protested. "You mock me. Gaultier is not here either."

Marie led her husband to the window. Suspicion rolled from him in waves. He expected a trick, but did not guess the truth as yet. He moved to her side with caution. His gaze followed her pointing finger and he frowned.

All that appeared on the curtain wall of the keep was the corpse of the executed prisoner hung from the parapet.

Twisting in the wind.

"There is only the prisoner," Royce protested. "What jest is this? I seek Gaultier!"

"And who was the condemned man?"

"The knight who would claim Haynesdale in my stead," Royce said with impatience. "I do not see Gaultier at all. Do not lie to me, woman!" He turned to march across the chamber. "I have no time for such ploys..."

Marie's laughter made him halt and glance back, wary anew. Aye, her smile troubled him deeply. She smiled a little more, savoring her victory. "Why do you think I requested that the prisoner be hooded for his execution?"

"Because women are weak. Because you could not bear to look upon your lover when he died. Because..." Royce fell silent and she knew the very instant that he realized the truth. He stared at her and spoke in a whisper. "Because it was not the prisoner who died."

"Nay," Marie agreed easily. "It was not."

Royce leaped forward and struck her with the back of his hand, doing so with such force that she fell to the floor. Vermin! Marie raised a hand to her burning cheek, her own anger redoubling.

279

"You ensured that the most trusted man in my ranks was executed!" he raged, his face livid. "How dare you meddle in such matters! How dare you defy me in this?" He made to seize her again, but Marie rose quickly to her feet.

She seized the blade, spun as he grabbed her elbow and stabbed hard into his gut. His eyes widened in astonishment as she jerked the blade higher and his blood flowed between them. "How dare you strike your lady wife?" she muttered, even as he glanced down in dismay.

"Marie!" he whispered.

It was a thin blade, a wickedly sharp one, and she drove it higher then twisted it deeply inside him. Royce coughed at the pain and blood came from his mouth as he staggered backward. He stared at her as if she were a stranger.

Emma watched from the portal.

"Viper," he managed to say. "You are all vipers."

Marie drove the knife deeper then pulled it out of him. He clearly thought she would attack him again for he took a step backward.

"Never let a man assault you and live to tell about it, Emma," she said quietly and saw fear flash in Royce's eyes. "Aye, husband, you will not walk out of this chamber."

"You cannot ensure otherwise," he protested, though she had already won. He tried to put distance between himself and that blade, but Marie pushed him with the flat of her hand and hooked her foot behind his ankle. He staggered backward, flailing for the wall, and his eyes widened in a most satisfying manner when he realized there was only empty space behind him.

The sill of the window collided with the back of his knees. He almost regained his balance, but Marie gave him a helpful push.

"Farewell, Royce," she whispered then he was gone, tumbling through the air. She leaned out in time to see him land hard on the snow that covered the moat. The force of impact broke the ice and his body sank into the dark hole.

Royce disappeared beneath the ice, only a red stain left on the snow, and did not reappear. Marie wiped her blade with one of his chemises, then cast the garment after him.

She pivoted to survey the chamber, certain it would suit her well. "Our fortune changes, Emma, and thus our strategy."

"Aye, my lady."

"There is no longer any cause to leave the keep built with my father's coin. It is as good as mine, and rightly so." Marie glanced at the road visible from the window and hoped the knight Bartholomew would soon return. "Please bring my possessions to this chamber. It shall be mine from this point forth."

"Aye, my lady." Emma curtseyed and left.

Marie smiled. Haynesdale would be hers and she would take a certain alluring knight to husband. Aye, the appeal of this holding grew by the moment.

In Royce's absence.

❧

There was no opportunity to speak with Bartholomew and tell him what she had learned of her own past. Anna hoped she would have many chances to talk to him once this was resolved. She gave a whistle when they drew nearer to the keep and Duncan and the others appeared out of the forest.

"We might have mistaken you for Royce's own men!" Duncan exclaimed, shaking Bartholomew's hand heartily. It turned out that the squire who had ridden back this way had not survived this bend in the road, for Duncan and the others had attacked him.

Royce would not be warned!

Duncan and the others cast the boy onto the cart and tied the steed with the others. The tale was shared of their capture of the cart, as well as the details of Royce's deceit and Bartholomew's plans.

To Anna's pleasure, he halted beside her again.

"Do not let your pleasure in Gaultier's demise show," Bartholomew advised her in a whisper. "Your thoughts are clearly read in your eyes, after all."

"Are they?"

He smiled and touched her cheek with a fingertip. With the slightest caress, he could awaken a glow within her. "Aye, you are the most forthright woman I have ever known. I admire that trait greatly, Anna, but do not let it betray us."

She parted her lips to share her good tidings, but Duncan came to return Bartholomew's own belt and sword to him. He exclaimed

281

with pleasure and accepted the weapons, then gave the command for them to depart.

They reached the keep and Anna did not look at the body hanging from the curtain wall, given Bartholomew's advice. The guards at the gate opened the portcullis with only a cursory survey of their party, laughing and jesting that the outcasts in the forest had been so foolish. "But where is William?" demanded one.

"His horse went lame," Bartholomew said with easy confidence. "He follows at a walk." He laughed then. "The forests are clear of brigands so there is no peril."

The porters laughed with him.

The company passed through the gates and Anna gave Percy a nudge. The second cart was loaded and left to one side, the horses harnessed to it in preparation. She saw at a glance that they were Royce's younger and swifter steeds. All those trunks! They had to contain gold and silver!

But there was not a one of them that looked large enough to hold the reliquary. The villagers gathered closer together and those of them dressed as Royce's men gruffly commanded them to cluster into a group.

"Out of the way, out of the way, you lot of ruffians," Duncan said with some impatience, keeping the ruse.

Bartholomew strode toward the hall. From the back, he looked a great deal like Gaultier, for he mimicked that man's walk. Once he disappeared into the hall, another sentry came toward them.

"Well, where is Stephen?" he demanded and Anna smelled the scent of horse upon him. He turned on Duncan. "If he fell, why did you not bring him back?" He frowned and peered more closely at Duncan, seizing him by the shoulder when he would have turned away. "Who are you?" he had time to demand, his voice rising high enough to attract the attention of other sentries, before Stewart sank a sword blade into his back.

But it was too late. A hue and a cry erupted, squires and sentries turning upon the new arrivals. "And the battle begins," Duncan muttered. 'Drop your ropes and seize your weapons!"

The villagers immediately shook free of their bonds and took up weapons from the wagon. The boys opened the trunks and began to throw rocks at the baron's men. Anna grabbed her crossbow from the cart and took aim at a sentry on the high wall. He had been aiming at Duncan. She killed him with a single bolt, and his body fell over the wall to the opposite side. Royce's men moved quickly and she knew they would not have much time.

Shouting erupted on all sides and the battle was fierce. Servants flowed out of the hall, the cook waving a knife and the castellan a sword of his own. The squires proved to be fierce fighters and better trained than the villagers. Blood began to flow, but Anna was worried about Father Ignatius.

There was no movement from the chapel.

"Get the other wagon through the gate," she commanded Percy. "And loose the steeds that they can run."

The boys hastened to do her bidding, the others defending Percy as he scurried toward the wagon. Anna shot another sentry who was aiming into the group, but only damaged his shoulder. He leaped down the wooden scaffolding lashed to the inside of the curtain wall, seized another arrow. To her dismay, he struck a flint and lit a bundle of cloth on the end of the arrow. Anna fired at him with a retrieved bolt, but it did not fly true.

His burning arrowhead landed in a pile of straw behind the second cart. The straw ignited, then tumbled and the fire spread to the clothing of those battling in the bailey. Anna shouted a warning, then ran to the chapel. The wagon laden with the king's taxes moved toward the gates, Percy shouting to the horses.

"Father Ignatius!" she cried and tried the door to the chapel. It was locked. Was he gone? Was the reliquary safe? She had time to hope before the priest replied.

"I have the reliquary, Anna, but the door was locked against me."

"What of your keys?"

"Lady Marie took them. Sir Royce has the only others."

"The solar," Anna whispered. "They will be in the solar." She spoke again to the priest. "There is a battle, Father, and a fire in the bailey. I will be back as quickly as I can."

"Go, child!" he urged. "Go! Bartholomew is garbed as Gaultier."

"I know! He is with us."

"Praise be," murmured the priest even as Anna ran. She retrieved three bolts on her way across the bailey and narrowly missed being shot herself. She fired at the assailant, then ducked through the portal to the hall.

That was when she heard the portcullis fall.

She glanced back as the horses halted with a whinny at the gates. Squires swarmed the cart and the villagers fought back with gusto.

Would they be trapped inside the bailey until they were hunted down?

Nay, it could not be!

She raced up the stairs to the solar, hoping she could save Father Ignatius in time.

⁊⚭

The tower was so quiet, compared to the sound of battle in the bailey below.

Bartholomew climbed the stairs slowly, halfway convinced that the pounding of his heart would reveal him.

He flattened himself against the wall as the servants from the kitchens raced through the hall and poured into the bailey through the portal he had just used. Where were Lady Marie and her maid? Where was Royce? He wagered the baron was in his high chamber.

There was no sentry at the base of the stairs nor one at the first turn. Bartholomew paused, listening, then drew his blade before continuing.

There was no one in the chamber that he and Anna had shared.

There was no one in Lady Marie's chamber. In fact, the portal stood open and the contents looked to be in disarray. Trunks were open and some fabric on the floor. Was this the usual state of her chamber, or had something befallen her?

Bartholomew stood in the corridor, but heard no sounds from above. Could he truly ascend to Royce's solar without being challenged?

He reached the summit of the stairs and found the portal to that highest chamber open. He paused, then stepped inside. There were satchels and small trunks on the floor and a woman standing at the window with her back to him. She wore a cloak, the hood raised over her head.

"Lady Marie?" he asked softly. She did not reply. He stepped into the room and spun when the door was slammed behind him.

He jumped back from the darting dagger held by Marie's maid and froze at the feel of a second blade against his back.

"Take off your helm," Marie said.

Bartholomew removed it and cast it aside, then felt the breath of her laughter.

"You are returned!" she declared. "And our future can begin this very day." She gestured and the knife point was removed from his back. "Leave him, Emma, and continue with your labor."

"Aye, my lady." The girl appeared to be moving Marie's garment into the trunks in the chamber and flinging men's garb on the floor.

Bartholomew turned back to Marie. "I do not understand. What is this?"

"We will be wedded this very day," Marie declared.

"But you *are* wed, my lady."

Marie's eyes danced. "Nay, I am widowed, and this time, I will choose my spouse." She leaned closer, her delight evident. "I choose you."

"But what happened to Royce?"

"He fell," Marie said with a shrug. She drew Bartholomew to the window and from this angle, he could see the place where a man's body had broken through the ice on the moat. He also could see those from the new village thronging the gate and guessed that the portcullis was closed, for they did not move inside.

Were the others trapped? He had to assist them!

He turned from the window, only to find Marie confronting him with a thin knife. "Surely you do not mean to decline my offer?" she said and he watched Emma slide a small chest into a sturdy sack. She moved covertly, as if to evade her mistress's attention and he wondered what was in the trunk.

And what she meant to do with it.

"I mean only to fetch the priest, of course," Bartholomew said.

"He is safely in the chapel," Marie said. "With Agnes and the reliquary." She smiled. "I had intended to flee, but now we might remain here," she said. "I find the view much improved from this tower room." She chuckled darkly. "And you need not fear that you might share Royce's fate."

In truth, Bartholomew did wonder just how Royce had fallen from a chamber he knew so well. The glint in Marie's eyes suggested that the baron had had assistance.

He chuckled, appearing more confident than he felt. "Nay, I will not be so fool as to fall out of my own window!"

Marie's smile broadened. "I meant that you should not have to fear that your wife will present you a daughter who was fathered by the Captain of the Guard."

Bartholomew blinked. "I do not understand." Did he hear a footfall on the stairs? Emma backed into the corridor slowly, the sack held behind herself. The bulge within it was larger, and he guessed she had added to its contents. What was the maid's scheme? He could smell fire and hear shouts, which did naught but add to his concerns.

Marie laughed, oblivious to her maid's actions. "Nor did Royce, poor man. He never listened to servants, but they know all. It is folly to ignore them." Her eyes shone. "Royce's first wife conceived by the Captain of the Guard, who was the youngest son of the Duke of Arsent. Even better, she told Royce that the babe had died when it had not."

The story had to have some relevance but Bartholomew could not guess what it was. He wished she would hasten the telling. "Why?"

"Perhaps because Royce had discovered the affair and had her lover executed." She bit her lip. "Perhaps she no longer trusted her lord husband." She met Bartholomew's gaze. "Perhaps the girl resembled her father. There must have been a reason for her to trade her babe with the stillborn daughter born to the smith's wife."

Bartholomew was astonished.

"But the smith is dead, as is his wife, and the girl died two years ago. Royce never knew that Anna, the smith's daughter, was truly the babe of his own wife, but the cook told me of it. Perhaps one of the servants aided in Anna's escape, but she could never have survived the abuse Gaultier visited upon her." Marie smiled again. "But I will be faithful, sir, so long as you are not cruel."

"That seems a fair wager," Bartholomew said and bent over her hand. How could he escape this situation?

"Provided you survive this day," Emma said with such malice that they both turned. She seized the door and slammed it, a key turning audibly in the lock. "It would suit me well to see you burn with the rest of this place, you selfish viper!"

"Emma! What have I ever done to you?"

"Eight years in this place," the maid cried from the corridor beyond. "Eight years past the end of the world, eight years with only the venom of you and your demands." Her voice rose in fury. "And what is Agnes' reward at the end of it all? She died for your indiscretion, yet all you could do was defile her body, shaming her memory with the appearance that she carried a child out of wedlock. You deserve no loyalty from me or any other."

Marie shook the door handle. "Emma! I command that you open this portal."

"And your command will be defied."

"Emma!"

Bartholomew surveyed the chamber. He supposed they could knot the bed curtains and lower themselves out the window, though he was not certain the cloth would bear the weight. There was no rope to be seen.

Marie spun and noticed the missing trunks. "Emma! Did you steal my coin?"

"It is mine now, my lady," the maid sneered. "And may it make me more happy than it has done you." Her footsteps sounded on the stairs, then she grunted and Bartholomew heard her fall. She swore and there were sounds of a struggle. He peered through the keyhole in time to see Anna fighting with the maid on the stairs. That Emma desired to keep hold of the sack of coin above all else betrayed her.

Anna ripped the ring of keys from the maid's girdle. She cast them at the door, shouting his name. They clattered against the door and fell to the floor on the other side.

Bartholomew's dagger barely slid through the space. He managed to catch the loop of the key ring and flick it under the door. He seized the keys, then unlocked the portal.

Emma had forced Anna against the wall, her one hand clutching a fistful of Anna's hair. Anna's crossbow was on the floor, some distance away from them. Emma raised the sack of coin, prepared to strike Anna in the head with it.

Bartholomew flung his knife. Emma froze, the knife buried between her shoulders, then the sack of coin fell from her grasp. Silver spilled across the floor.

Anna wriggled free as the maid's body fell, then snatched for her crossbow. Bartholomew tossed the keys in his hand so that they jingled and when Anna looked his way, cast them to her. She snatched them out of the air with a triumphant smile.

"Who is this?" Marie demanded from behind Bartholomew. "She looks like the smith's daughter."

"Aye, she is, though you have just told me that she is nobly born. I thank you for those tidings."

Bartholomew felt the thin dagger at his back and froze. "You will not abandon me here," Marie whispered.

He saw that Anna had loaded a bolt and held her gaze for a moment. Her lips set and he knew he could trust her aim.

"I suppose you are right." Bartholomew winked, knowing Marie would not be able to see his expression. He then ducked and Anna fired, the bolt striking Marie in the chest.

She staggered backward, her surprise clear. Her fingers rose to the wound and she stared at the blood on her hand. "You reject me."

"I will never take such a traitorous woman to wife."

"You will never take any woman to wife," Marie vowed. She seized a bell hung inside Royce's door and rang it, ensuring that the noise was loud and long.

Men shouted from below and there were footfalls on the stairs. Anna ran to Bartholomew as he retrieved his dagger. He seized her hand and she grabbed the sack of coin as he sought a means of escape.

"There!" he said, pointing to a ladder at one end of the corridor. They climbed it in haste and he shoved open the trap door in the ceiling above it. He could smell the smoke rising from the bailey. He leaped on to the parapet, then aided Anna to follow. He kicked the trap door shut and pivoted to face the sentries who came to attack.

They were only two, and one was injured.

"The bailey burns!" Anna whispered. "All will be lost."

"Fergus arrives," Bartholomew said, pointing to the plume of dust approaching Haynesdale. Even at a distance, he could see the white tabards of the Templars with their distinctive red crosses. "All will be saved!"

One sentry shouted and aimed his bow at them. Bartholomew tugged Anna toward the stairs against the interior of the curtain wall, a plan forming in his mind.

૨**

Anna did not share Bartholomew's confidence, but she trusted him.

The guards blocked them from the wooden scaffold that was obviously his destination. He swung his sword and injured one, then gave her his dagger so she could defend his back. She wished there was room to load her crossbow, but the men were upon them. The smoke rising from the bailey was thick and she could not fully see what was happening below. She feared for all of the villagers, for Percy, for Duncan, and for Father Ignatius.

How could Bartholomew scheme to save them? She knew he had a plan for he moved with purpose, battling their way closer to those stairs. Why would he descend into the bailey? They would only die with the others! And Fergus would not be able to aid them with the portcullis closed against him.

Then Bartholomew slashed at the binding the scaffold to the curtain wall, using his sword to cut the ropes. He spun to cross swords with another attacker, then pivoted to slice another set of bonds. Anna could see his intent, but not understand it. She ducked beneath the swinging blades and cut another rope lashing, then moved to the fourth and final one that she could see. A pair of squires were scrambling up the steps, intent on aiding their fellows, and she thought Bartholomew might mean to eliminate any assistance.

Instead, he caught her around the waist when the last bond was cut and kicked hard at the scaffolding. It eased away from the wall, teetering slightly. Another bond below broke even as the squires shouted in dismay.

Bartholomew cast her a cocky grin, then leaped at the wooden stairs, flinging their combined weight sideways against it. The wood creaked and groaned, then the entire structure fell into the bailey.

With them atop it.

The squires screamed. Anna braced herself for the impact and had the breath stolen from her chest when they crashed into the bailey. The fire leaped from the straw to the wooden structure, spreading with dangerous speed. Horses whinnied in fear and serving maids ran from the hall in terror.

"The portcullis!" Bartholomew roared and Anna heard a surge of activity. "Fergus arrives!"

Duncan bellowed, the villagers cheered, and the battle became more frantic.

"Father Ignatius," Bartholomew bade her, then swung his blade at a pair of attackers. He battled his way toward the gate, dodging fire and mayhem, shouting encouragement. His very presence fortified the villagers, giving them new strength and resolve.

Anna raced to the chapel and unlocked the portal with shaking hands. Father Ignatius had the reliquary bundled against his chest. Without a word, they ran for the portal. The smoke was thick near the ground, but she spied Stewart and Edgar on the back of the second wagon. She shouted and the two men grabbed Father Ignatius and pulled him aboard.

The high tower erupted in flame and a woman screamed.

The portcullis creaked and the villagers cheered as it opened. The horses harnessed to the wagon needed no encouragement to surge through the gate and away from the fire. The untethered horses raced after them, the villagers spilling forth to safety with them. Anna dared to breathe a sigh of relief when Bartholomew swung through the gate after the last of them and scooped her off her feet.

Father Ignatius bared the treasure in his possession and kissed its golden surface, his gratitude more than echoed in the hearts of those around them.

2⪰

The villagers were tired and some were injured. Rowe the carpenter had been killed and was deeply mourned. Many of the other villagers had been hurt but Finan in the old village tended them well. Children ran to collect such stores and food as was available and they shared it all, gathering around a bonfire lit in the midst of the new village. The keep burned slowly and thoroughly, but in Bartholomew's view, all of value had been claimed from within it. He made the boys promise to stay out of the ruins.

Esme brought her chickens from the forest and Regan shared the cheese from her goats. The herd of goats grazed near the company. Stories were exchanged and comfort given. Rabbits were roasted over the flames and Bartholomew knew that he would have to hunt on the morrow to ensure that all could feast as they should.

They had become too thin, the people of Haynesdale. He sat, watching and listening, savoring the tales and the camaraderie, knowing that sooner or later, his decision would be expected.

Of course, it was Anna who asked it of him.

She walked toward him, her features illuminated by the firelight, the resolve in her gaze prompting his admiration. She halted before him, then fell to one knee, offering his father's ring on the palm of one hand.

Again.

"Only a king can make a baron, Anna," he reminded her quietly.

She met his gaze, her own steady and clear. "What will you do?"

The company fell silent, their attention fixed upon him, their manner expectant.

Bartholomew stood to address them. "The king is owed his taxes from the holding of Haynesdale," he said. "I would deliver them to him, though it is likely his court is convened in Anjou in these days. Kings muster for crusade and he will consult with Philip of France." He stood and shed the tabard that had belonged to Gaultier, flinging it into the bonfire. "While I am there, I will request that the seal of Haynesdale be granted to me, in respect for my lineage."

Anna glanced over her shoulder as Percy appeared beside her. He carried the sack of coin that Anna had claimed from the solar. He dropped to one knee beside Anna and offered it to Bartholomew.

"For the escheat," Anna said.

"Nay," Bartholomew said. "This coin was gathered from all of you, leaving you in poverty and hunger. If you give it to me, Anna, I will return it to the villagers. As Father Ignatius has argued, you did not receive protection or justice in exchange for your taxes paid. This coin is rightly yours."

They murmured then, and he realized that his decision had been anticipated by Anna's triumphant smile. "We have agreed that we would see our taxes spent in this manner," she said. "And that if you made this argument, it would only win our support more fully."

She bowed her head. "Praise be that the true son is returned, and there will be justice in Haynesdale again."

The villagers cheered and Fergus applauded, his pleasure in Bartholomew's changed fortunes most clear. Duncan held the reliquary again, and Bartholomew knew they would continue to Killairic as planned.

He raised his voice, addressing all of the company. "The men of my father's line were renowned for their ability to blend old and new, to strike a balance between tradition and innovation. And here, I would continue this legacy. I will take the taxes to the king, that he has his rightful due, and I will gladly accept your offering of the coin for the escheat. I would grant you justice and defend you to the best of my abilities, if I am so fortunate as to win the king's approval. But I suggest this onto you, that if Anna, the daughter of the youngest son of the Duke of Arsent and the Lady of Haynesdale, will have me as her wedded spouse, the king may find that blending of old and new most compelling of all."

The villagers hooted and stamped their feet at this notion, but Anna stood tall, her manner wary. "You would wed me to gain Haynesdale?" she asked quietly. "Because of the name of my father?"

"I would wed you because I love you," he replied. "And I would wed you this very night, before we know the king's decree, so that you have no doubt of my reason. If King Henry has plans for this holding, wedding you might stand between me and Haynesdale. I think the risk a fair one, for I would rather live without Haynesdale's seal than without the lady I love by my side." He smiled at the way she blinked back her tears, noting that as ever, her thoughts were easily read.

He had to tease her then. "Assuming, of course, that you will have me, Anna, even knowing our quest to the king might not end in success."

"He will not dare to defy our will," she said hotly, then smiled as she offered her hand. "I am glad to put my hand in that of such a man of honor."

Bartholomew grinned and caught her close, swinging her around as the company cheered their approval. Father Ignatius cleared a path to them, intent upon supervising the exchange of vows, but Bartholomew claimed a potent kiss first.

"I love you," Anna whispered when he let her speak. "I think I loved you from the first, even when I thought you the most vexing man alive."

"Aye, you had a similar appeal," he agreed with a grin. "Lady mine."

Anna's expression turned mischievous. "Perhaps we are well suited then."

"I think there is little doubt of that."

Their gazes clung and Bartholomew saw the glory of the future in her eyes. Then Father Ignatius cleared his throat and they turned as one, her hand upon his, and pledged their love to each other. The stars were shining overhead, the bonfire was sending sparks into the night, the keep burned and a new one would be built. Bartholomew felt the spirits of his ancestors around him and the sense of homecoming he had yearned to feel now filled his heart with hope and tranquility.

Because of the bold woman who stood beside him, for she had stolen not just the Templar treasure but his own heart.

It would be hers forevermore.

Thursday, March 17, 1188

Feast Day of
Saint Joseph of Arimethea
and the Martyrs of Alexandria.

Chapter Fifteen

Châmont-sur-Maine

It had seemed that naught could go wrong, but when the day came for Bartholomew to plead his case before King Henry, Anna was fearful of the result.

Perhaps it was simply that she was not in the habit of meeting kings.

Much less asking for their favors.

She and Bartholomew had journeyed south, with Leila and Timothy to aid them, after leaving Fergus in charge of Haynesdale. There was much to done, for Bartholomew wished to rebuild his father's keep and restore the village to its former site. The villagers were enthusiastic and had begun the labor quickly. Their memory would be of aid to Fergus in directing the work, and Bartholomew had declared himself confident in his friend's administration. Duncan, too, had remained at Haynesdale, for his place was with Fergus until that knight was safely home again.

Bartholomew carried several trunks of coins south to make his plea to the king. Cenric had needed to be restrained to ensure he did not follow them, but Bartholomew said the journey would be too much for him. He had rubbed the dog's ears and vowed to return, and Anna halfway thought the beast understood him.

The weather had been fair, and despite Anna's concerns, their crossing to France had been uneventful. She alone of the party had never journeyed so far, but Bartholomew explained much to her and took her to many churches along the way. He taught her French as they journeyed, and though her efforts had made them all laugh at first, her skills improved daily. She also had to learn to comport herself like a noblewoman, and Leila had assisted her with that.

Still, by the time they reached Gaston's abode, Anna had been certain she would make a mistake that would cost Bartholomew dearly. She hoped that wedding her would not be the mistake that cost him all, for the whim of kings could not be anticipated.

Ysmaine had been gracious in her welcome and polite in her few suggestions, which had bolstered Anna's confidence yet more. Ysmaine's maid Radegunde had immediately spied that Anna was with child, confirming Anna's own suspicions. Ysmaine was rounder yet, and the two knights congratulated each other on their good fortune.

It was Gaston who sent word to Anjou, inviting the king to visit. That astonished Anna, for she thought people went to kings, but to her further amazement, King Henry accepted the invitation.

For two days hence.

The kitchens descended into a frenzy of baking, roasting, stewing, and saucemaking. The lady Ysmaine laughed that only a fool would cross that threshold willingly. The seneschal had the strewing herbs changed twice in the great hall—for he did not care for the scent of the first ones—and the wood stacked high beside the fireplaces. Banners were hung and minstrels were hired, and the parade of meat to the kitchens was sufficient to make Anna's eyes round.

There were swans and peacocks to be served, as well as venison and a roast boar, countless egg dishes and fine tarts. There was wine and there was ale, fresh bread and many cheeses. She could not believe the bounty of Gaston's larders and pantries.

It was just before noon on the chosen day that the entire household was gathered before the gates of Châmont-sur-Maine to welcome the king's party. Gaston and Ysmaine stood by the very portal, with Anna and Bartholomew to one side, then all of the household standing in order of rank. The villeins lined the road through the village, and some measure of rank was displayed there for the tradesmen and the guild members were closest to Gaston's household. All were dressed in their best, and each stood a little taller when the fanfare was heard announcing the king's arrival.

At first glimpse of the king, they all bowed low.

Anna could not help but steal glimpses of the king's party, in their rich robes, riding magnificent horses. She had never seen the like, and she caught Bartholomew smiling at her awe. She supposed her thoughts were as clear to him as ever.

Even the saddles of the steeds were embellished, wrought of

colored leather, hung with richly embroidered caparisons, even hung with silver bells. Mail and scabbards gleamed, the armor and weapons more likely to see a fine company of guests than a bloody battlefield.

The king himself was aged, but not as old as Anna might have expected. His hair was silver and his legs were bowed, doubtless from all the time he spent in the saddle. He dismounted with a grimace that was so fleeting she might have imagined it. He greeted Gaston with a warmth and familiarity that was evident to Anna even though she could not readily follow his quick French.

She was astonished that she stayed in the home of a man who was friendly with the king himself!

Then the king paused before Bartholomew. Anna felt her gaze upon him, but kept her head bowed until he gestured. She watched him survey Bartholomew. "And so the son of Nicholas of Haynesdale is finally found," the king said in English that bore a slight French accent. "I never imagined that Gabriella would have allowed you to be lost for good."

"You knew them, sire?"

The king smiled. "I arranged their match, Luc Bartholomew. Is it true that the mark is burned into your flesh? It seemed such a fanciful tale."

"It is, my lord."

"Yet the ring is lost."

"Nay, my lord," Anna dared to say. She tugged the lace from her chemise, noting how avidly the king watched her bodice for the sight of the ring. "It was entrusted to my family's care by Lady Gabriella."

The king lifted the ring, turning it so that the wyvern rampant caught the light. He smiled a little. "I remember it well. See the mark inside? Nicholas had the date inscribed when I granted Haynesdale to him, after his father's demise." He nodded. "He was a good man." He loosed the ring and it fell on its lace to Anna's breast, then eyed Bartholomew. "And this is your lady wife?"

"Aye, sir. Daughter of the Lady of Haynesdale who was wedded first to Royce Montclair and the youngest son of the Duke of Arsent."

"I wager there is a tale there," the king mused and Anna felt herself flush. "And yet, though she has the ring, you do not wear it."

"Only a king can make a baron of the realm, sir."

"And the king has always chosen the wife of the Baron of Haynesdale," Henry noted.

Anna's heart went cold.

"Forgive me, sire, if I have been presumptuous," Bartholomew said.

"You have been," the king replied, his manner stern. Then his gaze fell to Anna's belly. "And impetuous as well." He sighed and frowned. "Far be it from me to ensure that another bastard is born in my realm."

Anna gasped in delight at his implication. The king surveyed her and she wondered whether he realized the fullness of her relief.

Then Henry smiled at her, his eyes twinkling. "Fear not, I will not annul a match that has so obviously been consummated."

"I thank you, sire," Bartholomew said.

The king offered his hand to Bartholomew, who quickly bowed to kiss it. "I will need to see the mark, of course," he said. "And the escheat will have to be paid."

"I have coin for it, sire, as well as the taxes unpaid by the former Baron of Haynesdale."

"Your timing is most excellent," Henry said, then raised his voice to address all of those gathered before the gates. "There will be a crusade to the east to reclaim Jerusalem. I and King Philip and my son Richard will lead this venture, and I bid all of you to contribute to its financing as the new Baron of Haynesdale has shown the good sense to do." There was applause. "And I bid those of you who are hale to put your affairs in order and ride with us, the better to retrieve the Holy City from the grip of infidels!"

There was a cheer of enthusiasm and the king turned a knowing smile upon Anna. "I would wager that your new lady will not have you leave her bed so soon as this," he said to Bartholomew.

"And I would remain to see Haynesdale rebuilt, sire, for both village and hall have been plagued by fire."

The king sobered. "There will be taxes to fund the crusade. Do not imagine that you can shirk from paying your due."

"Of course not, my lord," Anna said, for she could remain silent no longer. "My husband wishes to have a license for an annual fair at Haynesdale, the better to enrich our coffers with tolls and tithes."

The king nodded. "We shall reflect upon the matter," he said, though his smile was approving. Anna saw Gaston nod once at Bartholomew, and guessed that he perceived the king to be inclined to agree.

Meanwhile, Henry inhaled deeply. "There is something in the air of Brittany that fosters a man's appetite. Here we stand at the gateway between Brittany and Anjou, and all I can consider is the scent of that roast boar. My lady Ysmaine, would you be so kind as to lead us to your board? Though it has been but a short ride, I find myself famished indeed."

"With the greatest pleasure, sire. You do us great honor with your presence." Then Ysmaine switched to French, her words falling so rapidly that Anna had no hope of following the conversation.

She took Bartholomew's elbow and his hand folded over hers. "Does that mean he approves?" she whispered and Bartholomew smiled at her.

"If all proceeds well, it shall be done."

"And why should it not?"

"There is no reason, Anna. Gaston considers the matter resolved, and I will take confidence in his view."

"Then Haynesdale will be yours!"

"Once the ring is on my finger." They passed beneath the gates, and Bartholomew bent to kiss her cheek. "But truly, the ring of greatest import is already upon my finger."

The sole one he wore was his wedding band, just as Anna wore just one. She smiled up at him, well content with her fate. "Ysmaine's maid thinks it will be a boy."

Bartholomew could not suppress his smile, and his eyes danced as she loved them best. "Whether it is boy or girl is of no import, Anna," he vowed. "For I am more than willing to try again to conceive an heir."

And in this matter, it must be said, Anna did fully agree with her lord spouse.

ॐ

Ready for more of the Champions of Saint Euphemia?

Read on for an excerpt from the next book in the series

The Crusader's Vow

A company of Templar knights, chosen by the Grand Master of the Temple in Jerusalem to deliver a sealed trunk to the Temple in Paris. A group of pilgrims seeking the protection of the Templars to return home as the Muslims prepare to besiege the city. A mysterious treasure that someone will even kill to possess...

Returning home to Scotland triumphant after his military service, and entrusted with the precious relic of the Templars, Fergus is more than ready to wed his beloved Isobel and begin their life together. To his dismay, Isobel has wed another in his absence, and he believes all of merit is stolen from his life—until Leila resolves to win the valiant highlander's heart for her own. She is convinced of her own success, until Isobel tempts Fergus anew.

It seemed that all was right with his fellows. Fergus would never have anticipated such a happy conclusion to events when they had left Jerusalem the previous summer. But on this fine spring evening, Bartholomew and Anna were returned, the signet ring of Haynesdale placed upon Bartholomew's finger by King Henry himself and the seal in his purse. They had a license to hold an annual fair and had returned to find the old keep of Haynesdale taking shape once more. Bartholomew had bought grain in York and the mill was turning even now, grinding flour from some of it while the rest would be sown in the fields that had already been plowed.

And now he returned home to Isobel. It would be four years since his departure, and Fergus was anxious to see his beloved again. He left the festivities in the great hall when the dancing began and stepped out into the night. The moon was full and the sky was clear.

Fergus smiled as he stared up at the glittering stars. Killairic — home — was so close, and there, every dream he yearned to fulfill. He wished, not for the first time, that his gift for foresight included his own future. He saw happiness for Bartholomew and Anna, just as he had seen it for Wulfe and Christina, and Gaston and Ysmaine. He saw babies in the futures of each of the couples, a number of children, their eyes filled with joy and mischief. He could even see his companion Duncan cradling a dark-haired child. But for himself? There was no glimmer of what the future held for him.

It had never concerned him before, but on this night, Fergus wondered what he would find when he arrived home. He hoped his father was well as yet, for he wanted days by the fire to tell the older man of all he had seen. He could not imagine his welcome from Isobel, who surely had been as impatient for his return as he had been. He wondered how Killairic itself had changed, if it had changed at all. There would have been births and deaths in the village during such a long time, but he hoped that those he wished most to see were hale.

Something troubled him, though he could not name it. Fergus decided it was impatience, no more than that, and strode toward the village. If he walked, he might sleep. Perhaps he might ride forth the next morning, since Bartholomew was returned.

His heart fluttered at the possibility and he resolved it would be so. He would see his fellows again at his own nuptials, to be sure, for they had vowed to come to Scotland. It could not be long before he and Isobel exchanged their vows.

A slight movement caught his eye and Fergus realized that he was not the only one to have left the celebration. Leila sat by the river, staring up at the moon. It still surprised him to see her in women's garb, though on this night, she wore no veil. Her dark hair had grown a little more since she had cut it shorter in Jerusalem and now it reached her chin. It shone like polished ebony in the moonlight. Her face was tipped up to the moon, and its light touched her features with silver. She did not seem to be aware of his presence, so he cleared his throat as he approached.

"You miss the dancing," he said when she glanced his way.

Leila smiled and moved along the log where she was seated, making room for him. "I do not know your dances."

"You could learn. I could teach you."

She chuckled. "And what will your betrothed think, if you arrive home not only with a Saracen woman in your company but one you have taught to dance?"

Fergus was startled. "I had not thought of it."

"She will believe you have brought home your whore," Leila said with conviction. "There is no need to reinforce that conclusion."

Fergus leaned forward, bracing his elbows on his knees, and looked at her. "You have been thinking of this."

"I have been thinking of many things." She gestured to the moon. "It is full, the eleventh full moon since we left Jerusalem."

"I suppose it is."

"I know it is. I have counted them."

He eyed her, hearing the sadness in her tone. "What does that mean, Leila?"

"It means that my cousin's son is a year old." She fell silent then.

"You miss your cousin?"

"Of course! We grew up together. She was the one whose hair I learned to braid and arrange." Leila sighed. "We lived in the same household, my uncle's home, after the death of my father. We might have been sisters, almost twin sisters, for we were born the same month."

As he listened, Fergus realized how little he knew about the woman who had joined their company in Jerusalem. "When did your father die?"

"When I was two summers of age." She took a shaking breath. "My mother died a year ago."

He saw the tear glisten on her cheek and wished he had the right to brush it away. "I would take you back to Palestine, if you wish to see your cousin again," he found himself saying. The offer was impulsive, but as soon as the words were uttered, Fergus knew it was true. What if Leila did return to the east? He would miss the opportunity he had lost in not learning more about her, to be sure. He could not imagine a future in which he never saw her again, yet realized in this moment, that it might well come to be.

Fergus had assumed she would stay once they reached Killairic, but had never considered what she would do there. He did not want anyone to think of her as a whore, though he saw the plausibility of that. It was not common for Fergus to feel like a fool, but in this moment, he did so.

He also felt as if he had failed the woman who had trusted him and served him loyally. His chest tightened and he did not know what to say to her, much less how he could make matters right.

Leila wiped her tears and touched the back of his hand with her fingertips. "I thank you for that, for you know the price of what you offer. But I cannot go back."

"Not even to see your cousin?"

"Especially not."

Fergus dared to acknowledge his own relief, even as he realized it was selfish. How would he feel when she wed another man? It was strange to admit that this possessiveness lurked within him, for he had no right to make any claim upon her.

Her conviction that others would see her as his whore was both troubling and titillating. It was all too easy to imagine a night of exploring Leila's charms, her throaty laughter and that smile that was both shy and knowing.

Clearly, he had been too long without Isobel's sweet touch.

He cleared his throat again. "Bartholomew said you were to be wed against your will, and that was why you wanted to leave Jerusalem."

Leila nodded and spoke mildly. "A marriage had been arranged."

"That happens to many."

"It does, and if I had known naught of the man, I would have accepted my uncle's word. But I knew him well and had heard much of his violence."

That she might have been wed to a man who might treat her with less than adoration sent fire through Fergus. "You should have told your uncle," he said, hearing his own outrage.

"I did! But the man in question was my second cousin and the alliance from the marriage was good for both families. Like the good man he is, my uncle dismissed the rumors that he believed to be malicious."

"You did not."

"He is fond of my cousin and has seen only his best." She turned to face him, her dark eyes filled with conviction. "But women do not lie to each other about such matters. The fact was I should not have known and I could not prove what I had heard."

This was intriguing. Leila had pretended to be a boy in order to tend horses at the Templar stables. It seemed that she had defied expectation in other ways. Fergus wanted to know more. "Who told you?"

"It does not matter now. I believed her, for once I had heard her tale, I also glimpsed the shadow in him."

"You knew to look."

She nodded. "And so I fled."

"Did your cousin with the infant boy know of your plan?"

Leila smiled. "She suggested it after my mother died. She knew I went to the Temple to help with the horses, because my uncle would not have approved and she helped to disguise my absences. She told me to find a knight there to aid me, preferably one who was leaving Jerusalem soon." She watched her own fingers as she pleated the fabric of her kirtle, and he knew she was reliving her fears in that moment. He wanted to draw her close and console her, but fought the urge for it was inappropriate. "But I only knew

Bartholomew. He was not inclined to help me."

"But I overheard you."

"You did." Leila met his gaze once more. "Thank you." She smiled at him and flushed a little, her eyes seeming to glow. Her lips parted and he found himself desiring a kiss.

Just one.

Though it was not his to take.

Leila did not avert her gaze and the air seemed to heat between them. Fergus felt keenly aware of Leila as a woman. He noted the ripe curve of her lips, the thick luster of her dark hair, the luminosity of her eyes, the sweet curve of her throat. She was tiny compared to him and delicately wrought, but achingly feminine. He had an urge to protect her, even as he was aware of her strength and resolve.

Fergus recognized that it had not been impulse alone, or even a need to do what was right, that had prompted his offer in Jerusalem to hide Leila in their party. She was both resilient and vulnerable, beautiful and strong, mysterious yet open. He had been intrigued by her when he had overheard that conversation, and more so when first he had glimpsed her. She had proven to be an asset to their party more than once, gave much and asked for little, yet as their gazes clung, he wanted to give her more.

Far more.

"Any regrets?" Fergus asked, his own voice husky.

"Only for what can never be," Leila admitted softly. "I would see my cousin again, but not return to Outremer. I would play with her son, but not risk my own future. I would wed, with my uncle's blessing, but not to the man he chose." She blinked quickly and shook her head once more. "I want the impossible, and so I fear that there is only disappointment ahead for me."

"Nay, not that." He had his arm around her waist before he realized what he did, and once her soft warmth was against him, he could not pull away.

"What do you see in my future days?" she asked. "Duncan says you can see what will come."

"Not on command. Only in dreams and glimpses."

She cast him a quick smile. "Do you lie because you have seen sorrow in my future, or is my future veiled?"

"I would never lie to you, Leila." He spoke with conviction, because it was true.

"Not even out of kindness?"

"Not even then."

She looked up at him, and her gaze lingered on his mouth. She ran the tip of her own tongue across her bottom lip, as if she hungered for his touch, then she took a deep breath and dropped her gaze, hiding her thoughts from him.

Fergus felt immediately bereft. "What will you do?" He lifted one hand when she did not reply. "Will you stay here at Haynesdale with Bartholomew and Anna? I know they would welcome you."

"I pledged to return to Killairic with you and I will keep my word." A smile touched her lips. "Even though I might well face the wrath of your betrothed."

"Isobel might not make the conclusion you expect."

"Then she is a fool," Leila said hotly and straightened beside him. "For any woman with blood in her veins would desire a man so loyal of heart as you, even if he were not wrought so tall and fine, nor possessed of such valor."

"Leila!" Fergus protested, surprised by her endorsement. "You know little of me..."

"After eleven months in each other's company, I know much of you, and all of it has merit." She looked up at him, her eyes flashing. "I admire you, my lord Fergus. You are the manner of man to whom I should like to pledge my troth."

Her confession made his heart leap and she must have seen his expression change.

She smiled ruefully. "You need not fear that I will act upon this, or that I will be more than your faithful servant," she continued more quietly. "But if the lady Isobel fails to see your merit, or dares to doubt your integrity, she will answer to me."

Fergus smiled at her ferocity, then his smile faded when Leila's hand landed on his thigh. His entire body went taut and desire rolled through him.

Leila's voice dropped low and her eyes were so dark as to be fathomless. "And if there is ever any deed you would desire of me, you have only to ask."

Fergus was honored and might have said as much, but he had no chance. For Leila caught her breath, then stretched up and touched her lips to his. He knew it was intended to be a chaste kiss, perhaps the sole one they would ever exchange, but her caress kindled a new fire within him. He found himself bending closer, unable to resist what she offered so freely. He cupped her nape in his hand and deepened their kiss.

When she opened her mouth to him, surrendering to their embrace, Fergus realized that Leila was not the sole one who wanted the impossible.

ठ♣

ક

The Crusader's Vow

is the fourth book in Claire Delacroix's
Champions of Saint Euphemia series.

Coming March 2017!

Visit Claire's website for more details.

ક

*Bestselling author Deborah Cooke sold her first romance novel in 1992–that medieval romance, **The Romance of the Rose**, was published by Harlequin Historicals in 1993 under the pseudonym Claire Delacroix. Since then, she has published more than fifty romance novels and numerous novellas in a wide variety of sub-genres under the names Claire Delacroix, Claire Cross and Deborah Cooke. **The Beauty** by Claire Delacroix, part of her successful Bride Quest series, was her first novel to land on the New York Times' List of Bestselling Books. In 2009, Deborah was the writer in residence at the Toronto Public Library, the first time they have hosted a residency focused on the romance genre. In 2012, she was honored with RWA's Mentor of the Year Award.*

*In addition to writing the **Champions of Saint Euphemia Series** of medieval romances as Claire Delacroix, Deborah also writes contemporary romance and paranormal romance as Deborah Cooke. She lives in Canada with her husband and far too many books.*

Learn more about Deborah's books and follow her blog at her website:
http://deborahcooke.com

Subscribe to Deborah's monthly newsletter for updates on new releases:
http://eepurl.com/UCUdf

Printed in Great Britain
by Amazon